THE TENTH JUSTICE

THE
TENTH
JUSTICE

BRAD MELTZER

ROB WEISBACH BOOKS
WILLIAM MORROW AND COMPANY, INC. NEW YORK

Published by Rob Weisbach Books
An Imprint of William Morrow and Company, Inc.
1350 Avenue of the Americas, New York, N.Y. 10019

Library of Congress Cataloging-in-Publication Data
Meltzer, Brad.
The tenth justice / Brad Meltzer. —1st ed.
p.   cm.
ISBN 0-688-15089-6 (hc)
I. Title.
PS3563.E4496T46   1997
813'.54—dc20   96-44815
CIP

Printed in the United States of America

First Edition

1 2 3 4 5 6 7 8 9 10

BOOK DESIGN BY RINA MIGLIACCIO

For Cori,
who changed my life
the moment she entered it

ACKNOWLEDGMENTS

I WISH TO THANK THE FOLLOWING PEOPLE FOR BEING involved with this book and, therefore, being involved with my life: Jill Kneerim, my agent, for her faith in me as a writer. Over the past four years, she has been an editor, an advisor, a cheerleader, and a confidante. Most importantly, she has been my friend. With sagacious (and sometimes prognostic) insight and down-to-earth sensibilities, she has offered me a relationship that I deeply treasure. If she never laughed at fraternal antics, we wouldn't be here today. Elaine Rogers, whose sales ability started the ball rolling—for that alone, I am forever in her debt; Sandy Missakian, whose sense of humor and tenacious negotiating abilities make my life much easier; Sharon Silva-Lamberson, for going beyond the call of duty and starting so much of this by enjoying it on her own (thanks, Sharon); Ike Williams and everyone else at The Palmer and Dodge Agency for all their support; Neil Stearns and everyone at the Dick Clark Film Group for their courage, commitment, and dedication. Neil, you and your crew were the first people to take a chance on me. I will never forget that.

I want to thank my parents, who have always given me tremendous amounts of love and have unknowingly provided me with years of good material; my sister, Bari, for her never-ending support; Ethan Kline and Noah Kuttler, who gave incredible amounts of time and energy to this book and all its details; Matt Oshinsky, Joel Rose, Chris Weiss, and Judd Winick for their tireless assistance and constant friendship; Professor Kellis Parker, for his expansive view of the law and unwavering aid; Kathy Bradley, for taking the time to help me during the planning stages and for giving me so many vivid details to work with; Chris Vasil, for his keen eye and generous nature; and the rest of my family and friends, whose names inhabit these pages.

Finally, I'd like to thank everyone at Rob Weisbach Books and William Morrow: Bill Wright, for his incredible enthusiasm; Jacqueline Deval, Michael Murphy, Lisa Queen, Lisa Rasmussen, and Sharyn Rosenblum, for their boundless energy and invaluable support; Colin Dickerman, for his reactions and suggestions; David Szanto, for his input on the manuscript and for helping with everything else that came his way; and all the wonderful people at Weisbach/Morrow who helped make this book a reality. Finally, I owe an enormous thank you to my editor and publisher, Rob Weisbach. Rob is one of the people in this world with true vision. He is a consummate editor whose commitment to his authors cannot be overstated. I am honored to be a part of his new imprint and even prouder to count him among my friends. Rob, I can never thank you enough for everything you've done: beyond endless enthusiasm, you've given me your faith.

In a capital full of classified matters, and full of leaks,
the Court keeps private matters private.
Reporters may speculate; but details of discussion
are never disclosed, and the vote is revealed
only when a decision is announced.

—THE SUPREME COURT HISTORICAL SOCIETY
Equal Justice Under Law

Five votes can do anything around here.

—WILLIAM BRENNAN
Supreme Court Justice

CHAPTER 1

BEN ADDISON WAS SWEATING. LIKE A PIG.

And it wasn't supposed to be this way.

In the past three hours, Ben had read the current issues of *The Washington Post*, *The New York Times*, *Law Week*, and *Legal Times*. Last night, before going to bed, he'd committed to memory every major Supreme Court case from the previous session. He'd also made a list of every Supreme Court opinion Justice Mason Hollis had ever written, and, to be safe, he'd reread Hollis's biography. No matter what the subject, Ben was convinced he was prepared for any topic Justice Hollis might raise. In his briefcase, he had packed two legal pads, four pens, two pencils, a pocket legal dictionary, a pocket thesaurus, and—since he'd heard that Supreme Court clerks typically work straight through lunch—a turkey sandwich. Without question, Ben Addison was ready.

But he was still sweating. Like a pig.

As he stood outside the Supreme Court, a half hour early for his first day on the job, he was entranced by the gleaming white columns of the nation's highest court. This is it, he thought, taking a deep breath. It's finally here. Running his hand through his recently cut brown hair, Ben climbed the wide marble stairs. He counted each step, in case Justice Hollis was curious how many stairs there were. Forty-four, he told himself, filing the information on a mental index card.

Ben dragged open the heavy bronze doors and entered the building. A security guard who sat next to a metal detector said, "Can I help you?"

"I'm Ben Addison. I'm here to clerk."

The guard found Ben's name on his clipboard. "Orientation doesn't start for another half hour."

"I like to be early," Ben said with a smile.

"Right." The guard rolled his eyes. "Go straight down the hall and make your first left. It's the first door on your right."

Lined with marble busts of past chief justices, the stark white Great Hall was as impressive as Ben had remembered. A sly smile lifted his cheeks as he passed each sculpture. "Hello, Supreme Court," he whispered to himself. "Hello, Ben," he answered.

Ben pulled open the large wooden door, expecting to see an empty room. Instead, he saw eight other law clerks. "Brown-nosers," he muttered to himself as he sat down in the only empty chair.

As inconspicuously as possible, Ben sized up his new colleagues. He recognized three of the eight clerks. On his far right was a well-dressed man with stylish, tortoiseshell-rimmed glasses who had been the articles editor of the *Stanford Law Review*. To his left was a tall black woman who was the former editor in chief of the *Harvard Law Review*. Ben had met both of them at a national Law Review conference at Yale. As Ben recalled, the Stanford man was a former reporter for the *Los Angeles Times,* while the Harvard woman used to be an Old Masters expert for Sotheby's. Angela was her name. Angela P-something. Finally, seated next to Ben was Joel Westman, a fellow classmate from Yale Law. A political analyst, Joel had spent his pre–law school years as a White House speechwriter. Nice résumés, Ben thought. Struggling to appear casual, he smiled and gave friendly nods to all three clerks; they nodded back.

Ben nervously tapped his foot against the plush carpet. Don't worry, he told himself. It'll be fine. You're as smart as anyone else. But as well-traveled? As well-heeled? That wasn't the point. Remember your lucky underwear, he reminded himself. He had bought the now fraying pair of red boxer shorts when he was a freshman at Columbia. He had worn them on the first day of every class, to every midterm, and on every important date. During finals, if he had exams on three consecutive days, the boxers would stay on for all of them. He had worn them throughout his three years at Yale and to every clerkship interview. Today's the day, he decided, that the lucky underwear comes through in the sacred halls of the Supreme Court.

A middle-aged man in a gray, pin-striped suit came in, carrying a stack of manila envelopes. He strode to the podium and counted heads. "I'm Reed Hughes," he said, solidly grabbing the sides of the podium. "On behalf of the Clerk's Office, I'd like to officially welcome you to the Supreme Court of the United States. At the risk of repeating information you're already familiar with, I thought it would be appropriate to tell you a little bit about what your next year here at the Court is going to be like."

Within seconds, four clerks pulled out pens and notebooks.

Pathetic, Ben thought, fighting the urge to take out his own notebook.

"As you know, each justice is permitted to hire two clerks to assist in the preparation of decisions," Hughes explained. "The nine of you starting today will join your nine co-clerks who started one month ago on July first. I realize that all eighteen of you have worked extremely hard to get where you are today. For most of your lives, you've been running a never-ending race to succeed. Let me tell you something I hope you'll take seriously. The race is over. You've won. You are law clerks of the Supreme Court of the United States."

"Did you get that down?" Ben whispered to Joel. "We're the clerks."

Joel shot Ben a look. "No one likes a smart-ass, Addison."

"The eighteen of you represent the best and the brightest of the legal community," Hughes continued. "After screening thousands of applications from the country's top law schools, the justices of this Court selected you. What does that mean? It means your lives are forever changed. Recruiters will offer you jobs, headhunters will take you out to expensive dinners, and potential employers will do everything in their power to hire you. You are members of the country's most elite fraternity. The current secretary of state was a Supreme Court clerk. So was the secretary of defense. Three of our nine Supreme Court justices were former Supreme Court clerks, which means that someone in this room has a pretty good shot at becoming a Supreme Court justice. From this moment on, you are the hottest property on the board. You're Boardwalk *and* Park Place. And that means you have power."

Easing back in his seat, Ben Addison was no longer sweating.

Hughes scanned his captivated audience. "Why am I telling you this? It's not so you can impress your friends. And it's certainly not to boost your ego. After dealing with clerks year after year, I know none of you has an ego problem. My goal is to prepare you for the responsibility you're about to encounter.

"This is an important job—probably more important than any job you'll ever have. For over two hundred years, the Supreme Court has steered our country through its greatest controversies. Congress may pass the laws, and the president may sign the laws, but it's the Supreme Court that decides the law. And starting today, that power is yours. Alongside the justices, you will draft decisions that change lives. Your input will constantly be sought, and your ideas will certainly be implemented. In many instances, the justices will rely entirely on your analysis. They'll base their opinions on your research. That means you affect what they see and what they know. There are nine justices on this Court. But your influence, the power that you hold, makes you the tenth justice."

Ben slowly nodded his head. He was mesmerized.

Hughes paused, carefully adjusting his glasses. "You are now charged with great responsibility. You must exercise it wisely. With that said, I know you'll take this commitment extremely seriously. If you have the right attitude, our clerkship program can change your life. Now, are there any questions?"

Not a single hand went up.

"Fine," Hughes said. "Then we can get you to your offices." As he distributed the envelopes, he explained, "Take the one with your name on it and pass the rest on. The envelopes contain your security card and your Court password. The card will let you into any Court entrance, while the password will get you on to your computer. Your secretary will show you how to log on. Any questions?" Again, not a single hand. "Good," Hughes said. "Then feel free to go to your office. The number is written on the front of the envelope." As the room emptied, Hughes called out, "If you have any questions, feel free to call me."

Ben headed for his office, the only one on the second floor. He had met Justice Hollis's former clerks there during his interview last year. Weaving his way back through the Great Hall, he raced toward the elevator. The elevator operator was an elderly woman with dyed, jet-black hair. Wearing a Court uniform that was too tight for her large frame, she worked a jigsaw puzzle on a small table outside the elevator.

"Second floor, please," Ben said. When the woman didn't respond, he added, "Ma'am, I'm trying to get upstairs. Can you please help—"

"Don't get in an uproar," she drawled, without looking up. "I'll be right with you." After finding a place for the puzzle piece in her hand, she finally looked up at Ben. "Okay, now, who're you here to see?"

"I'm clerking for Justice Hollis. I'm Ben Addison," he said, extending his hand.

"I don't care who you are, just tell me what floor you want to go to," she said as she walked into the elevator.

"Second," Ben said, dryly.

The second floor hallway was all marble, with red and gold carpet, but Ben barely noticed it. He was too busy looking for the room number that was written on his envelope. "Nice to see you, Justice Hollis," he said to himself. "Hi, Justice Hollis, nice to see you. How's everything, Justice Hollis? Nice robe, Justice Hollis—it fits great. Can I kiss your butt some more, Justice Hollis?" Finally, he saw room 2143. Outside the intricately carved mahogany doors, Ben wiped his hand on his pants hoping for a dry handshake. He grabbed the brass knob, opened the door, and stepped inside.

"I guess you're Ben." A woman in her late twenties peered over the newspaper she was reading. "Sorry you wasted the nice suit on me." Dressed in khaki shorts and a forest-green T-shirt, the woman tossed aside the paper and approached Ben, extending her hand. "Nice to meet you. I'm Lisa, your co-clerk for the year. I hope we don't hate each other, because we're going to be spending quite a bit of time together."

"Is the justice—"

"Let me show you our office," Lisa interrupted, pulling him into the room. "This is just the reception area. Nancy's out today, but she usually sits here. She's Hollis's secretary."

Lisa was petite with an athletic build, compact but elegant. A tiny nose balanced out thin lips and blue eyes. Lisa opened the door to a smaller room. "Here's our office. Pretty crappy, huh?"

"Unbelievable," Ben said, standing in the doorway. The office wasn't large, and it was sparsely decorated, but the intricate dark wood paneling that covered the walls gave it an instant sense of history. On the right-hand side of the office were built-in bookcases, which housed the clerks' personal library. Stocked with volumes of cases, treatises, and law journals, the room reminded Ben of the libraries that millionaires have in cheesy movies.

On the back wall hung the room's only picture—a photograph of the current justices. Taken when a new justice was appointed to the Court, the official photograph was always posed the same way: five justices seated and four justices standing. The chief justice sat in the middle, while everyone else was arranged according to their seniority on the Court. The oldest justice sat on the far left; the newest justice stood on the far right. Although the photo was only six months old, the justices' identical black robes and stoic stares made the current portrait almost indistinguishable from the dozens taken in years past.

Arranged on the navy and gold carpet were two antique wooden desks facing each other, two computers, a wall of file cabinets, a paper shredder, and a plush but well-worn scarlet sofa. Both desks were already submerged under a mountain of paper. "From what I can tell, the desks are from the early colonial period," Lisa explained. "They might've been used by some old justices. Either that, or they're replicas from someone's garage. What the hell do I know about antiques?"

As he followed her into the cramped but sophisticated office, Ben noticed Lisa was barefoot.

"I guess the justice isn't coming in today?" Ben pushed aside some papers and put his briefcase down on one of the desks.

"That's right. I'm sorry, I was supposed to call you last night. Most of the justices take off for the summer. Hollis won't be back until next month, so it's as casual as you want." Lisa leaned on Ben's desk. "So, what do you think?"

Ben surveyed the room. "The sofa looks comfortable."

"It's average at best. But it's more comfortable than these old chairs." Darting to the side of one of the gray metal file cabinets, Lisa said, "This, however, is the best part of the office. Check it out."

Pulling the cabinet away from the wall, Ben saw eighteen signatures written in black marker. "So these are Hollis's old clerks?" he asked, reading through the names that covered half of the cabinet.

"No, they're the original Mouseketeers," Lisa said. "Of course they're the old clerks."

"When do we sign?"

"No time like the present," Lisa said, pulling a black marker from her back pocket.

"Aren't we eager?" Ben laughed.

"Hey, you're lucky I waited for you." With a flourish, Lisa wrote her name on the side of the cabinet. Ben signed just below and pushed the file cabinet back against the wall. "I guess you started in July?" he asked.

"Yeah. I wish I could've traveled more."

"That's where I've been," Ben said. "I just got back from Europe two nights ago."

"Bully for you," Lisa said as she flopped down on the sofa. "So give me your vital stats—where you're from, where you went to school, hobbies, aspirations, all the juicy stuff."

"Do you want my measurements too, or just my shoe size?"

"I can see the measurements," Lisa shot back. "Small feet, medium hands, average build, big ego."

Ben laughed. "And everyone said my co-clerk would be a stiff," he said, taking off his jacket. Ben had an oval face and a less-than-impressive jaw, but he was still considered handsome, with intense deep-green eyes and light-brown hair that fell over his forehead. Rolling up his sleeves, he said, "I'm from Newton, Massachusetts; I went to Columbia for undergrad and Yale for law school; last year I clerked for Judge Stanley on the D.C. Circuit; and I eventually want to be a prosecutor."

"Boorrrrrrrring!" Lisa said, slouching back on the sofa. "Why don't you just give me your résumé? Tell me about yourself. Loves, hates, favorite foods, sex scandals, what your family's like. Anything."

"Are you always this nosy?" Ben asked as he sat on the corner of his desk.

"Hey, we're going to be living in this room for the next twelve months. We better start somewhere. Now, are you going to answer or not?"

"My mother is an executive for a computer company in Boston. She's the aggressive, street-smart power-mom who grew up in Brooklyn. My dad writes a liberal op-ed column for *The Boston Globe*. They both went to the University of Michigan and met in a sociology class. Their first conversation was a fight: My father went crazy when he heard my mom say that salary level had a direct correlation with intelligence."

"All right! Controversy!" Lisa said, sitting up straight.

"They get along really well, but we can't discuss politics in the house."

"So where do you fall politically?"

"I guess I'm somewhere between moderate and liberal," Ben said, drawing an imaginary line with his hands. "I'm the product of a bipartisan marriage."

"Any girlfriends?"

"No, I think my dad's pretty much narrowed it down to my mom."

"Funny."

"I live with my three best friends from high school."

"You ever been in love?"

"You ever been called intrusive?"

"Just answer the question," Lisa said.

"Only once, though I'm not sure I can call it love. After law school, I took a two-month trip around the world—Europe and Asia, Bangkok and Bali, Spain and Switzerland, everything I could see."

"I take it you like to travel."

"Very much. Anyway, in Spain, I met this woman named Jacqueline Ambrosio."

"How exotic. Was she a native?"

"Nope. She was a marketing consultant from Rhode Island. She was starting her travels in Spain, and I was at the end of my trip. We met in Salamanca, took a weekend trip to that beautiful little island, Majorca, and parted ways five days after we met."

"Please, you're breaking my heart," Lisa moaned. "And let me guess, you lost her address, could never find her again, and to this day, your heart aches for her."

"Actually, on my last day there, she told me she was married, and that she'd had a great time revisiting the single life. Apparently, her husband was flying in the next day."

Lisa paused a moment, then asked, "Is that story bullshit?"

"Not a bit."

"Wasn't she wearing a wedding ring?"

"Not when we were together."

"Well, then, it's a good story. But it definitely wasn't love."

"I never said it was," Ben said with a smile. "How about you? What's your story? Just the juicy stuff."

Lisa swung her feet up onto the red sofa. "I'm from Los Angeles, and I hate it there. I think it's the toilet of the great Western rest room. I went to Stanford undergrad and Stanford Law only because I enjoy being near my family."

"Boorrrrrrring!" Ben sang.

"Don't get your panties in a bunch. My dad is originally from L.A.; my mom's from Memphis. They met, and I swear this is true, at an Elvis convention in Las Vegas. They collect Elvis everything—plates, towels, napkin holders, we even have an Elvis Pez dispenser."

"They have Elvis Pez heads?"

"Some lunatic collector in Alabama put sideburns on a Fred Flintstone Pez, filed down the nose, and painted on sunglasses. My parents went nuts and paid two hundred bucks for it. Don't ask; they're total freaks."

"I don't suppose your middle name is . . ."

"You got it. Lisa Marie Schulman."

"That's fantastic," Ben said, impressed. "I've always wanted to scar my kids with a really funny name, like Thor or Ira."

"I highly recommend it. Being taunted throughout childhood is great for your self-esteem."

"Let me ask you this," Ben said. "Do you twirl spaghetti?"

Lisa raised one eyebrow, confused.

"I think there are two kinds of people in this world," Ben explained, "people who twirl spaghetti on their fork to make manageable bites, and those who slurp it up, getting it all over themselves. Which are you?"

"I slurp," Lisa said with a smile. "And when I was little, I didn't eat anything white, so my mom had to dye my milk and my eggs with food coloring."

"What?" Ben asked, laughing.

"I'm serious. I used to hate the color white, so she used to make my milk purple and my eggs red. It was tons of fun."

"You used to cut the hair off your Barbie dolls, didn't you?"

"As soon as I pulled them out of the box," Lisa said proudly. "The little bitches asked for it."

"Oh, I can see it now," Ben laughed. "We're gonna get along great."

After a ten-minute Metro ride to Dupont Circle, Ben climbed one of Washington's many oversized escalators and headed home. A block from the subway, he spotted Tough Guy Joey, the neighborhood's angriest street person. "Hey, Joey," Ben said.

"Screw you," Joey snapped. "Bite me."

"Here's some dinner," Ben said, handing Joey the turkey sandwich he had brought to work. "Lucky me, they feed you on the first day."

"Thanks, man," Joey said, grabbing the sandwich. "Drop dead. Eat shit."

"You got it," Ben said. Passing the worn but cozy brownstones that lined almost every block of his neighborhood, Ben watched the legion of young professionals rush home to dinner down Dupont Circle's tree-lined streets. Almost home, Ben inhaled deeply, indulging in the whiff of home cooking that always flowed from the red-brick house on the corner of his block. Ben's own house was a narrow, uninspired brownstone with a faded beige awning and a forty-eight-starred American flag. Although it was August, the front door was still covered with Halloween decorations. Ben's roommate Ober was quite proud of his decorating and had refused to take them down before they got another year's use out of them. When Ben finally walked through the door, Ober and Nathan were cooking dinner.

"How was it?" Ober asked. "Did you sue anybody?"

"It was great," Ben said. He dropped his briefcase by the closet and undid his tie. "The justice is away for the next two weeks, so my co-clerk and I just worked through some introductory stuff."

"Your co-clerk—what's he like?" Ober asked, adding pasta to his boiling water.

"She's a woman."

"What's she look like? Is she hot?"

"She's pretty cute," Ben said. "She's spunky, very straightforward. There's no sense of bullshit about her. She's got nice eyes, pretty short hair . . ."

"She's a lesbian," Ober declared. "No question about it."

"What's wrong with you?" Nathan asked as Ben shook his head.

"Short hair and straightforward?" Ober scoffed. "And you think she's not a lesbo?"

"She did offer to fix my car today," Ben added.

"See," Ober said, pointing to Ben. "She just met him and she's already strapping on the tool belt."

Ignoring his roommate, Ben opened the refrigerator. "What're you guys making?"

"Anita Bryant is boiling the pasta, and I'm making my stinking garlic sauce," Nathan said. His square shoulders didn't budge as he moved the large pot of spaghetti to the back burner of the stove. Military in his posture, Nathan was still wearing his tie even though he had been home for a half hour. "Throw some more pasta in—there's only twenty boxes in the cabinet." Carefully, he moved his sauce pan to the front burner. "So tell us how it was? What'd you do all day?"

"Until the Court officially opens, we spend most of our day writing memos for cert petitions," Ben explained. Looking to make sure his friends were still interested in the explanation, he continued, "Every day, the Court is flooded with petitions seeking certiorari, or 'cert.' When four justices grant cert, it means the Court will hear the case. To save time, we read through the cert petitions, put them into a standard memo format, and recommend whether the justice should grant or deny cert."

"So depending on how you write your memo, you can really affect whether the Court decides to hear a case," Nathan reasoned.

"You can say that, but I think that might be overstating our power,"

Ben said, dipping his finger into the sauce for a taste. "Every other chamber also gets to see the memo, so you're kept in check by that. So let's say an important case comes through that would really limit abortion rights. If I slant the memo and recommend that Justice Hollis deny cert, all the conservative justices would go screaming to Hollis, and I'd look like a fool."

"But I'm sure on a marginal case, no one will really notice—especially if you're the only one who reads the original petition," Nathan said.

"I don't know," Ben said, shaking his head and leaning against the counter. "I think your Napoleonic side is showing tonight. This is the Supreme Court. There's a fierce code of ethics that goes along with it."

"I still can't believe you're clerking for the Supreme Court," Ober said as he peeled garlic over the sink. "The Supreme-fucking-Court! I'm answering phones, and you're hanging out at the Supreme Court."

"I guess you didn't get your promotion," Ben said.

"They completely dicked me over," Ober said quietly. With two dimples that punctuated his pale cheeks and light freckles that dotted his nose, Ober was the only one of Ben's roommates who still looked like he was in college. "The whole reason I went to Senator Stevens's office was because they said I'd only answer phones for a few weeks. That was five months ago."

"Did you confront them?" Ben asked.

"I tried everything you said," Ober explained. "I just can't be as aggressive as you are."

"Did you at least threaten to quit?" Ben asked.

"I kinda hinted at it."

"*Hinted* at it?" Ben asked. "What'd they say?"

"They said they're sorry to hold me up, but they're gearing up for an election year. Plus, there are at least a hundred people who would take the job in a heartbeat. I think I might have to urinate on the personnel manager's desk."

"Now that's a good idea," Nathan said. "Urination is a solid response for a twenty-eight-year-old. I've always heard it's the best path to a promotion."

"You have to be more forceful," Ben said. "You have to make them think losing you would be the end of the world."

"And how do I do that?"

"You have to present the total package," Ben explained. Noticing Ober's white oxford shirt, he added, "And you have to dress the part. I told you before—don't wear that shirt. With your freckles and that blond hair, you look like a total kid."

"Then what am I supposed—"

"Here." Ben took off his jacket and handed it to Ober. When Ober put it on, Ben said, "That fits you pretty well. I want you to wear my suit and tie. It's a good make-an-impression suit. Tomorrow morning, you'll go back into work and ask again."

"I can't ask again," Ober said.

"Maybe you can write them a letter," Nathan suggested to Ober. "That way you don't have to do it face-to-face."

"Absolutely," Ben said. "If you want, I'll draft it with you. Between the three of us, you'll have a new job in no time."

"I don't know," Ober said. Taking off the jacket, he handed it back to Ben. "Maybe we should just forget about it."

"Don't get frustrated," Ben said. "We'll get you through it."

"Why don't you tell Ben your scratch-off story," Nathan said, hoping to change the subject.

"Oh, my God, I almost forgot! I'll be right back." Ober ran out of the kitchen and up the stairs.

"We've really got to help him," Ben said.

"I know," Nathan said. "Just let him tell his story—it'll put him in a good mood."

"Let me guess. Does it have anything to do with the lottery?"

"P. T. Barnum would've loved him like a son."

"How can he be so addicted?"

"I don't know why you're surprised," Nathan said. "You were in Europe for six weeks. Did you really expect the world to change while you were gone? Some things are immutable."

"What took you so long?" Ben asked when Ober returned.

"You'll see," Ober began, his hands hidden behind his back. "So there I am, walking home from work in a pissy mood. Suddenly, I see a new poster in the window of Paul's Grocery: WE GOT LOTTERY!"

"Grammar is everything at Paul's," Nathan interrupted.

Undeterred, Ober continued, "First I bought a scratch-off. I scratch it and I win a dollar, so I buy another ticket. Then I win two dollars!" His voice picked up speed. "Now I *know* I can't lose. So I get two more tickets and I lose on one and win another dollar on the second."

"This is where normal people stop," Nathan interrupted.

"So I get this last ticket!" Ober continued. "And I scratch it off, and I win three bucks, which I use to buy Snickers bars for all of us!" From behind his back, he threw Snickers at Ben and Nathan.

"Unreal," Nathan said as he opened his candy. "Do you realize that you jumped through every hoop that the lottery commission set up for you?"

"Who cares?" Ober asked. He swallowed a huge piece of his candy bar. "I haven't had a Snickers in months. I figured it'd be a nice way to celebrate Ben's first day of work."

A half hour later, the three friends were seated at the kitchen table. "Honeys, I'm home!" Eric announced as he kicked open the front door.

"Can he have worse timing?" Nathan put down his fork as Ben and Ober headed toward the living room.

"The good son has returned!" Eric announced as soon as he saw Ben.

"It's about time," Ben said. "I thought you ran away."

With a half-eaten sandwich in hand, Eric embraced his roommate. Wearing an unironed button-down and creased khakis, Eric was the sloppiest of the four. His thick black hair was never combed, and his face was rarely shaven. The darkness of his sparse beard was heightened by his bushy black eyebrows. Only a few millimeters from touching, they created the perception of a constantly furrowed brow. "Sorry about that," Eric said. "I've had a deadline every night this week."

"Every night?" Ben asked, confused. "For a monthly?"

"He doesn't know about your job," Nathan said, walking into the living room. "Remember? He hasn't been here for six weeks."

"No more *Washington Life* magazine?" Ben asked.

"No, sir," Eric said. He scratched his head with vigorous pride. "Just when I thought I was going to spend the rest of my journalistic career covering local antique shows and the best new restaurants, I get a call from the *Washington Herald*. They had a staff writer opening in the political bureau. I started two weeks ago."

"You're working for a bunch of right-wingers?" Ben asked.

"Hey, it may be this city's secondary paper, but it's got circulation of eighty thousand, and they're all mine!"

"That's fantastic." Ben slapped his friend on the back.

"And by the way," Eric said to Ober, "guess what they're putting on the crossword page?"

"Don't toy with me . . . a word jumble?" Ober said, grabbing Eric by the front of his shirt.

"WORD JUMBLE!" Eric screamed. "Starting next month!"

"WORD JUMBLE!" Ober repeated.

"JUM-BLE! JUM-BLE! JUM-BLE!" the two friends chanted.

"Ah, what entertains the ignorant," Nathan said, putting his arm around Ben's shoulder.

"I have to admit, I really missed this," Ben said.

"They don't have simpletons in Europe anymore?" Nathan asked.

"Funny," Ben said as he turned back to his jumble-obsessed roommates. "Hey, wonder twins, how about getting back to dinner?"

"I can't," Eric said. Taking another bite of his sandwich, he explained, "This is dinner for me. Tomorrow's edition beckons."

Later that evening, Nathan walked into Ben's room, which was arguably the best-decorated room in the house. With his antique oak desk, oak four-poster bed, and oak bookcase, Ben was the only one of the four roommates to actually care about matching anything. Nathan had once thought about working on his room, but he reconsidered when he realized he was doing it just because Ben had done it. Three professionally framed black-and-white pictures hung on the wall over Ben's bed: one of a half-completed Washington Monument, one of a half-completed Eiffel Tower, and one of a half-completed Statue of Liberty. Ben was a pack rat when it came to memorabilia. On his bookshelf were, among other things, the keys to his first car, a personalized belt buckle his grandfather had given him when he was nine years old, the hairnet Ober used to wear when he worked at Burger Heaven, the hideous tie Nathan had worn to his first day of work, the visitor's pass he'd been given when he interviewed with Justice Hollis, and his favorite—the gavel Judge Stanley had given him when his clerkship ended.

"Still catching up on your mail?" Nathan asked, noticing the stack of envelopes Ben was flipping through.

"It's amazing to see how much junk mail one person can amass in a six-week period," Ben said. "I've gotten three sweepstakes offers, about fifty catalogs, a dozen magazine offers, and remember last year when Ober was watching Miss Teen USA and he called the eight hundred number to order us applications? I'm still on their mailing list. Listen to this: 'Dear Ben Addison. Are you the next Miss Teen USA? Only the judges know for sure, but you can let the world know about your participation by ordering from our selection of Official Miss Teen USA products.' " Looking up from the letter, Ben added, "I think I'm going to order Ober a Miss Teen USA sports bra. Once he's on their mailing list as a buyer, he'll never get off."

"That's a fine idea," Nathan said, sitting down on Ben's bed.

"So, tell me, what else is going on around here?" Ben said, throwing aside the letter.

"Honestly, nothing is different. Eric's around less because he's always on deadline."

"I guess he still hasn't done the deed?"

"Nope, our fourth roommate still remains a virgin. And he still contends it's by choice—waiting until marriage and all that."

"I guess Ober's still riding him about it?" Ben asked, knowing the answer.

"He's been riding him since eleventh grade," Nathan said. He smoothed back his red hair, which he wore cropped short to disguise his receding hairline. Nathan was the first of the roommates to start losing his hair and if he was in the room, baldness and hairstyles were forbidden subjects. Extremely competitive, he didn't like to lose at anything, and to him, his retreating hairline undermined his entire appearance, eclipsing everything from his determined posture to his angular jaw.

"And this new job at the *Herald*? It seems like Eric's really happy with it."

"Are you kidding?" Nathan asked. "Eric's been flying since he got this position. He thinks he's king of the world."

"Do I detect a bit of jealousy?" Ben asked.

"Not at all," Nathan said. "He spent two years getting a graduate degree in journalism—I'm happy he's finally writing about something more than local yard sales. I just wish he was around more."

"Don't give me that," Ben teased. "You couldn't give a crap whether he's around more. You just don't like the fact that he's doing better than you are."

"First of all, he's not doing better than me. Second of all, I don't mind that he's doing well, I just wish he'd be a little less selfish about it."

"And jealousy rears its ugly visage."

"You know what I mean," Nathan said. "Whenever Eric takes on anything, he becomes obsessed with it. He did the same thing when he was in grad school, the same thing when he was writing for that literary magazine, and the same thing when he started at *Washington Life*. I know he thinks he's both Woodward *and* Bernstein, but I wish he'd pay a little more attention to his friends. As it is, I don't think I've had one solid conversation with him since he started this job. He doesn't have time for us anymore."

"You want to know what I think? I think you're way too competitive. You always have been; you always will be."

"This has nothing to do with my competitiveness. It has to do with friendship."

"Give him a break," Ben said. "He's still new there. I'm sure he's just trying to make a good impression."

"Maybe," Nathan said as he picked up a pencil from the desk and began to doodle.

"Forget that. How's life at the State Department?" Ben asked. "Have you taken over any Third World countries in the past few weeks?"

"Alas, no. It's been pretty much what I thought. My boss has been in South Africa for the past week, so it's been slow. But I think they want to keep me around. I figure they'll put me in the S/P in a few more months.''

"S/P?"

"The secretary's policy planning staff. They do all the policy work for the department. People from the S/P usually feed into the major think tanks.''

"You and a bunch of big brains pondering our existence, huh?''

"Someone's got to think about running the world,'' Nathan said as he doodled an outline of the United States. "Meanwhile, what about you? Your first day at the Supreme Court. That's no mall job.''

"I know,'' Ben said as he fidgeted with the clasp of his datebook. "I just hope I'm okay starting in August instead of July. I felt kind of lost today.''

"I'm sure it's fine,'' Nathan said. "You haven't missed a thing. Besides, your co-clerk had a month head start.''

"I guess,'' Ben said. He walked over to his bookshelf, and began to reorganize his books.

Nathan watched his friend for more than a minute. "It's okay to be nervous,'' he finally said. "It *is* the Supreme Court.''

"I know. It's just that everyone there is so damn smart. They can name every Court precedent for the past twenty years; I can name the original cast of *L.A. Law.* That's not going to get me far.''

Without knocking, Ober entered the room. "Who died?'' he asked, recognizing the anxiety on Ben's face.

"He's just worried that the Supreme Court will be intellectually intimidating,'' Nathan explained.

"Big deal,'' Ober said as he sat on Ben's bed. "Tell them you can name the entire cast of *L.A. Law.* That always impressed me.''

"I'm a dead man,'' Ben said as he continued to reorganize his books.

"Ben, stop with the books. You have nothing to worry about,'' Nathan said. "For your whole life, you've been at the top of the intellectual ladder. You went from Columbia, to Yale, to a clerkship with Judge Stanley. Now you're working for Justice Hollis, one of the best justices on the Supreme Court. Either all of your success is a fluke, or you're just stressing. Which do you think is more likely?''

"He's probably a fluke," Ober teased.

"Shut up, pinhead," Nathan scolded. "Ben, you're the ultimate over-achiever. You used to alphabetize the crayons in the Crayola Sixty-four box. You researched the aerodynamics of the whiffle ball . . ."

"He was the only one of us who didn't eat the Play-Doh," Ober added.

"Exactly," Nathan agreed. "Besides myself, you're the smartest person I know."

Now smiling, Ben turned toward Nathan. "I'm smarter."

Holding back his own laughter, Nathan said, "Three letters, buddy-boy: S-A-T."

"Just because you beat me by a measly hundred points on the SAT does not mean you're smarter," Ben said.

"The test does not lie," Nathan said as he walked to the door. "You may have the street-smarts, but when it comes to unbridled intellectu-alism, you can call me master. And Ober, when we were little, none of us ate the Play-Doh. We used to pretend to eat it, just to watch you."

As Nathan left the room, Ober turned toward Ben. When Ben started laughing, Ober shouted back, "I knew that!"

CHAPTER 2

AT SEVEN THE FOLLOWING MORNING, BEN WALKED INTO JUS-
tice Hollis's chambers wearing plaid shorts and a faded T-shirt. "BEN,
IS THAT YOU?" he heard Lisa shout from their office. "Get your ass
in here!"

"What's wrong?" Ben asked, running into the office. "Are you
okay?"

"You won't believe what just happened." Lisa's fingers were racing
through the Rolodex on her desk. "I got a call from the governor's
office in Missouri, and we have twenty-four hours to act on this application for a death penalty stay."

"What are you talking about?" Ben asked, throwing his briefcase on
his desk.

"Here it is!" Lisa proclaimed, pulling a card from the Rolodex. Turning to Ben, she explained, "There's a murderer in Missouri who killed
three little kids. He was sentenced to death about ten years ago and
his case has been appealed through the courts since then. The execution was set for October, but for some reason, the state bumped up
the date to tomorrow. He's allowed an appeal to the Supreme Court,
so we now have twenty-four hours to find Hollis and get his opinion."

"How do we reach him?" Ben asked.

"That's what I'm trying to figure out," Lisa said, holding out the

Rolodex card. "He left me the number where he was staying in Norway, but apparently he went traveling for a few days. I took his Rolodex from his office. I know he has a sister who lives in California, so I'm going to call her."

Ben picked up his phone, dialed information, and asked for the number of the U.S. Marshals Service. Looking at Lisa he said, "Every justice has to have a marshal with them at all times. They must know where he is."

"Hi, Mrs. Winston?" Lisa asked. "I'm so sorry to wake you, but I'm a clerk for Justice Hollis and we need to reach him. It's an emergency."

"Hello, is this the Marshals Service?" Ben asked. "This is Ben Addison calling from Justice Mason Hollis's chambers. We need to reach the justice. It's an emergency."

"She doesn't know where he is," Lisa said, hanging up her phone as Ben explained the situation to the Marshals Service.

"Uh-huh. Okay. Yes, definitely," Ben said.

Lisa smacked Ben on the arm. "What're they saying?"

"They know where he is," Ben said, hanging up. "They won't give us the number, but they're contacting him, and they'll have him call us."

"Did you tell them it's an emergency?" Lisa asked. Noticing the do-you-think-I'm-a-moron look on Ben's face, she said, "Sorry, just making sure."

Ten minutes later, the phone rang. Pulling it from its cradle, Ben calmly said, "Justice Hollis's chambers . . . Hello, Justice Hollis. How's Norway? Yes, I hear it's beautiful this time of year. No. Yes, the office is great. Lisa's been terrific. We just had a little emergency. A death penalty appeal just came through, and they want to execute the defendant tomorrow morning. So, uh, what should we do?" After scribbling some notes to himself, Ben finally said, "We'll call you there later this afternoon."

"What the hell did he say?" Lisa yelled as soon as Ben put down the phone.

"Here's what has to happen," Ben said, flipping the page on his pad to make a list. "First, we have to let every justice know that their votes are due by eight tomorrow morning. We need five votes to get a stay of execution. If only four vote for the stay, this guy dies tomorrow. Then, after we notify all the chambers, we have to write a memo recommending whether Hollis should vote to grant the stay."

"All the relevant case history will be in the lower federal court papers," Lisa said.

"Exactly. And he told me how to get those. He said we probably won't be done until early tomorrow morning, but he said he wants the completed memo by six A.M. tomorrow. I have his fax number." Flipping on his computer, Ben said, "I'll write the official request so we can get the court papers."

"I'll let all the other chambers know what's happening."

"After you tell them, make sure you put the whole story in a memo so they all have official notification," Ben said as Lisa darted for the door. "Then none of them can say they didn't know about it."

Lisa nodded and ran out.

An hour later, nine boxes of official court papers were delivered to the office. "We're dead," Ben said when he saw the boxes being wheeled in.

"There's no way we'll be able to read through all this by tonight," Lisa said.

Ben read the sides of the boxes, which were labeled by year. "How about I start with the oldest stuff, and you take the newest? I figure we'll hit the middle together sometime this winter."

Lisa agreed and the two began to plow through the mountain of papers.

At two P.M., Ben's phone rang. "Justice Hollis's chambers. This is Ben," he said.

"Hi Ben, this is Rick Fagen. I was a clerk for Justice Hollis three years ago. I was just calling to see how things were going. It's a tradition for the older clerks to give you a call every once in a while. I know things can seem imposing in the first few weeks."

"It's a hell of a time, all right," Ben said.

"Who is it?" Lisa asked.

Covering the phone, Ben whispered, "It's one of Hollis's old clerks."

"Perfect," Lisa said. "I got a call from a clerk last month. They totally know how to deal with this crap. Ask him what we should do."

"Rick, can I ask you a question?" Ben said. "We just got a death penalty case—"

"Unbelievable," Rick said. "They always do this early in the term. I assume Hollis is away?"

"Sunning and funning in Norway," Ben said. "And we have to read a truckload of documents to recommend whether he should grant a stay."

"Okay, here's what to do," Rick said, with a reassuring confidence in his voice. "If this case has been floating around for a few years, chances are you'll never be able to read all the supporting documents. You should concentrate on the legal issue this final appeal is based on. All the other issues are unimportant. What I'd do is go on to one of the legal databases and key your search to the single legal issue you're looking at. If it's habeas, do a habeas search; if it's a jury instruction question, do that. Westlaw is definitely the easiest way to—"

"I already went through Westlaw," Ben said. "The problem is the record's a mess. We can barely tell where to start."

"Just focus on the original trial transcript, since so much of the appeal is usually based on a screwup that happened at the lowest level. Have any of the other justices reported in yet?"

"No," Ben said, still writing down Rick's instructions. "It just came to us this morning."

"If you're lucky, five of the other justices will grant the stay before you guys are done. That way you don't even have to sweat it out."

"And what are the chances of that?" Ben asked as Lisa read over his shoulder.

"It depends on the issue. If it's a Fourth Amendment issue, Osterman and the conservative crew will never touch it. Dreiberg might pick it up, though. The key for you guys is that you understand you're not writing *your* opinion, you're writing Hollis's. You may think this defendant got screwed, but you have to base it on what Hollis might think. Traditionally, he won't touch a death penalty appeal unless it's an innovative legal issue. Otherwise, he's pretty happy to put his faith in the lower court's decision.''

''What if it's based on factual innocence?'' Ben asked, twisting the phone cord tightly around his finger.

''That depends on the facts,'' Rick said. ''If you have a case where the defendant was truly denied his rights, Hollis may take it. You have to be careful, though. You're not Sherlock Holmes, so don't think you can solve the case from your office. If the defendant maintains that he's factually innocent, you better be sure there's a mistake in his trial. Don't waste Hollis's time by just saying you have a hunch and that you feel it in your gut that the defendant didn't do it. Hollis has been sitting on the bench for twenty-three years. He may have a weak spot for First Amendment issues, but he doesn't give a squat about your hunch.''

After a long pause, Ben said, ''What if you really, really know that this guy is innocent? I mean, you feel it in your gut and your chest and your armpits. Everywhere.''

''It's your decision,'' Rick warned. ''If you're right, good for you. But if you're wrong, Hollis'll deny the stay and you wind up with egg on your face. It's not that big a deal, but since it's your first few weeks, I'd want to gain a bit more of his confidence before I crawled out on a limb.''

''So I should let this guy fry so I don't look bad?''

''Listen, I don't know the facts of the case,'' Rick said. ''I'm just saying pick your battles wisely. I have to run, but if you have any questions just give me a call.''

''Listen, thanks for the help,'' Ben said. ''We really appreciate it.'' After writing down Rick's number, Ben hung up the phone, turned on his computer, and reentered the Westlaw database.

At five-thirty P.M., Joel, one of Chief Justice Osterman's clerks, entered the office. ''We're out. Osterman's denying the stay.''

''So you're leaving now?'' Lisa looked up from her stack of papers.

''You got it,'' Joel said with a smug smile. ''Our day is done.''

As Joel walked out, Lisa shouted, ''I wish you a life ridden with hardship and a lingering death.''

"See you tomorrow," Joel sang. "Hope you're not wearing the same clothes."

Within the next three hours, Justice Gardner denied the stay, while Justices Veidt, Kovacs, Moloch, and Dreiberg all granted it.

"Three justices left, and all we need is one more yes vote," Ben said. "What are the chances this decision falls on us?"

"I don't want to talk about it," Lisa said, her eyes glued to the document in her hand. "I just need to stay focused, and this will all be over soon. I am calm. I am focused. I am the center of my universe and I am one with the document."

At eleven P.M., Lisa leaned back in her chair and screamed, "I can't take it anymore! I haven't moved for the past twelve hours!"

"What happened to being one with the universe?" Ben asked.

"Fuck the universe," she said, getting up from her chair and pacing around the office. "I hate the universe. I whiz on the universe. I am now one with anger, resentment, and hatred. Let's fry this bastard and go home."

"Now that's exactly the kind of jurisprudence we need to see more of on this Court."

Suddenly, the office door opened and Angela announced, "Both Blake and Flam are out. Stay denied. It's all on you."

Ben looked at Lisa, whose shoulders slumped in defeat. "So if we fry this guy, we can go home?"

Not long after midnight, Ben was sitting in front of his computer, his eyes fixed on his screen. "I don't see the proof here," he said for the third time in fifteen minutes. "I don't know this guy, I never met him, but I know the proof's not here."

"You don't know shit," Lisa said, stretched out on the sofa with her arms covering her eyes. "Now what do we want to say in this memo?"

"Let's give Hollis a brief overview of the facts, and we'll recommend he grant the stay based on factual innocence."

"We don't know this guy is innocent," Lisa said.

"This defendant did not receive a fair trial, and that's a fact." Ben stopped typing. "The arresting officer swears in the police report that he saw someone run out the back door of the house when the defendant was arrested. But when the defense tries to admit the officer's testimony, the trial judge denies the request saying it's inconsequential. That's ridiculous."

Lisa sat up on the sofa. "It's called judicial discretion. There's no reason to assume the judge was wrong."

"There is a reason," Ben said, turning his chair toward his co-clerk. "The defendant contends that this mystery figure was an alibi witness on the night of one of the murders."

"That still doesn't explain the other two murders," Lisa said. "Even if he didn't kill one child, he killed two others."

"You're missing the point." Ben's voice rose with irritation. "I'm not saying he's innocent of all the murders, but if he killed two people instead of three, he might not've gotten the death penalty. Maybe the jury would've sentenced him to life imprisonment instead."

"Ben, this guy killed two innocent children in one night. Even you admit that. If he didn't kill three, big fuckin' deal. He still deserves what he's getting."

"That's just your opinion," Ben said, jumping from his seat. "If the jury voted on three murders, that's different than two murders."

"But you don't even know if the officer's testimony would've gotten him off," Lisa interjected. "Maybe he still would've been found guilty."

"But maybe he wouldn't have," Ben waved his hands, exaggerating his point. "It's not up to us."

"Listen to yourself," Lisa said, getting up from her seat to stand face-to-face with Ben. "You can't redo every trial just because you would've done it differently. The jury heard the defendant's testimony. They heard him say there was an alibi witness who he couldn't get in touch with. They still convicted him of three murders. Just because a cop saw this mystery witness, that doesn't mean the witness was really an alibi. Whether the policeman's testimony was admitted or not, the alibi couldn't be found. Seeing a person who could potentially be an alibi doesn't add one iota of proof that an alibi existed.''

"But it does change the story the jury heard," Ben said. "I'm not saying the policeman's testimony would've proven the alibi, but it would've added some strength to the defendant's story that a mystery man existed. Before you go to your death, I think you should at least get every opportunity to prove your story."

"You just feel bad for this guy because you don't like the death penalty as a solution," Lisa said.

"That's exactly right," Ben said, cracking his knuckles. "I want to recommend Hollis take the case. If you don't agree, I understand, but it's worth it to me. If Hollis disagrees, the worst that happens is I look bad. Considering this guy's life is at stake, I'll risk it. If it makes you happy, I'll put only my name on the memo."

Lisa shook her head and put her hands on her hips. "Do you really feel that strongly about this asshole?''

Ben nodded.

"Fine, let's write the recommendation," Lisa said. "If Hollis disagrees, though, I kick your ass."

Returning to the computer, Ben smiled. "Deal."

"Hurry!" Lisa yelled at five-fifty A.M. Racing out the door with the newly printed, thirty-two-page recommendation, Ben headed straight for the fax machine in Hollis's private office. Twenty minutes later, he returned. "Can we be more tired?" he asked, smoothing back his now greasy hair from his forehead.

"I assume the fax went through okay?" Lisa asked. The bags under her eyes highlighted her own exhaustion.

Ben nodded and sat down next to her on the sofa.

Squinting up at her co-clerk, she said, "You really have a wussy beard."

"I do not," he said, running his hand across his light stubble.

"You do too. It's not a character flaw. It just means you're not a real man."

"You wish you knew how much of a man I am," Ben said, smiling.

An awkward silence filled the room. "You just flirted with me," Lisa said.

"What are you talking about?" Ben laughed.

"You did. You just flirted."

"I did not."

"Then what was that 'You wish you knew how much of a man I am'? You might as well have said, 'Check out my meat.' "

"That was it. You got me," Ben said sarcastically. "Hey, Lisa, let's end these games. Check out my meat."

"You wish I would," Lisa said with a smirk.

Ben pointed at Lisa. "Don't pull that with me, woman! That was you flirting with me. You just did it back!"

"You're crazy," Lisa said, laughing. "Listen, let's just forget this. We're not hooking up. We're both tired, and I'm in no mood to let mental exhaustion make me do something I'll regret."

"Exactly." Ben tilted his head back. "Though I promise you no one has ever regretted it."

"Lisa, wake up!" Ben said, shaking her awake.

"Wha?" she said as she sat up on the red sofa. "What time is it?"

"It's seven-thirty. I can't sleep. I keep thinking about this defendant. What if Hollis denies the stay because we did a crappy job? That means we killed him."

"We didn't kill anyone. We did the best we could and we made a sound recommendation."

"You think so?"

"Definitely. We did what we thought—"

The phone rang.

Ben jumped for it. "Hello? Hi, Justice Hollis. Did you get the fax okay?" Ben fell silent and Lisa slapped his arm, trying to elicit a reaction. "No, we understand," Ben said. "Yes, we know the process. Okay. I guess we'll see you in a month or so. Have a good day." Hanging up, Ben paused, looking at Lisa with a blank stare. "That's five votes! We got stayed!" he screamed.

They embraced and jumped around the office, chanting, "We got stayed! We got stayed!"

"I can't believe it!" Lisa said. "What else did he say?"

"He said he enjoyed our memo. He said the argument was persua-sive, our analysis was sound. He said we used the word 'moreover' too much, but he thought we were right on point. He's already called the governor's office in Missouri. We just have to make all the preparations to hear the case."

"I can't believe it."

"And y'know what the best part was? Hollis actually said, and I quote, 'These trial courts are a fuckin' pain in the keister.' "

"Hollis said 'fuckin'?"

"Right to me," Ben said with a wide smile. "This is a great fuckin' day."

CHAPTER 3

STANDING IN FRONT OF ARMAND'S PIZZERIA, BEN ENJOYED the cool late October breeze. As summer officially ended, so did Washington's unbearable humidity. Without his jacket, and with his shirt sleeves rolled up to his elbows, Ben relished the quiet that blanketed the area. Already forgetting the green of summer, he stared at the brown and orange hue that decorated the trees along Massachusetts Avenue. Relaxed, he waited for his lunch companion. After a few minutes, he felt a tap on the shoulder. "Ben?"

"Rick?" Ben asked, recognizing the voice of Justice Hollis's former clerk. Rick wore an olive-green suit and a paisley tie. His most noticeable features were his eyes, puffy and slightly bloodshot. With thin, blond hair that was combed to perfection, Rick was tall and rangy and older-looking than Ben had anticipated. "It's nice to finally have a face to put with your voice," Ben said as they shook hands. "After all the advice you've given me in the last two months, I figured it was time to find out what you look like."

"Same here," Rick said as they walked into the restaurant. "So how has Hollis been treating you?"

"He's fine," Ben said as they sat down at a table in the corner. "It's been about a month and a half since he got back from Norway, so I think I'm finally used to his idiosyncrasies."

"He can be extremely odd, don't you think? I never understood why he would write only with pencils. Do you think he's allergic to pens?"

"I think that's just part of his personality," Ben said. "In his mind, nothing is written in stone; it's all changeable. I just wish he wouldn't eat the erasers from his pencils."

"He still does that?" Rick laughed. "That used to make me sick."

"It's one thing to eat a clean eraser. I'm all for clean erasers. But he gnaws on the dirty ones. One time I saw him erase half a sheet of paper. There was rubber fallout all across the paper and the eraser itself was pitch-black. He put that sucker right in his mouth and started chewing. It came out with nothing but metal showing. His teeth were all black, it was nasty."

"Ah, yes, I do miss those days," Rick said, looking down at the menu.

"Don't even bother with the menu," Ben said. "There's only one thing to get here." Ben pointed to the unlimited pizza bar that was Armand's specialty. "All the pizza you can eat for only four ninety-nine. It's just about the greatest thing in the city as far as I'm concerned. I can't believe you never heard about this place."

"I clearly missed out," Rick said, surveying the various pizzas.

After giving the waiter their order, Ben and Rick walked up to the pizza bar and grabbed three slices each. When they returned to the table, Ben said, "Meanwhile, thanks again for the advice on the *Scott* case. I didn't realize Hollis was so adamant about ruling for defendants on those."

"Our fair justice has never seen a Sixth Amendment case he didn't like," Rick said. "By the way, how did that death penalty case turn out?"

"You know I'm not supposed to tell you that," Ben said, forcing a slight laugh. "We signed an ethics code—everything's confidential."

"I signed the same agreement," Rick said, folding up a slice of pizza covered with onion and garlic. "And I'm still bound by it. Believe me, I know what it's like to sit in those chambers. The responsibility never ends."

Ben looked over his shoulder, then leaned over to Rick. "We're working on the dissent. The justices voted five to four to fry him. It was a heartbreaker."

"Hey, don't let it get you down," Rick said. "You guys did a great job in setting up that case. You can't—"

"I know, I can't win them all," Ben said. "I just wish we could've saved that guy. He got screwed by the trial court."

"He's not the first, and he's certainly not the last," Rick said. "So what else are you working on? What's happening with the CMI merger? Doesn't that come down next week?"

"Actually, it probably won't come down for another few weeks. Blake and Osterman asked for more time to write their opinions. You know how it is—merger cases always wind up confusing everyone. It takes forever to sort through all the regulatory nonsense."

"So who wins?"

"It was actually pretty amazing," Ben said, once again checking over his shoulder. "When the justices were voting in Conference, it was five to four against CMI. At the last minute, Osterman took Dreiberg out of Conference and into his chambers. According to Osterman's clerks, Osterman then convinced her that the regulations ran in favor of CMI, making the merger with Lexcoll completely legal under the Sherman Antitrust Act. Charles Maxwell is going to skip to work when this decision comes down. Rumor says he's spent well over five million just on legal expenses to get the case up to the Court."

"Any idea what made Dreiberg switch?"

"None. You know how Osterman is. He probably leaned on Dreiberg intellectually and Dreiberg gave in. It's hard for the newest justice to stand up to the chief justice."

"Especially when she's a woman," Rick said.

Surprised by Rick's comment, Ben said, "I wouldn't say that. Even if Dreiberg were a man, she'd have a hard time facing Osterman head-on."

"I guess," Rick said.

"What time is she coming over?" Nathan asked, polishing his shoes on the living-room coffee table.

"She should be here any minute." As Ben was working on his own shoes, he noted Nathan's meticulous rubbing and buffing. "How about I just pay you to do mine?"

"This is a passing of tradition, boy," Nathan said. "From father to son. From son to friend. Polishing shoes is a part of life."

"I can't believe I'm doing this," Ben said, rubbing the black polish into the loafer. "I feel like my grandfather. I mean, only old people shine their own shoes. I'm probably aging as we speak."

"Age has nothing to do with it," Nathan said. "I've been self-polishing since I was twelve."

"Yeah, but you also iron your socks."

"Just my dress socks," Nathan corrected. "As if you're one to speak."

"Don't give me that," Ben said. "I may be organized, but you're King Anal."

Nathan brushed the side of his shoe and added a little spit. "In your dreams."

"Is that why your credit cards are alphabetized in your wallet? Or why none of the clothes in your closet can ever touch each other?"

"I just want everything to have its own personal space," Nathan explained.

"Sure you do—and it's not because you're a freak." Staring at the loafer on his right hand, Ben added, "If Lisa saw me doing this, she'd have a field day."

"I can't believe you still haven't brought her by."

"I think you'll really like her," Ben said. "She's got spunk."

"Then why don't you date her?"

"I can't," Ben said. "We're too close. It'd be like dating my sister." He slipped his feet into his gleaming loafers.

When the doorbell rang, Ben went to answer it. "Nice place," Lisa said as she stepped inside. "Better than I thought it'd be." Against the far wall in the living room sat a large, deep-blue couch. A smaller striped love seat served as a way station for jackets, briefcases, wallets, and keys. Both had been bought with the proceeds from the room-mates' first paychecks in Washington. Over the larger couch hung an enormous, empty gold frame, surrounding a splattering of red, blue, yellow, and green paint, which Eric had painted directly onto the wall when they first moved in. In Eric's words, it was "primary colors in action"; in Ben's words, "a nice first attempt—if you're into the whole Jackson Pollock thing." In Ober's words, "it didn't suck." Nathan proclaimed it "a disaster."

Ben walked into the living room with Lisa and introduced Nathan, who was still polishing his shoes.

"Nice to finally meet you," Lisa said. Sniffing the air and noting the shoeshine kit, she added, "If you guys want, we can go catch a movie. They have a senior citizens' discount."

"Make fun if you like," Ben said.

"Oh, I definitely like," she said, glancing around the room. "By the way, what's with the coffee table?" The coffee table in the center of the room was actually a poster of Elbridge Gerry—according to Ben, the country's worst vice president—mounted on a piece of Formica, resting on concrete blocks.

"That's the most politically obscure coffee table in town," Ben explained proudly. "Where else can you rest your feet on the face of someone who refused to sign the U.S. Constitution?"

"You're really freaky sometimes, y'know that?" Lisa said. Walking past the glass dining-room table that was set up between the kitchen and the living room, Lisa entered the kitchen and approached a calendar attached to the refrigerator. "Is this a Miss Teen USA calendar?" she asked, noticing the logo under the picture of a young girl in an evening gown. Flipping through the months, she said, "This is pathetic."

"I knew you were a flipper," Ben said, watching her from the living room. "There are two types of people in this world: those who never look ahead on a wall calendar so they can be surprised every month, and those who flip ahead, racing to see all the months at once."

Lisa headed back to the living room. "I thought you said there were only *two* types of people: spaghetti-twirlers and spaghetti-slurpers."

Ben paused, then eventually said, "Okay, there are four types."

Suddenly, Ober walked in the door. "I'm home! Is the lesbo here yet?"

"Actually, there are five types," Ben said.

As Ober approached Lisa, Ben shut his eyes and prepared for disaster. "You must be Ober." Lisa extended a hand. "That's funny. Ben said your palms would be much hairier."

As Nathan laughed, Ober said, "Really? He said you'd be more butch."

"He said you couldn't walk upright," Lisa countered.

"He said you could pee standing up."

"Cute," Lisa said. "He said you didn't have opposable thumbs."

"I don't get it," Ober said, stumped. "What's an opposable thumb?"

"If you didn't have them, you'd be hanging out with monkeys. Or reptiles. Maybe bacteria. Lower life forms—"

"Ooookay, I think we get the idea," Ben interrupted, stepping between his two friends. "I can see you two will get along great. Now what are we doing for dinner?"

"I thought Lisa was cooking for us," Ober said, taking a seat next to Nathan on the large couch. "No—that's right—she was going to fix my car."

"Don't start," Ben warned. "How about we order in some Chinese?" With a nod, the three agreed and Ben called in the order. As he hung up the phone, Lisa reached into her bag. "Ben, I meant to show you this." Pulling out a ten-page document, she explained, "I just pulled this off of Westlaw. It's our first published opinion."

Ben smiled as he read through the official document. "I can't believe it! These are our words! This is the law!"

"I still don't understand this," Nathan said. "You decide the cases for the justices? Is that legal?"

"We don't decide the cases. We just write the opinions," Ben explained, waving the document in the air. "Every Wednesday and Friday the justices have Conference, where they vote on the cases. Based on our memos and research, they determine what their decisions will be. Say there's a civil rights case before the Court. The justices vote and five think the defendant is liable, while four think he's not. He's therefore liable. But the decision doesn't just get announced. The actual opinion has to be assigned and written. That takes from one to six months. So if Hollis is assigned the opinion, he comes back from Conference and says to me and Lisa, 'We're writing the majority opinion; the defendant is liable. I'd like to see you approach it from a Fourteenth Amendment perspective.' We take a shot at it and hand it in to Hollis. Usually, he makes significant changes before it emerges in final form, but it's still primarily our work."

"And here it is," Lisa said, pulling the document from Ben's hands and giving it to Nathan. "Hollis decided this months ago, but it just came down this week."

"Very impressive," Nathan remarked.

"See this paragraph over here?" Lisa pointed to the page. "We worked on that for two days straight. Hollis didn't want to overrule one of his earlier decisions."

The doorbell rang. "Food. Food. Food," Ober said, running to the door.

"It's not the food," Ben called out. "We just ordered."

Ober opened the door, but was disappointed to discover Eric.

"Sorry, I forgot my keys at the office," Eric said, running his hands through his uncombed hair.

"Perfect," Ober said, excited. "C'mon, there's someone I want you to meet." Dragging Eric into the living room, Ober said, "Lisa, this is Eric. He's a virgin."

"You'll have to forgive him," Eric said as he shook Lisa's hand. "He's so proud of me, he can't contain himself."

"Nice to meet you," Lisa said. "I've heard a lot about you."

"You, too," Eric said.

Ignoring Ober, Ben asked Eric, "Do you want to have some dinner? We ordered Chinese. It should be here any minute."

"That'd be great," Eric said. "Meanwhile, have you heard about the CMI merger?"

"No. What?" Ben asked.

"I was in the newsroom when it came across the wire. Just as the market closed, Charles Maxwell bought another twenty percent of Lexcoll stock. Lexcoll stock shot up fourteen points in the closing three minutes, and investors are predicting CMI will rocket up thirty percent by nine-thirty-five tomorrow morning. The traders on the floor were ripping their hair out."

"Maxwell couldn't have known, could he?" Lisa asked Ben.

"No. No way," Ben said, a chill running down his back as he remembered his conversation with Rick. Maxwell couldn't have known, Ben told himself. "There's no way. It was a lucky guess. The Court's decision isn't completely unpredictable. Maxwell must've spoken with his legal experts."

"Whatever he knew," Eric said, "they're calling it the riskiest decision Maxwell's ever made. If he's right, he's a billionaire, but if the Court denies the merger, he's invested all of his money in the worst communication alliance in history."

When Ben arrived at work the next day, a memorandum was sitting on his desk. Addressed to all clerks, the memo stated that due to the recent circumstances regarding the CMI merger, everyone should be reminded that all Court information is extremely confidential and should not be released under any circumstances. Suddenly, Ben felt a hand on his shoulder. "Who the f—" he yelled, spinning around.

"Take it easy, big guy," Lisa said.

"You scared the shit out of me," Ben said, wiping his forehead.

"Can you believe this memo?" Lisa was holding up her own copy. "Who the hell do they think they are? Is this an accusation or what?"

"I don't think it's so bad," Ben said as he fidgeted with his tie. "I think it's just a reminder. I'm sure the press is all over them to see if Maxwell's guess was correct."

"Well, the decision's been pushed up to next week, so all the vultures will know soon enough it he's a guru or a goofball. Listen, I'm going to get some coffee. You want anything?"

Ben shook his head. When Lisa left the office, Ben went straight to his Rolodex and looked up Rick's number. After picking up the phone and dialing the number, he was surprised to hear a mechanical female voice say, "The number you have reached is no longer in service. Please check the number and dial again." Confused, he redialed, double-checking each digit. "The number you have reached is no longer in service. Please check the number and dial again."

Slamming down the phone, Ben crumpled the Rolodex card in his hand and threw it against the wall. Damn, he thought. What the hell do I do now? He picked up the phone, and quickly dialed information. "In D.C., I'm looking for the phone number of a Rick Fagen. F-A-G-E-N." Ben tapped his pen nervously.

"I'm sorry, sir," the operator said. "I have no Fagens listed."

"How about if I give you his old phone number? Can you see if there's a forwarding number?" Ben asked.

"I can try," the operator said. Ben ran to the other side of the room to retrieve the Rolodex card. "Sir, are you there?"

Ben raced back to his desk and sat in his chair. "I'm here." He read off Rick's old number.

"I'm sorry, sir," the operator said, "that number is no longer in service."

"I know that," Ben snapped. "That's why I asked if there was a forwarding number." Bristling, he asked, "Can you tell me where the bill was forwarded to?"

"I'm sorry, we cannot give out that information."

"Thanks," Ben said, hanging up the phone. In a full-fledged sweat, he put his forehead down on the desk. There must be an explanation for this, he told himself. Rick just moved. There's no reason to panic. There's nothing to be upset about. He redialed information and got the number for the phone company. "Hi, my name is Rick Fagen," Ben said to the operator. "I recently disconnected my number, and I think I might've given you the wrong forwarding address. Can you check it, because I don't want to be late on my payments."

"Let me transfer you to the accounts payable department, Mr. Fagen," the operator said.

"Can I help you?" the new operator asked.

Ben described his situation again.

"What was your old phone number?"

Ben read the number off the crumpled Rolodex card and waited. Finally, the operator said, "Mr. Fagen, I'm glad you called. You never left a forwarding address."

"Are you sure?" Ben picked up a pen. "What address do you have?"

"All we have is the old one," the operator said. "Seventeen eighty Rhode Island Avenue, Northwest. Apartment three seventeen."

"That's the old one, all right," Ben said, writing down the address. "Well, as soon as I have a new address, I'll be sure to let you know." Ben hung up, then slid back in his chair, trying to think of another way to track down Rick. After checking the index on the Supreme Court directory, he left the office and ran down the hallway. Ben raced down the suspended spiral staircase, an architectural marvel that was off limits to everyone but staff. Running through the Great Hall, he followed his mental road map of the Court's layout, weaving his way through the corridors to the personnel office.

"Can I help you?" a woman asked from behind the counter.

"Hi, I'm Ben Addison, a clerk with Justice Hollis. We were trying to have a reunion for all of Hollis's old clerks, and I remember filling out all that paperwork for this office when I first started. Do you happen to have a list of where some of the old clerks might live?"

"Oh, we've got everyone here," the woman said, proudly. "Since we do the security forms, we know every place you've lived in the past ten years."

"Well, all we need is the address of one past clerk. We have everyone else."

"Security card?" the woman requested.

Ben reached into the front pocket of his dress shirt, pulled out his Court I.D., and gave it to the woman. After swiping it through a small, electronic machine on her desk, she stared at her computer, waiting for Ben's security clearance to appear.

"C'mon," Ben thought, his thumbs tapping against the high counter.

"What's the clerk's name, honey?" the woman finally asked as she handed Ben his I.D. card.

"Rick Fagen," Ben said, returning the card to his shirt pocket. "I guess it could be under Richard."

After typing the name into the computer, the woman said, "I don't have anyone under that name as a clerk for Justice Hollis."

Surprised, Ben said, "Maybe our master list is wrong. Can you check the list of clerks for the other justices?"

As the woman reconfigured her search, Ben continued tapping.

"Sorry," the woman said, "I have no one under that name listed as a clerk."

"That's impossible," Ben said, his voice rising in panic.

"I'm telling you," the woman said, "I checked our entire personnel database. No one named Rick Fagen ever worked at the Supreme Court."

CHAPTER 4

BEN DARTED UP THE STAIRS, THEN SPRINTED FULL SPEED back to his office. He ran toward the farthest file cabinet and pulled it away from the wall. Rick Fagen's signature wasn't there. "Damn!" he yelled, punching a huge dent into the cabinet. "How could I be so stupid?" Turning around, Ben noticed the giant bouquet of red, yellow, and purple flowers on his desk. He pulled the card from the oversized wicker basket and opened the miniature envelope. "Thanks for all your help," he read. "Sincerely, Rick." Ben's stomach dropped. He felt like he was going to vomit. When the room started to spin, he put his head down on his desk. I'm in serious trouble, he thought. What the hell am I going to do?

Eventually catching his breath, Ben pushed aside the basket of flowers, picked up his phone, and called Nathan. "It's me," he said.

"Are you okay?" Nathan asked. "You sound like you're out of breath."

"Can you meet me at home?"

"It's not even ten o'clock."

"Nathan, please, can you meet me at home? It's important."

"Of course." Nathan sounded confused. "I'll leave right now, but what's going on?"

"I'll tell you when I see you," Ben said, and hung up.

Ben wrote a quick note for Lisa, grabbed his briefcase, and headed for the door. As he left the building, he saw Lisa walking up the steps of the Court. "Where're you going?" she asked.

"I'm having bad stomach cramps," Ben said. His face was ashen. "Can you tell Hollis I had to go home sick?"

"Of course. Are you okay?"

"I just need to go home."

When Ben entered the house, he walked straight up to his room, sat on the bed, and tried his best to relax. He slowed his breathing. He imagined a walk in a quiet forest. He thought about the silence of scuba diving. Keep calm, he told himself. It's okay. Worse things can happen. Cancer. The plague. Death. Unable to sit still, he paced inside the little room. Over and over he repeated the sequence of events. "Damn!" he finally said aloud. "How could I have been so stupid?" Moving back to the bed, he again tried to relax. It was no use. He wondered what he should do. Should he go to Hollis? If he did, he'd be fired on the spot. No, there had to be a better way out. As his mind played through the different alternatives, he kept coming back to the same conclusion: The first step was finding the person who caused this disaster. Ben knew he had to find Rick. His thoughts were interrupted when a car pulled into the driveway.

"Ben!" Nathan yelled from downstairs.

"I'm up here," Ben called.

Nathan dashed up the stairs two at a time and charged into Ben's room. "What happened?"

Ben sat on the bed, his head in his hands. "I totally blew it," he said.

"What? Tell me."

Ben raced through the story. "And I think this guy Rick might've leaked the info to Maxwell."

Nathan stared out the window. "You don't know that," he said. Speaking calmly and slowly, he explained, "There's no reason to believe the worst."

Looking up at his friend, Ben recognized Nathan's consoling-but-lying voice. "Nathan, I know Rick did it. No one risks millions on a guess like that. He even sent me flowers to say thank you. He set me up and I fell for it completely. It was easy for him. All he had to do was some quick research and make a call to the Court once the new clerks started. The justices aren't there; we're wet behind the ears. It's simple.''

''I don't understand.'' Nathan leaned on the windowsill. ''You never asked Hollis about Rick?''

''No way,'' Ben said. ''I didn't want Hollis knowing I was getting advice from the outside. Lisa and I have to look as smooth as possible.'' Ben's gaze dropped to the floor. ''FUCK!'' he yelled, pounding the bed. ''That was so damn *stupid* of me!''

''There's nothing you can do about it,'' Nathan said, trying his best to comfort his friend. ''Maybe we can try to find Rick. Do you have his phone number?''

''I already checked it. Disconnected. But I do have his address.''

''You really don't have to come,'' Ben said as he opened the door to Nathan's old maroon Volvo.

''You make me take off work, and then you want to dump me while you go check out this guy's house?'' Nathan asked. ''Forget about it.''

''It's not that I'm trying to leave you out of anything—''

''I know,'' Nathan said. ''And I'm not here because I'm afraid of being left out. I'm here because I want to help you.''

''I appreciate it,'' Ben said as Nathan pulled out of the driveway. ''I just didn't want to get you involved with my problems.''

Nathan drove up Seventeenth Street, and pulled into a parking spot a few blocks from the address. ''Let's walk up.''

Ben looked up at the dark clouds. ''Do you have an umbrella? It's about to pour.''

''There should be one under your seat,'' Nathan said.

Located near the city's business district, 1780 Rhode Island was a building displaced in time. Designed in the late 1970s, it was bilious green, eight stories tall, and had tinted, full-story glass windows. A sore thumb on any architectural hand. After pushing open the heavy glass doors, Ben and Nathan walked into the lobby and approached the doorman, who was sitting at a slightly rusted metal desk in the otherwise renovated surroundings.

"Can I help you?" the doorman asked.

"I'm here to see my brother, Rick Fagen," Ben said. "He's in apartment three seventeen."

The doorman stared at the two friends for a few seconds. Eventually he said, "Follow me." Ben and Nathan glanced at each other, hesitating for a moment. But when Nathan nodded approval to Ben, they fell into step behind the doorman. Leading them up a small set of steps and past the building's only elevator, the doorman turned down a long hallway that ran along the right side of the building. He stopped at a room marked PRIVATE and opened the door, leading them inside. "Take a seat," the doorman said, pointing to two worn leather sofas in the waiting area. Nathan and Ben obliged, and the doorman walked through another door, which looked like it led to an office.

"You think this'll work?" Nathan asked.

"Can't hurt to try," said Ben.

Nathan looked around the empty waiting area, paneled in fake knotty pine. "This place has Mafia written all over it," Nathan whispered.

"What are you talking about?"

"It does," Nathan said. "It smells musty like my cousin Lou's house. We should get out of here."

"You can go," Ben whispered. "I'm staying."

"This was a bad idea," Nathan said. "For all we know, Rick could be in that room."

Before Ben could respond, the doorman and a small man with a mustache stepped out of the office. "I'm the manager. Can I help you?"

"Hi, I'm Rick Fagen's brother," Ben said, extending a hand to the manager. "He told us to meet him here."

The manager ignored Ben's extended hand, and examined Ben and Nathan. Putting his hands in the pockets of his slacks, he smirked. "If you're his brother, how come you didn't know he moved out of here two weeks ago? Listen, people like their privacy here. If you think you're going to fool us, you'll have to make up a better line of bullshit than saying you're his brother. Now, unless you're cops, get the fuck out of here.''

The doorman opened the door, and roughly escorted Ben and Nathan outside. "I think that was pretty successful," Nathan said as the glass door closed behind them. Standing under the building's awning, Ben stared out into a furious downpour. Opening his umbrella, Nathan said, "Well, at least we won't get—"

"I'm a dead man," Ben said as he rushed into the rain, toward the car.

Throughout the drive back, Ben was silent. "C'mon, snap out of it," Nathan said when they returned home.

"I just need to think," Ben said, heading straight for the kitchen.

"You've been thinking for the past fifteen minutes. Say something."

"What do you want me to say?" Ben raised his voice. "I just got screwed, and I jeopardized my entire career. Boy, what a wonderful day!"

"Listen, don't take this out on me," Nathan said. From the refrigerator, he poured himself a glass of iced tea. "I'm here for you, and I'll do my best to help you, but don't make me your whipping boy."

"I'm sorry," Ben said as he sat at the small kitchen table. "It's just—I just—this's a disaster."

Nathan handed the iced tea to Ben. "That's okay. But let's at least do something. Focus your energy. How about we plan Rick's death?"

"I've been doing that for the past three hours," Ben said, clutching the glass. "So far, the best I can come up with is slicing off his eyelids and sitting him in front of a mirror. He'll go insane watching himself since he won't be able to shut his eyes."

"That's one way to deal with him."

"I'm not screwing around," Ben said. He took a gulp of tea. "I have to find this guy. If word gets out that I leaked a decision, my life is over. And without Rick, I can't prove my innocence. At least with him, I can try to prove his link with Maxwell. Otherwise, I don't know what else to do. Can't we put a search on him through the State Department?"

"Not without saying why we're looking for him. And if you do, you can say good-bye to your job."

"And my entire career."

"But we can do a confidential search," Nathan blurted, his voice racing with newfound confidence. "All we need is a member of Congress to—" Hopping off the counter and grabbing the phone, Nathan dialed Ober's number. "Hello, Ober? It's me. We need some serious help. Are you still answering constituents' letters?"

"Absolutely," Ober said. "I'm the master of junk mail."

"Then you still have access to the pen-signing machine that fakes the senator's signature?"

"Of course," Ober said. "Did you really think Senator Stevens signed your birthday card?"

"I need a favor," Nathan said. "I need you to write an official request on Senate letterhead. Address it to my attention at the State Department and ask that a confidential background check be done on— what's his name, Ben?"

"Richard or Rick Fagen," Ben said with a wry smile. "Here's his old phone number and address."

After relaying the information, Nathan told Ober, "Make sure that the letter says that all correspondence should go to me."

"What's this for?" Ober asked suspiciously.

"I'll tell you later," Nathan said. "Now's not the time."

"But isn't this illegal?" Ober asked.

"Kind of, but it's an emergency," Nathan said. "We need this information."

"Actually, I have a way around the illegal part," Ben said, grabbing the phone from Nathan. "Ober, it's me," he said. "Let me ask you a question: What do you do when a wacko writes a letter to the senator?"

"It depends," Ober said. "Serious death threats go straight to the Secret Service. But if it seems like the writer is just a regular wacko, we're supposed to use our discretion."

"Perfect," Ben said. "Then here's what you do: Write a fake death threat to the senator and sign it Rick Fagen. But make the letter a little weird. That way, if anyone ever asks why you opened the investigation, you'll give them the letter and say you were just trying to protect the senator's life."

"Nicely played," Nathan said, taking back the phone. "Ober, one last thing. Make sure we get a good signature on the autograph machine. You can spot those fake ones a mile away." Nathan said goodbye and hung up the phone. "Feeling a little better?"

"A little." Ben wiped his still-wet hair from his forehead. "By the way, thanks for coming home."

"You give the order, I follow it," Nathan said, saluting his friend.

Later that afternoon, the phone rang in Ben's room. "Hello?" he answered, stretching from his bed to pick up the receiver.

"Ben, it's Lisa. I just called to see how you were feeling."

"I'm doing okay," Ben said, uncomfortable about lying. "It was just some stomach cramps."

"Are you bullshitting me?" Lisa asked. "Because I'll come straight over there after work."

"I swear, I'm okay," Ben said, lying back on his bed and staring at the ceiling. "I have an upset stomach and I wasn't feeling well. Is that okay?"

"Sure. Fine," Lisa said. "So, how much have you missed me?"

"Tons. Now what happened today? Anything exciting?"

"Nothing really. Everyone's been talking about the Charles Maxwell case. Hollis is worried that once the decision is announced, everyone is going to scream that he had an inside source."

"It's definitely possible," Ben said as he fidgeted with the vertical blinds that covered his window.

"I guess," Lisa said. "I just think the media sucks Carter's left peanut. They cry conspiracy at the drop of a hat."

"Carter's left peanut?" Ben laughed. "What decade are you living in?"

"You never heard that? That's a famous saying."

"I'm sure it was," Ben said sarcastically, "back when there was an oil crisis."

"Listen, I don't need to be made fun of. I have better things to do. Meanwhile, who sent you the flowers?"

Quickly realizing he'd forgotten to throw away Rick's bouquet, Ben tried to stall. "What flowers?" he stammered.

"There's a giant basket sitting on your desk."

"They're probably from my mother. I told her I wasn't feeling well last night."

"Do you want me to open the card?" Lisa asked. "Because I can see the envelope right next to—"

"No!" Ben yelled. "Leave it alone."

"Sorry," Lisa said. "I didn't—"

"It's not your fault. I just don't like people opening my mail."

"Maybe I should take the week off from work," Ben said as he and Nathan made dinner.

"No way," Nathan said, dicing a large onion. "You don't want to call attention to yourself. The best thing you can do is just go about your business."

"I won't be able to concentrate, though. I have to find Rick. I have to—"

"Forget it," Nathan interrupted. "What are you going to do? Wander aimlessly around the city until you bump into him? If Ober opened the investigation correctly, we'll have some information by the end of the week." He pulled the lid off the rice cooker and a fragrant cloud of steam wafted into the room. "Have you decided whether you're going to tell Ober what happened?"

"I have to," Ben said as he set out two plates on the table. "He's my friend."

"He's also a moron," Nathan added.

"Yeah, but he's still my friend. And he has a right to know what that letter's about."

"How about Eric?" Nathan asked as he dumped the diced onion into a saucepan.

"I don't know. I don't want to drag everyone into this. It's bad enough you two are involved."

"I appreciate the concern, but I think you should tell Eric. Maybe some of his contacts at the paper can find out something about Rick's building."

"That's not a bad idea," Ben agreed.

"Have you thought about telling Hollis?"

"I can't," Ben said, shaking his head. "He'd lose all respect for me. Not to mention having to fire me for violating the Code of Ethics." As he put out forks and napkins on the table, he added, "I think I may tell Lisa, though."

"Bad idea," Nathan said. "Definitely a bad idea. You hardly even know her. What makes you think she won't turn you in?"

"She wouldn't," Ben said. "Lisa's a great friend. Besides, she has a right to know. She's spoken to Rick. For her safety alone, I have to tell her."

"She's in no danger. You don't have to say a thing."

"I do," Ben said. "It's the right thing to do. If the situation were reversed, I'd want her to tell me. Besides, with all those flowers Rick sent to the Court, it's clear that he isn't just going away. I think he's trying to tell me that he knows how to reach me—and if that's the case, I have to warn Lisa."

"Just be careful," Nathan said. "I would hate to see it backfire on . . . Damn!" Nathan missed a clove of the garlic he was chopping and sliced into his finger. "Son of a bitch!" he yelled.

"Are you okay?" Ben asked.

"Yeah, I'm fine," Nathan said. He ran his bleeding finger under the faucet. "It's just a tiny cut."

"Those're the ones that hurt the most."

Just then, Ober and Eric returned. "Home, crap home," Ober announced as he walked through the door. Heading straight for the kitchen, he looked at Nathan. "Now what was all that secrecy about today? What the hell happened?"

Holding his finger and looking at Ben, Nathan was silent.

"I got into a bit of trouble," Ben said, trying to be as casual as possible.

"It better be bad," Ober said. "Writing fake death threats to a senator could get me thrown in jail."

"You wrote a death threat to a senator?" Eric asked, stealing a slice of red pepper from the cutting board.

"I'll tell you what happened," Ben said, "but you have to swear you won't say a word." He quickly explained everything that had happened, including his and Nathan's encounter at Rick's old building.

"You're a dead man," Ober said. "They're probably plotting your death right now."

"I told you not to tell him," Nathan said to Ben.

"Eric, do you think you can find out anything about this building from people at work?" Ben asked.

"I'll try," Eric said, not meeting Ben's eyes.

"What?" Ben asked, noticing Eric's uneasiness.

"This is no joke," Eric said, sitting at the kitchen table. "This guy Rick, whoever he is, isn't some petty scam artist. You can't just walk up to Charles Maxwell and say, 'I've got a secret.' Rick's got to be connected."

"I'm sure he is," Ben said. "When we went to his building today, the manager wouldn't say a single word about him."

Eric paused for a minute, then said, "I know you may think this a crazy option, but if you want, you can go to the press with this."

"No way," Ben said. "If the Court learns I violated the ethics code, they have to fire me, and my career is ruined. And on top of that, I'd look like a fool in front of millions of people."

"You did get suckered pretty badly," Ober said as he reached for his own piece of red pepper.

"Thanks," Ben said. "Thanks for your support." He looked at Eric. "At this point, I still want to see what we can find out ourselves. My career is in enough jeopardy, and the last thing I want to do is publicize that fact."

"Whatever you want," Eric said. "It's your life."

When Ben returned to work the next day, he immediately searched for the card from the floral bouquet. Ripping up the tiny note, Ben thought about what to do with the basket. He didn't want to keep it around, but was afraid that if he threw it away, Lisa would be even more curious. He eventually put the bouquet on top of one of the file cabinets. That way, he could decorate the office and say the flowers were from his mother.

Even without the flowers, Ben's desk was still covered with paper. Amid the piles of cert petitions were drafts of forthcoming decisions.

Each set of documents was enclosed in a brown folder marked "Confidential—Justice Hollis's Chambers Only." Although there was nothing to prevent anyone from opening a folder, Hollis was convinced that the moral consequences would deter potential peekers. Each folder was also labeled with a yellow Post-it, which Ben and Lisa used to identify the status of a document. Not a single opinion went to Hollis until both were satisfied with its content. Quickly scanning the Post-its, Ben was surprised to see one marked "First Draft—*Kramer* decision."

Lisa entered the office. "Morning, sick boy. How're you feeling?"

"I'm fine." Holding the Kramer folder in his hand, he said, "You didn't have to do this. I was assigned the first draft."

"I know, but you were sick, and I had some free time on my hands, so I figured—"

"You didn't have to write a full extra opinion, though. You have enough to do."

"Forget about it," Lisa said. "I wanted to help you. I did it. It's done. Be grateful."

Waiting until Lisa sat at her desk, Ben smiled. "Thank you."

At noon, Lisa and Ben walked down to Union Station for lunch. After years of languishing in ruin, the station was once again a tourist haven. Under the linked barrel-vaulted ceilings, between the statues and columns and sculptures and archways, more than a hundred upscale shops had popped up, along with a multiplex movie theater and, of course, a food court. Every time he walked through, it made Ben sick.

Lisa and Ben skirted the massive groups of tourists and grabbed a table in the corner of the food court. "Are you okay?" Lisa asked, watching Ben pick at his french fries.

"I'm fine. There's just something I have to tell you."

"Wait a minute. If you're about to tell me you're in love with me, I may vomit."

"It's not that," Ben said. "You wish it was that." Wiping his hands with a napkin, he asked, "Remember Rick? Hollis's old clerk?" Lisa nodded. "About three weeks ago I casually told Rick the outcome of the *CMI* case. A few days later, you know what happened—Maxwell risked all his money on a legal victory. When I tried to find Rick, he'd disappeared." Lisa's mouth dropped open. "Rick Fagen was never a clerk for the Supreme Court. The number he gave me is disconnected; he's moved out of his apartment building; he's gone."

"Are you fucking kidding me?" Lisa said, her sandwich still in her hand. "Why the hell did you tell him the decision?"

"We were just bullshitting about it one day," Ben said defensively. "He said he was curious about it and I told him. Every time we needed advice he helped us. I couldn't say no."

"But you're never supposed to let out a decision," Lisa said, raising her voice.

"Listen, I screwed up. I know it," Ben said. "But he totally suckered me in. Believe me, you would've done the same thing. It was a perfect setup."

"I can't believe this."

"Lisa, calm down. I told you this because I trust you. You won't say anything, will you?"

Lisa put down her sandwich and looked at her co-clerk. "This is serious stuff, Ben. We can't just sit on this."

"I know. But until I can prove it was Rick, I want to keep this low profile. Nathan is having the State Department run a search on him, and Eric is asking his newspaper contacts for info about the apartment building where Rick lived."

"We should tell Hollis."

"I'm not telling Hollis," Ben insisted. He leaned toward Lisa. "Believe me, I was up all night about this. If I go to Hollis, I'm fired. Even if I meant no harm, I violated the ethics code. If I'm fired, my whole life is over."

After a long pause, Lisa asked, "Why did you tell me this?"

"Because I didn't want to see you get hurt, too. I don't know if Rick's targeting every clerk or if I'm his one and only Sucker of the Year. I don't expect you to lie for me, and I never want to get you into trouble. I wanted you to know because you're my friend."

Lisa was silent for a minute. "So those flowers you got yesterday—they weren't from your mom, were they?"

"They were from Rick. I wanted to tell you yesterday, but I just . . ."

"Did you check the basket for bugs?"

"What do you mean?"

"You know—bugs, listening devices."

"You don't think—"

"Let's get out of here," Lisa said, pushing her chair away from the table and grabbing her bag.

The two clerks ran up the escalator and dashed out of Union Station. Watching them from the opposite corner of the food court, Rick leaned back in his chair. "Where are they going?" he asked.

"I couldn't hear," Rick's associate said as he approached the table. "But did you see the panic on their faces? They don't know where to run."

Rick smiled. "The funny thing is, it's only going to get worse."

Racing down First Street, Ben and Lisa didn't say a word until they returned to the Court. "Hey, guys," Nancy said as they marched past her desk. "How was lunch?"

"Good," Ben said.

"Fine," Lisa said.

They darted into their office and slammed the door behind them. They headed straight for the file cabinet, where Ben grabbed the large wicker basket. When he put it on the sofa, they rolled up their sleeves and methodically ripped the enormous bouquet apart. Flower by flower, they crushed every corolla and scrutinized every stem. Twenty-two roses, fourteen irises, eleven lilies, and four stems of freesias later, the sofa, as well as half of the office floor, was covered with the picked-apart remains of a previously well-organized floral arrangement. They found nothing. "It has to be in here," Lisa said. "There's no other reason to send flowers."

"Maybe he just wanted me to worry," Ben suggested. "Or maybe he's playing with my mind."

As Lisa wiped off the sofa, Ben reexamined the pile of flowers. For fifteen minutes, they repeated their inspection of each individual bloom. Then they ripped apart the basket itself. Again, nothing.

"Damn," Ben said, pushing the pulpy mess from the sofa. "It's impossible."

"I don't think we missed anything."

Ben leaned back on the sofa. "Of course we didn't miss anything. We just wasted our time."

"It's okay. You know we had to do this. I mean, what if we really did find something?"

"But we didn't," Ben said, nervously picking at the sofa's worn fabric. "We can't find anything."

Lisa lightly put her hand on his shoulder. "It's okay to be scared about this."

"It's just that my life—"

"I know what's at stake," Lisa said. "And this is more than you should have to deal with. But we'll get you through it."

"I don't want you to get involved. I only told you to warn you."

"Too late, baby," Lisa chided, her hand still on Ben's shoulder. "Now, are we going to sit here all day or are we going to try to find this guy?"

Looking at his co-clerk, Ben forced a smile. "You're a good friend, Lisa Marie. If I go to jail, I'm taking you with me."

Later in the week, Ben, Lisa, and Ober waited for Nathan to return from work. In the living room of Ben's house, Ben and Ober sat on the large blue couch, while Lisa sat alone on the love seat, her feet up on the cushions. "I don't understand it," Lisa said. "It's almost nine o'clock. Where the hell is he?"

"He said the search request would be finished by around seven or eight," Ben said, looking at his watch. "Maybe it's just running a little late."

"Maybe he was captured by Rick and his band of rogue clerks," Ober suggested as he clipped his toenails. "Now we'll have to go rescue them using makeshift weapons made from common kitchen appliances."

"What's wrong with you?" Ben asked, looking at his roommate.

"It's just a thought," Ober said.

Lisa tried to change the subject. "I still don't understand how you all managed to wind up in Washington. All of my friends are scattered around the country.''

"It's actually pretty simple," Ben explained. "Nathan, Eric, and I are all interested in politics, so Washington seemed like the right choice. Ober came because he didn't want to be left out.''

"That's not true," Ober said, looking up from his feet. "I came here because I believe in Senator Stevens.''

"That can't possibly be true," Lisa said. "You don't know squat about Stevens.''

"I know plenty about Stevens.''

"Name one thing you know about him," Lisa challenged. "Pick any platform and explain it.''

After a long pause, Ober laughed. "He's against crime and he's pro-children.''

"That's a revolutionary thought," Lisa said. "And here I thought Stevens ran on the always popular pro-crime, anti-children platform.''

"Leave him alone," Ben added. "Ober is a man of unusual knowledge. He knows more than he lets on.''

"I find that hard to believe," Lisa said.

"Believe it," Ober said. "For example, I know how to tell if a set of dice is balanced correctly.''

"Dice?''

"Yeah, dice. Like the dice you use in a board game.''

"Over the past few years, Ober has been the most—shall we say— entrepreneurial of the four of us," Ben explained. "Right after college, he and his father invented a board game that they thought would sweep the nation. Hence, the dice knowledge.''

"*You* invented a board game?" Lisa asked.

"Actually, my dad came up with the idea. It was called—''

"Speculation—The Game of Cunning and Guile," Ben and Ober said simultaneously.

"That was it," Ober said. "It was this super-intense strategy game. It had everything: pawns, bluffing, power moves, everything a good game should have.''

"And what happened?''

"Everyone hated it," Ober said. "They said it was too boring. After a year and a half, we were out of business, and I went through an illustrious sampling of the lower-tier job market. In three years, I was everything from a house painter to a marketing aide to a public relations assistant."

"If you're such a failure, how'd you get the job in the Senate?"

"That was all Ben," Ober said. "When he heard there was an opening in Senator Stevens's office, he wrote me a cover letter, put together my résumé so it sounded super-political, and prepped me for the interview. A week later, I got the job. And the rest is congressional history."

"So how do you tell if dice are fixed?" Lisa asked.

"I'm not telling you," Ober said. "Start your own game company."

Rolling her eyes, Lisa turned back to Ben. "So you went to law school, Eric went to grad school, and bizarro here played with his dice. What'd Nathan do before he joined the public sector?"

"He was a Fulbright scholar, so after college, he spent two years at Tokyo University studying international trade. After that, he worked for a Japanese high-tech company in their foreign markets department. Then he came back to the States and started working his way up the State Department ladder. My guess is he'll—" Ben broke off as Nathan came in.

"Speak of the devil," Lisa said. "It's Nathan-san himself."

"Well?" Ben asked anxiously as soon as Nathan walked in the door.

"Nothing," Nathan said, throwing a thick file folder to Ben. "They found four hundred fifty-seven Richard Fagens. Only twelve matched the age and physical description, and only two had criminal records. Neither of them had any type of legal background, and both were still incarcerated. I called the research center, and they said that Rick was probably using an alias. Until we find his real name, we'll never find him."

"Shit," Ben said, flipping through the useless documents.

"By the way," Nathan said to Ober, "they ran a check on Senator Stevens's signature, and it cleared as genuine. I thought you used the signature machine."

"I did," Ober said proudly. "I just bumped my butt against it while it was signing. It's the best way to make the signature look real."

"Good show," Nathan said, impressed.

"I have my moments," Ober said, looking back at his feet.

Watching Ben nervously look through the documents, Lisa turned to him. "Don't get yourself crazy. That doesn't mean we're done."

"We still haven't heard from Eric," Nathan added. "Hopefully, he'll have some information on the building."

At a quarter after ten, Eric returned home. Ben, Lisa, Nathan, and Ober were all watching television, trying to pass the time. "What took you so long?" Ben asked, pointing the remote and shutting off the TV.

"I'm only fifteen minutes late. I had to finish editing a story," Eric explained. "Do we have anything to eat?"

"Did you find anything on the building?" Nathan asked as Eric headed toward the kitchen.

"Oh, yeah," Eric said, turning back toward the living room. "I almost forgot. Seventeen eighty Rhode Island is not a good place. I asked some of the beat guys what the story was, and they said it's pretty sleazy."

"It smelled pretty sleazy," Nathan said.

"It's owned by a guy named Mickey Strauss," Eric explained. "Mickey is slime. Two years ago, they found two guys shot dead in there. Last year, there was this huge drug ring operating out of the place, but Mickey said he never knew anything about it. The guys at the office said that if a Mack truck came barreling through his office and straight across his desk, Mickey would swear he never saw it. Rick's smart as shit for picking that place—he obviously knows Mickey won't rat on him."

"We have to get in there," Ben said, standing up. "Maybe the leases have Rick's real name on them."

"Why would they?" Lisa asked. "If this place is so high security, why would there even be leases?"

All four roommates stared at Lisa. "She's got a point," Nathan finally said.

"That doesn't mean the leases don't exist," Ben said, walking to the door. "And that's all we have to go on at this point."

"Where are you going?" Eric asked as he turned toward the kitchen. "They're not going to let you waltz right in."

"It shouldn't be too hard," Ben said, his hand on the doorknob. "All they have is some stupid doorman guarding the place."

"And one security camera," Nathan added.

Ben turned back toward the living room. "There was a camera?"

"It was one of those old ones," Nathan explained. "Right above the office door. But that's hardly an impossible obstacle."

"What if we deliver a pizza to the building?" Ober asked. "That'll get us in."

"No, it won't," Ben said. "The office is probably empty, so there's no one to receive the pizza."

"But at least that'll get us past the doorman and into the building," Ober said. "Then all we have to do is pick the lock to the office."

"It'll never work," Ben said. "Unless you're an expert locksmith, we don't have a chance of picking the lock on our own. We have to somehow get the doorman to let us into the office."

"Excuse me," Lisa interrupted. "I hate to burst your bubble, but have you guys realized that what you're planning is illegal?"

"I told you you shouldn't have invited her," Ober said. "She's ruining everything."

Ignoring Ober, Lisa shot Ben a cold stare. "This isn't make-believe. You break into that building, and you're breaking the law. You of all people should realize that."

"I don't feel like I have a choice," Ben said nervously.

"Then you'd better think about the consequences," Lisa said. "If you get caught, you're out of a job. You'll be disbarred. Your career'll be ruined. All over a stupid breaking and entering offense."

"It won't be breaking and entering," Ben said defensively. "If we get the doorman to let us in, we have his permission."

"But you're lying to get in," Lisa said.

"So then the most we'll get is unlawful entry."

"Well, that's real bright," Lisa said. "Why don't you just—"

"What do you want me to do?" Ben asked, his voice wavering. "I have to get in there. If it gets out that I leaked information to an outsider, my career is ruined anyway. At least this way I have a chance of preventing that. If you don't like it, I understand, but please don't lecture me on it. This is hard enough as it is." Turning to his roommates, he said, "Any other ideas?"

"What if we dress up as exterminators and say we have to spray the office for roaches?" Ober said.

"And where do we get all this exterminator equipment?" Nathan asked. "Or do we just show up dressed in jeans and carrying flashlights and hope they don't notice?"

"What if we dress up like painters?" Ober asked. "It'll be just like *The Sting*. The doorman'll let us in, and instead of painting, we'll raid the files."

"If you really want to do this, I have an idea," Lisa interrupted. "Instead of taking the low road first, why don't we try to get in semi-legally? We can walk right up to the doorman and offer him a bribe. Then we'll give him Rick's apartment number and ask him to go check the leases for us. That way we're not the ones breaking and entering."

"That's not a bad idea," Nathan admitted.

"What's the worst that can happen?" Ben asked, shrugging his shoulders. "The guard says no?"

"How about they recognize you and they kill you?" Eric said, returning from the kitchen with a roast-beef sandwich in hand.

"They'll never recognize us," Nathan said. "There's no way the doorman that was there during the day is still there at night."

"And what if he is?" Eric asked.

"We'll pretend we have the wrong building," Nathan said. Noticing Ben's prolonged silence, he asked, "Are you okay?"

"I'm fine," Ben said unconvincingly. Turning to Lisa, he added, "I can understand if you don't want to come."

"Don't pull that macho shit on me," Lisa said. "I'm coming."

"What happened to all your worries about getting arrested?" Ben asked.

"We both know conspiracy law," Lisa said. "Just by being here, I'm involved."

"I can't go," Eric said, swallowing a bite of roast beef. "I have to go back to the paper to finish my story."

"What do you mean, you're not going?" Nathan asked. "Ben needs—"

"What am I supposed to do?" Eric asked. "I have a story."

"Don't worry about it," Ben said. "But if you don't hear from us by two in the morning, call the police."

*　　*　　*

At midnight, the friends looked for a parking spot around the corner from the building. "This city is the worst," Nathan said. "Thousands of people. Thousands of cars. Twelve parking spots."

Ben studied the drizzle that tapped the windshield. "This is going to be a disaster."

"Now you're having second thoughts?" Lisa asked from the backseat. "What happened? Your brain suddenly started working again?"

"I'm not having second thoughts," Ben said, turning around in his seat. "I'm just nervous. Is that okay?"

"Don't worry about it," Ober said. "You'll be fine."

Convinced he would never find a spot, Nathan pulled into a small alley next to the building. "Do you have the money?" he asked, shutting the engine off.

"I have it," Ben said, feeling his right jacket pocket for the first hundred and his left jacket pocket for an additional two hundred.

"I still think I should go," Nathan said.

"Stop taking it personally," Ben said. "I told you before: Lisa and I are going. They're more likely to believe a man and a woman."

"Says who?" Ober asked.

"Says me," Ben said. "Now stop whining about it. It's no big deal." He grabbed an umbrella from below the front seat, opened the door, and got out of the car. Lisa followed.

Walking toward the building, Ben held the umbrella over Lisa. "Are you sure you want to do this?" Lisa asked.

"Not really," Ben said.

"Then why don't we turn around and—"

"You know I can't," Ben pleaded. "I have to find Rick. Right now, this is the best way to do that. If you want to leave . . ."

"I'm here," Lisa reassured him. "As long as we keep it legal, I'll be here."

When they reached the building, Ben was surprised to find the front door locked. Lisa pressed her face against the glass to get a better view of the interior. "Buzz," she instructed. "He's in there."

Moments later, a buzzer sounded, allowing Ben to pull open the door. Confidently and calmly, Ben and Lisa approached the night guard, who was sitting at his metal desk. "What's wrong?" the guard asked. "Don't you have a key?"

"We don't actually live here," Ben explained.

"Then who do you want to see?" the guard asked, picking up his phone.

"We don't want to see anyone," Ben said. "We have a favor to ask."

The guard hung up the phone. "I'm listening."

"My wife and I are looking for her brother, who used to live here. He has some money of ours, and as you can imagine, we're trying to get it back." Ben pulled out the five twenty-dollar bills from his right pocket and put them on the guard's desk. "We were wondering if you could help us find his lease or his forwarding address. Either piece of information would be extremely helpful."

Staring intensely at Ben and Lisa, the guard said, "There aren't any leases."

"How about a forwarding address?" Ben asked. "Can you check the Rolodex for us?"

"There are no files on anyone," the guard said. "No Rolodex. Nothing."

"Can you double-check to be safe?" Ben asked. "Maybe there's something in the office." He threw another hundred dollars on the desk. "His apartment was number three seventeen. All I need is his name or address. No one will ever know."

"If he's your brother, why do you need his name?" the guard asked suspiciously.

"Listen, do you really need to know the answer to that?" Lisa jumped in. "This is easy money. Do you want it or not?"

The guard continued to stare at the two clerks. Finally, he picked up the money. "Make it three hundred and I'll do it." Ben threw another hundred on the desk. Pocketing the money, the guard stood from his chair and opened the top drawer of his desk. He then pulled out a gun and pointed it at Ben and Lisa. "I'll count to three."

"What'd we do?" Ben asked, raising his hands in the air.

"I know who you are," the guard said. "Now get the hell out of here."

"Just relax," Lisa said.

The guard pulled back the hammer on his gun. "Get out! Now!"

Turning around, the two clerks quickly walked to the door. When they got outside, they ran.

"Get us out of here," Ben said when he and Lisa got back into the car.

"What's wrong?" Nathan asked as he started the engine. "Did you get the lease?"

"Drive. Just drive," Ben said nervously. "I don't want to talk about it."

At twelve-thirty, the roommates returned home. "What happened?" Eric asked from the sofa, remote control in hand.

"We didn't get a thing," Nathan said, collapsing on the big couch. "Ben's a wanted man in that building."

"And we lost three hundred dollars," Ober added, taking off his sweatshirt and throwing it on the couch.

"Where's Lisa?" Eric asked.

"We dropped her off at home," Ben said. "There was nothing else to talk about."

"From what the guard said, there were no leases and no records of the building's tenants," Nathan explained. "The way I see it, Rick is even more sophisticated than we thought."

"So that's it?" Eric asked. "You're done with your search?"

"Not at all," Ben said, walking up the stairs. "We're just getting started."

CHAPTER 5

"HI, MY NAME IS RICK FAGEN, AND I WAS WONDERING IF YOU could help me out," Ben said in his most diplomatic voice. "I recently disconnected my phone, but I still haven't paid the bill, and I think it's because you still don't have my new address."

"What was your old phone number, sir?" After typing in Rick's old number, the phone company employee said, "Mr. Fagen, you are correct. We still don't have a forwarding address for you. If you'll give me your new address, we'll be happy to send you a duplicate bill."

"That'd be great," Ben said. "My new address is Post Office Box 1227, Washington, D.C. 20037."

"Mr. Fagen, you should receive this bill in the next few weeks," the employee said. "Is there anything else I can help you with today?"

"Actually, I have one last favor," Ben said. "I just realized that when I moved, I misplaced all my old phone bills, which I need for tax purposes. Is it possible to get duplicates of those as well?"

"Certainly," the employee said. "Let me just make a note of that here, and we'll get those to you. Is there anything else I can help you with?"

"Nope. I think that's it. Thanks for your help." When he hung up the phone, Ben looked up at Lisa who was sitting across from him.

"Do you think the bills will really help?" she asked.

"Not really," Ben said. "I don't think Rick is dumb enough to call anyone important on a traceable phone. My guess is he was constantly mobile and worked most of his deals on a cell phone. The local number was probably just for me."

"That was smart to get the P.O. box," Lisa said, in an effort to cheer him up.

"Whatever," Ben said. "If anyone's watching that phone line, they already know I'm involved."

"You don't know that," Lisa said. Looking at her watch, she added, "It's almost ten. We should probably head over."

"I don't feel like it," Ben said, suddenly irritated.

"Are you crazy?" she asked. "They're handing down the *CMI* decision. Don't you want to see the crowd's reaction?"

Ben was silent.

"Well, you're coming anyway," she said, grabbing his hand. "We're not supposed to miss decisions."

Although the justices returned to work in early September, and the fall term officially began on the first Monday in October, it wasn't until early November—when the first decisions were announced—that the energy of the Court reached critical mass. While oral arguments were heard throughout the week, decisions were handed down at precisely ten A.M. on every subsequent Monday. Open to the public, the decision sessions were always packed with tourists, press, and friends of the Court. On a typical decision day, the line began to form outside the Court at eight in the morning. For a more popular case, the lines started at six. When the *Webster* abortion case was handed down in 1989, local entrepreneurs found that both tourists and press would pay big money to have others wait in line for them. The result was an underground line-sitting business that covered all major media events on Capitol Hill. In anticipation of the *CMI* decision, the professional sitters had started lining up almost a day in advance.

At approximately nine in the morning, the restless crowds were finally led into the building. While the groups were herded through the Great Hall and two separate metal detectors, Ben and Lisa walked straight into the main courtroom. "I love this," Lisa said as she watched the lines of tourists who were slowly being seated.

Ben was hardly enthusiastic to see Charles Maxwell's impending victory, but he had to acknowledge the excitement of a decision day. Reporters swarmed into the tiny press area on the left side of the courtroom. It was the only place in the room where observers were allowed to take notes, although there were no recording devices allowed. Armed guards escorted tourists and other observers into the twelve rows of benches in the center of the room, where they all eagerly awaited the arrival of the justices. Everyone spoke in hushed whispers, which added a buzz of energy to the room. On the right was a seating area reserved for family and friends of the justices, as well as a small private area for the Supreme Court clerks.

"They're all sheep," Ben said, looking at the packed courtroom. "They just come to see the spectacle and then they leave. They don't care about the consequences. To them it's just a tourist attraction."

"Lighten up," Lisa said. Still thrilled by the pomp and circumstance, she watched the clock tick toward ten.

Ben fixed his eyes on the marble frieze over the main entrance, which the justices faced. It displayed the Powers of Evil—Corruption and Deceit—offset by the Powers of Good—Security, Charity, and Peace, with Justice flanked by Wisdom and Truth.

Following Ben's gaze, Lisa asked, "So, does art imitate life?"

"Funny," Ben shot back.

At exactly three minutes before ten, a buzzer summoned the justices to the conference room, where they prepared to enter the courtroom. Behind the burgundy velvet curtain, the justices ceremonially shook hands with each other. It was a custom instituted by Chief Justice Fuller early in the Court's history, to show that "harmony of aims if not views is the Court's guiding principle." At precisely ten o'clock, the marshal banged his gavel, and every person in the room rose to his feet.

"The Honorable, the Chief Justice and the Associate Justices of the Supreme Court of the United States!" the marshal announced. Within seconds, the nine justices strode through openings in the curtain and moved to their respective chairs.

No matter how many times she saw it happen, Lisa was always awed by the simultaneous arrival of all nine justices. "I love this," she whispered to Ben. "It's like watching the arrival of the All-Star team."

"Shhhh!" Ben said, unable to remove his eyes from center stage.

The room faced the nine chairs of the justices. Made of matching black leather, the chairs were specially designed to fit each justice's particular body type. As the justices took their seats, the marshal announced, "Oyez! Oyez! Oyez! All persons having business before the Honorable, the Supreme Court of the United States, are admonished to draw near and give their attention, for the Court is now sitting. God save the United States and this Honorable Court!" Once again the gavel fell, and everyone took his seat.

Chief Justice Osterman sat in the center seat. "Today we will be handing down the decisions in *United States* v. *CMI and Lexcoll,* as well as *Tennessee* v. *Shreve.* Justice Blake will be reading both of our decisions today."

"Thank you, Mr. Chief Justice," Blake responded. Appointed to the Court nearly ten years ago, Blake was a South Carolina judge whose Southern drawl was still as strong as the day he first took the bench. Primed for the *CMI* decision, the spectators held their collective breath. Reading from the prepared statement sheet, Blake said, "In the case of *State of Tennessee* v. *Shreve,* we find for the plaintiff and uphold the decision of the Supreme Court of Tennessee." Knowing full well that the crowd was starving for the *CMI* decision, Blake took his time announcing the findings of the Court.

When Blake finished the *Tennessee* case, he sat back in his chair and shifted his weight. Clearing his throat, he reached for one of the pewter mugs that were in front of every justice. He poured himself a glass of water and prepared to read the next case. Wiping the corner of his mouth with a handkerchief, Blake smirked. "In the case of *United States* v. *CMI and Lexcoll,* we believe that although the two companies will become a major communications conglomerate, there is no predatory conduct with the intent to monopolize. For this reason, the merger of the two corporations does not violate the Sherman Antitrust Act. We therefore find for the defendant and affirm the decision of the Court of Appeals."

A sharp murmur shot through the crowd as observers acknowledged the cunning of Charles Maxwell's recent decision to increase his holdings in Lexcoll. Then, seconds after the decision was read, the Clerk's

Office turned off its intercom to the courtroom and notified the Information Office that the decision had become public. Immediately, the seven-person staff of the Information Office handed out copies of the official decision to the assembled reporters who waited in the basement office, while two computer staffers posted the decision on various legal computer networks. Inside the courtroom, the print media took notes on the mood of the justices. Outside the Court, at least two dozen television reporters vied for stand-up space, hoping to be the first to break the story on air. By the time Justice Blake had finished explaining the Court's reasoning, more than 3,760 people had their own copies of the decision, while 6 million people had heard the outcome of the case. As the marshal officially closed the session, the media were exhausted, Charles Maxwell was a genius, and Ben was devastated.

"Crap," Ben said as he and Lisa walked through the mob of people exiting the courtroom.

"Why are you surprised? You've known the outcome of the case for months."

"Let's just get out of here," Ben said, pushing his way through the crowd. As they swiped their I.D. cards through a small machine, two bulletproof doors opened, and the co-clerks were granted access to the first floor's private office area. Taking one of the less-trafficked staircases, they walked upstairs and returned to their office. "I just can't believe it," Ben said as soon as the door closed behind him. "Maxwell becomes a captain of industry because a schmuck law clerk couldn't keep his mouth shut." Taking off his suit jacket, he hung it on the back of his chair. "Maybe Eric was right. Maybe I should go to the press."

"No way," Lisa said. She grabbed a brown folder from her desk and walked to the back of the office. Turning on the paper shredder, she fed the entire stack of paper to the machine. She never destroyed her old versions of an opinion until the opinion was actually announced. "First, you have no proof, so they'll think you're crazy. Second, if they do believe you, you've just sacrificed your entire career."

"But Maxwell would be revealed."

"Are you crazy? You'd give up your life just to be spiteful?"

"It's the right thing to do," Ben said, slumping on the office sofa. "I can't find Rick; we may never see him again; it's impossible to track him. It's the only way to resolve this mess."

Lisa walked over to the couch and stared down at Ben. "What the hell is wrong with you? You're acting like the whole world is about to end. It was a mistake. You blew it. You got conned. But you didn't do it on purpose. You were outsmarted—"

"And that pisses me off," Ben shot back, sitting up straight.

"Is that it? You're mad because someone finally outsmarted you? This whole feeling-sorry-for-yourself deal is based on the fact that you were intellectually beaten?"

"You don't understand."

"I definitely understand, Ben. You're mad because he beat you on the I.Q. test." Lisa sat down next to him on the sofa. "Get your head out of your ass. It's not your fault. You weren't stupid or gullible. You did what any smart person would've done. You just got set up. Rick played you and you have to accept that."

"Can't I just sulk a little more?"

"You get thirty more seconds," Lisa said, looking down at her watch. She waited. "Okay, time's up. You done?"

"How'd the decision go today?" Eric asked Ben later that night as they sat in front of the television.

"It was fine. What was the *Washington Herald*'s take on the whole affair?"

"They went crazy with it," Eric explained between mouthfuls of cereal. "Wait until you see tomorrow's edition. The front page has a massive picture of Maxwell minutes after the decision. He's wearing this shit-eating grin that just about makes you want to vomit."

"Great."

"And the Sunday edition is running a massive piece on him. The guy is getting better press than the pope."

"Great," Ben repeated, flipping through channels. He stopped on CNN, then caught a glimpse of Maxwell and continued flipping.

"CMI stock flew up almost seventeen points by the end of closing today."

"Great. Eric, can you go to the kitchen and get me a knife? I want to gouge my eyes out."

"Oedipus, huh?" Eric said, shoveling another spoonful of cereal into his mouth. "That'd be a good look for you."

Without warning, Ober walked into the house singing, "Guess who's stopped answering phones in Senator Stevens's office?"

"You got a promotion?" Eric asked, jumping up to embrace his friend.

Nathan strolled in behind Ober. "He got the promotion?" Ben asked.

"You won't believe this one," Nathan said. "Ober, tell the story."

"Oh, you've got to hear this," Ober said. "This is mondo."

"Mondo?" Eric laughed. "This isn't L.A. Get out of here with that crazy talk."

"Just let him tell the story," Ben said.

"Here's the story," Ober began. "Remember when you had me write that fake death threat from Rick to Senator Stevens?" Ben nodded. "Apparently, the staff director found out that I started a State Department computer search on Rick. Last week, she came up to me and asked me why I did it, so I told her I was just being cautious—that I didn't think it was a real death threat, but I wanted to be extra safe. This week, she calls me into her office and tells me that I'm their newest legislative assistant. I'll be responding to all of the constituent complaints on zoning laws and orange juice subsidies."

"Clearly, you're at the forefront of Stevens's re-election campaign," Ben said.

"It gets better," Nathan said. "Ober, show them the letter."

"Oh, yeah," Ober said, opening the leather briefcase his parents had bought him for graduation. He pulled out a single piece of paper and handed it to Ben.

"Dear William," Ben read aloud as he stood in the living room. "Thank you so much for your follow-up efforts on the recent threat on my life. Your actions are a shining example of the kind of initiative few people are willing to take. I hope you know how much I appreciate all of your work. Marcia tells me you are doing a wonderful job. Keep up the fight."

"Read the closing," Ober said, laughing.

"Your friend, Paul."

"He signed it 'Paul'?" Eric asked, grabbing the letter from Ben's hands.

"And I'm his friend," Ober said.

"This is unbelievable," Ben said.

"Unprecedented," Nathan said.

"Unheard of."

"Impossible."

"It's fantastic!" Ben continued.

"They're mondo stupid!" Ober shouted. "And I got a promotion out of it!"

As Ober and Eric danced around the room, Ben asked, "Have you ever read 'The Emperor's New Clothes'?"

"Exactly," Nathan said as the phone rang.

"Hold on a second." Ben walked to the kitchen to get the phone. Picking up the receiver, he answered, "Hello?"

"Hello, Benjamin."

"Hi, Mom," Ben said.

"Benjamin, let me ask you a question. Did you have anything to do with that Charles Maxwell decision that came down today?"

"Not really," Ben said, rolling his eyes. "That was handled by another justice's clerks."

"But you knew the decision before it happened, didn't you?" she asked.

"Of course, Mom. I knew it three months ago."

"Thank you," Sheila Addison said. "Now why don't you tell your father because he'll never believe it if I say it. The man thinks that just because he's a columnist, he knows everything."

"Mom, is there anything else?" Ben asked. "We're in the middle of celebrating. Ober just got a promotion."

"Good for him!" Sheila said. "Oh, Barbara will be so proud. Put him on the phone, I want to say hello."

"I'm not putting him on the phone," Ben said.

"Well, tell him I better see him when you guys come home for Thanksgiving. By the way, do you know if you're coming in Tuesday or Wednesday yet?"

"It's still three weeks away. I have no idea," Ben said. Hoping to change the subject he asked, "What else is going on at home?"

"Nothing really," Sheila said. "I got a piece of mail for you today. It looked like an important bill, so I didn't know if you wanted me to open it before I sent it to you.''

"Who's it from?" Ben asked.

"The return address says 'Mailboxes and Things.' It has a big stamp on it that says 'Second Notice.' "

Recognizing the name of the store where he had opened his P.O. box, Ben was confused. He'd already paid them in advance, he thought. "Open it," he said.

"It's definitely a bill," she said. "It says that if you don't pay the balance, your P.O. box, number thirteen twenty-seven, will be closed, and your mail confiscated. Why do you have a P.O. box, Benjamin?"

"What was the number of the box?" Ben asked, ignoring his mother's question.

"Thirteen twenty-seven."

"It must be a mistake. That's not my box."

"Should I send you the bill?"

"No, I'll just go down there tomorrow to fix it. Listen, I really have to go. Give my love to Dad." Ben hung up the phone and returned to the living room.

"Are you coming out with us?" Ober asked. "We're going to celebrate my promotion."

"Of course I'm coming," Ben said, grabbing his coat from the hall closet. "Miracles like this happen only once a decade."

Walking into Boosin's Bar, Ober inhaled the smell of stale beer and smoldering cigarettes. "Ahhh, there's nothing like bar whiff," he said. "I feel like I'm back in college." Their regular haunt since they had arrived in D.C., Boosin's was the second home for much of Washington's young shirt-and-tie crowd. It wasn't long before they were approached by their regular waitress at their usual spot in the back.

"Hey, Tina," Ben said.

"What's happening?" she asked.

"Ober got promoted today. We're hoping to fill him with so much beer that he falls down and vomits in joyous celebration."

"I'll see what I can do," she said as she headed to the bar. She returned with two pitchers and four glasses. After filling each of the roommates' glasses, Nathan raised his glass in a toast.

"To Ober. May dumb luck embrace you in all of your travails."

After the friends toasted, Ben put his hand on Ober's shoulder. "I'm really proud of you, my friend."

"Wow, a compliment from the Job Guru himself."

"I'm serious," Ben said. "No matter how it happened, we all know you deserve that promotion."

"I don't know," Ober said. "I mean, I'm still not a Supreme Court clerk."

"You don't have to be a clerk," Ben said. "All you have to do is be yourself."

"And always let your conscience be your guide!" Eric and Nathan sang.

A half hour later, Ober was tapped on the shoulder by a beautiful brown-haired woman, dressed in a jet-black designer pantsuit. "Do you mind if we join you?" she asked.

"Lila!" Ober shouted. "What are you doing here?" After getting up to hug the stranger, he looked at his roommates and explained, "This is Lila Jospin. We used to fool around in college."

"That's a wonderful introduction," Ben said. Shaking Lila's hand, he said, "You are obviously a woman of fine taste. Nice to meet you."

"You, too," Lila said.

"Looks like you brought some friends. How many are you?" Ober asked as he began to pull together tables to make more room.

"There are four of us," Lila said as her three friends approached the table.

"Perfect," Ober said. "Absolutely perfect."

At seven-thirty Tuesday morning, Ben entered the office. "You're late," Lisa said as he collapsed on the sofa.

"I'm tired," he said.

"Where were you last night? Drowning your sorrows in beer?"

"Last night, I'll have you know, there were no sorrows to be found. Last night was full of joy."

"So you went out to a bar, found a woman, and took her home. Big deal. Who do you think you are, William the Conqueror?"

"Actually, I picture myself more as Magellan. He was so much more regal and imposing—a true visionary. Like myself, he was a Renaissance man living in a world that rarely understood him."

"Actually, he was a misogynist barbarian who barely understood what he had found. In that sense, you are alike." Leaning back in her chair, Lisa put her hands behind her head. "So, aren't you going to ask me how my date went last night?"

"*You* had a date?" Ben asked, raising an eyebrow.

"What's so surprising about that? I'm a strong woman with needs of her own."

"Why didn't you tell me you were going on a date?"

"Because you'd tease me about it."

"I'm still going to tease you about it. Now tell me, who was the poor victim?"

"His name is Jonathan Kord. He works in Senator Greiff's office."

"Oh my God! Jonathan Kord? I know that guy! A friend of mine, may she rest in peace, went out with him."

"You don't know him," Lisa said, grabbing a handful of paper clips and throwing them at Ben.

"I don't need to. With a name like Jonathan, I can tell he's stale."

"What are you talking about? Jonathan's a great name. His friends all call him Jon."

"But he goes by Jonathan, doesn't he?" Lisa was silent. "I knew it!" Ben shouted. "He's stale."

"He didn't taste stale," Lisa shot back.

"Whoa, whoa, whoa," Ben said, sitting up straight on the sofa. "Did you really get some play last night?"

"I might've," Lisa teased. "But even if I didn't, I get to know that you're jealous."

"I'm not jealous."

"Then why does your face match the sofa?"

"Trust me, I'm not jealous. Now tell me what happened."

"It wasn't much. We went to dinner and then we walked around the Washington Monument."

"Oh, please," Ben said, throwing his hands in the air. "This guy played you like a fiddle. He buys you dinner and then takes you to walk around a giant erection? What kind of message does that send?"

"I paid for dinner, stud-boy. And it was my idea to go to the Monument."

"Now that's a date," Ben said, nodding his head. "I'm impressed." He crossed his arms and said, "Go on."

"And then I dropped him off."

"That's it?" Ben asked suspiciously. "You took him out and dropped him off?"

"I don't know," Lisa said, her eyes focused on her feet. "I think I scared him off. I might've been too aggressive."

"You? Aggressive?"

"No, I was definitely too aggressive," Lisa said, suddenly serious. "I think he was really intimidated when I told him that I could teach him a thing or two in bed."

"You said that?" Ben blurted.

"See, I knew I was too aggressive."

"Lisa, don't beat yourself up. You were just being yourself. You can't be faulted for that. You're an aggressive woman, and most men are intimidated by aggressive women. You've seen the talk shows—the average guy in America wants a complacent, weaker woman, simply because they've been taught to feel threatened by strong women."

"Okay, Freud. Now where does that leave me?"

"You're left with much less to choose from, but the quality of those men is three hundred percent better than the average loser. The gene pool you're fishing from is more confident, more sophisticated, more intelligent . . ."

"They're men like yourself," Lisa said sarcastically.

"Exactly. We're a new breed of men. We're not afraid to let our feelings show. We like strong women. Sexually, we enjoy being dominated."

"You're not afraid to cry at the end of the Rocky movies," Lisa added.

"Correct. And we like the smell of potpourri."

"Well, I hate to burst your bubble, but what if I don't want the sensitive type? What if I want a big, dumb jock who'll be fun to fool around with, and who won't care if I don't call him?"

"You like big jocks?"

"For a few thrills, sure. I'd never marry one, but they're fun to hook up with."

Confused, Ben scratched his forehead. "How can you like big jocks? How can you go to bed with someone who just thinks of you as a sexual conquest?"

"Let me tell you something, the sexual conquest is a two-way street, and I'm driving a Ferrari."

Laughing, Ben said, "I take back what I said before. You're way too aggressive to find a man. You'll probably be lonely for the rest of your life." Getting up from the sofa, Ben flipped through the newest pile of paper on his desk. "What's happening today?"

"A whole new batch of cert petitions just came in. Hollis wants us to really tear through them since he expects we'll write the opinion for the *Grinnell* decision."

"They didn't vote on that already, did they?"

"Take a look at your watch, moron," Lisa said. "Conference isn't until tomorrow. Hollis doesn't think they'll even get to it, but it'll definitely be done by next week. Osterman's been stalling. And Justice Veidt's clerks said Veidt's on the fence, so Osterman has been working on him since the cert petition came in."

"What's wrong with Veidt? Do you think he has a thing for Osterman?"

"I doubt it," Lisa said. "Veidt's an intellectually unimpressive justice who knows he was selected because he was confirmable. I think he figures that by hanging with the chief justice, it'll give him some credibility."

"That could be," Ben said, "but my way's much cooler. Can you imagine? Two Supreme Court justices caught in a sordid love affair? How great would that be?"

"It'd sure be more interesting than reading cert petitions all day."

After a quick lunch in the Court's cafeteria, Ben walked down to Mailboxes & Things on Constitution Avenue. Time to break out the overcoat, he thought as a chilly November wind pulled the last leaves from the trees. Fighting off the impending arrival of winter, Ben blew warm air into his cupped hands. Within ten minutes, he arrived at the store, which was painted red, white, and blue—the color scheme of choice for so many D.C. vendors.

"Can I help you?" a cashier wearing a turtleneck asked.

"Yes, I received an overdue payment notice for a P.O. box. Not only did I pay for my box in advance, but the number on the bill wasn't my box."

"Oh, I'm sure we just made a mistake," the cashier said. "Let me look up your name."

"My name is Be—" Catching himself, Ben remembered the fake name he'd given to open the box. "My name is Alvy Singer."

"Singer, Singer . . ." the cashier said, looking through his files. "Here it is." He pulled out the file and continued, "You opened box twelve twenty-seven on October twenty-eighth, and you paid for that in advance. You then opened box thirteen twenty-seven on October twenty-ninth, requesting that you be billed for it." Reading the file, the cashier added, "It says here you also paid an extra twenty-five-dollar lock fee so that both boxes could be opened with the same key."

"Of course, how stupid of me," Ben said, wiping away the cold sweat that had suddenly formed on his forehead.

"Would you like to pay your balance today?"

"Sure. That's fine," Ben said. He pulled out his wallet and paid the bill.

When he reached the room of P.O. boxes, Ben was in a full-fledged panic. Looking around, he was relieved no one was watching him. He pulled the key from his pocket and opened his box, 1227. Empty. Directly under his was box 1327. Inserting his key, he opened the box. Inside was a single manila envelope. Taking out the envelope, he locked the box and walked to a small counter.

Inside the envelope was a single typed sheet of paper. "Dear Ben," he read. "I'm sorry I haven't been in touch, but, as you've probably guessed, I've been quite busy. Needless to say, all went extremely well. I realize you're frustrated with what's happened, but please stop trying to find me. You're wasting your time. Tearing apart my flowers was useless, your bribery attempt at my old apartment was pathetic, and as far as your telephone bill idea—do you really believe I would make important calls on a line so easily traceable? Come on, now. Since you still haven't gone to the authorities, I assume you understand the consequences to your own career should you reveal your story.

"At this point in time, I propose a truce. If you are interested, please meet me at Two Quail on Saturday at eight P.M. The reservation has been made under your name. If you do need to contact me, please feel free to use our P.O. box, number 1327. Yours, Rick."

Ben stuffed the letter back into the envelope, left the store, and walked briskly back to the Court. How the hell does he know everything? he asked himself. Bounding up the Court's steps, Ben waved his I.D. card at the guard and sidestepped the metal detector. Within a minute, he was charging through the reception area on the way to his office. Slamming the door behind him, he threw the envelope on Lisa's desk. "You won't believe it," he said.

"Where did you get this?" Lisa asked as she read the letter.

"He opened a P.O. box right under mine—under my fake name," Ben said, his voice shaking.

"How did he know you had a P.O. box?" Holding up her hand, Lisa stopped Ben from answering. "Let me finish reading this first." Eventually looking up, she asked, "Okay, now, how did he know you had a P.O. box?"

"How did he know my fake name? How did he know what we did with the flowers? How did he know I called the phone company? How did he know we broke into his old apartment building? He knows my parents' address, for Chrissakes! He billed me for the P.O. box at my parents' house!"

"Calm down a second," Lisa said, putting her reading glasses on the desk. "Let's think about this."

"If he goes near my family, I swear I'll kill him. I'll fucking kill him."

"Relax, I'm sure he did that just to scare you."

"Well, it's working," Ben said, taking off his suit jacket. "He's obviously been following me for the last month of my life. He knows everything I do, everywhere I go. He knows where my family lives . . ."

"You have to calm down. Let me think for a minute."

Pacing up and down the office, Ben remained silent.

"I can understand that he knew we broke into the apartment building, but I don't understand how he knew about the phone bill. Both times you called the phone company, you called from his office, didn't you?'' When Ben nodded, she added, ''I doubt he's tapped the phone in here. I mean, this's the Supreme Court.''

''There's no way he could tap this phone—not with the security system we have here,'' Ben agreed. ''But how did he know what we did with the flowers? We're the only ones that knew about that.''

Still focused on the phone bills, Lisa said, ''Most likely, he didn't change his address on purpose. Then he just waited to see what we did. The phone company probably told him you ordered a copy of the bill.'' After pausing to reflect, she continued, ''I just can't believe he knew we'd do that.''

''This guy is no dummy,'' Ben said, unable to stand still.

''Do you really think he has someone following you?''

''How should I know? How else would he know my fake name for the P.O. box?''

''Are you going to meet with him?''

''Of course,'' Ben said. ''This guy is all mine. I'm gonna nail his ass to the wall.''

''You sound like a bad TV movie,'' Lisa said. ''I think you should come up with a serious plan first.''

''Definitely,'' Ben agreed. Sitting at his desk, he pulled out a sheet of paper. ''I'd like to get everyone together for a little brainstorming session. Can we do it at your place?''

''Why my place?''

''Because I think he might have my house bugged.''

''Listen, you have to calm down,'' Lisa said. ''This isn't *The Firm*.''

''This guy has the resources to reach Charles Maxwell, he pulls off one of the greatest insider information scams of the decade, and you're telling me he doesn't have the resources to bug my crappy house with its nonexistent alarm system?''

''Fine,'' Lisa said. ''We'll meet at my apartment.'' Rising from her seat, she walked over to Ben and leaned on his desk. ''Meanwhile, want to hear some fresh gossip?''

''I'm not in the mood.''

''Okay. Fine. Then I won't tell you that Justice Blake is stepping down.''

"That's nothing new," Ben said. "People have been saying that for years."

"But now it's official," Lisa said. "He gave his notice today to Osterman."

"Are you serious?" Ben asked as his raised eyebrows creased his forehead.

"Scout's honor."

"Is this confirmed, or is it just what you heard?"

"Let's put it this way—when you were at lunch, Hollis came down here and told me Blake just gave notice of his resignation. He's calling the president this afternoon and the press will be notified within the next week or two. You think that source is trustworthy enough for you?"

"If Hollis said it, it's the gospel."

"The thing is, I don't think most of the justices have told their clerks, so keep it a secret. Hollis said it was just for our information."

"What else did he say?" Ben asked.

"He said that *Grinnell* won't be decided until the end of the week. Justice Veidt still hasn't responded, and all the conservatives have pushed it back so they can work on getting him aboard."

"Excellent gossip," Ben admitted. "Sounds like Hollis was running at the mouth today."

"You know how he is," Lisa said. "Sometimes he won't say a word, and other times he won't shut up. Today was just a good day."

"So I guess that means we won't be working on *Grinnell* this week."

"That's what I wanted to tell you," Lisa said, slapping Ben's desk. "Since Blake is stepping down, he's going to be lightening his workload. So he's no longer writing the *Pacheco* v. *Rhode Island* decision."

"And I suppose we are?" Ben asked. Lisa nodded. "Why do we have to do it? That's a solid bankruptcy issue. It's a good case."

"It's a good case, but it's not a great case. Hollis said that when a justice steps down, he gets the pick of the litter when it comes to cases. All the other justices defer to him so he can make his last great pronouncements on the law."

"So that means he'll get all the best cases this session?"

"Pretty much," Lisa said. "He can't write all of them, but I'm sure he'll get a good number."

"That's great," Ben said sarcastically. "Did Hollis say when Blake's office would send us the materials?"

"The Clerk's Office will transfer them later today."

Turning on his computer, Ben said, "And Hollis still hasn't looked over our *Oshinsky* opinion."

"Actually, he did," Lisa said, passing Ben a stack of paper.

"And still not satisfied," Ben said, unable to avoid the bright red marks covering the front page of the document. "What is this, draft six?"

"Seven if you count our original outline."

"He's never going to be happy with this decision," Ben said. "I think we should just realize that and move on."

"You have to stop complaining," Lisa said. "It's not that bad."

"Are you kidding? We get here at seven every morning, we have four pending cases that we're simultaneously working on, a fifth that a retiring justice just passed off on us, and now a sixth case arriving just as soon as Veidt caves in to the conservatives. At the same time, we have a dozen or so cert petitions to get through every week. How much busier can we be?"

"I don't know," Lisa said. "I guess we could also be involved in a chase for a psychotic mastermind who's trying to undermine the entire court system."

At nine-thirty that evening, Ben and Lisa arrived at Lisa's apartment, which was a short walk from the Tenleytown Metro. Ober and Nathan were waiting in front of the drab brick apartment building. "What took you so long?" Ober asked as they walked inside. "You said to meet at nine."

"Sorry," Ben said sharply. "We were only busting our asses rewriting history at the Supreme Court. Some of us aren't lucky enough to have jobs that end at five."

"Hey, who crapped in your Apple Jacks?" Nathan asked as they stepped into an elevator. "We're the ones trying to help you."

Getting out on the fourth floor, they walked down the hallway and eventually reached Lisa's apartment. "I'm sorry," Ben said to Ober as Lisa opened the door. "I didn't mean to snap like that."

"Here we are," Lisa said. "It's not much, but it's mine." Sparsely decorated, the living room consisted of a worn brown leather couch, a coffee table, and a desk, which was actually a piece of finished wood balanced on two small file cabinets. Both the coffee table and desk were submerged under papers. On the wall opposite the sofa was a huge picture of cats playing poker. Over the couch were two portraits done on black velvet, one of the *Mona Lisa,* the other a Smurf standing next to a flower.

"Nice art," Ben said, intrigued to see how his co-clerk lived.

"I'm into neo-garbage," Lisa said. "The trashier, the better. The Smurf is the prize of my collection. I won it at a carnival."

"This is actually a pretty cool place," Ober said.

"You sound surprised," Lisa said. "Were you expecting pink and purple satin pillows thrown everywhere?"

"I'm not sure," Ober said. "I think I was expecting maxi pads and other feminine hygiene products."

"Expecting or hoping?" Nathan asked as he took a seat on the couch.

Lisa threw her attaché case full of Court documents on her desk and headed toward the kitchen. "Does anyone want something to eat or drink?"

"I'll take a rack of lamb and a white wine spritzer," Ober said.

"Where's Eric?" Ben asked, sitting on the couch.

"He's working late tonight," Ober said. "He said he's sorry he couldn't make it."

"Typical," Ben said.

"Are you okay with this?" Nathan asked, watching Ben rifle through the magazines on the coffee table.

"Huh?" Ben asked. "Yeah, I'm fine. I just want to get started."

Lisa pulled a chair from the kitchen, put it down in the living room, and faced the couch. "What I don't understand is why Rick sent you the letter through *his* P.O. box. He could've just mailed it, or better yet, he could've put the letter in your box."

"I was thinking about that," Ben said. "I think Rick was just showing off. In that one action, he ripped apart my new plan and sent the message that my attempts at secrecy were a joke."

"What I can't understand is why he wants a truce," Ober said. "It's obvious you have no chance of catching him. In a way, you're nothing more than an annoyance." Looking at Ben, he added, "No offense."

"I think he wants information," Nathan said.

"I agree," Ben said. "There's no reason on earth why Rick needs a truce with me."

"Do you think he wants you to tell him another decision?" Lisa asked.

Ben continued to flip through the magazines. "That's the only thing I can imagine."

"Then I think we should assume that's what he's going to ask you when you go to the restaurant on Saturday."

"You're going to meet with him?" Lisa asked.

"Of course I'm going to meet with him," Ben said. "You think I'm going to let him get away from me? He's mine come Saturday."

"And how do you propose to do that?" Lisa asked.

"I'm not sure. That's where I was hoping you'd help. I was thinking about videotaping him at the restaurant, or something like that."

"I got it!" Ober yelled. "What if one of us dresses up like a waiter and somehow gets his wineglass, which will be covered in his fingerprints."

"And then what?" Lisa asked. "We'll run it through our computers in the Batcave?"

"We can send it through Nathan at the State Department."

"I say we take surveillance pictures of him as he enters the restaurant," Nathan said. "We'll have a positive I.D. on this guy in no time."

"I know the perfect spot for you to wait," Ben said as his voice raced with excitement. "There's an outdoor café right across the street from the restaurant."

"We can go buy a night lens for the camera," Ober said, rising from the couch.

"And we can wear cool disguises with trench coats and hats and fake mustaches," Lisa said sarcastically. "You all have to relax. That won't do you any good."

"Oh, it won't?" Ben asked. "And I assume you'll tell us why."

"So what if you have a few pictures of him? You're still in the same position you're in right now. Even if you have Rick's real name, you can't turn him in—unless we want Ben to go to jail too."

As silence swept through the room, Nathan said, "The woman speaks the truth."

"We have to somehow get him to proposition you about a new case," Lisa suggested. "If he does that, then we can get him for bribing a public official."

"Ben's not a public official," Ober said.

"He's a federal employee," Lisa said. "By bribing him, Rick will be attempting to interfere with the United States government. That's a federal offense, and it'll get him put away for at least a couple of years."

"Hold on a second," Nathan said. "What's to prevent Rick from striking a plea bargain with the authorities? For all we know, he can point to the *CMI* case and offer up Ben on a silver platter, saying that the Supreme Court clerk is the mastermind behind the whole scheme. Then Rick walks free, and Ben gets indicted—all because of our great plan."

"Rick would never do that," Lisa said. "The *CMI* decision is probably the best thing that ever happened to him. He probably made at least a couple million dollars on that deal. If he turns in Ben, or even attracts any attention toward CMI, the SEC will be all over Charles Maxwell's ass, even more than they are now. I'm sure Rick understands that it's better for him to do a few years for bribery on this second decision than to lose all his money and risk the wrath of Maxwell. He's not playing with small fish. CMI will eat him alive."

"I'm impressed," Nathan admitted.

"And you didn't think she was smart," Ben said, crossing his arms as he looked at Ober.

"Wait a minute," Lisa said to Ober. "You didn't think I was smart?"

"I didn't—" Ober began.

"You?" Lisa persisted, rising from her chair. "When we were playing Scrabble last week, you tried to use the word 'duh,' and you think *I'm* stupid?"

" 'Duh' is a word," Ober said.

"It's not a word!" Lisa said. "It's a slang expression used by primates in the late twentieth century. It's nonsense. Noise. Stupidity. But it's not a word."

"It's a word," Ober repeated.

"You can fight later," Ben interrupted. "Right now I want to think about the plan. It sounds like our best bet is to nail him on the bribery charge. It's not the greatest revenge, but it's the best we can do. Now how are we going to catch him?"

"What if you wear a wire?" Nathan said. "I might be able to get one from some of my buddies who work in security."

"Can you definitely get one?" Ben asked.

"If not, you'll wear a tape recorder," Lisa said. "Either way, he's on tape."

"I still think wc should get some pictures of him," Ober said.

"You just want to wear a disguise," Lisa said.

"I definitely want to wear a disguise," Ober admitted. "But I also think it'd be smart to get some physical proof of what Rick looks like."

"That's actually not a bad call," Ben admitted. "Eventually, the authorities are going to have to bring him in. We might as well let them know what he looks like." When he saw Lisa scrunch up her nose, Ben asked, "What's wrong?"

"Huh?" she asked. "No, it's nothing."

"Don't give me that," Ben said. "I know that look. What are you worried about?"

"Well, I can't help but think—shouldn't we go directly to the authorities with this? I mean, we're getting way out of our league. We might be better off asking for help."

"No way," Ben said. "If I do that, it means I might as well kiss my job good-bye. Besides, even if I went to the police, Rick would see us coming a mile away."

"What makes you think that?" Lisa asked.

"Are you kidding?" Ben asked. "For the past month he's watched our every move. Besides, it's not like we're doing anything so sophisticated. We're just trying to get his voice on tape. It's not like wc're trying to invade his hidden sanctuary located on a private island."

Lisa turned to Ober. "Don't worry. Rick doesn't really have a private island. It's just a figure of speech."

"No duh," Ober shot back.

"I'm serious, though," Ben said. "If things get hairy, we can call in help. But until then, I'd like to try this by ourselves."

CHAPTER 6

THE FOLLOWING DAY, BEN AND LISA WORKED NONSTOP ON four different decisions. After three months together, the two clerks had developed an efficient method for writing opinions. The better of the two at crafting original arguments, Ben always composed the first draft of the decision. With an aggressive writing style and uncompromising persistence, his opinions always barreled forward from introduction to conclusion. Lisa was the impeccable analyst. Ben said she had X-ray vision since she was able to see the holes in the most well-reasoned arguments. So after Ben presented his completed first draft, Lisa's editing skills went to work. A stickler for detail and the superior logician, she usually wrote twenty-page responses to Ben's forty-page decisions. When they'd finished their rewrite, the opinion went to Hollis.

At six o'clock, Ben shut off his computer and grabbed his jacket from the closet.

"Where are you going?" Lisa asked, looking up from the desk.

"I have a dinner date I can't break. Eric's aunt and uncle have been inviting us over since I got back from Europe."

"But I still haven't seen your first draft of the *Russell* decision."

"It's almost done. You'll have a finished draft by tomorrow at lunch."

"I better."

"You will. I promise." As Ben walked to the door, his phone rang. Assuming it was Eric calling with another excuse about why he'd be late, Ben ran back to his desk and picked up the receiver. "This is Ben," he said.

"Hey, Ben," Rick said. "How's everything going?"

"What the hell do you want?" Ben asked, recognizing the voice.

"Nothing," Rick said. "I just wanted to know what you're up to. I understand you have a big dinner date tonight."

"Are we still on for Saturday? Because—"

Rick hung up.

Ben slammed down the receiver.

"What's wrong? Who was that?"

"It was Rick," Ben said, rushing to the door.

"What'd he—" Before Lisa finished her question, Ben was gone.

Ben ran down the Court's forty-four steps and impatiently waited for his ride to arrive. At five after six, Eric and Ober pulled up in Eric's car. Ben was silent as he got into the pale gray Honda.

"I thought of the best name for a Mexican restaurant today," Ober excitedly announced, turning around in his seat. "I'm going to call it Tequila Mockingbird."

Ben didn't say a word.

"Sorry I'm late," Eric said. "I was—"

"Where's Nathan?" Ben interrupted.

"We're picking him up at home. I figured you three would want to change before dinner. Aunt Katie doesn't require a shirt and tie." Looking in the rearview mirror, Eric noticed the scowl on Ben's face. "What's wrong?"

"Nothing," Ben said. "I don't want to talk about it."

"Are you—"

"I don't want to talk about it," Ben repeated.

Glancing at Ober, Eric shrugged his shoulders and headed home.

"You're late," Nathan proclaimed the moment the door opened. Walking inside, Ben headed straight to the kitchen.

"What's wrong with him?" Nathan asked.

"He wouldn't say," Eric said. "I think something happened at work." Sitting on the love seat, Eric asked, "Were you waiting long?"

"I want you to know it still amazes me that you are consistently five minutes late to everything," Nathan said, looking at his watch. "I mean, I can set my watch to your lateness."

Unaccustomed to a close shave, Eric rubbed his face. "I'm not late," he said. "You're messed up because you set your watch ten minutes ahead."

"Don't even start with that," Nathan said. "On my watch you're fifteen minutes late, but you're still five minutes late in real time."

"I'll never understand that," Ober said. "If you know your watch is always ten minutes ahead, then what good does it do you?"

"Au contraire, my simpleminded friend. I don't pay attention to the—"

"Who opened my mail?" Ben interrupted. He stood in the doorway, holding up the pile of envelopes.

"It was like that in the mailbox," Nathan said.

"Was anyone else's mail opened?" Ben asked.

"Just yours," Nathan said. "You think it was Rick?"

Ben loosened his tie and unbuttoned his collar. "I don't know what else to think. He called me today right when I was leaving work. And he knew about our dinner tonight."

"Were any of the letters important?"

"None of them. They're all either bills or junk mail."

"I don't mean to be inconsiderate, but if we're late for dinner, Aunt Katie will never let us hear the end of it," Eric said.

"I'm not going to dinner," Ben said.

"Why?" Eric asked. "Just because someone opened your mail?"

"No, because I'm terrified Rick was checking up on me." Ben put his mail on the kitchen counter and poured himself a glass of water. "Maybe he was planning on breaking in here when we were gone."

"If he wanted to break in, he would've done it when he opened your mail," Eric said. "Don't let him wreck your life like this. He's just trying to make you crazy."

"Then I'll have to be crazy," Ben said. "Go without me and tell Katie I'm sorry. I wouldn't be any fun tonight, anyway."

"Are you sure?" Eric asked.

"Go," Ben said. "I'll be fine here."

Realizing that Ben wasn't about to change his mind, the three friends walked to the door. "We'll see you later."

The moment the door closed, Ben picked up his mail again. Shuffling through the envelopes, he found the only one without a return address. He pulled the letter from the envelope and reread the five words written in thick black Magic Marker: TRUST YOUR FRIENDS? SINCERELY, RICK. As he stared at the short message, Ben wondered whether the letter was a taunting warning or a simple question. Feeling both guilty and regretful for not telling his roommates about the letter, Ben crumpled it in a tight fist. How the hell did I let him do this to me? he wondered. Now he's got me suspecting my closest friends.

Ben threw the rest of the mail back on the counter, stepped into the dining room, and leaned on the large glass table. Don't even think it's one of them. There's no way it's one of them, he reassured himself. If I don't trust them, who can I trust? Staring at his reflection in the smudged glass, he replayed all the important events in his mind. He thought about every piece of information Rick had. He recalled every other person who was also privy to the information. He then came up with a logical way for Rick to find out about each piece. If the house is bugged, he thought, he could've heard us talking about Aunt Katie's dinner. And I told Nathan about the flowers. He could've overheard that as well. With a well-hidden microphone, Rick could've overheard everything. Staring down at the glass table, Ben nodded to himself. That's the most logical explanation. That's how he—

At the base of the glass table, Ben spotted a small dark object. On his knees in a matter of seconds, Ben closely examined the object. It was nothing. A clump of dirt from someone's shoes. Undeterred, Ben tilted the table and searched under each leg for Rick's microphone. Then he looked at each chair. He turned over the couches, lifted the cushions, squeezed the pillows, flipped the coffee table, ran his hands along the back of every picture frame, examined the television, turned over the VCR, inspected every videotape, pulled apart the closet, checked the pockets of every coat, opened every umbrella, peeked into baseball gloves, peered into tennis-ball cans, looked behind the toilet, cleared out the refrigerator, picked through all the cabinets, lifted every appliance, emptied every drawer, scrutinized every lamp, and took apart every phone. By the time he was finished, the first floor of the house was a shambles. And still nothing.

Hold it together, Ben told himself, his shirt soaked with sweat. Don't lose it. After rearranging the kitchen, the bathroom, the dining room, and the living room, Ben collapsed on the large sofa. He lay facedown; his right arm sagged to the floor and his fingers picked at the carpet. Catching his breath, Ben reached his conclusion. No matter what, you have to trust your friends. That's the only way to stay sane. Trust your friends.

When Ben's roommates arrived back at the house, Nathan headed for the bathroom, Ober headed for the kitchen, and Eric slumped in front of the television. Hearing the front door slam, Ben left his room and headed downstairs. He found Ober digging into a pint of ice cream. "How can you possibly be hungry?" Ben asked. "Didn't you just eat a full meal?"

"I'm a growing boy," Ober said.

Nathan returned to the living room. "How are you feeling?" he asked Ben. "Still worried about Rick?"

"Of course I'm still worried. But I've calmed down. I just needed the time alone." He joined Eric on the large couch. "How was dinner?"

"You missed it," Ober said, still picking at the pint of ice cream. "Eric's aunt is hotter than ever!"

"Can we stop talking about her?" Eric pleaded.

"Listen, we can understand why you feel the need to be protective, but you have to face facts," Nathan said. "Your aunt is steamy."

"I don't understand," Eric said. "She's not even that pretty."

"You'll never understand," Nathan said. "It's her aura. It speaks to us."

"Does she still have that picture of herself in a bikini on the refrigerator?" Ben asked.

Ober smiled. "Not anymore." Reaching into his back pocket, he pulled out the photo and threw it to Ben. "I figured you needed a little pick-me-up."

"You *stole* the picture from her refrigerator?" Eric asked, looking over Ben's shoulder.

"We borrowed it," Ober said. "We'll give it back. I just wanted to show Ben what he missed."

"*Hello*, perverts," Eric said. "This is my aunt we're talking about."

"What would happen if you had sex with her?" Ober asked. "Would your kids be mutants or something?"

"What's the word again for kids who are born from inbreeding?" Nathan asked.

"I think they're called 'Obers,' " Eric said.

"Now that's funny," Ober said. "That's a real laugh riot."

Comforted by the camaraderie, Ben was even more convinced that the letter was just Rick's way of playing mind games. He passed the photo to Nathan and put his hand on Eric's shoulder. "I meant to tell you, I have a good bit of gossip for you. But you have to keep it secret until I say it's okay."

"Let 'er rip," Eric said, watching Nathan fawn over the picture of his aunt.

"Let's just say that if you had to have a journalistic hunch in the next few days, I'd start asking around about an old Supreme Court justice."

"Blake's finally retiring?" Eric asked.

"You didn't hear a word from me," Ben said. "All I'm saying is that if you want to impress your editors with your sense of intuition, that's the path I'd start sniffing."

"Thanks," Eric smiled.

"Is what you told him illegal?" Ober asked, looking up from his now melting ice cream.

"Of course it's not illegal," Ben said. "It's just friendly advice."

"Because if it was illegal, I'd be forced to make a citizen's arrest." When Ben shook his head, Ober said, "I'm serious. I'd arrest the both of you."

"Ober, if you got me arrested, I'd call your boss and tell her you faxed me a photocopy of your penis last week."

"So?" Ober said.

"And then I'd tell her you were the one who sideswiped her car at the office barbecue last July."

"So?"

"And then I'd call all your overdue credit cards and give them your real address *and* your daytime telephone number."

Ober paused. "So?"

"And then I'd tell Eric that you're constantly stealing *his* quarters to do *your* laundry."

"You're what?" Eric asked.

"Oh, he's so full of sh—"

"That's where all my quarters went!"

"Good night," Ben said, standing from the couch. "Time for bed."

At six-thirty the next morning, Ben walked into the kitchen for breakfast. "Morning," he said to Nathan, always the earliest riser.

Folding the newspaper on the table, Nathan pushed aside his bowl of cereal. "I think you should see this."

"What is it?" Ben asked, pouring himself a glass of orange juice. "Read it to me."

"I think you should read it," Nathan said.

Ben picked up the paper. The headline blared, INVESTIGATION OPENED AFTER HIGH COURT'S CMI DECISION. Quickly, he read, "A high-level source at the Supreme Court revealed that an official investigation has been opened to dismiss rumors of wrongdoing during the recent CMI decision. After Charles Maxwell risked millions on the outcome of the case, critics from Wall Street to Washington have suspected foul play. As a result, the Court has begun 'a high level and thorough investigation.' According to the source, 'Everyone who knew the outcome in advance, from the printing department to the law clerks, will be thoroughly questioned.'"

Ben ground his teeth. "This is a bunch of crap," he said, throwing the paper on the table. "There's no investigation. They're just trying to create some controversy."

"Did you see the byline?"

When he read the words "By Eric Stroman," Ben's stomach dropped. "I don't believe this."

"Just relax," Nathan said, putting a hand on Ben's shoulder.

"That motherfucker!" Ben screamed, ripping up the paper. He ran out of the room and shot up the stairs. "ERIC! WAKE THE HELL UP!"

"Just calm down," Nathan called, following his friend.

Ben kicked open the door to Eric's room. The bed was empty. Nathan breathed a sigh of relief. "Where the hell is he?" Ben asked. A white envelope lay in the middle of Eric's unmade bed, with Ben's name written on the outside.

As Ben opened the envelope, Ober staggered into the room, wearing nothing but a pair of boxer shorts. "What the hell is going on?" he asked, rubbing his eyes.

"Don't ask," Nathan warned.

"I'll tell you what happened," Ben announced, ignoring the card in his hand. "Our piece-of-shit roommate wrote a story on page five of the newspaper about potential wrongdoings at the Court. He then went on to wrongly report that an investigation has been opened, and that members of the staff are suspected of leaking information to Charles Maxwell before the decision was handed down. In other words, he fucked me. If there wasn't an investigation before, there is one now. And if there was one before, he just forced Court security to turn the heat up."

"No way," Ober said.

"Just relax," Nathan said. "What's the card say?"

"Dear Ben," he read. "At this point, I'm sure you're raging mad. I hope you'll give me a chance to explain. I'm sorry I had to leave so early this morning, but I had some stuff to do at work. Always your friend, Eric."

"Oh, please," Ben said, passing the card to Nathan. "He hasn't been up before noon for a whole year, and today he had to go in early? He ran out on me."

"It sounds like there's an explanation," Nathan said, passing the card to Ober.

"What could he possibly say?" Ben asked. "What explanation could possibly excuse this? 'Sorry, we had some space to fill, so I decided to dick you over'?"

"Maybe they needed to fill in for the word jumble," Ober said.

"Ober, don't screw around with this," Ben warned. "This is serious for me. This story could get me fired." Ben was silent as he leaned on Eric's dresser. Watching their friend, Nathan and Ober said nothing. "DAMN!" Ben screamed, pushing a stack of papers from Eric's dresser. "They're definitely investigating now. They can't ignore this."

"You have to speak to him," Nathan said. "Give him a call."

Looking at his watch, Ben said, "I'm late. I have to go." He marched down the stairs, grabbed his overcoat from the closet, and stormed out of the house.

"This will not be a pretty one," Nathan said when the door slammed shut.

"Did you know about this?" Ober asked.

"Of course I didn't know," Nathan said.

"I knew," Ober said, sitting on Eric's bed.

"You knew?" Nathan asked. "You knew and you didn't stop him?"

"There was no stopping him," Ober explained. "You know how Eric gets when he's in reporter mode. He's out to win the Pulitzer."

"Did you at least say something to him?"

"Of course," Ober said. "He wouldn't listen. Besides, it was too late. He told me last night."

"I'll tell you one thing, their friendship is over," Nathan said, picking up the knocked-over papers. "And Ben is not a person you want as your enemy."

"He's definitely going to kill him," Ober said.

"Absolutely. He'll never forgive this. And no matter how long it takes him, he's going to make sure Eric's miserable."

"Maybe we should make up a flyer for a new roommate," Ober said,

"Actually, why don't you do that at work today? It'll say: Wanted, semi-messy roommate to replace our old dead one. Must be willing to live with one genius, one monkey, and one Supreme Court clerk who's recently acquired a taste for blood."

As he approached the Supreme Court, Ben struggled to calm himself. Taking deep, slow breaths, he climbed the stairs and entered the marble edifice. Biting the inside of his cheek, he showed his I.D. and walked around the metal detector. He made every attempt to appear calm, taking extra-small strides to slow himself down. Walking through reception, he was relieved to see that Nancy wasn't in yet. As he entered his and Lisa's office, he lightly shut the door behind him.

"I guess you saw it," Lisa said, the paper open on her desk.

"I don't want to talk about it," Ben said, heading directly for his desk. "He's a dead man."

"Have you talked to him?"

"He ran out before I got up. Has anyone said anything yet?"

"Nothing so far. It's only seven, though. The day is young."

"That's just great. Thanks for that piece of advice."

"Listen, it's only the *Washington Herald*. Everyone in this town knows it's a right-wing, lunatic paper. No one takes it seriously." Getting no response from Ben, she added, "It didn't even make the front page."

"Terrific. I'm thrilled."

"Listen, it could be worse. At least he didn't say that it was a clerk."

"Well then, I'm tickled-fuckin'-pink," Ben said, his voice rising. "It's all okay now. I don't have to worry. My career is just perfect. Thanks, Sally Sunshine, for showing me the way."

"Listen, I don't need your asshole tone," Lisa yelled across the desk. "I was just trying to help."

"Well, sorry if I'm not in the mood."

"It has nothing to do with being in the mood," she said. "If you want to be miserable, go right ahead. But *don't* take it out on me."

"I'm sorry," Ben said, leaning back in his chair. "I really am. I'm just scared about this whole thing."

"And you deserve to be. I'd want to kick the crap out of him."

"I have no idea what to do."

"Well, I hate to be the one to say this, but there's not a lot you can do about it now. We have to get the *Russell* decision done, and I still haven't seen your first draft."

"Can't you do it?"

"Oh, don't even think that," Lisa warned. "I'm your friend, and I'm here whenever you want to talk, but don't think you're getting out of your work just so you can sulk all day."

"C'mon. I'd do it for you."

"Are you crazy? While you're writing *Russell* and *Pacheco*, I'm editing *Oshinsky*, and *Lowell Corp.*, and *Pacific Royal*, and *Schopf*. And we haven't even started working on *Grinnell*, which is scheduled to be announced at the end of the month."

"So what are you saying?"

"What I'm saying is, don't leave work and run down to the *Washington Herald* to confront your roommate, which I know you've been planning to do since you saw the damn article."

Ben fought a smile. "That's not what I was thinking."

"Oh, really?"

"I was going to wait until lunch to go down there."

At eleven-thirty, Ben's phone rang. "Hello, Justice Hollis's chambers," he said, picking up the receiver.

"Ben Addison? This is the Supreme Court security office. We need to speak to you. We believe you may be leaking information to the public."

"E-excuse me?" Ben said, panicking.

"Just kidding!" Ober said. "It's just me."

"Don't do that! You scared the shit out of me."

"Oh, relax," Ober said. "You have nothing to worry about."

"What do you want?"

"Eric called me. He said he'd like to talk to you tonight."

"What time?"

"Eight, if that's okay with you."

"That's fine. I'll see him then."

"Who was it?" Lisa asked, noticing the irritated look on Ben's face. "Just Ober."

A half hour later, the phone rang again. "Hello, Justice Hollis's chambers," Ben said.

"Is this Ben Addison?" a voice asked.

"Yes," Ben said, annoyed to be pulled away from the *Russell* opinion.

"Hi, Mr. Addison. My name is Diana Martin, and I'm with *The Washington Post*. I was wondering if you had any comment on the story in this morning's *Herald*."

"Listen, if you work with Ober, tell him to bite me."

"Mr. Addison, I think you have me confused with someone else. As I said, I'm with *The Washington Post.* I'd be happy to fax over my press credentials. In fact, if you'd like, perhaps we could meet for lunch and talk this over."

Sitting up straight in his chair, Ben knocked over the coffee on his desk. "How can I help you today, Ms. Martin?" he asked as Lisa pulled a pile of napkins from her left-hand drawer.

"Well, as I said, I was wondering if you had any comment on the story in today's *Herald.*"

As Ben lifted piles of paper from his desk, Lisa dabbed away the coffee. "I'm sorry," Ben said. "I have no idea what you're talking about."

"In this morning's *Washington Herald,* there was a story about a possible leaking of information during the recent *CMI* decision. I was wondering if you had anything you'd like to say about it. If you'd like, I'll keep your identity secret. You'll be an unidentified source."

Ben opened his top drawer and pulled out a small stack of papers. Searching through the stack and trying to avoid bumping into Lisa, Ben quickly found what he was looking for. Reading verbatim from the sheet titled "Response to Press," he said, "I appreciate your concern on this matter, but as a clerk of the Supreme Court of the United States, I am not permitted to reveal any information to the press."

"So are you saying that there is an investigation taking place, but that you just can't talk about it?"

"Ms. Martin, I have nothing further to say," Ben said, throwing aside the sheet. "Thanks for your time." As Ben hung up the phone, Lisa finished soaking up the coffee. "Thanks for the help," he said, wiping the remaining liquid from under his pencil sharpener.

"No problem," Lisa said. She walked back to her desk. "Was that really the press?"

"I don't believe it," Ben said. "It was *The Washington Post.*"

"What'd they say?"

"They asked me about the story. I almost shit in my pants."

"It sounded like you were fine," Lisa said. "You did the right thing. That's what the press sheet was designed for."

"When I got this in August, I never thought I'd have to use it," Ben said, putting the sheet back in his top drawer. "Do you think they know?"

"No. They probably called everyone. I'm sure they know that the clerks are the easiest ones to get information from."

"I really think they know. They have to know."

"They don't know a thing," she said. "In fact, I'm surprised we haven't gotten more calls from the press. I'd heard that we'd be called before every big decision."

"They haven't called you," Ben said. "Explain that, Miss Optimis—" Lisa's phone rang.

Lisa smiled. "Hello, Justice Hollis's chambers." As Ben listened, she said, "Yeah, I really can't talk now. Can I call you back later? Yeah, now's a bad time."

"Who was that?" Ben asked as Lisa hung up the phone.

"Just an old friend from law school." Walking over to Ben's desk, she said, "Listen, don't let this get you down. I'm sure they're just going through their list. I'll get called."

"Whatever," Ben said. "It's no big deal. I mean, they're the press. They're supposed to find these things out. It's their job to wreck my life."

"Ben, your life is far from wrecked."

"Listen, I don't need the pep talk. I know what I got into, and I'll figure a way out of it."

"It's not a matter of figuring a way out of it. You're not in trouble. No one knows it's you. Besides, worse comes to worst, you can always wait tables."

"That's very funny," Ben said, heading for the door.

"Where are you going?"

"I have a stupid lunch meeting with the firm I worked at two summers ago."

"A recruitment lunch?"

"I imagine."

"Why are you going?" Lisa asked. "If you want to be a prosecutor, you don't have to go to a firm. You should just go to the U.S. Attorney's Office."

"I wish. But the U.S. Attorney's Office won't help me pay off all the debt I have from law school."

"You still have law school debt? I thought your parents were wealthy executives?"

"My mom's an executive, but my family doesn't have that kind of money. Anyway, I wanted to pay my own way."

"You did?"

"It's my responsibility. I'm the one who went to law school, I'm the one who gets the benefit. Why should they pay the bill?"

"So how much debt do you have?"

"From law school, about ninety-two thousand dollars." Lisa's mouth fell open. "And that's not including the eight thousand that I paid off in the past two years."

"Haven't you ever heard of financial aid?"

"Absolutely," Ben said. "That's how I got the loans."

"I still don't understand why you didn't let your parents—"

"It's a long story," Ben said. "In the end, they couldn't afford to do much, and I wanted to make it easier on them. That's it." Looking down at his watch, he said, "I really have to go. I'm late."

Ben jumped into a cab outside the courthouse and headed to Gray's, home of Washington's premier power lunches. Although many of the city's most important meetings were still held in dimly lit restaurants that smelled of cigar smoke, brandy, and barely cooked steak, Gray's attracted executives and congressional leaders who actually wanted to be seen at lunch. Of course, it still had four private rooms in the back for patrons who wanted to be more discreet. With oversized glass tables balanced on geometrical steel bases, and chairs draped with white slip-covers, the main dining room was arranged in a large circle, to facilitate celebrity spotting. The restaurant was decorated in stark black and white, giving it a minimalist look that was almost too ultramodern for downtown D.C.

Once inside, Ben tightened his tie and looked for Adrian Alcott. Alcott was the hiring partner for Wayne & Portnoy, one of the city's most established firms, and the place where Ben had worked during the summer after his second year of law school. As a summer associate at Wayne, he was taken by the recruiting committee to baseball games at Camden Yards, concerts at the Kennedy Center, and lunches and dinners at the best eateries on K Street. The summer was capped by a yachting excursion for the entire firm—more than four hundred people sailed away on two magnificent yachts. Knowing that they had attracted the best and the brightest from America's top law schools, the firm tried to make sure they kept them. For the summer associates who were still choosing between competing firms, the evening at sea was the ultimate hard sell.

All eighteen summer associates had gone on to yearlong judicial clerkships after they graduated from law school. The firm expected its associates to clerk for a year, knowing that they would gain invaluable experience that could be used when they eventually joined the firm. And to make sure the recruits did not forget Wayne & Portnoy during their clerkship year, the firm made bimonthly phone calls to each would-be associate to see how his or her year was going. Eventually, seventeen clerks returned to the firm. Ben went to the Supreme Court. When the firm found out their eighteenth summer associate had been offered a Supreme Court clerkship, the phone calls tripled and the free lunches began. To the city's most prestigious law firms, Supreme Court clerks were human badges of honor. Of Wayne & Portnoy's four hundred fifty-seven lawyers, ten were former Supreme Court clerks. Today, Adrian Alcott was hoping to make it eleven.

"Hello, Mr. Addison," Alcott said with a warm smile as Ben approached the table in one of the back rooms of the restaurant. "Please, join us." Alcott was tall and slender, and his long frame was capped by thick blond hair. With a smile that he flashed at every opportunity, Alcott was the firm's best recruiting tool. He loved Wayne & Portnoy, and his gracious and charming nature had convinced more than one quarter of the firm that they loved it, too. "Ben, this is Christopher Nash. He was a clerk for Justice Blake four years ago, and I thought it'd be nice for you to speak to someone who's been through the process."

"Nice to meet you," Ben said, shaking Nash's hand. Nash looked like the typical Blake clerk: weasely and white, with an Andover or Exeter in his background.

"So, how's the Big House treating you?" Nash asked. "Everything the way I left it?"

"Absolutely," Ben said, immediately annoyed by Nash's attempt at coolness.

"You picked a great year to be at the Court," Nash said. "This CMI thing has the whole place in an uproar."

"It's definitely been exciting," Ben said.

"So what do you think?" Alcott asked. "Did Maxwell know?"

"I have no idea," Ben said with a strained smile. "They don't tell the clerks the important stuff."

"Right. Of course," Alcott said, opening up his menu. "So, what shall we have for lunch? The snapper here is wonderful."

Looking at Ben, Nash said, "I have to tell you, the Court is the world's most exciting place to work, but there is nothing like a free lunch at an expensive restaurant. When it comes to food, I'm like a kid in a candy store."

Struggling to pay attention to the conversation, Ben thought about the various possibilities for escaping lunch. I bet if I set fire to the curtains, I could lose them in the confusion, he thought, staring at the menu.

"I'm not sure if you know, but we're going to be in front of you real soon," Alcott said. "We're representing the respondent in the *Mirsky* case. Our oral arguments are set for January."

"You have to put in a good word for us," Nash said, laughing along with Alcott.

Maybe I could start choking on mineral water, Ben thought. That would shut them up real quick.

"So what's the Court working on now?" Alcott asked.

"Hey, don't even think it," Nash jumped in as one of their two waiters placed a tiny appetizer of blackened bass on his plate. "He can't say anything. Court business is extremely confidential. When your clerkship is over, they even make you shred any documents you still have."

"Is that right?" Alcott said.

"Definitely. The place is airtight." Looking at Ben, Nash said, "How's Justice Blake doing? Still as cranky as ever?"

"That's him," Ben said. "The most miserable man on the Court."

"I spoke to him recently. I've been calling every once in a while to give advice to his current clerks, Arthur and Steve. They seem nice."

"They're really nice," Ben said.

"I just try to be helpful," Nash said, as a waiter refilled his water. "I know how crazy it can get there."

"Do most clerks call their former chambers?" Ben asked, taking a roll.

"Some do," Nash said. "It depends. I think all of Blake's clerks do because a year with Blake can be such a miserable experience."

"He works them like dogs."

"That's Blake. I think all of his former clerks are bonded by knowing that we've all lived through a year with him. Have any of Hollis's old clerks called you?"

"No," Ben said bluntly. "That's why I was curious."

"Wait, let me think. Who was clerking for Hollis when I was there? Oh, I remember, one of them was Stu Bailey. He's a great guy. He works at Winick and Trudeau now."

Alcott looked annoyed at the mention of Wayne & Portnoy's rival firm.

"I'm actually not surprised no one's called," Nash added. "Hollis makes you work, but deep down, he's a big teddy bear."

"Is that right?" Alcott asked.

"That's not a bad description," Ben agreed.

"Have you had any encounters with Osterman's clerks?"

"Not really," Ben said. "They're the only clerks who really keep to themselves."

"Unbelievable!" Nash said, banging the table. "Nothing changes." Nash leaned toward Ben and lowered his voice. "When I was there, Osterman's clerks were the worst, most obnoxious, conservative cranks in the whole Court. And the rumor I heard was that all of Osterman's clerks were part of this tiny network. They all keep in touch, and they have a secret meeting once a year."

"I never heard this," Ben said with a smile.

"I'm not joking," Nash said. "I heard they used to call themselves The Cabal, and the older clerks would teach the younger clerks how to sway decisions to their own agenda. I'm serious," he added, noticing

Ben's doubtful expression. "You know how much influence you can have if you want it. When you write a decision, for the most part you can structure it your own way. You can emphasize certain points, or make other points extra ambiguous. It's a subtle gesture of power, but it's still power."

"Yeah, but you really can't do anything the justice doesn't want in the first place."

"That was the scary part. People said Osterman knew about all this and he just turned his back on it—letting his clerks do what they wanted."

"I think that's how Hitler trained his militia," Ben said as a waiter refilled the table's breadbasket.

"Didn't I tell you this guy knows what it's like?" Alcott said to Ben as he pointed at Nash.

"So tell me," Ben said, "how's everything at Wayne?"

"Fantastic," Alcott said, putting both elbows on the table. "We just took on NFL Properties as a client, so if you need any tickets to a Redskins game, you let me know. In fact, any game in the whole country, whenever you want. We also took on Evian, so every water cooler in the firm has sparkling fresh Evian water."

"That's great," Ben said, noticing that Alcott had paused for his reaction.

"And the pro bono department recently started doing work for the Children's Defense Fund."

"There are no free benefits from them," Nash laughed.

Shooting Nash a look, Alcott said, "But we do get invited to their annual convention, where the president usually speaks."

"That's great," Ben said. "I'm on their mailing list because I did some work with them during law school."

"Did you really?" Alcott asked. "Then we'll have to get you in on this. Whenever you have some free time, let me know, and I'll get you in to see the chairperson. She's a wonderful woman. Very charismatic."

"Meanwhile, did you tell him about the Supreme Court bonus?" Nash asked.

Alcott smiled. "Ben, this one is wonderful. The hiring committee recently met to reevaluate compensation packages for first-year associates. Since we've always given bonuses to associates who have clerkship experience, we thought we should add another bonus if the candidate also clerks for the Supreme Court. So in addition to that number I gave you last week, you can add another ten thousand. It's only for the first year, but we think it's a nice token."

Staring at his plate, Ben wondered how he could take a $38,000-a-year job with the U.S. Attorney's Office when a $100,000 job was staring him in the face and buying him an expensive lunch.

"Listen, you don't have to decide now," Alcott said. "We know it's a hard choice. I'll be honest, we know you can write your ticket any-where, but we want you at Wayne and Portnoy. You've been with us for one summer; you know our style. It's a relaxed atmosphere. We work hard when we have to, but we try to enjoy all the perks our profession allows us. If you come to us, I can assure you that at least twenty percent of your work will be on pro bono cases, so you can still give a great deal back to the community. Obviously, this isn't the last time we'll be speaking this year, but I do want to keep you informed about your choices."

"I appreciate it," Ben said. "You make it hard to say no."

"Good," Alcott said, closing his menu. "With that said, let's order some expensive food."

When Ben returned to the office, Lisa was still sitting at her com-puter. "How was lunch?"

"It was great," Ben said, lying on the sofa and patting his stomach. "I had the best snapper I've eaten in my entire life. It was crusted with macadamia nuts and covered with the most tantalizing lemon-butter sauce. Unreal."

"So let me ask you, how does it feel to sell your soul for a piece of fish and some designer butter?"

"Don't even start with me. *I'm* at least deciding whether to go to a firm. *You're* the one who's already decided to say yes, Ms. Faustus."

"Damn right I'm selling out. I've got a Saab to think about."

"Your soul for a car. How tainted you've become."

"Trust me, you'll be right behind me. Guar-an-teed!"

"First of all, I won't be right behind you, because there's no amount of money in the world that can get me to live in Los Angeles. I heard that when you enter the city, the toll booths there accept dimes, nickels, quarters, and your integrity. Second of all, even if I do go to a firm, I'll be going for ten thousand dollars more than you will."

"You will not," Lisa said.

"I will too."

"Will not."

"Okay," Ben said, putting his hands behind his head. "Then I guess they didn't just promise me an extra ten grand as a bonus for being a Supreme Court clerk."

"Are you kidding me? You get ten grand more for working here? That's bullshit. I have to get my firm on the line. I want more money. I'll do whatever it takes. I'll convince them I'm a bleeding heart who wants to save the world."

Laughing, Ben said, "Let me ask you a question: Can we be more disgusting at this particular moment? Wait, do we have any death penalty cases coming up this week? Maybe we can kill someone for being poor."

"You really have the worst liberal guilt I've ever seen," Lisa said. "We're going to be wealthy. Big deal. We worked hard to get where we are."

"I know," Ben said, "but we had so many advantages . . ."

". . . that other kids never had. Yeah, yeah, yeah," Lisa said, playing an imaginary violin. "Listen, I don't know what suburb you grew up in, but I grew up in a normal middle-class family. During bad years, we were lower middle class. I went to public school and no one cut the crusts off my Wonder bread. How much class can my parents have— they met at Graceland, and they still tell people about it."

"Y'know, there are two kinds of people in life," Ben said, sitting up. "Those who cut the crust off their bread and those who—"

The ringing of Lisa's phone cut off Ben's sentence. "Hold on a second, I think that's my pimp. He's selling all of my intellectual skills to the highest bidder." Picking up the receiver, she said, "Hello, Justice Hollis's chambers." After a second she grinned and mouthed the words *Washington Post.* Then she pulled out her press sheet. "I appreciate your concern on this matter, but as a clerk of the Supreme Court of the United States, I am not permitted to reveal any information to the press." Lisa hung up the phone and sat back in her chair. "Are you happy now? I'm a suspect with you."

"Yeah, but you were always a suspect. Your whole family is a bunch of shady thieves."

"I resent you using the word 'thieves.' We prefer the word 'scoundrels.' " Walking to the door, she continued, "I'm going to give Hollis our *Oshinsky* opinion. Hopefully, he'll approve it by the end of today."

"Good luck," he said as Lisa left the room. Ben picked up the phone and dialed Nathan's number.

"The Administrator's Office," Nathan said.

"Is that how you answer the phone? No wonder our government's a bureaucratic mess."

"Did you just get back from lunch with the castrating lawyers?" Nathan asked.

"You got it."

"I knew there had to be a reason you were so excited. What did they try to buy you with this time?"

"An extra ten grand."

"Are you serious? I was joking. Man, I'm in the wrong profession."

"No, no. You have it much better off. Sitting around and thinking about social problems is probably the best way to solve them. And don't forget, you beat me by a hundred points on the SAT, which, now that I think of it, is the square root of ten thousand."

"Rot in Hades, capitalist sloth."

"Listen, I meant to ask you, have you gotten all the stuff we need for Saturday?"

"I'm on it," Nathan said. "Rick won't know what to do when we're done with him."

"Is the plan done?"

"It's pretty much the same as we first discussed."

"I guess we're set then," Ben said. "We should probably meet tomorrow night just to do a run-through."

"That's fine. By the way, I'll assume you haven't spoken to Eric yet?"

"Nope. We're meeting tonight at eight to have it out."

"Ben, do me a favor. Go easy on him."

"I'm fine. I'm completely calm."

"Yeah, but did you hear what I said? Go easy on him. He's still your friend."

"Listen, I have to go," Ben said, stretching. "I have to work on these opinions." Hanging up the phone, Ben pulled his chair up to his desk. He opened the brown folder marked "*Russell* decision" and pulled out his first draft. Staring at the pages, he wondered if Osterman's clerks really swayed opinions to their own agenda. No way, he thought. That story has urban myth written all over it. Lisa's phone rang. He reached across the desk and picked it up. "Hello, Justice Hollis's chambers."

"Hi, I'm looking for a Lisa Schulman. Do I have the right extension?"

"You do." Ben pulled the phone toward his own desk. "She just stepped out for a minute. Can I take a message?"

"Can you tell her Diana Martin of *The Washington Post* called her, and if she could give me a call back that'd be great."

Puzzled, Ben said, "I guess she has your number?"

"No, no. She doesn't even know me. Let me give it to you."

After writing down the number, Ben hung up the phone and sat back in his chair. For the next half hour, he stared at the pages of the *Russell* decision.

At three o'clock, Lisa returned to the office. "We're done," she sang as she entered the room, throwing a manila file folder on her desk. "He loved it! Oshinsky is O'history!" Taking one look at Ben, she asked, "What?"

"I have a message to give you. Diana Martin of *The Washington Post* called. She wants you to call her."

"Ben, I can expl—"

"Don't bother," he said, throwing Diana's number on her desk. "I won't believe it."

"Ben, don't be so damn stubborn."

"Why not? All my other friends picked today to dick me over. Why can't I be a little bit stubborn? In fact, I think I'm entitled to be a full-fledged jerk today."

"Well, you're doing a great job of *that*. And let me ask you a question: Why were you even answering my line?"

"Don't even think of turning this one around," he said, jumping from his seat. "Your phone rang; I picked it up. Period. What's your excuse?"

Lisa looked at her feet. "I was worried that you would be crazy if I didn't get a phone call from the *Post*, so I had a friend of mine make that first call to me and I pretended it was the reporter. I was trying to make you feel better."

Ben fell silent. "You really did that for me?"

"I did it because I pity you," she said with a smile.

"That's not a bad excuse."

"C'mon, you can't be mad."

"You're lucky this time," he said, pointing at Lisa. "Next time you try to be nice, I'm gonna really get pissed."

At seven-thirty, Ben packed up his briefcase and left the office. Walking downstairs, he thought about his forthcoming confrontation with Eric. If he has no explanation, he's dead, Ben thought as he swiped his card through the security door on the first floor. Even if he has an explanation, he's dead. As he passed the marble statues in the Great Hall, Ben heard the security guard at the front entrance mumble something into his walkie-talkie. When the guard got out of his seat, Ben wondered what was wrong. Slowly, he approached the entrance. The guard looked at his clipboard. At the last second, Ben decided to turn around. Heading back the way he came, he swiped his card through the security door he had just left, reentering the north wing of the Court. He hurried toward the unmanned side door that exited to the north side of the building. As he approached the door, he heard the echo of footsteps behind him. Only the guilty run, he thought, remembering the advice from his criminal law professor. As he approached the exit, he once again prepared to swipe his I.D. card. Forcing it though the machine that would let him reach the exit, he was surprised when he didn't hear the usual click of access. Again he tried the card. Nothing.

"Ben, can we speak with you for a moment?"

Ben jumped. Turning around, he saw a man in a gray wool suit coming toward him.

"Do you have a moment?" the man asked.

"Uh, is there a problem?" Ben stuttered.

"If you would just follow me." Ben followed the man back to the front entrance. As they walked through the Great Hall, Ben loosened his tie. When they reached the front of the building, they took the elevator to the basement. Known to Court staff as Disneyland, the basement of the Supreme Court contained a snack bar, cafeteria, movie theater, gift shop, and exhibits on the history of the Court.

As Ben passed the giant statue of John Marshall, he tightened his jaw and tried his best to remain calm. On the west side of the building were the only basement offices: those of the marshals, who were in charge of all security for the Court. Entering through the main door, Ben walked through the maze of tiny cubicles and was escorted to the far left-hand corner of the room. Stopping in the doorway of a large office, Ben waited behind his guide. A heavy man in a blue pin-striped suit sat behind a faux antique desk.

"Come on in," he said. His round face was highlighted by a fat, pockmarked nose and a beard peppered with gray. The smell of the office revealed his taste for cigars. Decorating the front of his desk was an extensive collection of batteries. "Do me a favor, close the door," the man said, motioning to Ben's escort. He tilted back in his leather chair as the door slammed shut. "So you're Ben Addison," he said. "Please. Sit."

"Is there some sort of problem?" Ben asked nervously as he sat in one of the two seats in front of the desk. He kept his breathing slow and steady, trying to look unfazed.

"That's what we're trying to figure out," the man said as Ben's escort sat in the other chair. "In case you don't know me, I'm Carl Lungen, chief marshal here at the Court. I oversee all of our security here. This is Dennis Fisk, our deputy marshal," Lungen said, indicating Ben's gray-suited escort. "The reason we brought you here today is because we have some questions that we hope you can answer about a story that appeared in today's *Washington Herald.* If you're not aware of the story, let me say that it suggests the possibility that the recent *CMI* decision was leaked to Mr. Charles Maxwell. Are you with me so far?''

''I saw the story,'' Ben said, annoyed by Lungen's condescending tone.

''Good,'' Lungen said, grabbing a 1980 Energizer. ''You see, Ben, this story suggests that the security of this Court has been compromised. As you can imagine, this reflects poorly on our office. Luckily, we have a very close friend at the *Herald,* and after a phone call to this friend, I was informed that the author of the story was a new reporter to the paper. I was also informed that this reporter happens to live with one of our clerks. That clerk is you. So, you can imagine my desire to meet you face-to-face.''

''I know what you're thinking,'' Ben said, ''but I had nothing to do with the story.''

''So you're telling me that you don't know of anyone leaking information from this Court?''

''No one.''

''Then why did your friend write that story?''

''I don't know. To be honest, that's exactly where I was headed when you pulled me down here. The first I heard of the story was at seven o'clock this morning. When I went to confront my roommate about it, he was gone.''

''Ben, I'm going to ask you again. Do you know of anyone leaking information from this Court?''

''No, I don't. I swear, I don't know of anyone.''

Lungen placed the battery back in line with the others. He stared at Ben. After a pause, Ben said, ''My only guess is that he was trying to make a good impression on his editors. I mean, he knows that we know the opinions in advance. From there he can write whatever he wants. You know the *Herald,* they print anything.'' As his voice picked up strength, he continued, ''And if Eric had a single shred of proof, do you really think they'd run it on page five? The story is complete conjecture. You read it; all it does is present the possibility of an inside source to explain Maxwell's lucky guess. It could've appeared on the op-ed page.''

''Ben, do you know what would happen if we found out you were lying?'' Lungen asked, placing his hands flat on his desk. ''Naturally, you'd be removed from your position. If that happened, my guess is that the press would pick it up immediately. Whether you were responsible or not, I'd wager that you'd be implicated as the source that leaked to Maxwell. After that, I'd say your career would be over, and your only work would be as an adviser to the TV movie that tells the world your story.''

''Why don't you just cooperate with us?'' Fisk asked in a calm, soothing voice. Fisk was rugged-looking, with chiseled features offset by a bad complexion and a poorly fitted suit. Fisk's strong Chicago accent flattened his *A*'s and rounded his *O*'s. ''If you let us, you know we can help you with this.''

''Listen, I don't need the good-cop-bad-cop routine,'' Ben said, a rush of adrenaline keeping his voice from cracking. ''If I leaked the story to Eric, I'd be a complete moron. I mean, no offense to you guys, but it doesn't take a genius to figure out Eric and I are roommates. Does it make any sense for me to ask my roommate to write a story that will not only jeopardize my career, but will also call attention to myself?'' Letting the logic of the argument sink in, he added, ''The story is bullshit. Eric probably wanted attention and—''

''We didn't say you asked Eric to write the story,'' Fisk interrupted. ''We just think you're the one that gave him the information.''

''I didn't say word one to him. Believe me, I've been extremely careful about what I've said around everyone, Eric especially.''

''But you did tell Eric that Blake is retiring, didn't you?''

Ben bit the inside of his cheek. Lungen continued, ''Don't bullshit us, Ben. My friend at the *Herald* said there's a story running tomorrow about Blake stepping down. The *Herald* wouldn't run it without a solid source, and Eric fingered you.''

Crossing his arms to look confident, Ben knew he was losing control. ''I admit I told him about Blake. I told him we'd be releasing the information later this week. But I didn't tell him about—''

''You admit that you purposely leaked information from this Court about Blake, and yet you expect us to believe you about Maxwell?'' Lungen asked.

''You know there's a difference,'' Ben said. ''The Blake thing was common knowledge. It was hardly confidential information. What you're talking about with Maxwell is on a totally different level."

"That's exactly our point," Lungen said. "Now, would you like to start over?"

Determined not to show his frustration, Ben said, "Look, I swear, I don't know anything about Maxwell. If I did, do you really think I'd be sitting here, talking to you? If I leaked the decision to Maxwell, I'd be on a beach in Greece right now, counting my ten-million-dollar fee."

"Ben, let me tell you what we think. We agree you probably didn't leak anything to Eric. That'd be stupid, and frankly, we expect better from you. You probably didn't personally leak any information to Maxwell, either. As you said, if you did, you wouldn't need to work anymore. Our fear, however, is that you may've heard something from your co-clerk, or from a clerk in another office, about someone else leaking information. You casually mention this to Eric, or maybe he overhears it, and suddenly we have a major scandal on our hands. At this point, though, the only person we do have is you."

"I'm telling you: I have no idea of anyone, including myself, leaking information from this Court."

"What about Blake's resignation?"

"You know what I mean—substantial information concerning legal decisions. When I first started at the Court, I explained to my roommates that I knew all the information in advance. But they never cared—not even Eric. The only way I can figure it is that Eric created this hypothetical situation to get published. Ask your friend at the *Herald*. You said they wouldn't run the Blake resignation story unless they had a good source. What was the source for Eric's story about Maxwell?"

Lungen was silent.

"Eric wouldn't name his source, would he?" Ben asked. "You obviously asked your friend."

"No," said Lungen, looking away.

"So you didn't know it was me, but you still grilled me just to be sure?" Ben asked, shaking his head.

"Ben, the *Herald* may not know the source, but they definitely believe Eric has one. If that story ran, there's got to be some truth behind it."

"Weren't you ever told not to believe everything you read?"

"Don't be a smart-ass," Lungen said. "Until I'm sure what happened, this isn't a closed issue."

"Well, until you're sure what happened, I'm out of here." Ben stood to leave.

"I'm not playing around," Lungen warned, standing. "If you think you're so innocent—"

"I *am* innocent."

"Would you be willing to take a lie detector test to back that up?"

Pausing, Ben knew there was only one answer that would satisfy Lungen. In his most confident tone, he answered, "If that's what it takes."

"You should realize one thing," Fisk interrupted. "Even if we believe you, there's no reason to assume the rest of the world will. Carl's friend at the *Herald* said they received calls from every major newspaper about Eric's story. They didn't realize what they were getting into when they ran that sucker."

"Why don't you demand a retraction?" Ben asked.

"We demanded one first thing this morning," Lungen explained. "Apparently, since the article only suggests the possibility of a leak, the paper doesn't care that it's unsubstantiated."

"Do you think other papers will pick it up?"

"Now you know what we're worried about," Lungen said. "From what we hear, the press won't touch the story until they have a source. It doesn't have to be a good source. It can be a janitor, a secretary, a clerk, anyone. But as soon as they get a source, they'll tear whoever's responsible apart. To be honest, they may never get a source. But you never know. Some cafeteria worker might be pissed at how tight her hairnet is, and the next thing we know, she's on the evening news telling the world how she overheard someone talking to someone else.

"For the next few weeks, although it may not get much play in the press, I'll guarantee you that every journalism grad in town will be digging around this place hoping to blow it wide open. And if I were you, I'd be worried, because thanks to your roommate, the easiest person to finger in this disaster is you."

"Thanks," Ben said wryly, struggling to suppress his anxiety. "Can I go now?"

"I'm serious."

"I understand," Ben said, moving to the door.

"One more thing before you leave," Fisk said. "If you are going to confront Eric about his story, I'd appreciate it if you could come back here tomorrow morning, in case anything new pops up."

"We'll see," Ben said, sidestepping him and edging out the door.

After Ben left the room, Lungen looked to Fisk. "What'd you think?"

"You know how I feel," Fisk said. "I hate clerks. They all think because they were picked to work at the Supreme Court, their shit doesn't stink anymore."

"That's very helpful," Lungen said. "Now what'd you think of Ben?"

"I got what I expected. He's obviously a bright kid, and I think he laid it out pretty well. He's not dumb enough to help Eric write that story, but that doesn't mean Eric is full of shit either. Why? What was your take?"

"I'm not sure. I wish Ben was a bit more nervous."

"He was definitely calm," Fisk agreed. "So he's either telling the truth, or he's one of the best bullshit artists I've ever seen."

"I really think he was as surprised by the article as we were. And my friend at the *Herald* said they grilled Eric for a source. He never came close to naming one, though."

Pausing for a moment, Fisk finally said, "I don't like these kids."

"Fisk, you don't like anyone who's smarter than you."

"I'm dead serious about this. I say that no matter what happens, we watch this guy very carefully."

CHAPTER 7

WHEN OBER RETURNED HOME, HE WAS SURPRISED TO SEE NAthan and Eric sitting silently on the large blue couch. "Where's Ben?" he asked, looking at his watch. "I thought you guys were going to blows at eight."

"He must be stuck at the office," Nathan surmised, looking up at Ober. "Did you get a haircut?"

"Absolutely," Ober said, running his fingers through his blond hair. "You guys have to go to this barber. A guy in my office recommended him—he cuts all these senators' hair. He once cut Jimmy Carter's hair. Anyway, his name is Murray Simone, King of Hair." Brushing his neck to remove some remnant clippings, he continued, "Naturally, I made up the 'King of Hair' part—his name's just Murray Simone."

"We get the idea," Nathan said, immediately annoyed by the hair talk. "Finish the story."

"So I go into the abode of Murray Simone, King of Hair, and I tell him that I like the top long and the sides short, and how I hate it when the top's short. He surveys the terrain, and then he looks into the mirror and says to me, 'What I'm gonna do for you is I'm gonna give you a short haircut, WITH ATTITUDE!'" Laughing at the mention of Murray's words, Ober almost knocked himself over. "How funny is that? 'I'm gonna give you a short haircut, WITH ATTITUDE.'" Touching his hair, he continued, "So what do you think? Did Murray Simone, King of Hair, give me attitude? I think so." Looking at himself in the glass of a nearby picture frame, Ober said, "I have ATTITUDE!"

"Ober, maybe now's not the time," Nathan said, staring at Eric.

"Cheer up," Ober said to Eric. "Your life's only lasting another few hours—you might as well enjoy it."

"Can you just shut up?" Eric asked, raising his voice.

"Don't take it out on me," Ober said, standing in the middle of the living room. "I didn't dick over my friend."

"Asshole," Eric yelled, "why don't you—"

"Ober, just shut up," Nathan interrupted. "Both of you, relax."

"Don't forget what I said, though," Ober said. "Murray Simone, King of Hair. And tell him I sent you." When he heard a key in the front door, Ober leaped on the large blue couch and stared at Eric. "Round One. Ding. Ding."

Ben stormed through the front door to find Ober, Nathan, and Eric on the couch. "So? What's the explanation?" Ben said, crossing his arms.

"Ben, I know you're mad," Eric said. "Just let me explain."

"Go right ahead," Ben said. "That's what I'm waiting for."

"I can't tell you if you're pissed. You're going to be mad at me no matter what I say."

"Eric, even if I was in a good mood, I'm going to be mad."

"I told you he'd made up his mind," Eric said, turning to Nathan.

"Ben, just give him a chance," Nathan pleaded.

"You have a chance," Ben said, still staring down at Eric. "Just go. I've been waiting all day." When Eric was silent, Ben added, "C'mon, tell me. I'll keep an open mind."

"Fine," Eric said. "I just want you to know that when you told me about what happened with Rick and the Maxwell decision, I never thought about saying a word. I mean, we've been friends since third grade. I'd never turn you in or let anything damage our friendship. And I certainly wouldn't write something that I thought would get you in trouble. But you have to understand the position I was in. I've been working at the *Herald* for almost five months, and I haven't done anything but edit excerpts from the *Congressional Record*. The editors wanted to transfer me down to the Style section, and when the CMI thing happened, I couldn't pass it up. I'm the low man on the totem pole, and I had to give them something. So I gave them that.''

"That's it?'' Ben asked when Eric paused. "That's your *reason?* You might've gotten transferred to the Style section?'' Ben's voice boomed. "You tell me that there's an explanation for your actions, and that's what you come up with? Eric, you are a piece of shit!''

"My job was at stake.''

"So you risked my job to save yours?'' Ben yelled. "You think that's the answer to the problem?''

"You don't get it. I wasn't risking *your* job,'' Eric said.

"Oh, no?'' Ben asked in disbelief. "Don't you realize what you—''

"You know there's no way you'll get caught,'' Eric said. "They'll never find Rick, and we won't tell. You can't get hurt by this.''

"Well then, today's my lucky day,'' Ben said. "Thanks, Eric! Since they'll never find Rick, I'm off the hook. Do you have any idea why I was late getting here? It's because for the past hour, I was getting grilled by the Marshals Office at the Court. And in case you're totally clueless, the marshals are responsible for all Court security. They sat me down and raked me over the coals about my involvement with the CMI leak. The head of security wanted to know about my relationship with you, since his friend at the *Herald* said we were roommates. He said that if they find out I'm involved, I'll be fired. They want me to take a lie detector test to prove my innocence, and they'd love nothing more than to throw me to the press and watch them rip me apart.''

"Oh, shit,'' Nathan said.

"Oh, shit is right,'' Ben repeated. Pointing his finger in Eric's face, he continued, "And since it's obvious you didn't take a single moment to anticipate the consequences of writing that story, you should also know that every paper in the country called the Court today to find out if it was true. At this point, they won't turn me in, but they say it's only a matter of time before the press finds a source who'll talk. And I don't think it will take long before someone puts the story together with the fact that you and I are roommates.''

"All I did was write about a possibility,'' Eric said.

"No. All you did was plant a seed in everyone's mind. Since that rag you write for doesn't give a crap about reality, they ran it. The result screws no one but me."

"But I didn't even give a source," Eric said.

"IT DOESN'T MATTER!" Ben yelled. "Get your head out of your ass. Not giving a source just means it takes longer for them to investigate."

"Listen, don't get mad at me," Eric said, getting up from the couch.

"Then who the hell should I be mad at?" Ben asked, throwing his hands in the air.

"Well, I'm not the one who leaked information from the Court. I hate to burst your bubble, but what you did *was* illegal. I didn't make it up."

Ben shoved Eric in the chest. "You selfish son of a—"

Nathan jumped up, knocking over the coffee table, and wedged himself between the two friends. "This is not turning into a rumble. Both of you, relax."

Clenching his fists, Ben stepped back from Nathan. "You really are a lowlife," he said to Eric.

"Don't pull that with me," Eric said, his voice racing. "You have no idea what I was going through. You always have everything handed to you. You have no idea what it's like to struggle on your own. My editor was breathing down my ass for a source. I didn't care, though. I never once named you! Never!"

"Then how did the Marshals Office know that I was the source for your story about Blake's resignation?"

Eric was silent.

"What's the matter? You don't have an answer for that one?"

"The Blake story was different and you know it," Eric shot back. "For CMI, I didn't say a word. No matter what they said, I wouldn't give them a source. My editor told me people would call me a hack. But I kept quiet."

"Well, you're just the best friend a guy could have. Maybe next week you can do me a real favor and slice my throat. That'll be the greatest."

"I'm serious," Eric said. "I was flooded with calls today. I got calls from *Newsweek, Time, USA Today, The New York Times.* You name it, I got a call from it. And I could have blown your story to any one of them.

I could ride this one to fame and fortune. I could write a book about the whole thing. I'd have movie deals, a syndicated column, the whole world if I blew the lid off this one. You know it's true—"

Before Eric could finish his sentence, Ben rushed toward him and pushed him against the back wall of the room, holding him by the front of his shirt. "You say one word, and I swear I'll rip your fucking heart out!"

"Ben, let go!" Nathan demanded as he and Ober pried him off of Eric.

Straightening his shirt, Eric said, "Listen, I understand you're pissed, but that was good journalism. The point is, I protected your ass, *and* I wrote a page five story my first time out."

"If you killed your mother, you'd make page one," Ben screamed. "Does that mean you should do it? You didn't blow this story open. You would've been clueless unless I told you. So don't fucking act like you're doing me any favors by not signing away the movie rights!"

Taking a deep breath, Eric said, "Ben, do you have any idea how hard this CMI thing has been on me? From the moment you told me about how Maxwell got the info, I wanted to write the story. I waited, though. I waited until all the smoke cleared, until all the papers were finished obsessing over Maxwell and the decision. I waited until all the hoopla was over. And all I ran was a small piece that tried to explain it."

"Do you hear what you're saying?" Ben asked, shaking his head. "Are you trying to say I should thank you for waiting a bit before you put the knife in my back? Do you have any idea how warped that logic is?"

"I don't know why you're so crazy. They'll never be able to prove—"

"That's not the damn point!" Ben yelled. "Stop rationalizing your actions and think for a second! You knew this would happen. You knew it, and you didn't care."

"Ben, I never meant for you to get in trouble. What do you want me to say? I'm sorry. I'm sorry a million times. What the hell else do you want?"

"I want you out of this house."

"What?" Eric asked.

"Ben, you can't do that," Ober said, his voice cracking.

Ben looked at Eric. "You heard me. I want your ass out of this house." As Eric shook his head in disbelief, Ben continued, "I'm not joking, Eric. This isn't some silly high school fight. I don't want you in my life anymore. I don't trust you, I don't like you, and I no longer need you as a friend."

"What if I won't leave?"

"Then I will," Ben said. "Our lease is up on the first of the year. That gives you a month and a half to find a new place. If you want to fight me on it, we'll take a vote. If no one wants to vote, we'll flip a coin. Either way, I refuse to have you in my life anymore." Turning his back to his friends, Ben stormed up the stairs to his room.

"Eric, just let him cool off."

"I don't want to talk about it," Eric said, walking to the front door. "I'll be at the paper if anyone needs me."

When the door slammed, the room was silent. "I really think he's serious," Nathan finally said.

"He can't kick him out of the house," Ober said. "We can't let him do that."

"What's wrong with you?" Nathan asked, surprised by Ober's reaction.

"We can't let him break us up. When I moved here, it was to be with the four of us."

"Ober, you have to relax."

"Do you think he'll really kick Eric out?"

"I don't know," Nathan said. "But when he went flying toward Eric, I thought Ben was going to kill him. This isn't an easy thing to forgive."

"You have to talk to him," Ober said. "Promise me you'll talk to him." When he saw Nathan heading toward the stairs, he asked, "Where are you going?"

"To talk to Ben."

"Are you going to talk about Eric?"

"No, I'm going to talk about Murray Simone, King of Hair."

*   *   *

"What'd he say?" Lisa asked the moment Ben arrived at work the next morning.

"It was a disaster," Ben said, hanging his coat in the closet. "He had no excuse."

"Nothing?" Lisa asked. "He didn't even make up an excuse?"

Ben grabbed the cup of coffee from Lisa's desk and took a sip. "He tried to tell me he was going to get demoted, but it was pathetic."

"Did you at least take a swing at him?"

"Lisa, I'll have you know, I'm a man of words, not violence."

"But didn't you want to rip his face off? Didn't you want to just bust his teeth in? Didn't you—"

"I get the idea," he said, fidgeting with his red and gold tie.

Wait a minute," Lisa said. "You hit him, didn't you?"

"I didn't hit him."

"Ben, don't lie to me. . . ."

"I just threw him into the wall, threatened him a bit, and told him to move out."

"All right, Mr. Tough Guy!" Lisa said. "Give me all the gore."

"It wasn't anything. I just lost it for a second."

"I can't believe it. I can't even imagine you losing it."

"And why's that?"

"Because you're such a wuss."

"Oh, and you're so tough?"

"Trust me, I kick ass when I have to. And given time, I'll kick your little ass as well."

"Lisa, I don't want to hear your sadomasochistic fantasies in the office. That's sexual harassment, and it's against the law." Ben's phone rang. "Hello, Justice Hollis's chambers," he answered.

"Ben, is it okay to call you now?"

"Mom? Is everything okay?"

"Yes, everything's fine. Are you in court?"

"No, we don't have court on Fridays," Ben said nervously. "Why? What's wrong at home?"

"Well, I was wondering if there was something you had to tell me," his mother said.

Either she was talking about Eric's story or she'd gotten another letter from Rick. Either way, Ben saw trouble. Hoping to pry before he gave up any information, Ben said, "I'm not sure what you mean."

"Benjamin, don't play games with me. Now, do you have anything you've been meaning to tell me?"

"Mom, I have no idea what you're talking about."

"Well, then, perhaps you can explain why I had to hear secondhand from Barbara that you have a very serious girlfriend."

"Oh, my God," Ben said as Lisa looked up from her desk. "Mom, I don't have a serious girlfriend. Ober's mom doesn't know what she's talking about."

"Don't lie to me, Benjamin."

"Mom, I swear I'm not lying."

"Then who was the woman your friends were raving about at Katie's house last week?"

"They were probably talking about my co-clerk," Ben said, frowning at Lisa.

"You're sleeping with your co-clerk?"

"I'm not sleeping with anybod— Mom, I'm not sleeping with Lisa. Nathan and Ober were just joking around with Aunt Katie. We're just co-workers."

"Well, Ober seemed to say it was more than just a working relationship."

"When did you speak to Ober?"

"This morning. You had already left for work. What time do you go in anyway? They must be working you like a dog there."

"It's the Supreme Court. We tend to work hard," Ben said. "Now tell me what Ober said."

"That's none of your business. William and I had a wonderful conversation. Now, tell me, is this co-clerk from Washington?"

"No. She's from Los Angeles."

"Is she there now?"

"No, she's not here now," Ben said, looking up at Lisa. "She's taking depositions."

"HI, MRS. ADDISON!" Lisa called out.

"I knew she was there!" Ben's mother said. "Put her on the phone."

"Mom, I'm not putting her on. Get it through your head."

"Ask her if she's going home for Thanksgiving."

"Mom—"

"If I need to, I'll get her number from Ober and call her myself."

Laughing, Ben said, "Lisa, my mom wants to know if you're going home for Thanksgiving." Ben mouthed the words "Say yes."

"No, I'm completely free!" Lisa shouted.

"Wonderful," Ben's mother said. "Tell her she's invited to spend it with us. She'll come home with you."

Glancing over at Lisa, Ben said, "My mother wants me to tell you that she's glad you're going to be alone on Thanksgiving. She hopes you have a miserable night, and that your heat gets turned off, and that you die alone without the comfort of family and friends."

"Benjamin!"

"She wants you to come home for Thanksgiving."

"I'd love to," Lisa said, sticking out her tongue at Ben.

"Great," Ben said, turning back to the phone. "Mom, you may want to prepare an extra turkey or two. I don't know if Ober told you, but Lisa eats like a cow and a horse and a whole barnyard of animals."

"If you're seeing her, I want to meet her," his mother said.

"Fine, I give in. You caught us. We're going out. Mom, this one's the one. Lisa and I are in love, and she's pregnant, and we're thinking of naming the baby Hercules, after Aunt Flo."

"That's not funny," his mother said.

"Listen, I really have to go."

"Just tell me one last thing: What happened between you and Eric?"

"Mom, nothing happened. Why? Who said something happened?"

"Ober."

Closing his eyes, Ben spoke in a calm voice. "Nothing happened between me and Eric. We just had a small argument. That's it. We'll make up later tonight."

"Just remember what I said to you when you left for college: 'There's nothing like childhood friends.' "

"That's great, Mom. Thanks for sharing that for the eighty-fourth time. Can I go now?"

"So Lisa is coming to Thanksgiving?"

"Yes, Mom. Thanks to your meddling, she'll be there."

"Wonderful. I'll call you later. I love you."

"I love you, too. Say hi to Dad." Hanging up, Ben turned to Lisa. "You really think you're smart, don't you? Well, guess again, missy, because you just made the biggest mistake of your life. In your infinite wisdom, you've just gotten yourself invited to the seventeenth circle of hell—my house for dinner."

"I can't wait."

"Hold on," Ben said, pulling out a small pad from his top drawer. "I have to write this one down." As he scribbled on the little pad, he announced, "On Friday, November twenty-first, Lisa Marie Schulman said 'I can't wait,' as she referred to her upcoming meal of death."

"It'll be fun," she said.

" 'It'll be fun,' " Ben said as he added that phrase to the pad. "I think that's what Napoleon said right before he went to Waterloo."

"Ben, my family is still impressed with the Lava lamp. How much worse can your family be?"

"I'd say a great deal worse. A world of worse. Maybe a whole universe of worse."

"Just stop it already."

"Lisa, I'm not exaggerating. My parents are mutants. They're sick, bizarro freaks who were spawned to bring guilt and angst to all the innocent children of Earth."

"Well, I can't wait to meet them. They sound like wonderful people."

" 'They sound like wonderful people,' " Ben said as he resumed his writing on the pad of paper. "Ho, boy, I can't wait until you eat these words."

"Whatever you say," Lisa said, opening up one of the many brown folders on her desk. "Meanwhile, have you finished with the *Russell* opinion? You said you'd have it done two days ago."

"Don't rush me. It needs more work." Ben returned the pad to his desk. "And by the way, can we meet at your house tonight? I want to go over my meeting with Rick before tomorrow."

"Absolutely. Oh, and Ben? I don't mean to be a dick, but I really do need the *Russell* decision."

"Lisa, I said I'd get it to you. What do you want?"

"I want you to finish it. I believe you when you say you're working on it, but you've been doing the first draft for over two weeks now."

"Well, I'm sorry I had a busy week, but my life's been a bit chaotic lately."

"Don't pull that with me," Lisa scolded. "You know I completely sympathize with everything you've had to deal with. All I'm saying is that you have to do your best to ignore it all. Like it or not, this Court is more important than whatever's going on in your life."

Ben was seething as he turned to a clean page of his legal pad. "Fine. I understand. Let me get to work now."

"Ben, stop it. What do you want me to do?"

"How about being a bit more understanding!" he shouted. "It's easy for you to be diligent, but I'm the one who's chasing the psychopath. Every time my mom calls, I'm terrified he's contacted my family. On top of all that, my friend betrayed me and the Marshals Office is threatening me—and the week's not over yet."

"Y'know, for one second, I wish you could see things from another perspective besides your own."

"And I suppose your perspective is the optimum one?"

"I'm serious," Lisa said. "Hollis knows I always go over the decisions before he sees them, so he's gotten used to asking me for them. For the past week, he's been asking me, and I've been making up excuses. On Tuesday, I said we were working on a few points. On Wednesday, I said we still hadn't resolved them. Yesterday, I avoided him completely. I don't know what to tell him today. We're in this together, and I don't mind taking the fall with you, but this is stupid. *Russell* is a nonsense procedural issue. Hollis told us exactly how he saw this one, but we're dragging our feet on it. Just finish it and give it to me. Even if you're halfway done, give it to me and I'll touch it up. I just have to hand him something by the end of today. I'm sorry if that means I have to ride you, but at this point it's the only way you'll take me seriously."

Ben stared at his legal pad. "I'm sorry," he said coldly. "You're absolutely right. I'll have it for you before lunch."

"Ben, I—"

"No explanation's necessary. You're right. If I couldn't get it done on time I should've passed it to you."

"That's all I was trying to say."

*   *   *

"Are you ready for tomorrow?"

Looking in the mirror, Rick pulled his tie into a perfect knot. "Of course I'm ready. The real question is: Will Ben be ready?"

"You know he's plotting against you."

Dissatisfied with the length of his tie, Rick undid the knot and started over. "He can do whatever he wants. I'm not worried."

"How can you be so confident?"

Rick turned away from the mirror. "Because I understand Ben. After that disaster with Eric, he's going to have a hard time saying no to my offer."

At a quarter to one, Lisa returned to the office carrying a small brown bag. She pulled out two cups of coffee, a bran muffin, and a chocolate croissant. "Lunchtime. Eat up," she said, handing Ben the croissant and one of the coffees.

Twenty minutes later, Ben still hadn't touched the coffee or the croissant. A half hour after that, he finally looked up from his computer screen. "One Supreme Court decision coming up," he announced as the laser printer started to hum.

"Great," Lisa said as she walked to the printer. When she had picked up all seventeen pages, she returned to her desk and pulled out her red pen. As Ben watched her expression from his desk, Lisa read the decision, her red pen primed for corrections. Slowly and meticulously, she scrutinized each page, placing it facedown on her desk. After fifteen minutes, she turned over the final page and looked up at Ben.

"So?" Ben asked, picking at his croissant. "What'd you think?"

"Ben, this is a phenomenal job," Lisa said as she turned over the pile and shuffled the pages. "Usually, I hack your first drafts up. My pen only touched the paper twice."

"Three times, actually," he said. Walking over to Lisa's desk, he grabbed the small pile of paper and searched for her corrections.

"It was just grammatical stuff." Lisa leaned back in her chair. "I'm amazed, though. This first draft is like one of our third drafts."

"Well, this time I was trying."

"Why the hell don't you try like that the rest of the time? Usually you do an excellent job, but this is a finished product. You probably saved us a whole extra day of work."

"It was an easy case," Ben said. "It's not that big a deal. I just work well under pressure."

"I should get pissed off more often." Lisa got out of her seat, took the pages back from Ben, and put them in one of Hollis's brown folders. "I'm going to walk this over to Hollis as is. Hopefully we can be done with it by this afternoon."

"That's fine," Ben said, pulling his black overcoat from the closet. "I have to run to the restaurant, but I'll be back within an hour."

"Planning for tomorrow?" Lisa asked.

"Absolutely," he said. "At this point, I'm not leaving anything to chance."

At three-thirty, Lisa returned to the office. "That's it. We're done with *Russell*," she announced as she tossed the seventeen-page document on Ben's desk.

"He liked it?"

"Did he like it? Let's put it this way. At one point I had to wipe away the drool that was hanging off his lower lip."

"Be serious."

"I'm not joking," she said. "Hollis loved it. He said it was well argued, and organized exactly the way he wanted. He especially liked the conclusion, where you called the dissent 'an attempt to empty the endless ocean of logic with a thimble.' "

"He's keeping that? I thought for sure he would cut it. He always cuts my metaphors-as-insults."

"Well, he liked this one. Apparently he thinks Osterman is out of his mind in the dissent."

"Damn," Ben said, slapping the desk. "If I'd known he was going to be open to wordplay, I'd have come up with something even better. I was thinking of saying that the dissent is 'trying to piss on the inferno of common sense.' "

"I don't think that one would have flown," Lisa suggested.

"Why not?" Ben asked. "You don't think he'd agree with the parallel I'm drawing between common sense and fire?"

"I don't think Hollis wants to go down in history as being the first justice to ever use the word 'piss' in one of his opinions. He's crazy like that."

"Maybe you're right," Ben said, flipping through the seventeen-page document. "So tell me what else Hollis said."

"Nothing really. He's happy we're done with *Russell* because he says that *Grinnell* will almost definitely be decided tonight."

"How does he know it'll be assigned to him?"

"He already spoke to Moloch and Kovacs, and they don't want to touch it. Whether he's in the majority or the dissent, Hollis'll be the most senior justice who wants to write the decision."

"Any word yet on whether Veidt has hopped the fence?"

"They'll know tomorrow. Hollis said Veidt is having dinner with Osterman and Blake tonight."

"Ah, another Supreme Court case is going to be decided based on how hard one justice schmoozes another."

"Welcome to Washington."

"Gee, thanks," Ben said. "You're so politically astute. *Now* I know how this town works. And all along I foolishly thought it was democracy that ran our nation."

"Listen, when I first got to law school, I always used to say that if the Supreme Court was really about true justice, then every issue, no matter who was on the Court, would come out with the same result. If *Roe* v. *Wade* granted abortion rights in 1973, then the decision shouldn't be overturned just because some conservative justices came onto the Court. But over time, I've realized that that's the beauty of the law. We decide each case individually. No fact pattern is exactly the same, and every justice takes all the different facts into account. If we wanted the same decision every time, we wouldn't need judges—we'd get robots we could plug the facts into, who could reach the same cold, logical decision. But who the hell wants a robot deciding their life?"

"That depends—are they conservative or liberal robots?"

"That's exactly my point. Stop seeing everything in black and white. No two people see anything exactly the same way. That's what makes it great. We sacrifice ourselves to people's particular mores, but we gain an individualized judicial system. I mean, would you really want to live in a world where there were no Ostermans or Veidts?''

"Actually, I probably would," Ben said. "But I guess that would also mean that the entire madras golf pants market would crash."

"Ben, be serious."

"I know, I know," he said, picking at the hardened remains of his croissant. "But that doesn't mean I can't be annoyed when a case is decided on personal politics."

"No, you should definitely be annoyed. But just realize that the personal side of the judicial process also provides a lot of benefits that ensure democracy as we know it."

"That's wonderful, General Washington. I'll keep that in mind every time I tell the story of how Veidt sold his vote away."

CHAPTER 8

LATER THAT EVENING, BEN AND LISA RETURNED TO LISA'S apartment, where they found Ober and Nathan waiting outside. "Where the hell were you guys?" Ober asked, running in place. "We're freezing out here."

"Why didn't you wait in the lobby?" Lisa asked.

"Because the asshole doorman wouldn't let us. He said if our host wasn't here, we had to wait outside."

"You've got to be kidding me." Lisa stormed into the building and approached the smiling doorman. "Why the hell do you have my guests waiting outside?"

"Ma'am, their party was not here."

"I'm their party," she proclaimed. "And if I'm five minutes late, I don't want my friends waiting out in the cold."

"Ma'am, you may be their host, but we do have rules in this building, and no guests are admitted without their host's approval. As doorman, it is my job to ensure that there is no loitering in our lobby."

"Oh, it is?"

"Yes, ma'am, it is," the doorman barked. "The tenants' association has given me full authority to remove loiterers, vagrants, and other criminal characters from this vicinity."

"Are you sure about that?" Lisa asked.

"Oh, no," Ben said, peeking through his fingers. "This is about to get ugly."

"Let me tell you a few things," Lisa said, her finger pointed in the doorman's face. "First, I don't care who you are, but the moment you have my guests in this building, they become your guests. And if you think you're authorized to let guests stand out in the cold, you've got your head up your ass. This may not be the frozen tundra, but it's still cold out there. Second, general loitering laws are illegal, since they allow mall cops like you to randomly discriminate against whomever you like. So if you don't have solid, real reasons to suspect my friends, I suggest you keep your mouth shut. Finally, if you are calling my friends vagrants or criminals, I'll haul you into court on defamation charges just to piss you off. I won't win the case, but I'll have a great time wasting your time and money as you argue your way out of it. Now, unless you have anything else to say, I'm going to go upstairs. Have I made myself clear?"

"Certainly," the doorman said, flustered. Turning to Nathan and Ober, he added, "And I apologize for any misunderstanding."

"I accept your apology," Ober said as the friends walked into the elevator.

"Was that really necessary?" Ben asked.

"That was fantastic!" Ober yelled.

"He pisses me off," Lisa said. "You give guys like him a tiny bit of authority, and they think they're dictators."

"Yeah, but I think you made him wet his pants," Ben said.

"I was impressed with the clarity of your argument," Nathan said, looking at Lisa with new respect.

"Thank you," Lisa said, as the elevator door opened.

Walking into the apartment, Lisa flipped on the lights and put her briefcase on her desk. "What's that smell?" Ben asked as he headed toward the living room.

Sniffing the air, Ober said, "It smells so . . . feminine."

"It's potpourri," Lisa said. "I just put it out. Do you like it?"

"I'm enchanted," Ober said.

"I guess you guys aren't used to a home that doesn't smell like feet." As Lisa turned toward her bedroom, she added, "I'll be right back."

Minutes later, she returned to the living room wearing sweatpants and her favorite Stanford T-shirt. "Ready to start?" she asked, sitting down next to Ben on the sofa.

"Here's the story." Ben opened his briefcase and pulled out a yellow legal pad and a pen. "Rick and I are meeting tomorrow. The only reason I can think of for the meeting is that Rick still wants something, and the only thing he can want is information."

"But you don't know this for sure," Lisa said.

"It's the only logical reason. I mean, I don't think he wants to talk politics."

"Maybe he just wants to torture you over how big a sucker you were last time," Ober said.

"I don't think that's it," Ben said, shooting a scowl at Ober.

"But why would he want more information if he already made a million dollars from the *CMI* decision?" Nathan asked. He sat on the sofa and placed a small blue duffel bag on the floor.

"We have no idea how much he made on *CMI*. He may've made ten million or he may've made ten thousand. The problem is, we don't know his background. If he isn't wealthy already, then he probably didn't have a great deal of money to invest in the CMI stock before it shot up. All of his winnings might've come from a fee Maxwell gave him."

"But I'm sure that's a tidy sum," Nathan said.

"It probably is," Ben said, "but I wouldn't underestimate the power of greed. If Rick made a million his first time out, I'm sure he'd love to make ten million the next. Now, we don't know that he's going to ask me for more information, but if he does, I think our best option is to follow Lisa's original plan and try to get it all on tape."

"If he does proposition you, he's sure to offer you some money for the information. Obviously, he's not going to be able to trick you out of the information again."

"You never know, though," Ober said. "Ben can be pretty naive when he wants to be."

Ignoring his roommate, Ben said, "And if he does offer me money, we'll get the bribe on tape. Then we'll at least be able to prove that he bribed a government official."

"I don't understand one thing," Nathan said. "If you do get Rick on tape, how are you going to use it against him? By turning it over to the authorities, you'll reveal your own involvement as well as his."

"I know," Ben said. "But at this point, I'm more concerned with the fact that he'll always have my involvement to dangle over my head. If I get something on him, he can't use that information against me. Although it's not the optimal situation, we'll at least be on a level playing field. Otherwise, I'll never be safe."

"Did you get the taping equipment?" Lisa asked Nathan.

Nathan pulled the small blue duffel bag onto his lap and unzipped it. "Here's our wireless microphone. And just so you know, it's equipment like this that makes the United States the enduring superpower of our time."

"That's great, Colonel," Ben said. "Who'd you get it from?"

"This friend of mine who works down in security. I was hoping he could get us the state-of-the-art stuff, but this was the best he could do. Without authorization, the best equipment never leaves the security room."

"Does he have those microphones that are built into your cuff links?" Ober asked.

"Those are fantastic," Nathan agreed. "I was hoping for the poison darts that shoot out of your watch, but this was the best he could do." Rising from his chair, he pulled the various wires from the bag. Looking over at Ben, he said, "Stand up and take off your shirt."

"Woooooooo!" Lisa howled as Ben unbuttoned his dress shirt.

"Wait until you see his bod," Ober said. "The man has no chest hair."

"Hey, at least I don't have the Isle of Capri on my chest," Ben said as he stood topless in the living room. Looking at Lisa, he explained, "Ober is hairless except for a great island right in the middle of his chest."

"Wrong," Ober said.

"Take off your shirt," Ben challenged.

"There's no need for that," Ober smiled. "But, trust me, it's not shaped like the Isle of Capri."

"Let me figure out how this works," Nathan said, struggling to untangle the wires.

"I hate to admit it," Lisa said, "but you have a sexy bod." As Ben tried to fight back a blush, she continued, "I'm serious. I didn't think you had one, but you have a great chest." Looking at Ober, she said, "I think I'm actually turned on."

"Well, I have that effect on people," Ober said.

"Here we go," Nathan said, looking over at Ben. "Why are you blushing?" he asked.

"Just show me how this thing works," Ben said.

"Okay. You take this Velcro strap and you wrap it around your chest. The microphones are built into this," Nathan explained, pointing to two tiny bumps in the wide strap. "This is your battery source," he said, tapping a larger protrusion on the back of the strap. "It should last at least eight hours and I just put that battery in, so it'll be fine." He pulled a thick black box from the bag. "This is the receiver. It has a cassette deck in it, so we can tape the whole conversation."

"Is it on?" Ben asked.

"It should be." Nathan raised the antennae on the box and flipped a few knobs. "Go in the other room and say something."

As Ben walked toward Lisa's bedroom, the three friends waited in silence, staring at the black box. Suddenly they heard, "Here I am in Lisa's bedroom. The satin sheets come as no surprise, but I am shocked to see a picture of myself right next to her bed."

"DON'T TOUCH MY BED!" she yelled.

"And wait . . . what's this? There are remnants of lipstick marks around my face. Oh, Lisa, you are so very, very sad."

"GET OUT OF MY ROOM!"

"Wait, is this her underwear drawer? Yes, I think it is, boys!"

As Lisa jumped from the sofa, Ben turned the corner and entered the living room. Hitting rewind, Nathan waited a moment and hit play. ". . . bedroom. The satin sheets come as no surprise, but—"

"It works," Nathan said.

Ben took off the microphone and put on his shirt. "So all I have to do is talk normally, and everything should come through?"

"Yep."

"Maybe you should stuff it into your underwear just in case Rick decides to pat you down," Ober suggested.

"I don't know if that's such a good idea," Nathan said. "If you do that, I think we'll lose a lot of clarity." Shutting off the receiver, he added, "The only other thing I should tell you is that since it's cordless, it has only about a hundred-yard radius."

"That should be fine," Ben said, buttoning his shirt. "We're meeting at Two Quail, a tony restaurant on Massachusetts Avenue. I went there today during lunch just to scope it out. It's a small place and it has only one window that faces the street. But there's a Thai restaurant across the street that you guys can wait in."

"I know the one you're talking about," Nathan said. "Bangkok Orchid."

"That's the one," Ben said. "I figure you and Ober should get there at about seven. I'm supposed to meet Rick at eight. They're right across the street from each other, so we should definitely be in range."

"Is there anything that might interfere with the microphone?" Lisa asked. "Shortwave transmissions? Satellite dishes? Anything like that?"

"My friend said it should be fine," Nathan said. "It's not the best equipment, but it's still reliable."

"Y'know what we need?" Ober said, excited. "We should have a password. Just in case something goes wrong, it'll be our signal that you need help."

"That's not a bad idea," Ben said, returning to his seat on the couch.

"How about if the password is 'What's your damage, Heather?' " Ober asked.

"No way," Ben said. "It has to be something that I can easily work into the conversation, and it can't look like I'm panicking."

"How about 'travesty of justice'?" Nathan asked.

"What about 'electric cheese'?" Ober said.

"How the hell can I work that in?" Ben asked. "Please don't kill me, and can I please have some electric cheese?"

" 'Crimes against humanity,' " Nathan said.

" 'Devil Dogs,' " Ober said.

"How about if I just scream, 'Help me, unimaginative roommates! Help me!' " Ben said.

"Why don't you use the word 'bingo'?" Lisa asked. "It's easy to work into a sentence, and it always works in the movies."

"That's ridiculous," Ober said. "Name one movie that used bingo as the password."

"Lots of them."

"Name one," Ober challenged.

"I don't care if it works in the movies," Ben interrupted. "Bingo's the password. If I say 'bingo,' you guys come running."

"That should take care of the bribing part," Lisa said. "The only other thing we have to worry about is getting his picture taken so we can I.D. him."

"This should take care of that," Nathan said, pulling out a telescopic lens from the duffel. "It'll fit on my camera, and it should give us all the pictures we want of this asshole."

"We need detailed pictures, though," Lisa said.

"Trust me, this puppy'll show us the blackheads on his nose. It even has a built-in infrared filter." Nathan looked at Ben and added, "I just need to know who to photograph. I've never seen Rick before."

"I took care of that today," Ben said. "Two Quail has one table that sits in front of the main window. Rick and I will be seated at that table, so all you have to do is snap pictures of the guy I'm sitting with."

"And what if you don't get seated at that table?" Nathan asked.

"We'll be there. During lunch, when I went to scope out the restaurant, I gave the maître d' a hundred bucks to make sure that my party is seated at that table."

"You blew another hundred bucks?" Ober asked.

"When I got there, there was already a reservation in my name," Ben said. "It was pretty spooky."

"You'll be fine," Nathan said, repacking the microphone in the duffel.

"I was just thinking," Lisa interrupted. "What if Rick doesn't ask for the info?"

Ben shrugged his shoulders. "I guess we'll just have to be happy with the pictures we get. If we can I.D. him, we'll be able to finger him if he decides to act against me. And then we can at least link him with whoever his next Charles Maxwell is."

"Speaking of which," Nathan said, "do you have any idea what case he might ask for?"

"I was thinking about that," Lisa said. "The *American Steel* case is a big money issue. That one's got to be worth at least a couple of million."

"No way," Ben insisted. "As far as I'm concerned, there's only one it could be: *Grinnell.*"

"You think?" Lisa asked.

"I'm sure," Ben said. "That case is a potential gold mine."

"How about clueing us legally impaired spectators in?" Nathan said.

"Howard Grinnell and a bunch of other investors own a gigantic old church in downtown Manhattan. About three years ago, they decided to tear down the church to build a new restaurant and shopping complex—just what New York needs. When they went to the zoning board for approval on their demolition plans, word got out, and the New-York Historical Society and a bunch of religious groups asserted that the church was a historic landmark and couldn't be destroyed. After major lobbying by everyone involved, the church was officially declared a landmark, and therefore was protected by the city. Grinnell and his investors eventually sued New York, saying that by not allowing them to build on their land, the rezoning was a taking of their property."

"According to the Takings Clause of the Constitution," Lisa interjected, "the state cannot take land without paying the owner a reasonable value for it. In this case, the value is the money the property would have brought in if it was made into a skyscraper."

"But I thought you said it was rezoned," Nathan said. "How is zoning a taking?"

"That's exactly the question," Ben said. "Zoning isn't considered a taking as long as the zoning furthers important community interests. For example, a city can zone an area of land as residential to keep away commercial developers and to ensure that a community thrives. That's fair zoning. The issue here is whether preserving a historic landmark furthers the community's interests."

"It obviously does," Lisa said, "since the landmark is part of the community. It helps protect the history of the community, and it also helps attract tourists to the community."

"That's one way to look at it," Ben said. Looking back to Nathan, he explained, "Lisa and I disagree on this one. I think it's definitely a taking. Just look at the facts: This investment group paid millions of dollars for this property, which, when they bought it, was allowed to have commercial development on it. They should have been able to rely on that information. Instead, Lisa thinks it's okay for the government to come in and say, 'Sorry, we changed our minds. You can't build anything here and, moreover, you can't even touch the church since it's a historic landmark.' That's crazy. The government just waltzed in and effectively took the land from the owners. Grinnell and Company now have a dingy old church that's basically worthless."

"It's not worthless. Now they own a historic landmark."

"Lisa, no one is coming to New York City to see this run-down church. It's not Disney World. They can't charge admission. They're stuck with it as is."

"If the land needs so much protection, why doesn't the government just pay Grinnell for it?" Nathan asked. "Why should a private citizen have to bear the burden of paying for a historic site that everyone else enjoys for free?"

"There you go," Ben said. "I told you you should've gone to law school."

"But the owner still owns a historic monument," Lisa said.

"Big deal," Ben said. "What are the bragging rights going to get you? If you can't make money from it, you've got fifty million dollars sunk into a stamp collection you can't sell."

"What's wrong with that?" Lisa asked. "Otherwise, we bulldoze history so we can have more strip malls."

"Listen, I don't want to sound like Scrooge here, but history doesn't pay the bills. This group invested millions of dollars because they relied on the city's zoning. If the city changes its mind, then the city should compensate whoever it screws. Period."

"Ben, you're saying we should—"

"Okay, I think we get the idea," Nathan interrupted. "I'm sure you two can go at it all night, but some of us have work tomorrow."

"Besides, it's not our decision," Ben said. "Hollis and crew will tell us what to write, and that'll be it."

"Precisely," Nathan said, closing his duffel. "So let's wrap this up. Is there anything else we need to discuss?"

"I think that's about it," Ben said. "Let's hope it goes well tomorrow."

"And if it doesn't, I just hope you don't freak out and become a sick and twisted version of yourself," Ober said.

"What are you talking about?" Lisa asked.

"Oh, no," Ben moaned. "Not the Batman theory."

"What?" Lisa asked.

"I don't know if you'll be able to handle it," Ober said.

"I'll take my chances."

Slapping his hands together, Ober said, "The theory is based on the idea that your whole life can fall apart in one bad day."

"And how does this relate to Batman?" Lisa asked skeptically.

"Think about how Bruce Wayne became Batman: His parents were shot to death in front of his eyes. On that day, he lost his entire life and had to become something different to stay sane. Same thing with Robin—his parents died on the trapeze. Now think about the villains: The Joker fell in a vat of acid and was betrayed by those he trusted. Two-Face was hit with a vial of acid. In the movies, Catwoman was pushed out of a window and the Riddler lost his job. All it takes is one bad day to step over to the side of obsessive madness."

"That's a wonderful theory, but there's one flaw," Ben said.

"And what's that?"

"It's that THOSE PEOPLE AREN'T REAL! THEY'RE COMIC BOOK CHARACTERS!" Ben yelled, sending Nathan and Lisa into hysterics.

"So?" Ober asked.

"So, I'm not that worried about whether I'll want to get myself a Bat-a-rang or become Gotham City's newest villain. For some silly reason, I don't think your theory applies to real life."

"You say that now," Ober said, "but you have no idea what tomorrow will bring."

"You're right," Ben said. "I may not know what tomorrow will bring, but I'm pretty sure it won't be a cape and a utility belt."

When Ben, Nathan, and Ober returned home, they found Eric sitting at the dining-room table, writing. "Where were you guys?" he asked, putting down his pen. "I was starting to get worried."

"We were—"

"Nowhere," Ben interrupted.

"Ben, can you just stop it?" Eric asked.

"No, I can't just stop it," Ben said, walking into the kitchen to get a drink. "You started it, and now you have to deal with it."

"I said I'm sorry. What the hell else do you want?"

"What do I want?" Ben asked, pouring himself a glass of cold water. "Let's see: I want trust. I want respect."

"Forget about it," Nathan said, taking a seat next to Eric. "Everyone just go to bed."

"Oh, and Ober," Ben said, "I don't appreciate you telling my mother about Eric's and my argument. It's none of her business."

Ober sat on the couch, leafing through a magazine. "I just said it was a tiny disagreement."

"Now why did you have to tell my mother that?" Ben asked. "Was that really necessary?"

"You know how she is," Ober said. "She started grilling me on what was going on. She's relentless. It was like she could smell that something was wrong. That was the only thing I said, though. I swear."

"Are you sure?"

"I'm positive. After that, I was strong."

"Then why did she tell me that you also confirmed the rumor that I was sleeping with my co-clerk?"

A wide smile spread across Ober's face. "That one I told her just for fun."

"Thank you," Ben said sarcastically. "Because of your idiocy, Lisa is now invited to my house for Thanksgiving."

"She's going to your house for Thanksgiving?" Ober laughed. "She'll be eaten alive there! Oh, is this great, or what?"

"You may want to tell Lisa to wear a bulletproof vest," Eric said.

Shooting a scowl at Eric, Ben turned back to Ober. "Just wait until I get your mom on the phone." Picking up the blue duffel that was at Nathan's feet, Ben headed toward the stairs. "You may want to bring the straitjacket back from the cleaners, just in case."

CHAPTER 9

AT NOON THE NEXT DAY, LISA ENTERED THE OFFICE AND AN-
nounced, "They postponed it again."

"How?" Ben asked, looking up from one of over two dozen cert petitions piled on his desk. "It's Saturday—the justices aren't even here."

"Osterman just called Joel from home. They still haven't decided it."

"Unbelievable," Ben said. "What was the reason? Do they want to
make *Grinnell* the most drawn-out decision in history?"

"They actually made the deadline next Tuesday."

"They moved Conference from Wednesday to Tuesday?"

"Just for next week," Lisa explained. "They wanted to make sure
everyone had off the day before Thanksgiving, so it has to be decided
by then."

"That was nice," Ben admitted.

"They have their moments," she said. Lisa sat down on the sofa and
took off her shoes. She looked at her watch. "Only eight hours until
the big meeting. Are you getting scared?"

"I definitely have butterflies."

"At least now you don't have to worry about being tricked into revealing the *Grinnell* decision."

"I learned my lesson, thanks," Ben said curtly.

"Don't take it personally."

"How can I not take it personally?" Ben asked.

"I'm not saying you'd blurt it out," she said, "but your face might give it away if he asked you how the decision came out."

"My dear, when one has a poker face like my own, one does not worry about giving things away."

"In your little mind, do you really believe you have a great poker face?"

"I *know* I have a great poker face." Ben gave her a stone-cold stare.

"That's your poker face? You look constipated."

"I look fierce," Ben said, fighting to keep his features at full intensity. "I'm a wolf on the hunt. I'm prowling. I'm sleek."

"You're dreaming. If I saw someone looking at me like that, I'd think they were severely medicated."

Coming out of character, Ben wagged a finger. "Don't underestimate the power of a medicated stare. That's how we won the Cold War."

"Whatever you say."

"I'm serious," he said. "And Reagan's entire reelection campaign was based on the success of the medicated stare."

"I'm not listening to you."

"If that's the way you want to be, I should tell you that denial is a terrible psychological deterrent. It harms you in ways you cannot imagine."

"It's okay," Lisa said. "I like to live life on the edge."

At seven-thirty that evening, Ben packed up his briefcase and took his coat from the closet. "You all ready?" Lisa asked.

"I think so," Ben said. He put his coat on his desk and felt his chest, checking for the fifth time that his microphone was properly attached. "I think that's it," he added, once again grabbing his coat. "As long as Nathan does his job, this should all work out. By tomorrow, we'll have a bribery charge and a positive I.D."

"Call me when everything is finished. Good luck," Lisa said, leaning over to Ben and giving him a kiss on the cheek.

Ben smiled. "How hard did you have to fight your urge to slip me the tongue?"

"I could barely restrain myself," she said. As Ben walked to the door, she added, "Just make sure you get Rick to proposition you. Without that, all we have are some pictures of two men eating dinner."

"Consider it done."

As Ben headed up Massachusetts Avenue, his mind was flooded with anxiety. Looking for people who might be following him, he glanced over his shoulder at two-minute intervals. The November night was cold—freezing to Washingtonians—and he turned up the collar of his coat. I come from Boston, he thought. This weather shouldn't bother me. Half a block away from the Thai restaurant, Ben glanced over his shoulder. No one. Then he started speaking into his chest. "Breaker One-Nine, Breaker One-Nine, do you read me? This here's Ober's father, Robert Oberman, and I was wondering if my son is still lightweight in the brain. Do you read me?" As he approached Two Quail, he saw that the window table was empty. He once again peered over his shoulder. Still nothing. Finally, he glanced in the window of the Thai place and saw the disguised figures of Nathan and Ober. The two friends wore Washington, D.C., sweatshirts and matching mesh baseball caps from the Smithsonian. With cameras by their sides, they fit in perfectly with the late-fall tourist crowd. Nathan gave Ben a small but unmistakable thumbs-up to let him know that the receiver was working.

Walking up the stairs to Two Quail, Ben wondered what time Rick would show up. I'm sure he'll be a little late, he thought.

Located in an old brownstone behind Capitol Hill, Two Quail was unassuming. All that identified it as a restaurant was the tiny burgundy and white sign above the entrance. What it lacked in elegance on the outside, it made up for with its opulent interior. Filled with antique furniture, Two Quail was designed to resemble a family home, where every room was a dining room. To further the lived-in look, the tables in the restaurant offered unusual seating arrangements: sculptural sofas, Art Deco love seats, antique wingback chairs, and refinished, upholstered benches. Ben approached the maître d', who was dressed in black wool pants and a black cashmere turtleneck. "Hi, my name is

Ben Addison. I'm supposed to meet a friend here in about five minutes.''

Looking down his list, the maître d' said, "Yes, Mr. Addison, we have a reservation for two at eight o'clock. Would you like to sit now, or would you rather wait for your friend?"

"If it's okay, I'd rather sit now."

"Of course. Right this way." He led Ben to the table by the window. "Enjoy your meal," he said as he placed a menu in front of him.

"I'm in," Ben whispered into his chest. "Can you still hear me?" From his vantage point, Ben could make out a distinct nod from his friends in the restaurant across the street.

"What's he saying?" Ober asked.

"Hold on a second," Nathan said, focusing on the voice that came through the tiny earplug he was wearing. "He asked if we can hear him." Nodding his head, Nathan forced a smile and said to Ober, "Now all we have to do is wait."

At a quarter after eight, Rick still hadn't arrived. Where the hell is he? Ben wondered, taking a thin breadstick from the basket at the center of the table. Maybe he's not coming. Maybe he saw right through our plan. No, there's no way. He'll be here. The skinny bastard's greedy. He'll definitely be here.

"Can I get you something from the bar?" the waiter asked.

"Huh?" Ben asked, startled.

"Can I bring you a drink while you're waiting?"

Ben looked down and saw that he had crumbled the breadstick into tiny pieces that were now dispersed across the starched white tablecloth. "No. No, thank you."

"He looks worried," Ober said, peering through the telescopic lens of Nathan's camera.

"Of course he's worried," Nathan said. "Rick's fifteen minutes late."

"Do you think he'll show?"

"How should I know?" Nathan asked. "I don't know this guy."

Five minutes later, the waiter approached Ben. "Are you Mr. Addison?"

"Yes," Ben said. Without saying a word, the waiter handed Ben a folded piece of paper. Opening it, he read the handwritten note that said: "Ben, how about moving this party elsewhere? Those tourists across the street are starting to make me nervous. Follow your waiter to the back of the restaurant, and I'll take care of the rest. Naturally, I'll understand if you don't want to come, but if you don't, this will be the end of our dialogue. Rick."

When Ben looked up, the waiter said, "You can follow me, sir."

"Where do you think he's going?" Ober asked as Ben left the table.

"I have no idea," Nathan said. "He hasn't said a word. Maybe he's just going to the bathroom."

As he moved toward the back of the restaurant, Ben said to the waiter, "Y'know, here I thought I was going to have a nice relaxing dinner. Then, all of a sudden, bingo, I get a note that says to step outside. Can you imagine my surprise?"

"Holy shit, he's in trouble," Nathan said, picking up his camera and racing to put on his coat.

"What'd he say?" Ober asked as he followed Nathan's lead.

"Just grab your camera," Nathan said. Dashing out the front door, the two friends ran across the street and into Two Quail. As they entered the restaurant, they were stopped by the maître d'. "Can I help you?"

"Where's the guy who was sitting at this table?" Nathan pointed.

"I think he went to the bathroom," he said.

Rushing past him, Nathan ran through the restaurant. "Where's the bathroom?" he yelled as he bumped into a busboy.

"Over there," the busboy said, pointing Nathan to the back of the restaurant.

Nathan charged into the bathroom and pulled open each of the stalls. "Shit," he said, seeing that both were empty. Leaving the bathroom, he ran into Ober. "He's not in there," Nathan said, standing in a small corridor in the back of the restaurant. Looking around, he saw an emergency exit at the end of the corridor. Nathan and Ober ran toward the door, pushed it open, and found themselves in the back alley behind the restaurant. Down the block, they saw a departing black limousine. "Quick, gimme my camera," Nathan said. Ober handed it over. Nathan snapped four quick pictures as the car raced out of sight. "Damn!" he yelled as it disappeared around a corner.

"Could you make out the license plate?" Ober asked.

"I couldn't see it, but the camera should've gotten it. Hopefully, we can enlarge the picture." Nathan pulled the receiver from his duffel bag, put the earplug back in his ear, and turned on the receiver.

"I don't think it's going to help," Ober said.

Surprised to hear Ober's statement in both ears, Nathan looked up and saw Ober lifting Ben's microphone from the pavement. "Damn!" Nathan said, pulling the plug from his ear.

"Do you think he'll be okay?" Ober asked.

"He'll be fine," Nathan said without much conviction. "I'm sure he's fine." When he was positive that the car was out of sight, Nathan turned and yelled, "Lisa, did you get it?"

"I got 'em!" Lisa yelled, standing up as she pushed open the cover of the dark green dumpster next to the back exit. As Nathan and Ober approached, she handed them her own camera and hopped out of the dumpster. "I got everything! The limo driver, Rick, the license plate— you name it."

"I just wish we had the audio," Nathan said, rewinding Lisa's camera.

"Don't worry about it," Lisa said. "At least we'll be able to get an I.D. now."

"Thank God you were hiding in the dumpster," Ober added.

"It was Ben's idea," Lisa said. "He knew Rick would spot you guys in a heartbeat.'' Wiping bits of random filth from her jeans, she added, ''I just wish I didn't have to be the one sitting in that smelly rathole.''

''Rick wouldn't have made a move if he couldn't account for me and Ober,'' Nathan said as the three friends walked down the alleyway. ''Now, are you sure you got clear shots of Rick?'' he asked, holding both cameras.

''Absolutely,'' Lisa said. ''The windows were tinted, but Ben made Rick roll them down before he got into the car.''

''Speaking of which,'' Nathan said, ''are we sure he's safe? Because if he's not, I'd be happy calling the police.''

''Don't call the police just yet,'' Lisa said as they reached the street. ''As far as we know, Rick's just after information.''

''Long time no speak,'' Ben said to Rick as they sat in the back of the limousine. ''I guess you've been pretty busy lately.''

''You could say that,'' Rick said, smoothing his beige cashmere coat against his expensive brown tweed pants.

''And I guess you've moved up in the world since then. I'm impressed. A whole limo just for me.''

''Well, we thought you deserved the best.''

''Y'know, I should also say thank you to your driver.'' Ben tapped on the glass partition that separated him from their chauffeur. ''He really gave me a great pat-down before I got in the car.''

''It was my idea to frisk you,'' Rick confessed. ''To be honest, he said you didn't have the resourcefulness to get a wireless mike.''

''He said that about me?'' Ben said, tapping the glass a bit harder. When the driver looked over his shoulder, Ben put up his middle finger. Turning back to Rick, he said, ''I'm sorry. Where were we?''

''You're a bit more tense than I remember,'' Rick said. He ran his hand over his perfectly combed blond hair.

''Well, you know what working in the Supreme Court does to you,'' Ben said. ''Oh, I forgot, you didn't work there. My mistake.''

''Ben, I know you're upset. And I understand—''

''No. You don't. That is, unless you were ever dicked over for some quick cash by someone you trusted.''

"Don't be so judgmental. You know nothing about my life," Rick snapped. "I'm sorry I had to do that to you, but at that point I wasn't sure whether I could trust you."

"So that's why we're riding around right now? Now you can trust me?"

"I didn't say that. I simply thought you deserved an explanation."

"So what's your explanation? You went to Maxwell with the information you stole from me and made yourself a few million dollars. What else is there to say?"

"Are you really that sure of my actions?"

"I'm pretty sure," Ben said. "Last time we met, you spent four ninety-nine at an all-you-can-eat pizza place. Now, we're cruising around in a limo, and you're decked out for a movie premiere. Add that to the fact that Maxwell made one of the riskiest wagers in telecommunications history, and I'd say we've got the full picture. Am I wrong?"

"Why are you so obsessed with right and wrong?" Rick asked. "That's your problem, y'know. You always want the black-and-white answer. But life is all grays, my friend—"

"Rick, why did you want to meet with me?" Ben interrupted.

"I'm just chatting with an old friend. I know you've been through some hardships lately, and I wanted to make sure you're okay."

"And what hardships are those?" Ben asked, wondering exactly what Rick knew.

"First, your roommate uses you to advance his journalism career, then you get interrogated by the Marshals Office, and your plan to get me on tape falls apart. All in all, I'd say you've been having a pretty terrible week. Am I wrong?"

"It's been hectic, but manageable."

"Now that's an optimistic way to look at it," Rick said with a smirk. "Let me ask you something, Ben. Have your investigations into my background turned up anything yet? As I said in my letter, the phone bill trick was clever, but that attempt at my old apartment was embarrassing. I mean, from a man of your intellect, I expect real thinking."

"Well, besides the wireless microphone that's built into my cuff links, I'd say I was doing terribly. But since I have that, I'd say I'm pretty happy."

"You should be so lucky," Rick said with a forced laugh.

Noticing Rick's discomfort, Ben pulled a handkerchief from his suit pocket and handed it to him. "You may want to wipe your brow. You look terribly unprofessional."

"You really love it when you think the victory is yours, don't you? But if you even had the slightest hint of a communicator on you, I'd know about it. I have way too much invested in my business to risk it all on a stupid mistake." Noticing the slight sweat that now covered Ben's forehead, Rick handed back the handkerchief. "Cuff-link microphones—who do you think you are? James Bond?"

"Rick, if you're so well informed, tell me why you need to risk being caught with me."

"As I said, I'm simply checking up on an old friend. Now tell me, how's everything at the Court?"

"It's fine. I've written over thirty decisions since the session began. At least twelve of them could've made you over a million dollars." Ben stared at Rick, unflinching. "Don't insult my intelligence. Tell me what you want and name your price."

"Oh, you'd love to have it in a neat little package, wouldn't you?" Rick said. "I know you're in a tough position. When this year started, you were poised for stardom. But because of this disaster with Eric, you've put your entire career at risk. If the press links you to Eric, you'll be eaten alive. No matter what the D.C. law firms have offered you, if you're suspected of leaking information, there isn't a firm in the country that'll touch you. Which means these next few weeks will be risky ones for you."

"Is that a threat?"

"Not at all. In fact, I'm here to suggest a truce. You know what I need. I'm pretty sure that's always been clear to you. In return, I'll make sure you're handsomely rewarded."

"You'll have to forgive me—I'm not up on my criminal-speak. How much is 'handsomely' these days?"

"Three million dollars," Rick said curtly. "I assume that'll be enough to bury all your fears about your financial future."

"Have you been smoking some of the money you made? Why the hell would I take money from you? Right now, my life is fine. The press is a little suspicious, but otherwise, they're calm. But if I take the money, I'm definitely screwed. If a clerk shows up with three million bucks, someone's liable to get a bit suspicious."

"Ben, you're screwed either way. You may have no problems with the press at the moment, but as I said, it's only a matter of time before they link you with Eric. When that happens, I hope you're prepared. Take the money—at least you'll be ready for the disaster that will become your life."

"You're right—if the press links us, I'm dead. But there's no guarantee they'll find out. If my bank account suddenly hits three mil, though, I'm guaranteed to raise a few eyebrows. At that point, I might as well admit guilt."

"Now you're getting caught up in semantics. Do you really believe I'd be dumb enough to just show up with a bag of money at your doorstep? Your three million dollars will be put into an account that no one but ourselves will ever be able to find."

"Of course—the Swiss bank account. How stupid of me."

"Ben, this isn't a game. This is real life here. If you want to risk your existence on the unlikely possibility of media incompetence, be my guest. But I know you're more of a pragmatist than that. Unless you take the money, you risk losing everything. I hope you'll choose a more secure future."

"And if I don't help you, how do I know you won't blackmail me?"

Rick looked coldly across at his passenger. "You don't. But blackmail doesn't solve any of our problems. Revealing your link with these decisions means risking my own indictment as well. As you know, if the truth comes out, the world's largest magnifying glass will be turned on all of us. While it's easy to outsmart a single Supreme Court clerk, it's not as easy to sidestep the SEC and the resources of an unrelenting media."

"And if I say no?"

"Then I'll find someone to say yes," Rick said. "Believe me, it won't be hard."

"Is there a particular decision you have in mind?"

"*Grinnell* v. *New York* is one. There are others."

"And when do you want the information?"

"Get it to me at least three weeks before the decision is announced. The earlier the better."

Ben picked at a hole in the leather seat. "How does it feel to know you're going to hell?"

"Don't get on a moral high horse with me," Rick said. "It's easy to be honest when you're on top. Try starting the race from the back of the pack."

"Cry me a river."

"I'm serious. If I were you, I'd be less concerned with ethics and more concerned about securing your future. There isn't much demand for out-of-work legal geniuses."

"Let me ask you one last question," Ben said. "How'd you get all the information about me?"

"That would be telling. You know the line—about magicians revealing their tricks."

"That's a good one. You're so original. So what else do we have to talk about?"

"I believe that's it."

"You should know one thing," Ben said. "Ever since they lowered my security clearance, the marshals have been watching me pretty hard."

"I don't think your recent drop in security status will affect anything," Rick said. "In the future, if you need to reach me, you can contact me through our P.O. box."

"By the way, that P.O. box thing was a pretty good trick. I was impressed."

"Doesn't take much," Rick said sarcastically. Pushing the intercom button on the side of the door, he said to the driver, "As soon as you see a good place, I want to let our guest out."

"One last thing," Rick said as the driver pulled to the side of the road. "Please take out your contact lenses."

"What?"

"You heard me. Take out your contacts. I'd prefer that you didn't memorize our license plate."

"These things cost a hundred bucks," Ben said as he took out his left lens.

"I don't want to keep them," Rick said. "I only want them out of your eyes."

When he saw that Ben was holding both lenses, Rick opened the door and let him out. "Thanks for dinner," Ben said sarcastically. Rick slammed the door and the limo sped off. Squinting hard, Ben struggled in vain to read the plates. "Asshole."

"Where the hell is he?" Nathan asked.

"I'm sure he's fine," Ober said, bent over and staring into the refrigerator. "He and Rick just went for a ride."

"How can you be so damn calm?" Nathan asked.

"I'm not," Ober said, selecting a soda. "But what do you want me to do? He'll be home when he gets home." As he opened the can, he added, "You don't think Rick kidnapped him and threw him off a pier, do you?"

"Of course not," Nathan said, walking into the kitchen. "Rick isn't some petty criminal. If he wanted to eliminate Ben as a witness, he would've put a bullet in his brain a few days after the decision came down. Rick's after more information." Nathan washed his hands in the sink. He then shut off the water and paused. "Ober, do you trust Lisa?"

"What are you talking about?"

"I'm serious," Nathan said, drying his hands with a dish towel. "Do you trust Lisa?"

"Of course I trust her," Ober said, sitting at the dining room table. "She makes me crazy, but I definitely trust her. Why? What are you thinking?"

"I'm thinking that someone had to tip off Rick. You don't just get lucky and guess our entire plan. Even if he did spot the two of us, how did he know about the microphone? As far as I can figure, either Rick has all of us bugged, or he has an inside person telling him what we're up to."

"That's not true. Maybe he actually realizes that Ben is a worthy opponent. In that case, he could've just been trying to be cautious."

"Maybe," Nathan said.

"Anyway, why would you suspect Lisa?" Ober asked.

"Because, besides Ben, only the three of us knew the plan. So if someone's leaking, it's either you, me, or Lisa."

"Well, it's not me," Ober said defensively.

"I didn't say it was you. I said it was Lisa."

"Do you think she'd really do that?"

"How should I know?" Nathan asked. "But don't you think it was weird that she wanted to go home rather than come here and wait with us?"

"She wanted to take a shower. She smelled."

"She could've showered here. Besides, what do we really know about her?"

"We know Ben's been working with her for the past four months, and he doesn't have a bad word to say about her."

"That's just because he's hot for her. Sex will always obscure good judgment. Always."

"I don't know about that," Ober said, shaking his head. "I don't really think Lisa could be involved."

Suddenly, the front door opened and Ben walked in.

The questions started flying: "What happened?" "Where'd he take you?" "Are you okay?"

"I'm fine," Ben said, his hands cupped together. "I just need some contact solution." Turning toward the bathroom, he explained, "Mastermind made me take out my contacts so I couldn't make out his license plates."

"Well, it doesn't matter what you saw, because we got everything," Nathan said as Ben reinserted his lenses. "We got some shots of the limo, and Lisa got everything else."

"Where is she?" Ben asked. As he blinked his contacts into place, saline-solution tears ran down his face.

"She went home to shower," Ober explained.

"Did she see Rick when he opened the window?" Ben asked.

"She said she did. She took a whole roll of film."

"Did you bring it in yet? Are they clear shots? We can probably enlarge them."

"Already taken care of," Nathan said. "We took them to the place around the corner. They were closing, so the pictures won't be ready until tomorrow. As soon as we pick them up, I'll bring them into work. We'll have an I.D. in no time."

"So what'd he say?" Ober asked. "What happened?"

"You saw the whole story," Ben said, still struggling with his contacts. "Just like we thought, he fucking knew everything. When I was sitting at the table, he slipped me a note saying that I should meet him outside since he didn't want to be photographed by the two of you. I almost shit my pants."

"So he did know we were there," Nathan said. "Did you save the note? Maybe we can analyze it for fingerprints or do a handwriting analysis."

"Forget about it," Ben said. "The limo driver took it away from me right before he patted me down for the microphone."

"I told you—" Ober began.

"I don't want to hear it," Ben said angrily.

"Take a seat," Nathan said.

"I can't," Ben said, leaning on the kitchen table. "I'm too wound up." Running his hands through his hair, he added, "I can't believe this. Now we have no audio. If we'd given him a power drill, I don't think he could've screwed us harder."

"What else did he say?"

"He wants the *Grinnell* decision, and he said he'd pay me three million dollars if I gave it to him."

"Three million?" Ober asked.

"Did you tell him no?" Nathan asked.

"Of course not," Ben said. "I did exactly what we talked about. I told him I'd think about it."

"When did you talk about that?" Ober asked. "I don't remember that."

"Last night," Ben said. "You were down here talking to Eric."

"How come you didn't invite me?"

"I just said—you were with Eric," Ben explained. "Sorry."

"About Eric—" Ober began.

"Ober, I know it upsets you, but I really don't want to talk about it," Ben said. "It's a dead issue, so drop it already."

"Do you think Rick believed that you were interested?" Nathan asked.

"Absolutely. He said if I'm linked to Eric, I'm screwed. So if I don't take the money, I'd be a fool."

Nathan paused for a moment. "You would be."

"I know," Ben said. Pushing himself away from the table, Ben walked toward the kitchen. "The only other thing that freaked me out was how much information he had on me. He knew everything. He knew about Eric and the Marshals Office. He even mentioned something about my meeting with my firm," Ben said as he picked up the phone.

"Who're you calling?" Nathan asked suspiciously.

"Lisa," Ben said. "I want to tell her what happened." Noticing the odd look on both Nathan's and Ober's faces, Ben asked, "Why? What's wrong?"

Nathan was silent.

"He thinks Lisa might be leaking information to Rick," Ober explained.

"You've got to be kidding me," Ben said, hanging up the phone. Coming back into the dining room, he asked, "You don't really believe that, do you?"

"It's definitely possible," Nathan said. "How else do you explain how Rick knew about everything?"

"It's not that hard to figure out," Ben reasoned. "He knows Eric's name, so he probably saw his story in the paper."

"And how did he know about our entire plan?"

"He might've seen you guys across the street."

"That's what I said," Ober said.

"But what about the rest? What about the marshals? And your firm? And the mikes?" Nathan asked. "C'mon, Ben, don't be blind to this."

"I'm not being blind," Ben insisted. "Trust me, I've been thinking about this since the beginning. I just don't think it's Lisa, though. She'd never do that to me."

"You barely know her," Nathan said. "You have no idea what she would and wouldn't do."

"She's a good friend," Ben said. "I guarantee she wouldn't do that. Besides, just because Rick is unbelievably resourceful doesn't mean that one of my close friends is responsible."

"Eric's been your close friend for two decades and he had no problem selling you out. How can you say Lisa wouldn't do the same?"

"Because Lisa's a better person than Eric is. I know she seems like a loudmouth to you guys, but she has integrity. Trust me, she'd never do it."

"Ben, now you're being stupid," Nathan said, rising from his seat. "If you think she wouldn't sell you out, you're wrong. Everyone has their price, and she's no exception. If you started thinking with your real head, you'd see how right I am."

"No. No way," Ben insisted, shaking his head. "If Lisa was leaking information, Rick would be better informed than he was. He knew about things that have gone on, but he only knew about them in a general sense. He really didn't have any details."

"You don't know that for sure."

"Yes, I do," Ben said. "I dangled our red herring and he snapped it up."

"He fell for the security clearance?" Nathan asked.

"Hook, line, and sinker."

"That's interesting," Nathan said.

"What security clearance?" Ober asked, confused. "What the hell are you talking about?"

"Last night, we were talking strategy," Ben explained, "so Nathan and I said that I should say something happened when it really didn't. If Rick said he knew about it, we'd know to what extent he was bluffing his way through some of this crap. So I told him that the Marshals Office knocked down my security clearance, which they didn't. And Rick said he knew about it."

"Great move," Ober said, impressed.

"It definitely was," Ben said. "But I still want to know how Rick had even the little information he had."

"I think he has us bugged," Ober said.

"I still think it could be Lisa," Nathan said.

"I don't want to hear about it," Ben said, walking up to his room. "I have way too much to worry about, and I don't want to have to start suspecting my closest friends." When he got into his bedroom, Ben closed the door behind him, picked up the phone, and dialed Lisa's home number.

"Ben?" she answered anxiously.

"Relax, I'm fine," he said, looking under his desk for anything that resembled a microphone.

"What happened? Are you okay? Did he proposition you?"

"He definitely wants info," Ben said. After a full explanation of the last few hours, he continued, "So all we have left are the pictures that you and Nathan snapped as we drove away. Hopefully, those'll be enough."

"When will they be done?"

"They'll be ready tomorrow morning," Ben said, searching under every piece of his memorabilia collection. "Nathan gave them to some place around the corner. But if those don't come out, we're back where we started."

"They'll come out," Lisa said. "Once Nathan runs the photos and the license plates through the State Department, we'll have everything we need."

"I guess," Ben said.

"So you're calm? You're not crazy?"

"I'm completely calm," he said, crawling on the floor and searching under his bed. "Lisa, by the way, thanks for hanging in the dumpster. We would've been lost without you."

"Don't sweat it. That's what I'm here for."

"I know, but I just wanted to say thank you."

"Any time," Lisa said, hanging up the phone.

Later that evening, Nathan walked into Ben's room. Ben was sitting at his desk, slumped in his chair and staring at the wall. "How're you doing?" Nathan asked.

"I'm okay. Just trying to figure this whole thing out."

"Any ideas?"

Ben slowly shook his head. "Not really."

"You don't really need to stay involved with this bullshit," Nathan said as he sat on Ben's bed. "I mean, you can just walk away. The only thing hurt is your pride."

"It's not about pride," Ben said, still slumped over. "Rick will always have information that can damage my career. If I walk away, I'll never know when he'll be back to dangle it in front of my face. At least if we get something on him, we can counteract whatever blackmail he might think of in the future." Ben opened the top drawer of his desk and pulled out a pencil. "Besides, I want this guy."

"Not to be a pessimist, but have you thought about turning yourself in and explaining the situation to the police? I mean, it's not like you leaked the information on purpose. Rick tricked you out of it."

"I've definitely thought about that," Ben said. "But it doesn't matter how Rick got the information from me. If they found out I released a decision, they'd have to kick me off the Court."

"Yeah, but it's not like you'd go to jail—there was no criminal intent on your part."

"If a clerk got fired from the Supreme Court, it'd make every paper in the country. The media eats up Court scandals faster than my family eats dessert. And if that happened, my entire career would be finished. I'd be disbarred and I'd never be able to practice law again."

"I think you're just worried that you'd lose your Golden Boy status."

"You're probably right. I've busted my ass to get where I am. The last thing I want to do is throw it all away by confessing. No offense, but that doesn't sound like the optimal solution."

"I'm just exploring all your options," Nathan said. "You know I'll support you no matter what you decide to do."

Early the next morning, Ben knocked on Nathan's door. "Do you have the receipt for the pictures? I want to go pick them up."

"Hold on a second," Nathan said, bent over as he tied the laces on his sneakers. "I'll go down with you."

Nathan untied his laces and retied them again. "C'mon," Ben said. "How many times have you tied them already? Four? Five? Six? You have a sickness, y'know that?"

"I just like the perfect knot," Nathan said, still bent over. "Excuse me for being a perfectionist."

"You're not a perfectionist. You're the poster boy for next year's obsessive-compulsive calendar."

"There. Done."

"Now *that's* a beautiful bow," Ben said, staring at his roommate's shoes. "Wonderful job."

"Jealous," Nathan said as they headed downstairs to get their coats. "By the way, my mother's been bothering me all week. Are you coming over to dinner the night before Thanksgiving?"

"Who's going to be there?" Ben asked, buttoning his coat.

"Well, it'll be my family, the four of us, and Lisa, if she's coming."

"What do you mean, the four of us? I'm not eating with Eric."

"C'mon," Nathan pleaded, opening the front door. "Now you're being immature."

"I'm not being immature. I just want to enjoy my time at your house. If Eric's there, I won't. It's as simple as that."

"What do you want me to do?" Nathan asked. "Should I tell him he can't come? Should I invite everyone and leave him out? Besides, if he's not invited, our mothers'll never leave us alone. They'll want to know the whole story, start to finish."

Silent until they reached the corner, Ben said, "Fine. He can come."

"Thank you," Nathan said, breathing a sigh of relief. "I'm glad your forgiving side won out."

"Don't think this has anything to do with forgiveness. I just weighed my hatred for Eric against the consequences of maternal interrogation. From there it was no contest. Moms are undefeated."

Ben and Nathan walked three more blocks until they reached Rob's Camera and Video. As they approached the store, Ben said, "We'll probably have to enlarge the photo."

"It won't be a problem. They can do that within an hour. I'm more worried that the license won't give us good information."

"It definitely will. Even if it only gives us a limo company, that's a start." Ben opened the door for his friend and followed him inside.

Nathan pulled out the two ticket stubs and handed them to one of the two female clerks waiting behind the counter. "We have some pictures to pick up."

As one of the clerks took the stubs to the photo bins, the other looked at Ben. "Did you go to Maryland undergrad? Because you look really familiar."

"I'm sorry, I didn't," Ben said. "My friend did, though. He got a degree in shoelace tying." Pointing to Nathan's feet, he asked, "Have you ever seen anything tied so tight in your whole life? I mean, besides him?"

The clerk leaned over the counter. "That *is* a nice bow."

"I'm sorry," the other clerk said, shuffling though the envelopes of finished photos. "When did we say your pictures would be ready?"

"You said to pick them up this morning," Nathan said. "They were under the last name Oberman. Two rolls of film."

The clerk shook her head. "I can't find them here. Hold on a second." The clerk flipped through a small looseleaf binder and stopped on a page. "Wait, I found them. They were picked up about an hour ago by your friend."

A chill ran down Ben's back. "What friend?"

"Oh, I remember that guy. I helped him," the other clerk said. "He said that if you came in, we should tell you that he already picked up the photos."

"This wouldn't happen to be a tall guy with blond hair and droopy eyes?" Ben asked.

"That's him," she said. "He was so sweet."

"Fuck!" Ben said, banging the glass counter.

"Relax," Nathan said. Looking at the perplexed clerks, Nathan explained, "That wasn't our friend. You gave our pictures to someone who shouldn't have seen them."

"I'm so sorry," the clerk said. "I didn't mean—"

"Don't worry about it," Nathan said.

"What do you mean, don't worry about it?" Ben yelled. Turning to the clerks, he asked, "Don't you have a policy about picking film up? Don't you always ask for a receipt?"

"He knew the name—he said you guys were friends."

"Do you keep any negatives on file?" Ben shot back. "Anything at all in case someone walks off with your pictures?"

"No. The negatives go right back to the customer."

"I don't fuckin' believe this," Ben said, walking to the door.

"You don't happen to have security cameras here, do you?" Nathan asked. "Something that might've snapped a picture of our friend?"

"I'm sorry, we don't," the clerk said. "They were stolen when we were robbed last March."

"Unbelievable," Ben said as he left the store.

Waving to the clerks, Nathan said, "Thanks for your help," and walked outside. Running to catch up with Ben, he said, "I'm sorry. I shouldn't have left the photos in there overnight."

"It's not your fault," Ben said. "I should've seen this one a mile away. This was just dumb. I could've been here early this morning."

"How do you think he knew? Do you think there was someone following us when we left you at the restaurant?" As he struggled to keep pace with his friend, Nathan asked, "Did you tell Lisa where the photos were?"

Ben was silent.

"You told her, didn't you?"

Again, silence.

"Answer me," Nathan demanded. "Did you tell Lisa about the photos?"

Coming to an abrupt halt, Ben threw his arms in the air and screamed, "YES! I TOLD HER! What the hell do you want me to say? I told her they were at a camera store a few blocks away!"

"Now why'd you do that? I told you—"

"I told her because I trust her. And when I speak to her, I don't worry about guarding my thoughts—she's my friend. So no matter what you say, until you have proof that it's Lisa, I won't believe a single bit of your conjecture."

"What kind of proof are you waiting for? If she put a knife in your back, you'd say it wasn't her because you didn't see her with your own two eyes."

"Lisa has nothing to gain by talking to Rick. If she was after the money, she'd leak the decisions to Rick herself."

"Is that what you think?" Nathan asked. "What about this scenario: Rick and Lisa are conspiring, and Lisa is leaking the decisions to Rick. The only problem is that if word gets out that information is leaking, there's no fall guy. Enter one befuddled clerk named Benjamin Addison. Get enough information on him, and if anything ever goes wrong, you have an instant scapegoat. All they need to do is keep amassing evidence of your involvement."

Ben walked silently for almost a block. Finally, he said, "I don't agree with you, but I understand what you're saying. When we get back from Thanksgiving, I'll be happy to talk about it, but until then, I want to enjoy my time at home. Lisa'll be with me and I refuse to suspect her the entire weekend."

"Then maybe you shouldn't take her home with you," Nathan said.

"Get it out of your head. She's got her ticket and she's coming home. That's the end of the discussion."

"It's your life," Nathan said.

CHAPTER 10

"THEY DECIDED *GRINNELL,*" BEN SAID, COMING INTO THE office carrying a stack of books.

"How do you know?" Lisa asked, looking up from the paperwork on her desk. "Conference isn't over yet."

"Oh, yes, it is," Ben said, dumping the books on Lisa's desk. "Osterman just buzzed his clerks and told them they'll be writing the majority. Veidt finally went to the dark side."

"Says who?"

"I just saw one of Blake's clerks in the elevator. He had the biggest shit-eating grin on his face. Historical-monument-destroying prick."

"I can't believe this." Lisa picked up the phone. "Where's Hollis? How come no one told us?"

"I don't think now's such a good time to call. He's probably pissed about it."

"Are we definitely doing the dissent?" Lisa asked, returning the phone to its cradle.

"That's my guess. I'm not sure, though."

"Why're you so upset?" Lisa asked. "I thought you were in favor of seeing it as a taking of property."

"I am," Ben said. "I just don't like seeing the vampires win. They played dirty on this one."

"Did they say what the final vote was?"

"It was five to four. Apparently Osterman convinced Veidt that if New York's zoning was allowed to protect the church, Grinnell and the other owners were going to bear a disproportionate burden."

"So Osterman's decision is based on a disproportionality argument? Are you sure it isn't challenging the legality of zoning?"

Shaking his head, Ben said, "If they attacked the zoning directly, they couldn't get all the votes they needed for a majority. Blake's clerk said that was the only way they could get Veidt on board. So Osterman's decision is going to say that the benefits of historic monuments are enjoyed by the whole city. Therefore, the preservation of such monuments is a burden that should be borne by the city, not by individuals."

"So if New York wants to protect the church, it's going to have to pay Grinnell and Associates the expected future value of the property?"

"You got it," Ben said. "Grinnell just got the golden ticket, and he doesn't even know it. He's going to reap all the profits of a mall complex that he's never going to have to build. That should teach the city to interfere with a private citizen."

"How can you think that's fair? This was so obviously planned by Grinnell. He bought that property with a constitutional lawyer at his side. He knew the city would freak if he said he was going to raze a church to open a mall. And the bigger he said his plans were, the more he knew he'd collect if the Court went his way."

"C'mon," Ben said. "This case took three years to reach us. You don't really believe the whole transaction was legal speculation?"

"I don't think it was all speculation, but I do think Howard Grinnell is a piece of shit. You read the record—he's an uptight greedy developer who was born with a silver stick up his ass."

"That was in the record?" Ben asked. "I never saw that."

"You know what I mean. I just can't believe Veidt was such a coward," Lisa said, flipping her legal pad to a clean page. "We have to write a scathing dissent for this. I want to limit this decision as much as possible."

"Don't worry. Veidt's lack of enthusiasm limits their opinion to this set of facts. By the time we're done with it, this decision will look like it came out of a traffic court."

Lisa put her pencil down and took a deep breath. While a halfhearted vote by a justice ensured victory in the case at hand, it usually also led to a halfhearted decision. And if history was any indicator, halfhearted decisions rarely made strong legal precedents.

"Besides," Ben said, "this decision will be overruled in a year. When Blake steps down, you know we're going to get a liberal justice."

"I know," Lisa admitted. "It'll just annoy me to see Grinnell take home all that cash." Looking up from her desk, she added, "Have you thought about how Rick fits into all this?"

"I haven't figured it out yet, but my guess is that if he knew the decision, he'd try to buy a piece of Grinnell's action."

"Have you decided whether you're going to tell him? Or is there a new plan to catch him on tape?"

"I'm not sure," Ben said. "I just have to survive Thanksgiving with my family."

"Where the hell is Ober?" Ben asked Nathan as the two friends stood in their living room, suitcases by their sides.

"He probably got lost on his way home," Nathan said. "The simple-minded are easily confused."

"I say we leave his ass," Lisa said, returning from the kitchen with a can of soda in her hand. "Maybe we'll get lucky and he'll miss the flight."

"Trust me, we don't want that," Ben warned. "If he misses the plane, his mother will be on our backs all weekend." Ben screeched in imitation of Ober's mom: "You've forgotten my baby! Where's my baby?"

"He's an only child," Nathan explained to Lisa. "His mom's a bit possessed."

"You mean *possessive*," Ben corrected.

"Oh, yes, I mean *possessive*. Silly me," Nathan said, repeating the friends' old high school joke.

"GET ME OUT OF HERE!" Ober announced, flinging open the front door.

"Where the hell were you?" Ben asked.

"There was an emergency at the office," Nathan said sarcastically. "There was an outburst of rowdy orange-juice-subsidy letter writers who needed swift attention."

Ober pointed at Lisa. "I didn't know you were flying with us."

"And she's not even paying for it," Ben said. "My parents are picking up the tab."

"Are you kidding me?" Ober asked. "If I knew free airfare was involved, I'd have told your mom that *I* was sleeping with you."

"I appreciate that," Ben said. "Now can we get out of here?"

Ober grabbed his suitcase from his room and returned to the living room. "Where's Eric?" he asked.

"ERIC!" Nathan called out. "WE'RE LEAVING!"

Eric walked down the stairs with a navy duffel bag and joined the group without saying a word to anyone. They all packed into Nathan's Volvo and headed for National Airport.

"They're going to lose our luggage," Lisa said, after the skycap loaded their bags onto a dolly and rolled them toward the conveyor belt.

"What makes you say that?" Ben asked.

"I just saw what Scrooge here tipped him," Lisa said, pointing at Ober.

"How much did you tip him?" Nathan asked, watching to make sure that his bags were loaded on the conveyor.

"I gave him a dollar," Ober said.

"You gave him one dollar for five bags?" Ben asked.

"Good-bye, suitcase, it was nice knowing you!" Lisa called to her luggage.

"What's wrong with a dollar?" Eric asked.

"For one bag, nothing," Ben said. "But if you have five bags for five different people, a dollar tip says, 'Throw these bags in a volcano. I have no use for them.'"

"Just relax," Eric said as the group walked inside the terminal. Turning to Ober, he added, "Nothing'll happen. You'll see."

With only two days until Thanksgiving, National Airport was swarming with people. Fighting the irate crowds, the friends made their way through the X-ray machine and toward their gate.

Ober scanned the row of shops and eateries that lined the terminal. "I'll be right back," he said as he took off in a mad dash.

"Lottery tickets," Ben said to Lisa.

As the remainder of the group arrived at the boarding gate, they waited at the back of a single, weaving line. Eventually, Ober returned, red-faced and breathing heavily. "Let me guess," Ben said. "You won."

"First I bought one ticket and I lost," Ober explained. "Then I bought another ticket and I lost. Then, I bought a third ticket—"

"And you lost," Nathan said.

". . . and I lost," Ober repeated. "But then, I bought the fourth magical, wonderful ticket . . ."

"And you won."

". . . AND I WON!" Ober screamed as everyone in line turned around. "I WON TWENTY BUCKS RIGHT THERE!"

"He has a small chemical imbalance," Ben explained to the onlookers. "With a little medication, he'll be fine."

"You won twenty bucks?" Nathan asked. "What'd you buy us?"

"I didn't buy you squat," Ober said. "If you want to make fun of the lottery, you will not reap its rewards."

"You won twenty bucks and you didn't buy your friends anything?" Ben asked. "I'm starving here."

"Me, too," Eric said. "I'm going to grab a slice of pizza. Does anyone want anything?"

"I'll take a slice," Ober said.

"Make it two," Nathan said.

"Make it three," Lisa said.

"Ben, do you want a slice?" Eric asked.

"No," Ben said, looking away. "Thanks."

When Eric stepped away from the line, Ober tapped Ben on the shoulder. "Don't be such a hard-ass. He's trying his best to make up."

"Too bad," Ben said. "I'm not ready to make up right now."

"Just be nice," Nathan begged. "Even if it's only for the weekend."

"Don't worry," Ben said. "I'll be fine."

"Are you nervous yet?" Ben asked, when the plane landed in Boston.

"A little," Lisa said, wiping her palms on her jeans.

"You should be," Ober said. "Because Sheila Addison is about to eat you alive."

"Did you bring the garlic and the wooden stake?" Nathan asked.

"If you ever feel like there's a lull in the conversation, just look her straight in the eye and say, 'Are you my mommy?' You can always use that in a pinch," Ben said.

"I'm sure it'll be fine," Lisa said.

Shaking his head, Ben said, "Just remember—you wanted to come here. I tried to persuade you to stay home. Therefore, all blood is on your hands."

"I think I'll be able to handle it," Lisa said.

When the plane reached the gate, the narrow aisle filled with people. Ben got up from his seat, but was unable to stand upright in his row. Cocking his head to the right, he crossed his arms and waited impatiently. Directly behind him, Eric was stuck in the same position. "Don't you just love this?" Eric asked, forcing a laugh.

"Actually, I hate it," Ben said.

"Listen, can we just pretend it didn't happen?" Eric asked. "It'll make for a nicer weekend."

"No, Eric, we can't pretend it didn't happen." Ben scowled. "No matter how much you want to make it go away, it's going to be with us for a long while."

"Why? Why can't we just start over? I'm sorry already. I'm sorry it happened."

"You make it sound as if it happened by itself," Ben said. "But in case you didn't realize, you're the one responsible. You did it. Understand?"

"Big deal. I did it—I'll live with it. Why can't you?"

Noticing the passengers who started to stare, Ben lowered his voice. "Because I don't like you anymore. Get that through your damn skull and leave me alone." As the passengers began to disembark, Ben inched closer toward the aisle. Eventually able to straighten his neck, he stood between Lisa and Nathan.

"What was that all about?" Nathan asked.

"Nothing," Ben said.

"Is there anything else you forgot to tell me about your family?" Lisa asked.

"Just one thing," he said, taking a deep breath and smiling at the thought of the coming weekend. "Don't touch my father's plate when he's eating. He's very territorial."

"Ben, be serious."

"You're on your own, missy. Just keep your head down at all times."

As they moved through the terminal, Lisa searched the crowd, hoping to identify Ben's family. Suddenly, a voice screamed out, "Yooohooo! Benjamin! Nathan!"

"Oh, God, it's Ober's mom," Ben whispered to Lisa, nodding in the direction of a frosted-blond head bobbing in the crowd. The woman was frantically waving her hands. "Be careful," he said. "She may try to put a scrunchie on you."

The five friends made their way through the crowds and watched as Ober was enveloped by his mother's hug. Wearing an extra long purple sweatshirt and a pair of black leggings, Barbara Oberman could barely contain herself. "William! I missed you more than words!" She squeezed Ober with all her might. "Nathan!" she said, moving toward the group of friends. "Eric! Ben!" She wrapped her arms around each one, a human hugging assembly line. "And you must be Lisa," Ober's mother said, extending her hand. "You should know that you're the first girlfriend Ben's brought home since—what was her name?—Lindsay something."

"Lindsay Lucas," Ober sang. "The psycho from Long Island."

"Whatever happened to her?" Nathan asked.

"Last I heard, she had hurt herself in a terrible Skee-Ball accident," Ober said.

His face red, Ben interrupted, "Mrs. Oberman, do you know where my dad is?"

"He and your mom are working late," she said. "I'll drop you off at home. Nathan, Eric, I told your parents I'd pick you up as well. I have the minivan." After they retrieved their baggage, the small group walked to the parking lot and loaded their belongings into the podlike cherry-red minivan.

Pulling off at the West Newton exit, the van left the Massachusetts Turnpike and entered suburbia. Armed and stocked with roving rent-a-cops, the community was determined to remain a safe, clean neighborhood, no matter what the cost. As the minivan followed the curving streets, Ben said, "On your left, you can see Dr. MacKenzie's house— of the Newton MacKenzies. Naturally it's the biggest house in Newton."

"He's the best plastic surgeon," Ober's mother explained.

"This place is unbelievable," Lisa said, looking around. "I've seen suburbia and it's driving a Volvo."

After dropping off Eric and Nathan, the Oberman shuttle pulled up to Ben's house.

"So what are the sleeping arrangements for tonight?" Ober asked as he opened the door.

"Funny," Ben said as he and Lisa climbed out of the van. "Thanks for the ride, Mrs. Oberman."

"You're welcome. Tell your mom I say hi."

"I definitely will," Ben said. "And by the way, I'd watch your son while he's home. He's been so busy at work, he hasn't been eating well."

"I knew you looked skinny!" Ober's mother said as Ben shut the door and Ober scowled out the window.

"Now that was downright mean," Lisa said.

"He deserved it," Ben said as he walked up the path to his house.

Lisa looked up at the modest Colonial-style home. "Nice place."

As they approached the front steps, the front door opened. "Benjamin!" his mother said. She opened her arms and gave him a long embrace. "You look terrific," she said. "A bit thin, but otherwise terrific. And you must be Lisa," she said, extending her hand.

"Nice to meet you," Lisa said.

"In case you didn't guess, this is my mom," Ben said. "She's the malevolent evil one I was telling you about."

"Don't be such a smart-ass," Ben's mother said. "I'm trying to make a good impression." Without question, Ben had inherited his mother's features: her strong eyes, her quizzical eyebrows, the way her nose crinkled when she laughed. Even their mannerisms seemed to mirror each other. For every quick remark Ben had, his mother had a stronger retort.

Carrying his packed-to-capacity nylon bag, Ben followed Lisa and his mother into the house. When they reached the living room, Mrs. Addison called out, "Michael! They're here!" From out of the kitchen, Ben's father appeared, dressed in jeans and a beat-up old Michigan T-shirt.

"Nice to meet you, Mr. Addison. I'm Lisa."

Taking Lisa's hand, he said, "Please, call me Michael. Mr. Addison's my dumpy old dad."

His hair was longer than Lisa had expected. It must be the old-hippie thing, she thought.

"Why don't you bring Lisa's bags upstairs," Ben's mother said to Ben. "I wasn't sure how you two wanted to do the sleeping arrangements, so . . ."

"Mom, we're not even dating," Ben said.

"Well, excuse me, Mr. Bachelor," Ben's mother said. She turned to Lisa and added, "He says you two aren't dating, but he hasn't brought home a woman since Lindsay—what was her name?"

"Lindsay Lucas," Ben and Lisa said together.

Smiling, Ben's mother said, "I see you've already had this discussion."

"I refuse to explain," Ben said. Grabbing Lisa's bag, he walked toward the stairs. "I'll be right back." Walking up to his old room, Ben inhaled the smells of his childhood. It felt good and familiar and safe to be back, he decided. As with every other visit home, he marveled at the illusion that everything around him had gotten smaller—from his old bed, to his old desk, to the Albert Einstein poster on his wall. After a quick trip to the bathroom, he put Lisa's bags in the guest room and then walked down to the kitchen.

"Awwwww," he heard Lisa say as he entered the room. "You were so cute!"

"You've got to be kidding me," Ben said. "Baby pictures already? What'd it take, two whole minutes? That's a new record for you, Mom."

"Leave her alone," Lisa said, still engrossed in the photos.

"You should see some of the home movies we have," Ben's father added.

"Don't even think of it, Dad," Ben warned. "Home movies have at least a one-night waiting period."

"So tell me more about Ben as a little kid," Lisa said.

"Tell her about the time I lit Jimmy Eisenberg on fire."

"Oh, shush," Ben's mother said. Turning back to Lisa, she continued, "He was so bright. He learned to read when he was two. And by the time he was four, he used to read Michael's articles."

"He found a spelling mistake in one of my final drafts," Ben's father said proudly. "Tell Lisa about the time you found him up on the roof."

"Now that's a story," Ben's mother said. "When Ben was five, it was late one night, and I couldn't find him. I was frantic—"

"Mom, *you* were frantic?" Ben asked.

"I was frantic, looking everywhere for him. I was pulling my hair out. Suddenly, I hear this sound on the roof. Let me tell you, my heart dropped. I ran up through the attic and opened the door to the roof, and there's Benjamin, wearing his little pajamas and holding a rope in his hand. So I scream, 'Benjamin, what the hell do you think you're doing out here?' And he says to me, 'Mommy, I was just trying to lasso the moon.' "

"Awwwwww," Lisa said. "Ever the little overachiever."

"Oh, well—show's over," Ben said, leaving the kitchen. "Good night."

"Benjamin, come back here," Ben's mother said.

Scanning through the pictures, Lisa looked up and asked, "Is this little guy your brother?"

"Yeah," Ben said with a smile. He then looked over at both his mother and father.

Confused, Lisa was silent.

"That's Daniel. He passed away when he was twelve," Ben's father said. "He had leukemia."

"I'm sorry," Lisa said. "I didn't know."

"And now you do," Ben said, trying to make Lisa feel comfortable. Standing behind her, he put his hands on her shoulders. "Don't worry about it. It's okay."

"He was a terrific young man," Ben's mother said proudly. "You would've really gotten along."

"Thanks," Lisa said, unsure of what else to say.

"Maybe we should call it a night." Ben looked at his watch. "It's close to midnight."

"That's a good idea," Ben's mother said, stacking the photo albums in a neat pile. "What do you two have planned for tomorrow?"

"I think we're going to spend the day in the city. Lisa's never been to Boston. And we're supposed to go over to Nathan's house for dinner.''

"That's right," his mother said, getting up from her seat by the kitchen table. "Joan told me that. Just make sure we see you for at least a few hours."

"We will, Mom. Don't worry."

"Nice to meet you both," Lisa said as she and Ben left the kitchen.

Neither Ben nor Lisa said a word until they reached the second floor. "I'm sorry about bringing up your brother," Lisa finally said as they entered the guest room.

"It's okay," Ben said warmly. "It's been a while, so we can handle it."

"It must've been a painful loss."

Sitting on the white Formica desk in the corner of the room, Ben explained, "It was really terrible. He was diagnosed with childhood diabetes when he was ten. And that just led to complications when the leukemia came. He was a medical mess."

"How old were you when he died?"

"Fourteen," Ben said, propping his feet up on the chair below the desk. "It was the worst time in my life. I couldn't sleep for months—I had to start speaking to one of my dad's friends who was a family psychologist. My mother was a wreck. In fact, if it wasn't for my father, we'd probably all be in the nuthouse at this point. He really kept it together then."

"Your parents are great," Lisa said, sitting on the bed.

"They definitely are," Ben admitted.

"I'm just surprised you turned out as well as you did," Lisa added. "I mean, lassoing Earth's favorite satellite—that can make you a little nuts."

"Ho-ho. You're a riot."

Lisa kicked off her sneakers. "So tell me what happened with you and Eric on the plane. He didn't say a word the whole way here."

"Nothing. I told him off. I don't want to have to deal with his crap anymore."

"Good," Lisa said. "I was worried you were going to actually forgive him over time."

"No way," Ben said. "I love my friends. I'd do anything for any of them. I'd do anything for you. But life is too short to waste your time on assholes."

"I don't even think it's about being an asshole. I think his actions were a violation of your trust. As far as I'm concerned, that's the single worst thing you can do to a friend."

"Listen, you don't have to tell me. Between Rick and Eric, trust has been the Problem Virtue of the Year."

At noon the next day, Ben came down to the kitchen, where he saw Lisa and his mother talking. "Well, well, look who finally decided to join us," Ben's mother said as she cut vegetables for the following night's Thanksgiving dinner. Not fooled by Ben's recent shower and his close shave, she could see the still-tired look in her son's eyes. "What time were you two up until last night?"

"Probably around four," Lisa said.

Ben's mother dropped her knife on the cutting board and stared.

"Mom, calm yourself," Ben said, rolling his eyes. "We were just talking. Is that okay?"

"It's none of my business," his mother said. "I didn't say a word."

"You didn't need to." Turning to Lisa, he said, "How are you so awake?"

"I can't sleep late," Lisa explained. "I've been up since seven."

In mid-yawn, Ben stretched toward the ceiling. "You're crazy. Sleeping is the source of life."

Suddenly, the telephone rang. "Hello?" Ben's mother said, turning away from her vegetable slicing. Pausing for a moment, she responded, "Yes, he's right here. Hold on one second." She turned to Ben. "It's for you. It's someone named Rick."

The color drained from Ben's face. Surprised at her son's reaction, Ben's mother handed him the phone. Ben stretched the phone cord so that he was almost standing in the other room. "Hello?"

"Hey, Ben," Rick said. "How's everything at home?"

Pulling the cord even farther, Ben moved into the dining room. "What do you want?"

"Nothing," Rick said. "I just wanted to make sure everything was okay there. And I wanted to wish you and your family a lovely Thanksgiving. Is that okay?"

"No, it's not okay," Ben said, struggling to keep his voice low. "I'm hanging up the phone now. If you want to talk to me, call me when I get back to D.C. Otherwise, stay the hell away from my family."

"Ben, I just want you and your family to have an enjoyable Thanksgiv—"

Ben hung up the phone and forced a smile as he walked back into the kitchen.

"Is everything okay?" his mother asked. "Who was that on the phone? Who's Rick?"

"It's just a friend from the Court," Ben said. "We were having this argument about this case, and he wanted to talk about it. It's no big deal."

"Benjamin, don't lie to me," his mother said.

"Mom, I'm not lying!" Ben insisted. "It's this jerk from work that I always disagree with. It's fine. We'll work it out."

Before she could say a word, Ben was out of the room. "Lisa, c'mon!" he yelled from the front door.

Getting in his mother's car, Ben was silent, his lips pursed in anger. He was already inching the car out of the driveway by the time Lisa opened the door and jumped inside.

"Don't worry about stopping," Lisa said as Ben pulled out of the driveway. "I'm fine." Getting no response, she asked, "So what'd he say?"

"Nothing. He was just being an asshole."

"I assumed that," Lisa said. "Now tell me what he said."

"I really don't want to talk about it," Ben said. "I just want to enjoy myself today."

"Just tell me . . ."

"Please," Ben pleaded. "Let's just forget about it."

Lisa was silent until they turned onto the Massachusetts Turnpike. "Are you at least going to tell me where we're going?"

Taking a deep breath, Ben said, "First, we're going to Beacon Hill, where you will not only see some of our fair city's best architecture, but you will also partake in a Vito's upside-down pizza."

"An upside-down what?"

"We'll be eating at a restaurant called Vito's, where they serve two slices of pizza facing each other. Now stop ruining the story." Resuming his calm, narrating voice, he continued, "After that, we will walk through the Boston Common and into the heart of downtown."

"Are we going by the *Cheers* bar?"

"No, we are not going by the *Cheers* bar. This isn't the Freedom Trail. You'll see this city like a native. Naturally, that will mean that you'll miss the U.S.S. *Constitution,* the *Cheers* bar, Faneuil Hall, and all the other touristy nonsense that people love to snap pictures of, but you'll be a better person for it."

"I feel enlightened already."

"And if you're lucky, I'll show you my favorite spot in the whole city."

"We're going to the library?"

"I can stop the car anytime," Ben said.

"I'll be good. I promise," Lisa said, pulling an imaginary zipper across her lips.

At four-thirty that afternoon, Ben pulled the car into a small, graveled lot off Memorial Drive. Theirs was the only car in the tiny lot. Lisa looked around suspiciously. "If this is your old make-out place, I'm gonna be sick."

"It's not my old make-out place," Ben said, turning off the engine. "I told you, I'm bringing you to my favorite spot in the city. Did I lie to you about anything so far?"

"There were no skateboarders at Copley Square."

"It's freezing out," Ben said. "Besides that, though."

"The performers in Harvard Square sucked."

"The best ones come out at night. Besides that."

Thinking for a minute, she eventually said, "No, you have not lied about anything else."

"Then follow me," Ben said, getting out of the car. He walked against the cold wind that blew off the river and headed toward a narrow bicycle path that ran along the lot. The view from the concrete path was obstructed by a fence of aged and rotted wood currently covered with various spray-painted slogans. At a corner on the path, the wall ended, and Lisa could see that they were walking toward the Charles River. The walkway turned from concrete to wood, leading to a medium-sized boathouse next to the Charles. "This used to belong to Boston University," Ben explained. "It housed all the equipment for the crew team. All the schools have them up and down the river: Harvard, MIT, Boston College, Northeastern, they're all along here somewhere. And when B.U. raised enough money, they abandoned this shack for state-of-the-art headquarters closer to their campus." As he walked to the edge of the dock, he pointed to his right. "From here, we'll be able to see the sunset bathe the city in light. And that makes this the best spot in the city. The tour is finished. Tah-dah!" he said, turning around and taking a bow.

Lisa sat down and let her feet dangle off the edge of the dock. "You were right. This place is fantastic."

"Eric's older brother found it, and he showed it to us," Ben said, sitting next to Lisa. "This is where I was when I wrote my college essay to get into Columbia, and it's where I wrote my essay to get into Yale."

"We should've brought the *Grinnell* decision with us."

Ben glanced at his watch. "We'll be able to see the sunset in about twenty minutes."

"This city gets dark too early. It's only four-thirty."

"Wait until the dead of winter," Ben said. "It's pitch-black by four-fifteen. By having the country's earliest sunset, we also get the highest winter suicide rate."

"Now that's something to be proud of." Silent for the next few minutes, they waited for the sun to descend on Boston's gray horizon. When she saw Ben staring at her, Lisa raised an eyebrow. "You're thinking about kissing me, aren't you?"

"You wish," Ben said, drawing back.

"Oh, please," Lisa said. "You have that fawning look in your eyes."

"Lisa, I realize I've brought you to a magical place, but not all fantasies come true here."

"Don't pull that crap with me," Lisa said, pointing at Ben. "You have the same look you had the night we worked on the death penalty case."

"That severely-tired-so-my-exhaustion-is-mistaken-for-passion look? I think you're right—that's exactly the same look I had then."

"Forget it," Lisa said, shaking her head. "You're right. Let's just enjoy the sunset."

Leaning back on his elbows, Ben stared at the golden-orange hue that colored the top of the State House. After a few minutes, he asked, "Do you really think we'll be able to catch him?"

"I'm not sure," Lisa said, shrugging her shoulders. "I mean, I hope we can. He just always seems so prepared for us. Why?"

"Forget I asked." Ben sat up straight and brushed the dirt and pebbles from his hands. "Just drop it."

"C'mon, Ben. Is that your answer every time you get upset? Just tell me what you're thinking. I know you're scared shitless by this whole thing."

Ben was silent.

"And you ought to be."

"What do you want me to say?" Ben finally asked. "Of course I'm scared. My whole professional career is on the line. And at the one point when I'm finally calming down about it, the lowlife calls my house for no purpose except to unnerve me! Let's see, what else do you want to hear? That I have nightmares about it? That I can't get it out of my head? That I think I'm way out of my league? Washington is one thing, but it's different at home."

"How is it so different?" Lisa asked.

"My parents are here," Ben said. "That's it. Period. I don't want them involved in this."

"That's probably why Rick called," Lisa pointed out. "He knew it'd make you crazy."

"No? Really?" Ben said sarcastically. "And here I thought he was trying to establish a real friendship between us. After that nice ride in his limo, we have a ton of memories to look back and laugh about."

Lisa didn't respond.

"I'm sorry," Ben said, taking a deep breath. "Can we please start over?"

"Absolutely," Lisa said with a small smile. "So tell me; what'd Rick say?"

"He said he just wanted to wish me a happy Thanksgiving. I'm sure it's his way of saying, 'Don't forget what we talked about in the limo.' "

"We really should find him and beat the snot out of him," Lisa said, dangling her feet off the dock.

"You are so right," Ben said, leaning back on his hands.

"Y'know, if you ever want to talk about it, I'm an open ear."

"I appreciate it," Ben smiled. "Now, can we just enjoy the sunset?"

"Is everyone ready to eat?" Ben's mother asked at precisely seven the following evening.

"What about Dad?" Ben asked, putting out a pitcher of cold water and two bottles of soda.

"He called a little while ago. Someone slashed his back tires, so he's stuck at work."

"Slashed his tires? Is he okay?" Lisa asked.

"Do you want me to pick him up?" Ben asked.

"He's fine," Ben's mother said. "He said the tow truck would be there soon enough."

As Ben and Lisa took their places around the table, Ben's mother brought out a huge bowl of Caesar salad. "Pass me your bowls."

Suddenly, the door opened and Ben's father stepped inside. "Hi, everyone," he announced. He kissed everyone before sitting at the head of the table. "Good timing by me."

"That was quick," Ben's mother said.

"You won't believe what happened," Ben's father said, pulling off his tie. "Right after I called the towing company, I went outside to change the first tire. I figured that would save me time when they eventually came. Anyway, as I'm in the middle of putting on my spare, this guy drives up and notices that my other tire is flat. He offers me the spare in his car and even helps me put it on. And then when I offered to pay him, he said he couldn't take money for it—that it was Thanksgiving and all."

"What'd this guy look like?" Ben asked, hoping to sound casual.

"Blond hair, kind of preppy. Nothing special."

Lisa and Ben exchanged a look.

"Did he say anything else?" Ben tried to remain calm.

"Nope," Ben's father said, shoveling a mound of Caesar salad onto his plate. "He said he recognized me from my columns. And get this: He knew that you worked at the Supreme Court. He remembered that story Cary wrote about you—when you first got your clerkship."

As his palms grew slick with perspiration, Ben dropped his fork, which crashed against his plate.

"Are you okay?" Ben's mother asked.

Ben wiped his hands on his pants, picked up his fork, and quickly pulled himself together. "I'm fine. I just haven't eaten all day."

Surprised by the casualness of Ben's father's reaction, Lisa asked, "Are your tires slashed often?"

"Every once in a while. Whenever I write a column about corruption in the city government, my tires are slashed, my windows are shattered. That's the life of a columnist. Too many enemies."

"So this is probably no big deal," Lisa said, hoping Ben was listening.

"Not for me," Ben's father said proudly.

In no mood to hear Michael's speech about the life of a columnist, Ben's mother asked, "Anything else happen at work?"

"Not really," Ben's father said. "It was a pretty slow news day. Someone was shot downtown. There's a new police corruption exposé that's running tomorrow. And my son got engaged. Other than that, it was quiet."

"What?" Ben asked, snapping back into reality.

"Didn't you see today's paper?" Ben's father reached into his briefcase and pulled out a section of the newspaper. "It's on page twenty-seven," he said, handing it to Ben.

Opening the paper, Ben turned to the metro section. At the top of the first column was a large picture of Lisa. Underneath the picture, it said: "Margaret and Shep Schulman of Los Angeles announced the engagement of their daughter, Lisa Marie, to Benjamin Addison, son of Sheila and Michael Addison of Newton. A March wedding is planned." Ben yelled, "What the hell is this?"

"Let me see," Lisa said as she grabbed the paper. "Who would do this?"

"Idiot roommates," Ben whispered.

"Does this mean you're not getting married?" Ben's father asked.

"Oh, this is funny," Ben's mother said when Lisa passed her the paper. "Who did it? Ober? Nathan?"

"Who else?" Lisa said.

Ignoring his family's reaction, Ben couldn't get Rick out of his thoughts. "Ben, are you okay?" his father asked.

"Yeah, I'm fine," Ben said, turning to his father. Motioning toward the newspaper, he added, "I'm sorry about this. I didn't have a thing to do with it."

"No, it's fine," Ben's father said. "We like it when we're completely humiliated. Every self-respecting paper likes to be the victim of a mindless joke every once in a while."

"You didn't get in trouble for this, did you?"

"Of course not," Ben's father said. "But all day, people were asking me how come I didn't tell them you were engaged." As he finished his salad, he continued, "By the way, the president apparently has his short list to fill Blake's seat on the Court."

"Who's on it?" Ben asked, trying to put Rick out of his mind. "Kuttler. Redlich. Who else?"

"Your old friend Judge Stanley is rumored to be on it."

"It'll never happen," Ben said, waving his hand. "That's the fish he throws to the liberals. I'll bet a hundred bucks Stanley doesn't get it."

"Have you heard any rumors at the Court?" Ben's father asked.

"Nothing really feeds through there," Ben explained. "The president's staff calls some justices for recommendations, but that's just out of courtesy. Otherwise we hear what you hear."

"Oh, c'mon now," Ben's father said. "You work there. You must hear some rumors. Just this once—feed your dad some inside info."

"I said I don't know anything," Ben insisted. "And don't put me in that kind of position. Even if I did know something, I couldn't tell you."

"Relax," his father said. "I was only kidding."

"It was just a joke," Lisa said.

"Fine," Ben said, picking at his salad. "It was just a joke. I get it. Har har."

"Is everything okay at work?" Ben's mother asked.

"Everything's fine," Ben said. "Everything's wonderful."

"And what about that firm that's been recruiting you? Are they still interested?"

"Mom, everything is fine. I'm well on my way to the fast track of the legal world. Nothing can stop me. Now, can we just drop the subject?"

"No. What are you not telling me?" Turning to Lisa, Ben's mother asked, "What is he not telling me? You can tell me."

"Mom, leave Lisa alone," Ben demanded.

"Ben, there's no reason to raise your voice," Ben's father said.

"There is when she won't mind her own business," Ben said. "I said drop it."

"I don't need that tone at the table," Ben's mother said. "Either apologize or leave the room."

"Leave the room?" Ben asked, forcing a laugh. "Or what? You'll punish me? Spank me? Maybe you can take away my TV privileges. Or maybe I won't get a birthday party this year."

"Benjamin, I'd appreciate it if you'd excuse yourself from the table," his father said in a low voice.

Ben got up from his seat and stormed upstairs. "I'll be in my room."

At eight o'clock, the doorbell rang. "I'll get it," Ben's father said, pushing his chair away from the table. He opened the door and said, "Hey, fellas! C'mon in—we just reached dessert."

"Do I smell cretins?" Lisa asked, sniffing the air as Ober and Nathan approached the table.

"Hello, boys," Ben's mother said.

"Hello, Mrs. Addison," Ober said, fighting back a smile. "I hope you're all having a lovely Thanksgiving meal."

"We were," Lisa said.

"What brings you two over this evening?" Ben's mother asked.

"We just wanted to say hello. It's been so long since we've seen you or Mr. Addison," Ober said. "And, of course, we wanted to say congratulations on your son's engagement."

"That's right," Nathan said, patting Lisa on the back. "This is a big day for you. The best to you both."

"Very funny," Lisa said.

"Oh, c'mon," Nathan said. "Don't tell me you didn't find it funny—the big picture of you, the fake bio—it was genius."

"And it cost us almost a hundred bucks," Ober said.

"It was definitely funny," Lisa admitted. "I just hope you don't think there aren't going to be repercussions."

"Take it like a man," Ober said, squeezing in next to Lisa so that the two friends shared a seat. "Speaking of which, where is the groom-to-be?"

"He's up in his room pouting," Ben's mother explained.

Ten minutes later, Ober, Nathan, and Lisa walked into Ben's room. "Well, I guess my punishment's lifted," Ben said, sitting on his bed. "I have visitor privileges."

"Drop it already," Lisa said, flopping onto Ben's bed. "They just want to know what's bothering you."

"And if I want to tell them, I'll tell them," Ben shot back.

"Listen, don't get upset just because your parents are still treating you like a twelve-year-old," Lisa said. "That's what parents are supposed to do. It's their job. They can obviously tell something's wrong. Besides, you're kinda behaving like a twelve-year-old."

"Do you think Rick was the guy that approached my dad?" Ben asked. He explained the situation to Ober and Nathan.

"I don't know who it was, but I did think it was too much of a co-incidence," Lisa said.

"Why the hell is he doing this?" Ben asked.

"Why don't we stop talking about it?" Nathan suggested. "There's nothing we can do here, and there's nothing gained by watching you go crazy. When we get back, we'll sit down and plan a new strategy."

"But what if—" Ben began.

"Don't say it," Nathan interrupted. "Let's change the subject and move on."

"I have a new topic," Ober said, checking out the seven-year-old Albert Einstein calendar that was still attached to the wall. "Let's talk about why tomorrow is such a special day."

Ben thought for a moment, then said, "You are so damn pathetic sometimes."

"What?" Lisa asked, looking at Nathan.

"Tomorrow is the anniversary of the day Ober lost his virginity," Nathan explained.

"And I became the first of us to obtain that honor," Ober added, "which will forever annoy Grumpy here."

"Ben was about to do it with Lindsay Lucas," Nathan explained, "but since Ober wanted to be the first to lose it, he slept with Shelly Levine, the Skank Machine."

"You slept with her just to beat Ben?" Lisa asked.

"It wasn't just to beat Ben," Ober said. "I also wanted to get to know her better."

"He did it just to beat me," Ben said.

"And it's bothered him since," Ober said.

"You guys are sick," Lisa said. "You had a contest to see who had sex first."

"The only contest was in Ober's head," Ben said.

"But I pulled in the gold medal," Ober said. "Don't worry, though. Winning the silver is still nice."

"And what grade was this?" Lisa asked.

"Eleventh," the three friends said simultaneously.

"That's not that bad," Lisa said. "How about you, Nathan? When did you do the deed?"

"That's a pretty personal question," Nathan said. "When'd you lose yours?"

"I did it with Chris Weiss in tenth grade in his parents' bedroom. They were away for the weekend."

"All right! An early riser!" Ober said.

"Now, when'd you do it?" Lisa asked Nathan.

"Twelfth grade—" Nathan began.

"It was *after* twelfth," Ben corrected.

"It was the summer between twelfth grade and college," Nathan insisted. "Technically, that's still twelfth grade. And while it may be summer to us now, it was twelfth grade to me back then. It was me and Eleanore Sussman in a small hotel room down by the Jersey shore— my parents have a summer place there."

"Very tasteful," Lisa said. "Where'd you do it?" she asked Ben.

"Being the classiest of this trio, I took my date down to the B.U.

boathouse. With sleeping bags set up, we did it with style—under the stars and overlooking the city."

"And how about you?" Lisa asked Ober.

"Me and the Skank Machine went back to her house after a heavy night of drinking and did it in her very own, tastefully decorated bed-room."

"While her parents were in the next room," Ben added.

"They weren't," Lisa said.

"They didn't hear a thing," Ober said, sitting cross-legged on the floor.

"Speaking of great sex, why don't you have Ober tell you about the affair he had with his boss?" Nathan suggested.

"Absolutely." Ben started laughing. "That's a great—"

"It was not an affair," Ober interrupted. "It was a terrifying seduc-tion."

"It was an affair and you were a coward," Nathan said.

"Just tell the story," Lisa said.

"This all took place during Ober's brief stint as a public relations assistant," Ben explained.

"It was a P.R. boutique that specialized in the computer industry," Ober added.

"And Ober's supervisor," Ben continued in a deep, sexy voice, "let's just say that she specialized in *love*."

"Just get to the point," Ober begged. "She made a pass at me and I refused it. End of story."

"No, no, no," Nathan jumped in. "She made a pass at you, and you passed out."

"You what?" Lisa asked, laughing.

"She called him into her office and she was wearing nothing but a bra, underwear and black garters," Ben said. "Ober took one look at her and fell over unconscious."

"I was feeling sick all day," Ober explained dryly. "I got up too fast, and by the time I got to her office, I was lightheaded."

"More like intimidated," Nathan said.

"What'd she do when you passed out?" Lisa asked.

"I'm not sure," Ober said. "All I know is, when I woke up, she was fanning me with a file folder."

"But she was still undressed," Ben added. "Needless to say, though, she was turned off at that point. Fainting is the world's worst aphrodisiac."

"Can we move on to something else?" Ober asked.

"Oh, baby," Nathan said to Ben. "I really love your underwea—" Closing his eyes, Nathan fell to the floor.

"Wham, bam, unconscious, ma'am," Ben said.

"That's it. I'm out of here," Ober said. "If I wanted to be made fun of, I could've stayed home tonight."

"Can you drop me at home?" Nathan asked as Ober walked to the door.

Saying nothing, Ober left the room. "I'll take that length of silence as a yes," Nathan said, waving to Ben and Lisa. "See you guys later."

"See you later," Ben said as Nathan stepped out.

"You're so pathetic," Lisa said, poking Ben in the chest.

"What?"

"That place you took me to yesterday—the boathouse. You were trying to seduce me."

"Give me a break," Ben said. "I was doing no such thing."

Lisa squinted and in a low voice did her best Ben imitation. "Uh, I wrote my essay for Columbia here, and I wrote my essay for Yale here, and I lost—" Switching to a slightly deeper voice, she interrupted, "No, dumb-ass, don't tell her about the virginity thing—if she finds that out, she'll never go to bed with us."

"That's amazing." Ben laughed. "You've perfectly reproduced my exact thought process."

"It may not be exact, but it's close."

"Do you really believe that?" Ben asked.

"Am I wrong?"

"Do you really believe it?"

"Answer my question," Lisa said. "Tell me I'm wrong."

A deep flush spread over Ben's face. "I'm not saying you're completely right, but you're not on another planet."

"I knew it! You're so predictable."

"What are you talking about? I'm not predictable."

"Are you kidding me?" Lisa asked. "You're so predictable, I could set my watch to your—"

Before Lisa could finish her sentence, Ben leaned forward and pulled her into a deep, long kiss.

Surprised, Lisa pulled back a bit. "A kiss from Mr. Addison—I'm impressed. I didn't think you had it in you."

"Can you shut up?" Ben asked, kissing her again. As Ben wrapped his arms around Lisa, she pushed him backward onto the bed. Straddling him, Lisa furiously unbuttoned Ben's shirt.

". . . and let me tell you one more thing," Ober said, storming back into the room. "HOLY TONGUE-IN-HER-MOUTH, BATMAN!"

"I don't believe it," Nathan said.

"Do you mind?" Lisa said. "Some of us are trying to fool around."

"Oh, you will NEVER live this down," Ober warned, pulling the door closed, a wide smile spread across his face.

"What're you going to tell Lindsay Lucas?" Nathan called out as the door shut.

As his head fell back on the bed, Ben said, "Damn."

"Forget about it," Lisa said, leaning in and kissing his neck.

CHAPTER 11

"SO?" BEN ASKED.

"What?" Lisa asked, lying next to him.

"What'd you think?"

"About what?" Lisa said with a smile.

"About the fact that your clothes are decorating my floor. What else?"

"It was fine," Lisa said. "It was good."

Ben sat up in bed and shook his head. "Don't even think about playing that game with me, sister. You are *not* making me crazy with vague adjectives."

"What do you want me to say?" she asked. "It was phenomenal. World's greatest. You were an artist—I was your canvas."

"You suck, y'know that?"

"That's funny," Lisa said with a thin smirk. "You weren't complaining a half hour ago."

"It wasn't that great."

"Whatever you say," Lisa said, staring at the clothes that were thrown across the floor. Pointing to the corner of the room, she asked, "By the way, are those your lucky boxer shorts?"

"Luck had nothing to do with it."

"Awwww, did I upset you?" Lisa asked, running her fingers under Ben's chin.

"This was just dumb," Ben said, pulling away and leaning against the headboard of the bed. "I shouldn't have given you the satisfaction. Now all you're going to do is make sex jokes."

"Of course I'm going to make sex jokes," Lisa said. "That's my nature. What'd you think, we were going to start *going out*? That we'd be the sweethearts of the Court? This was for fun. I've been waiting to jump your bones since I met you."

"You're just saying that."

Lisa grabbed the back of his head and pulled him toward her. "I'm serious."

"But now the mystery's over."

"Listen, whenever you want to go again, I'm ready. I had a fantastic time."

"Oh, we're not going again. This was it," Ben said, pulling away. "Now we're going to feel uncomfortable around each other at work. And every time I see you, I'm going to imagine you naked."

"Big deal. I'm an adult. I can handle it. Besides, if you even think you can say no if I want to go again, you're nuts."

"You haven't seen the bounds of my willpower. Believe me, this was a one-time engagement."

"Whatever you say, dear," Lisa said, turning on her side and pulling the covers to her chin.

Early Sunday morning, the Addisons drove Ben and Lisa to the airport. Lisa hugged Ben's mother as Ben pulled their luggage from the trunk. "Thanks again for having me," Lisa said.

"It was our pleasure," Ben's mother said. "I'm glad we were finally able to meet you."

"I'll see you later, Mom," Ben said as he hugged his mother. Noticing the tears well up in her eyes, he added, "Don't cry. I'll see you soon."

"I'm fine," his mother said, clenching her jaw. "Have a safe trip back."

After checking their bags, Ben and Lisa walked toward their boarding gate. "Have you heard from Ober or Nathan yet?" Lisa asked.

"Nothing. Not a phone call or anything. They're definitely planning something."

When they arrived at the gate, Nathan, Ober, and Eric were waiting. Hesitantly, Ben approached his roommates. "How was everyone's weekend?"

"Fine," Nathan said.

"Great," Eric said.

"Fine," Ober said. "And yours?"

"It was fine," Ben said suspiciously. Looking around the airport, he stared back at Ober and Nathan. Finally, he said, "Okay, let's have it. Say whatever you want, but respond already. The suspense is killing me."

"Respond to what?" Ober asked.

"I know not of what you speak," Nathan said with a straight face.

"Don't give me that," Ben said. "C'mon, what'd you plan? Is someone going to pop out and throw rice at us? Is a marching band going to come parading through? What's happening?"

"Nothing's happening," Nathan said.

"Why's he getting so crazy?" Ober asked Nathan.

"I have no idea," Nathan said. "Looks like a classic case of paranoia to me."

After dropping Lisa at her apartment building, the four roommates returned home. The first one to reach the door, Ober pulled the pile of mail from their mailbox, dragged in his luggage, and threw the mail on the kitchen table. After dropping his bag by the closet, Eric walked back to the door. "I'll see you guys later. I have to go down to the paper."

The moment the door closed, Ober grabbed Ben's shoulders. "So how was she? I bet she's an animal in bed."

"You thought she was a lesbian," Ben said.

"I never said that," Ober said. "I said she was bisexual."

"Sure you did," Ben said.

Nathan sat on the couch. "I can't believe you guys did it. I mean, what were you thinking?"

"What do you mean by that?" Ben asked.

"I mean, I thought we had an understanding that after Thanksgiving, we'd make sure we could trust Lisa," Nathan said.

Standing in the middle of the room, Ben still hadn't taken off his jacket. "Don't start with that," he said. "I trust her."

"Ben, don't take this the wrong way, but I hope you're not letting a horny weekend get the best of you."

"Well, no offense, but I am going to take it the wrong way. I learned a lot about Lisa this weekend, and there's no way she's working with Rick against me."

"How do you know that?" Nathan challenged. "What additional information convinces you of that belief? You think that because you had sex you somehow know her better?"

"It's not just the sexual part. I know her better as a person."

"Ben, the only difference between this week and last week is that now you know what she looks like naked."

"That's not true," Ben said. "You weren't there this weekend, we had—"

"Stop talking about this weekend and listen to what I'm saying," Nathan said, rising from the couch. "For an intelligent person, you're being extremely stupid. If my theory's right, Lisa's doing exactly what she should be doing. Think about it! She's playing with both your heads!"

Silence swept the room. Ben walked over to the table and sorted through the pile of mail. Pulling out his own letters, he added, "At least Lisa is concerned with my problems."

"And what's that supposed to mean?" Nathan asked.

"It means that she spent the entire weekend talking with me about all this crap with Rick. All you guys did was waste your energy on stupid pranks."

"Now you're reaching," Nathan said. "You know how much time we've all invested in this. Both Ober and I have risked our jobs to catch Rick. And if that engagement announcement was anything, it was the best way we could think of to cheer you up. Besides, the only reason Lisa spends so much time talking to you is to see what you know."

"You don't know what you're talking about," Ben said, heading toward the stairs.

"Don't get upset and walk away," Nathan said. "Come back down here and deal with it."

Ignoring his roommate, Ben walked to his room.

"You should have known he was going to get defensive," Ober said when Ben was out of sight.

"Of course I knew he'd be defensive," Nathan said. "But tough shit. I'm looking out for him."

"I know what you're doing," Ober said, "but maybe you could have been more sensitive."

"*You* want *me* to be more sensitive?" Nathan laughed.

"I'm serious. Ben's really scared about this."

"Of course he's scared. I was the one who said it before Thanksgiving—sex will always interfere with rational thought. But it's time for Ben to wake up. He had his fun, and now it's time to face reality: Lisa can't be trusted."

"How was your trip?" Rick asked, talking into his cellular phone as he waited for his baggage at the airport carousel.

"Did you really have to follow us to Boston?"

"Of course," Rick explained. "I had to keep an eye on my investment."

"Well, I hope you're happy with the results. You've made him completely nuts."

"The thing with his father really freaked him out, huh?" Rick asked.

"That's the understatement of the year. Now he doesn't know who to trust."

"Does he suspect you?"

"I don't think so, but he's much harder to deal with. He barely spoke the whole way back."

Rick smiled and moved the phone to his other ear. "That's what happens when you know you're about to lose. You start taking it out on those closest to you."

When he entered his room, Ben threw the mail on his desk and slumped into his chair. It couldn't possibly be Lisa, he told himself, his thumbs tapping against the desktop in a disturbed drumbeat. Look at the facts. With everything you know about her, what are the chances she's some kind of double agent? No. It's impossible. There's no way.

As he replayed the details in his head, he turned the single, messy pile of mail into three more manageable stacks, creating one pile for bills, one for junk mail, and one for personal letters. Noticing a magazine offer addressed to Benjamin N. Addison, he knew that *Newsweek* had sold his name. Picking up another addressed to Benjamin L. Addison, he knew that the *Legal Times* had made some quick cash. When he saw one addressed to Benjamin C. Addison, he frowned, annoyed that his credit card company had done it, too. He'd specifically told them not to. As he made a mental notation to call the company, he noticed the top letter on the personal-letter pile. Picking up the plain white envelope, he was surprised to see that there was no return address, no stamp, and therefore no postmark.

Ben slid his thumb across the sealed flap, opened the envelope, and pulled out the short, typed letter. "Dear Ben: Hope your Thanksgiving was enjoyable—I'm sure I'll hear all about it. Sincerely, Rick."

Ben's heart beat faster as he reread the letter. He pushed himself away from the desk and left the room. Racing downstairs, he returned to the living room, where he saw Nathan hanging up the phone. "Who was that?" Ben asked.

"My mom," Nathan explained. "I just wanted to tell her we got home okay."

"This was hand-delivered while we were gone," Ben said, handing Nathan the letter. "There was no postage on the envelope." As Nathan read the short letter, Ober returned from the bathroom.

"What's up?" Ober asked.

Saying nothing, Nathan passed the letter to Ober, who quickly read it.

"Can I ask you a question in your office?" Ben asked, motioning Nathan and Ober toward the front door. Stepping outside, the three friends got into Nathan's car.

"When did you get that?" Nathan asked, slamming the car door shut.

"Just now," Ben said nervously. "What do you think about that last part? Where he says that he'll hear all about my Thanksgiving."

"You already know what I think," Nathan said. "If that's not a reference to Lisa, I don't know what is."

"I know. I know," Ben said. "But if he was in cahoots with Lisa, do you really think he'd blow her cover?"

"At this point, I think Rick is just playing with us," Nathan explained. "If he is secretly working with Lisa, he's enjoying the game. If he isn't plotting with her, he's got us worried by hinting that he is. Either way, he's playing on that fear, and either way, he's making us crazy. He obviously knows how much you care for her."

"Shit," Ben said, slouching down in the seat.

"Can I ask a question?" Ober said, leaning forward from the backseat. Without waiting for an answer, he asked, "Why are we in the car?"

Nathan shook his head. "Goofus, if Rick was close enough to hand-deliver a letter, and he knew we weren't home, chances are he took a stroll around our house."

"You think he broke in?" Ober asked.

"Why wouldn't he?" Ben said. "He knew he could look for any information we have on him. He could bug the house in complete privacy. He could do whatever he wanted. As far as I'm concerned, I wouldn't say another word in that house."

"So what do you want to do now?" Nathan asked.

"I think we really have to I.D. Rick—if we can get a photo and run it through the State Department, we'll be a lot closer to catching him."

"He obviously knew about our little photography plot," Nathan said.

"Exactly," Ben said. "So if I were him, I wouldn't risk another meeting with us until we hand him the decision. That means we're going to have to use a more unconventional way to find him." Sitting up in his seat, Ben continued, "All we really know about him is that he's between twenty-eight and thirty-eight years old, he's smart, and he knows what he's doing. Also, the way I figure it, Rick, if that's even his real name, has got to be a lawyer. He knows way too much about the law to be a layperson."

"Do they take your picture when you take the bar exam?" Nathan asked.

"That's exactly what I'm thinking," Ben said. "If we think about all the information we have on him, we can find someplace where he had his picture taken. And if we can find that picture, we should be able to I.D. him.''

"So what about the bar exam?''

"Some states don't take your picture,'' Ben said. "And I'm not sure if the Bar Association would even release the information.''

"What about driver's license photos?'' Ober asked.

"Too broad a category,'' Ben said. "Even if we knew what state he's from, it'd be too many people to search.'' While the three friends sat in the motionless car, they rubbed their hands together to keep warm. "I was thinking that if Rick is a lawyer, he had to go to law school. So his picture should be in a law school yearbook from the last ten to fifteen years. Since there are over a hundred law schools nationwide, there'd be too many to search, but I was thinking that we can limit our search to just the top dozen or so schools: Yale, Harvard, Stanford, Columbia, and so on. Rick's a snob—I'll bet he went to a top law school.''

"That's still a lot of photos to search through,'' Ober said.

"Not really,'' Ben explained. "If we take the top dozen schools and look only at the last fifteen years, that's only one hundred and eighty yearbooks. And there's an average of about four hundred students per class, so it's not that bad.''

"That's seventy-two thousand pictures,'' Nathan said, tapping his wrists against the steering wheel.

"Actually, it's only a little more than half of that,'' Ben said. "We don't have to look at the women.''

"What's this *we* crap?'' Ober asked. "You're the only one who can recognize him.''

"So I'll be looking through a lot of pictures,'' Ben said. "Do you have a better plan? If I can spot his picture, we'll have everything we need.''

"Can you even get all of the old yearbooks?'' Nathan asked.

"Of course,'' Ben said. "If I call a school and say that a Supreme Court justice would like to get some yearbooks, we'll have them by the end of the week. In law school, the justices are gods who walk among men.''

"Then that sounds like the best available option." Leaning forward on the steering wheel, Nathan added, "Now tell me what you think about the Lisa thing."

Ben stared at the letter in his hands. "I still don't think you're right, but at this point, I'm not taking any chances. I trust her, but I can live with leaving her out of the plan."

"That's all I ask," Nathan said. "The fewer people involved, the better."

Early Monday morning, Ben returned to the Court wearing his favorite blue suit, a freshly starched shirt, and his black wool overcoat. Although not as well rested as he'd hoped to be, he was relieved to be finished with the holiday. As soon as he was able to see a corner of the regal marble building, however, anxiety resurfaced. The Court was always a constant, and lately, so were Ben's problems. He made his way to his office, but paused before opening the door. Okay, he said to himself. Just play it cool with her. Nothing's changed; you're still friends, but you can't tell her about your plans with Rick. Worried that his face would reveal his distress, he shut his eyes and imagined Lisa naked. Fine, I'm calm, he thought as he opened the door. I'm a rock. I'm unshakable. Walking inside, he was not surprised to see Lisa, who always arrived before he did.

"Why the goofy grin?" Lisa asked as Ben sat down on the office sofa.

"Can't I just be happy to return to work? Is that so bad?"

"Don't give me that," Lisa said. "I've seen that look before. You're still thinking about Thanksgiving, aren't you?"

"Lisa, although you would like to believe that you are the center of my universe, I am sorry to say you are not. Besides, that look was a quiet-calm look. This look is a it's-nice-to-be-back look."

"That's not a nice-to-be-back look," she said. "It's your constipated-medicated-stare look."

"Constipation. Sex with you. Similar," Ben deadpanned.

"That was cute," Lisa said. "Easy, but effective." She leaned back in her chair. "By the way, since when are you so calm about our whole sex thing? I thought you didn't want to talk about it."

"I'm actually fine with it now. As long as it doesn't get in the way of things, I'll be fine."

"I'm fine with it as long as you're fine with it," she said. "So tell me what's going on. Have you thought about what you're doing with Rick?"

"No. Not really," Ben said, moving over to his desk. "I've been thinking more about writing *Grinnell* than I have been about that."

"Good." Lisa picked up a legal pad and followed Ben to his desk. "Because I've been thinking about all the ways to approach the dissent." Putting the note-filled pad in front of Ben, she explained, "Since Veidt won't go all the way with the Osterman crowd, I think we can really limit their decision to these facts. They'll say Grinnell is suffering a disproportionate burden, but we can say this applies only in rare cases involving certain historic monuments—that way we'll—"

"Whoa, whoa, whoa," Ben said, trying to calm Lisa. "Relax a second. First I want to know when Hollis wants the decision."

"I got a note saying he wants our first draft done within the next ten days, and he wants the whole thing done before Christmas. They plan to announce the decision before the New Year."

"That gives us three weeks to get it done," Ben said, "assuming that he'll want his usual week to pass it around to the other justices."

"Fine," Lisa said. "Let's get started."

"*I* plan to get started," Ben said, picking up his own legal pad. "But if *you'd* like to suddenly be in charge of first drafts, be my guest."

"Oh, don't give me that sarcasm. I'm sorry if I crossed your intellectual line in the sand by giving you some suggestions."

"All I'm saying is that since we've been here, I've been the one to formulate the attack. Then you get to punch holes in it and patch things up. And at this point, I'm not ready to write the *Grinnell* attack. Before I put a thing down on paper, I need to spend at least two days in the library researching background information for this case. I'm sorry if you're all ready to write it off the top of your head, but that's not how a good decision is written. This isn't high school debate."

"Don't pick a fight with me over this. Now can we talk about the opinion?"

"Hello? Have you been listening?" Ben asked. "I just said I don't want to do that."

"Well, I want to," Lisa said.

"Why? So far, we've never done it that way. Why are you suddenly so obsessed with it now? It's just another opinion."

"Yeah, but this is the first decision we're writing where you think the other side is right," Lisa said.

"So that's what this is about?" Ben asked, raising an eyebrow. "You actually think I'm going to weaken our dissent so I can have a personal victory?"

"I didn't say—"

"You don't have to say it. I can see it on your face. You really think I'd do that, don't you?"

"You don't know what I'm thinking," Lisa said, walking back to her desk. "I just feel very strongly about this decision, so I'd like to take special care with it."

"Don't lie to me, because . . ."

"Ben, don't threaten me!" She threw her legal pad on her desk. "If you want to be a control freak on this one, go ahead. Be my guest."

Later in the week, Ben went to Mailboxes & Things to check his P.O. box. He was relieved to see that Rick's phone bills had finally arrived. When he turned over the envelope to open it, he saw a small note written on the back: "Hope these help. Rick."

"Damn," Ben whispered to himself. He tore open the envelope and pulled out the copies of Rick's bills. After scanning through them, he put the copies back in the envelope and returned to the Court. Relieved that his office was empty, he picked up the phone and dialed Nathan's number.

"Administrator's Office," Nathan answered.

"I just picked up Rick's phone bills."

"They took long enough," Nathan said. "What'd they say? Anything helpful?"

"Of course not," Ben said, flipping through the small pile of bills. "It's exactly what we thought. He must've had a cell phone for all his personal calls because the only calls on here are to my home number, my work number, and to operator assistance."

"He's definitely organized," Nathan admitted.

"I'm telling you," Ben said, tossing the bills on his desk, "I'm really worried that we'll never be able to find him."

"Don't say that. He's smart, but he can't be that smart."

"I used to think that, but I think he may be that smart."

"Don't get down on yourself. You ordered the yearbooks, didn't you?"

"I did it yesterday. They'll be here next week at the latest, which—" Suddenly, Lisa entered the office. Ben grabbed the phone bills and slid them into his desk drawer. "No, I definitely agree," he said to Nathan. "Ober gets pissed whenever we forget his birthday."

"Did Lisa just walk in?" Nathan asked.

"Oh, yes. Absolutely," Ben said. "That's why we should pretend we forgot it this year."

"Do not say a single word to her."

Looking at Lisa, Ben said, "Nathan says hi."

"Hey," Lisa said.

"She says hi back," Ben relayed. "Meanwhile, I have to go. Justice and righteousness call." Hanging up the phone, he turned to Lisa. "What's going on?"

"Nothing really," Lisa said. "You guys planning Ober's birthday?"

"Yeah," Ben said. "He gets pissed if we forget it, so we're all going to pretend we forgot it. Then we'll take him out to dinner or something."

"Wish him a happy birthday for me."

"I definitely will," Ben said as he fidgeted with some paper clips.

"Meanwhile, have you heard about the nomination?" Lisa walked over to Ben's desk and leaned on the corner. "Rumor has it that Kuttler's going to be the president's nominee."

"Says who?" Ben asked.

"Says Joel, who heard it directly from Osterman. Apparently, the president called Osterman as a courtesy. It's going to be announced tomorrow."

"If it is true, that's just sad. Kuttler's a poor choice."

"Why? Just because he's not a legal genius like you?"

"He doesn't have to be a legal genius, but I do expect him to be above the mean."

"Oh, c'mon. He's not an idiot."

"Of course he's not an idiot. But he's nothing special. He's okay. Average. Blah. A mop. A sieve . . ."

"I got it."

"You know what I mean, though. He's obviously bright, but I think that Supreme Court justices should be the absolute top of their field. They should be the most cutting-edge legal thinkers of their time."

"Well, welcome to reality, but the political process says otherwise. Unless you're confirmable, it doesn't matter what you scored on the I.Q. test." Lisa stood up from the corner of Ben's desk and headed back to her own. "What's wrong with you lately? You're constantly whining."

"I'm just having a bad day."

"Well, don't take it out on me," Lisa said. "It's not my fault."

Early the following morning, Ben walked downstairs to grab a quick breakfast. As soon as Ben entered the kitchen, Nathan asked, "Have you seen today's paper?"

"No," Ben said, pouring himself a bowl of cereal. "What happened? Eric write another story about me?"

"Close," Nathan said as he handed the front page of the paper to his roommate. The lead story's headline read: KUTTLER GETS THE NOD; PRESIDENT PICKS NOMINEE. Eric's name was on the byline.

"How'd he know about this?" Ben asked.

"It's no big deal," Nathan said casually. "Every paper carried the story. Apparently, the information was leaked last night."

When Ben saw a similar headline on *The Washington Post,* he breathed a small sigh of relief.

"I'm just impressed they let Eric cover such a big story," Nathan said.

"It *is* the Supreme Court," Ben said. "That's his specialty."

"Give him a break. He's been keeping his distance for the last month."

"Nathan, I'm not joking around with this. He's not getting a break, and my deadline still stands. If Eric doesn't move out by the New Year, I will. Either way, one of us is out of here."

"And who's going to pay for his part of the rent?"

"We can either find a new roommate or I'll pay for it myself."

"You'd actually pay double the rent, just so you wouldn't have to look at him? Are you sure that's the best solution?"

"What do you expect me to do? Give him a big hug and tell him all is forgiven? It's not happening. If this were a silly little spat between friends, that's one thing, but Eric went way beyond that. He—"

"Listen, I don't need the speech," Nathan interrupted. "I'm on your side. Ober's really upset by this and *he's* on your side. If you want Eric out of the house, that's your decision. I just want you to consider all your options." Flipping through the newspaper, Nathan asked, "Have you ever stopped to think what Eric might do back to you if you do make him move out?"

"What are you talking about?" Ben asked in disbelief.

"I'm just saying that if you made me move out, I'd be pretty pissed at you. Maybe I'd even write another story about you for revenge."

"I dare him to write another story," Ben said, seething. "I'd rip his head off. And then I'd—"

"Calm down," Nathan said. "He hasn't written anything. It was just a hypothetical."

Ben took a sip of his juice. "You don't really think he'd do that, do you?"

"If he did it once . . ."

"Are you telling me I should make up with him just so he doesn't hurt me further? Are you absolutely nuts?"

"I didn't say make up with him. I just think you should watch your back."

Ben waved hello to Nancy, Hollis's secretary, as he walked through her office on his way to his own. "Hi, Ben," Nancy smiled back. Nancy had worked for Hollis for almost twenty years. She'd been with him when he was a judge on the D.C. Circuit, and she was one of the five people in his office the day he found out about his nomination to the Court. A matronly woman with graying brown hair, Nancy would probably work for Hollis until the day he retired. As far as she was concerned, there was no more exciting job in the world.

Nancy picked up a large envelope from the corner of her desk and held it out for Ben. "This just came for you. By messenger—must be important."

"Thank you," Ben said, and headed for his office. Before he took off his coat, he ripped open the package. Inside was the current edition of the *Washington Herald*. Eric's byline was circled in red. Next to it was a handwritten message: "Still trust him?"

Asshole, Ben thought. Never lets me forget he's around. Ben tossed the newspaper in the garbage and saw a pink message sheet with Lisa's handwriting on it taped to his computer screen: "Call the Marshals Office. ASAP." He pulled the message from his computer, crumpled it up, and added it to the garbage. Taking a quick glance at the Court's telephone directory, he dialed. "Hi, this is Ben Addison, with Justice Hollis's chambers."

Seconds later, Carl Lungen, the chief marshal, was on the line. "Hello, Ben. How're you doing?" he asked.

"I'm fine," Ben said, struggling to remain calm. "What's happening there?"

"Nothing much," Lungen said. "I just happened to see that your roommate had another scoop, and it reminded me that we haven't spoken in a while."

"Listen, you know I didn't have a thing to do with that story," Ben shot back, raising his voice. "Every paper in the country carried it today."

"I didn't say you had anything to do with it," Lungen said. "I just said it made me think about you. The last time we spoke, you promised that you'd come see us after you confronted Eric."

"I never promised you that," Ben said. "Fisk asked me if I'd come. I said I'd think about it. Now, I don't mean to be abrupt, but is there anything else you want to talk about? I'm really busy here."

"Actually, we were wondering what happened with Eric."

As Lisa entered the room, Ben said, "Eric and I aren't talking anymore. He had no excuse for his actions, so I told him to fuck off. All he could say was that he wanted to help his career. Any more questions?"

"There was no other explanation for his actions?" Lungen asked.

Ben wrote the word "Marshals" on a scrap piece of paper and

passed it to Lisa. "If there was, he didn't tell me," Ben said. "Anything else?"

"One last thing," Lungen said. "We wanted to take you up on your offer to take that lie detector test."

Ben froze in his chair. "I don't see any reason why—"

"It's just precautionary. You know we're trying to keep this investigation low-key, so we haven't notified the justices yet. If you don't, though . . ."

"I'll take the test."

"Great," Lungen said. "We scheduled it for the twenty-third. Is that okay?"

"Sure. That's fine," Ben said. "That'll be fine."

"Great. We'll see you down here in two weeks. Say hello to Justice Hollis for me."

Ben hung up the phone and stared at his desk.

"What's wrong?" Lisa asked. "What'd they want?"

"They saw Eric's story about Kuttler's nomination, and they want me to take a lie detector test."

"No way," she said, throwing the scrap paper at Ben. "That was in every paper in the country. The announcement ceremony is today. The White House leaked it late last night so they could get two days of press out of it."

"Tell that to the marshals."

"They can't make you take a lie detector test," Lisa insisted. "It's a violation of privacy."

"Well, they scheduled it for the twenty-third. And I'm going to be there to take it."

"Why?"

"I have to take it," Ben said, rearranging a stack of papers on his desk. "If I don't, they'll tell Hollis everything they know, which'll definitely get me thrown out of here. And even if they're just bluffing about telling Hollis, if I don't take it, they'll be more suspicious than ever."

"I'll tell you when they'll be suspicious: when you fail the test."

"I won't fail the test," Ben insisted. "Those tests are beatable. That's why they're not admissible in court. They're not foolproof. At this point, I may've done something wrong, but I didn't do anything maliciously against the Court. If I keep a cool head, I bet I can pass it."

"If you say so," Lisa said, shaking her head. "But, I still think—"

"You know what? I just don't want to talk about it anymore."

"But—"

"I said drop it," Ben demanded, refusing to look at his co-clerk. "I'll deal with it."

Later that evening, Ben returned home covered in the first snow of the year. Wiping frozen clumps of hair from his eyes, he searched for the key to his front door and unlocked it.

"Put your stuff down, we're going out!" Ober shouted as he threw on his coat. Getting no reaction from Ben, Ober stopped and searched Ben's face. "What's wrong with you? You look like crap."

"Thanks." Ben dropped his briefcase on the floor and let his jacket slide from his arm.

"Tough day on the job, dear?"

"Terrible day," Ben said, undoing his tie and unbuttoning his collar. "The decision we're working on still isn't done. The Marshals Office is making me take a lie detector test. Rick's on the loose. I can't trust Lisa. My life is a mess."

"They're making you take a lie detector test?" Nathan asked. "They can't do that."

"I know they can't, but they'll tell Hollis if I don't."

"No offense, but are you coming with us or not?" Ober asked. "Nathan got promoted today and all we're doing is moping around here."

"You got the S/P job?" Ben asked. Nathan smiled. Ben gave him a bear hug. "Congratulations!"

"You are now looking at the newest member of the secretary of state's policy planning staff," Ober explained. "Whatever that is."

"From now on, I get to muck with all the major policy work that comes through our department," Nathan said.

"That is unbelievable!" Ben said. "I knew you'd get it. I hope you got a bigger office."

"Bigger office, bigger computer, slightly bigger salary."

"What more can you ask for?" Ben said. "And now I feel like a schmuck—here I was complaining when you had good news that you were waiting to tell me."

"Don't worry about it," Nathan said.

"Enough of this friendship crap," Ober said. "Let's go out and cel-ebrate!"

Ben ran to his room and changed into jeans and a chocolate-brown henley. "Where are we going?" he asked as he walked downstairs.

"Guess," Ober said.

"Are we really going there?"

"Hey, it's my promotion," Nathan said. "Now, c'mon, it closes at eight."

When the three friends arrived at the Smithsonian's National Air and Space Museum, they stepped through the large plate-glass doors and into the heart of the building. Within a minute, they were all gazing up at the Milestones of Flight exhibit. Among the collection of aero-dynamic marvels suspended from the roof were the Wright brothers' original flyer, the *Spirit of St. Louis*, and Nathan's favorite, *Glamorous Glennis*, the first airplane to fly faster than the speed of sound.

"How many flights did the Wright brothers take that first day?" Ben asked, reading a short exhibit card about the Wright brothers' first flight.

"Four," Nathan said.

"What was the day?"

"December seventeenth, 1903."

"Who flew first?"

"Orville flew first for twelve seconds," Nathan said, his eyes still fixed on the ceiling. "But Wilbur flew the longest with fifty-nine seconds."

"I still don't understand why you're so into this stuff," Ben said, looking at a replica of *Sputnik I*. "You have no science background, your father isn't in the military, your—"

"Can't you simply appreciate the wonders of technology?" Nathan asked. "Can your legal mind even comprehend such a thought? We're in the midst of science's greatest feat—escaping the bounds of our existence."

Ober walked over to an authentic moon rock brought back by the *Apollo 17* crew and rubbed the pale gray object. "This rock is so fake. It isn't from the moon."

"And you base this hypothesis on what?" Nathan asked. "Your vast knowledge of interplanetary geology?"

"It doesn't feel real," Ober explained. "It feels like it's completely fake." Turning around to the crowd of tourists that were walking near the exhibit, Ober announced loudly, "THIS ROCK IS FAKE! IT'S A HOAX!"

Putting his hand over the mouth of his roommate, Nathan said, "Can you be more embarrassing? What're you, ten years old?"

"He's twelve," Ben said. He rubbed the moon rock for himself and added, "It really doesn't feel real. It seems synthetic or plastic or something."

"See, I told you," Ober said.

"It's a real moon rock," Nathan insisted. "Read the sign. It was brought back by the crew of the *Apollo Seventeen*. It's nearly four billion years old."

"Maybe the real rock was radioactive, and when it killed a bunch of tourists, they replaced it with this smooth piece of junk," Ober said.

"I refuse to have this conversation," Nathan said. "The only reason it's smooth is because millions of goofball tourists like you feel the need to touch it."

Touching it one more time, Ober said, "It's so obviously not real. I want my money back."

Would you like to go to the next exhibit?" Nathan asked. "Is that what you're telling me?"

"I'm starving," Ober said. "I just want something to eat."

The roommates walked to the east end of the building and entered The Flight Line cafeteria. After filling their trays with premade sandwiches and plastic-wrapped desserts, they chose one of the cafeteria's empty tables. "Tell me about the lie detector. When do you have to take it?" Nathan asked.

"Two weeks from now."

"What if you fail it?"

"I have no idea," Ben said, unwrapping his roast beef sandwich. "I assume that won't be a good thing, but they never said what would happen. I don't think they'll fire me on the spot, but I don't think it'll help my case. My main concern is that they don't tell Hollis. If it gets to him, he'll never trust me with anything."

"I don't understand why they picked today to call you. Was it because of Eric's story?"

"Of course," Ben said. "They said it reminded them that we hadn't spoken in a while."

"And I guess you haven't told Eric that."

"Absolutely not," Ben said. "He might write another story about it. All I have to do now is figure out a way to pass the test."

"Ben, I know I've asked this already," Ober asked, his voice uncharacteristically serious, "but are you sure you want Eric to move out?"

"You know how I feel," Ben said. "Let's leave it at that."

"But what if he—"

"The tests are beatable," Nathan interrupted, shooting Ober a look. "I'm sure of that. I saw a special on PBS about how the military gives soldiers special drugs that lets them beat them. It somehow calms their heart rates."

"I heard that if you remain calm and focus yourself, you can definitely beat it," Ben said. "The common criminal usually panics."

"But white-collar criminals like yourself can usually keep it together?" Nathan asked.

"That's really funny," Ben said. "You're a laugh riot."

"Maybe you can get those military drugs through the State Department," Ober suggested to Nathan. "Now that you're a big shot there, you should be able to get anything."

"I can definitely try," Nathan said. "It can't hurt to ask." Taking another bite of his burger, he said, "So, did Lisa say anything about this?"

"Can you stop with Lisa?" Ben pleaded. "Ever since we've been back from Thanksgiving, it's been impossible dealing with her. When she asks me about anything, I clam up."

"I told you it was a bad idea to have sex with her," Ober said, shaking his head.

"This has nothing to do with the sex part. We're both perfectly fine with that. I just feel like an asshole for lying to her. Maybe you can't understand, but Lisa's a good friend of mine. I know you don't trust her, but honestly, I do.''

''So go ahead and tell her whatever you want,'' Nathan said. ''Sleep with her every night. Dig yourself deeper. You're a grown man; it's your choice. I just want you to face reality.''

''Listen, I'm not complaining. I'm just saying it's uncomfortable to lie to someone's face.''

''Well, you better get good at it. You have a date with a lie detector in two weeks.''

Ignoring the light snow that melted on the car's front windshield, Rick watched the entrance to the Air and Space Museum. ''What's taking them so long?''

''I'm sure they're just looking around. Now get back to the real question: Are you sure you can get the decision?''

''Don't worry about it,'' Rick said, turning on the defroster. ''We'll definitely get it. My source tells me—''

''I wish you'd stop relying on this source. Simply being close to Ben doesn't mean a thing. We need—''

''Trust me, I know exactly what we need. And if we don't get the decision from our source, we can always get it from Ben. I should be meeting with him sometime next week—I'm just waiting for him to get back to me.''

''How do you know he'll agree to meet with you?''

Watching Ober, Nathan, and Ben leave the museum, Rick grinned. ''I know Ben. Given the opportunity to catch me, he can't resist. He values his career too much to let me walk all over it. Besides, even if he can't catch me, how many people can say no to a three-million-dollar finder's fee?''

CHAPTER 12

AT NOON THE NEXT DAY, BEN LEANED ON THE FILE CABINETS in the corner of the room, waiting for his first draft of the *Grinnell* dissent to roll out of the printer. Anxious to hand the opinion over to Lisa, he knew she would have to find it impressive. Wait until she sees it, he thought as the first page crawled out. This dissent is so strong, she won't know what to do with herself. First, apologies will flow freely. She'll beg for my forgiveness. She'll swear that she'll never doubt me again. Clearly, she'll say, "You are the superior writer." She'll then rip off her clothes and lie naked on the desk.

As Ben smiled to himself, Lisa burst through the door carrying two medium-sized boxes. She put them on the sofa. "Where were you? You missed the anniversary party for Blake."

"Big deal," Ben said, grabbing another sheet from the laser printer. "I couldn't care less that he's spent ten years on the Court. Besides, I really wanted to finish *Grinnell.* I was close to the end and I didn't want to stop the flow of genius that was oozing out of me and into my computer." As Lisa walked back to her desk, Ben asked, "What'd Blake do, anyway? Shake hands and thank everyone for their support?"

"Basically. But it was really nice. All the justices were there, and all the clerks and support staff. It was only about a half hour, but it was nice." Putting on her reading glasses, she added, "And you missed the inevitable confrontation between Osterman and Kovacs."

"Did they really go to blows?" Ben asked, curious about the rumored hatred between the ultra-conservative Osterman and the semi-liberal Kovacs.

"Nothing happened, but they're the only two who never talk to each other. And Joel told me that when Kovacs was originally appointed to the Court, Osterman greeted him by saying, 'I hope you realize you have a great deal of reading ahead of you.'"

"Stop it."

"I'm not joking," Lisa said. "It was obviously a crack at Kovacs's intelligence."

"And what'd Kovacs say back?"

"I have no idea. That's all Joel said."

"It's just so silly," Ben said. "Some of these justices are almost seventy years old and they still behave like children. They're like little kids in a sandbox."

"That's the way it works," Lisa said as she sat at her desk. "The old justices haze the new justices. It's like a geriatric fraternity. The newest justice gets the worst office, the worst seat on the bench, the worst section of seats reserved for their family. Even when the justices meet in Conference, the lowest-ranking justice is the one who has to answer the phone if it rings and answer the door if anyone knocks."

"That's not true, is it?"

"It's definitely true. Go down to the basement bookstore. It's written in all the books about the Court."

"I can't imagine it—justices hazing each other." In a deep voice, Ben imitated Osterman and barked, "Hey, Kovacs, I want my chambers cleaned and dusted before oral args tomorrow! And if you're not done, you're not getting the *Mirsky* dissent! Do you understand me?"

"Yes, sir, Mr. Osterman, sir!" Lisa said.

"What'd you call me?" Ben yelled.

"Yes, sir, Mr. *Chief Justice* Osterman, sir!" Lisa screamed.

Ben pulled another sheet from the laser printer. "I guess I can see that."

"Meanwhile, are you really finished with *Grinnell*?"

"It's right here," Ben said as the final sheet rolled out. He slapped the thirty-page document on Lisa's desk. "Hot off the press."

"By the way, those boxes came for you," Lisa said, pointing to the sofa. "There are seven more waiting in reception, but I couldn't carry them all."

Ben pulled his keys from his pocket and sliced open one of the boxes. Inside was a Columbia University Law School yearbook. Without saying a word, Ben closed the box and returned to his desk.

For the next half hour, he watched Lisa read his first draft, hoping to see a hint of reaction in her face. She'll be a fool if she doesn't like it, he thought. When she turned over the final sheet of the decision, Ben asked, "So? What do you think?"

"It's an excellent opinion," Lisa said as she put her reading glasses on the desk. "I'm definitely impressed. The fourth section is phenomenal. Pointing out the logical repercussions of the majority opinion is definitely the best way to shred it. Blake is going to be so pissed when he reads it."

"So I was right."

"Yes, yes. You were right. I'll never doubt you again, Master-of-All-That-Is-Clerking." Lisa pointed to the boxes on the couch. "Now what'd you get?"

"It's nothing."

"Just tell me what it is," Lisa said, moving toward the box.

Ben hopped out of his seat to stop her. "It's private," he said, holding the box closed. "No offense, but I don't want to talk about it."

"What's in it? A severed head? Sex toys? What's the big secret?"

"Leave it alone!" Ben pushed Lisa's hands away from the box.

Surprised by the intensity of Ben's objection, Lisa stepped away from her co-clerk.

"I'm sorry," Ben said. "I just don't want you touching it."

"If you don't trust me, say it to my face."

"Lisa, it's not that, I just—"

"Don't bullshit me. It insults both my intelligence and yours. It obviously has something to do with Rick. What else can be that important?"

"It has nothing to do with Rick."

"Then show me what's in the box."

"Lisa, I can't. I—"

"Ever since we got back from Thanksgiving, you've been acting creepy around me. I know it's not the sex—I give you more credit than that. But it's clear that you're hiding something."

"What am I hiding?" Ben asked.

"It's just the way you act. You're just . . . different. I can't explain it. It's some kind of Walden-like withdrawal. And then, when I walked in on your phone call last week, you said you were planning Ober's birthday party. When I first met Ober, he told me he was born in the summer. He was complaining that summer birthdays suck because everyone always forgets them, and you don't get any presents. Ben, in case you didn't realize, it's now December." Lisa stared at her co-clerk in silence.

"It's not that I don't trust you."

"Then tell me what's in the box."

"What?"

"You heard me. If you trust me so much, tell me what's in the box."

Ben reluctantly pulled open the carton. "They're just old yearbooks. I was hoping that if I could pick out Rick's picture, I'd have a better chance of identifying him."

Tapping her foot against the floor, Lisa looked like she was ready to explode, her face crimson with anger. She pulled her wallet from her desk drawer, stormed to the closet, grabbed her coat, and opened the door.

"Lisa, I didn't mean—"

She left the office, slamming the door behind her.

At eight that evening, Ben pounded on the front door of his house. "Open the door!" he yelled. Struggling to carry four boxes full of yearbooks, Ben felt his grip slipping. "Hurry up!"

"Hold on!" Nathan called out as he rushed to the door. "I'm coming!"

When Nathan opened the door, Ben staggered into the house and dropped the boxes on the couch. "There are a few more in the taxi. Can you help me carry them?"

Braving the cold without a jacket, Nathan ran to the taxi waiting in front of their house. He pulled three of the five boxes from the trunk of the car and ran back to the house, followed by Ben. Once inside, he said, "I assume these are the yearbooks."

"Most of them," Ben said as he took off his coat. "We're still missing Harvard's and Michigan's."

"I saw Blake's anniversary party on the news. Were you there for it?"

"No, I missed it," Ben said. "I was too busy getting reamed by Lisa. She was pissed because she finally realized I wasn't telling her about Rick anymore."

"How could she realize that?"

"Because she's smart," Ben said. "Unlike those grunts at the State Department, I work with brilliant, deductive people. When she saw the yearbooks, she realized things were going on without her, and she got a tad irate with me."

"So you told her about the yearbooks?"

"I had to. I thought it was the only way to show her I trusted her."

"And that didn't work?"

"Are you kidding? Now she has concrete proof I was hiding stuff."

"And so now the one person we don't trust not only knows about our newest plan but is also intensely mad at you?"

"That sums it up," Ben said. "Not a bad day at work, huh? Tomorrow, I think I'm going to smash a few mirrors to see if things can possibly get worse."

Ober walked through the door. "I have the single best idea for a new restaurant!" he announced. "Better than Tequila Mockingbird!"

"Looks like you don't have to wait until tomorrow," Nathan said.

"Here's the idea," he said, throwing his jacket on the dining room table. "It'll be the world's first non-Jewish delicatessen." As his arms flailed through the air, he explained, "There are way too many Jewish delis, and they all serve the same thing. But there are millions of people who don't want the typical pastrami and roast beef on rye. So I'm going to open 'Christ, That's a Good Sandwich,' the world's first non-Jewish deli. Every sandwich will be served on white bread, and everything comes with your choice of mayo or cheese. It'll be a gold mine!" Rubbing his hands together, he said, "If you guys want, you can be initial investors."

"Maybe you can get a cooperative crossover deal with Wonder bread," Nathan said.

"That's not a bad idea," Ober agreed. Noticing the sullen expression on Ben's face, he asked, "What's wrong with you?"

"Lisa found out that we were planning against Rick without her, and now she thinks we don't trust her."

"She's right," Ober said. "We don't."

"She also won't speak to Ben anymore. She hates him and wishes he'd disappear."

"Awwww, don't let that get you down." Ober sat next to Ben. "Lots of women hate me. It's not that bad."

"Why are you in such a good mood?" Ben asked, staring at his roommate. "I haven't seen you this manic since you ate that whole bottle of Flintstone vitamins."

"I'm just happy," Ober said, putting his arm around Ben. "I have good friends, a good home, a good job—" Ober noticed the boxes that covered the small couch. "Are those the yearbooks?"

"Those're them," Nathan said. "The proverbial straws that broke Lisa's back."

"I really wouldn't worry about her." Ober turned back to Ben. "You guys are good friends. You'll make up soon."

"It'll be fine," Nathan agreed. "I mean, look at you and Eric. You guys are making improvements by leaps and bounds."

An hour later, a large tomato and garlic pizza was delivered to the house. After everyone had grabbed a slice, the roommates turned their attention to the yearbooks scattered around the living room.

Dressed in gray sweatpants and a black-striped T-shirt, Ober sat with his feet up on the sofa. "I don't even understand why we have to do this," he moaned, staring at an old Stanford Law School yearbook. "I have no idea what Rick looks like. I've never seen him before."

"Just keep flipping," Ben said. "I told you what he looks like. He has a really thin head and permanent bags under his eyes."

"That's half the people in here," Ober complained. "No offense, but lawyers aren't the physical gems of society."

"You're looking because I need your help," Ben said. "If you see someone that fits the description, highlight their name. That way, there's less of a chance that I'll overlook them when I go through it."

"But you still have to look through them yourself," Ober said.

"Just shut up and look," Nathan said.

"These people are all starting to look the same," Ober said two hours later. "Every class is the same: bald guy, ugly guy, ugly girl, bald guy, ugly girl, bald girl."

"They're certainly not a pretty bunch," Nathan agreed.

"I think we should have a contest," Ober said. "The person that finds the ugliest picture wins."

"What do you win?" Ben asked.

"It doesn't matter," Nathan said, sitting up on the couch. "I just won. Take a look at this freak."

Passing the book to Ober, Nathan pointed to a picture of Ben from his days at Yale Law School. "Look at you," Ober said. "What'd you comb your hair with that morning? A rake?"

"It definitely wasn't my best hair day," Ben admitted, looking at the picture.

"I'll say," Ober said. "It looks like you slept with a small box around your hair. It's almost a perfect square."

"We should try to find Lisa's picture," Nathan said, moving toward the Stanford pile. "She graduated the same year as you, didn't she?" He flipped through the appropriate yearbook. "She's not in here," Nathan said after a minute. "She's apparently camera shy."

"Really?" Ben asked suspiciously.

"See for yourself," Nathan said, handing Ben the yearbook. "She's nowhere to be found."

Ben scanned through the last names that started with S. Finding no picture, he flipped to the back of the photo section and saw Lisa's name among the list of "Not Pictured" students. "Y'know what I was just thinking?" he finally asked. "What if . . ."

Before Ben could finish his thought, Eric opened the front door, stepped inside, and shook the snow from his hair. "It's almost midnight," Ober said, looking at his watch. "This is an early work night, even for you."

"What're you guys doing?" Eric asked, immediately noticing the yearbooks scattered around the room.

"If you don't mind, this is private," Ben said.

"Nice to see you, too," Eric said to Ben. "By the way, I wanted to talk to you about your note."

"There's nothing to talk about," Ben said. "Just let me know what your decision is. I won't fight you on it."

"But what about—"

"I don't want to discuss it now. So unless you have an answer, can you excuse us? I want to discuss something in private."

"Can we talk about it tomorrow?" Eric asked, scratching at the five o'clock shadow on his chin.

"No, I already told you what—"

"Ben, if you expect me to move out, the least you can do is spare half an hour. Now, can we please talk tomorrow?"

"Fine," Ben acquiesced, grabbing a piece of pizza crust from his plate. "I'll find you tomorrow."

As Eric walked up the stairs, Nathan asked, "What was that about?"

"I left him a note that said I wanted his decision as soon as possible. If he doesn't move out after New Year's, I will. I just need to know so I can start looking for a place."

"Ben, please don't do this," Ober pleaded. "You guys can work it out."

"No, we can't," Ben said. "We're way beyond working it out. I know the idea upsets you, but we can't all be best friends for the rest of our lives."

"Don't say that," Ober shot back angrily. "All you have to do is—"

"I don't have to do anything. Whatever Eric decides, I'm abiding by. I really don't care at this point."

"You don't care?" Ober asked. "How can you be so dense?"

"*I'm* dense?" Ben responded. "This is coming from the man who wants to open a non-Jewish deli, and who thinks Mussolini is a kind of pastry, *and* who thinks it's a federal crime that the Air and Space Museum doesn't sell bomb-pops! This is the person telling me *I'm* dense?"

Looking as if he had the wind knocked out of him, Ober was silent.

"What?" Ben asked.

Nathan turned to Ben. "Was that really necessar—"

"I'm not stupid," Ober said, his voice shaking. "I may not be as great as Super Ben Addison, but I'm not a moron."

"I'm sorry," Ben said defensively. "I was just trying to—"

"You were just trying to make yourself feel better," Ober interrupted, his eyes welling with tears. "You did what you always do—pick on Ober and get everyone laughing again. That's the best way to deal with a problem. Yes, sir, that's the best thing I can think of. Forget about the fact that I constantly take the fall. You just keep doing what you do best."

Caught off guard by Ober's outburst, Ben didn't know what to say. In all their years together, after all the teasing Ober had taken, it was the first time Ben had ever seen his friend crack. "Calm down," Ben began.

"I don't want to calm down," Ober said, wiping the tears from his cheeks. "You guys may get a big laugh out of it, but I'm sick of being court jester. I'm not a failure." Ober's face turned scarlet. "I'm not a failure and I refuse to be treated like one."

"No one thinks you're a failure," Nathan reassured his friend. "Now take a deep breath and relax."

Ober turned his head away.

"I'm really sorry," Ben said. "I never should've taken it out on you."

"Yeah, you're right," Ober said.

"I knew you were upset about Eric moving out, and I shouldn't have pushed your buttons like that."

"I'll get over it."

Silently staring at Ober, Ben wondered how a calm conversation had turned into such a disaster. He knew Ober was upset about Eric, but he could tell he had struck a deeper nerve in Ober's self-confidence. "You know I don't think you're a failure."

"I know," Ober said. "And I'm sorry for getting so crazy. It just really bothered me." Leaning forward on the couch, Ober took a deep breath and stared straight at the floor. "It's not even about Eric moving out. It's about the four of us. If we're all going to be together, the two of you have to work it out."

"To be honest, I don't think that's possible anymore," Ben said, sitting down next to Ober. "You have to be prepared for that possibility."

"Can't you just—"

"Ober, I'm doing the best I can."

"No, you're not."

"We don't have to go through this again," Ben said. "The choice is in Eric's hands now. Let's wait and see what happens."

"Fine—we'll wait," Ober said as he stood up from the couch. "But if you wreck these friendships, I want you to know I won't forgive you." Without saying another word, Ober walked upstairs.

When Ober was out of sight, Nathan looked over at Ben. "You really have to take it easy on him," Nathan said.

"I knew he was upset, but I didn't think it was that bad. When he started crying, I thought *I* was going to break down. I felt like someone had kicked me in the stomach."

"Does that mean you're changing your mind about Eric?"

"For Ober's sake I'd like to, but you know I can't. Right now, my main concern is still catching Rick and getting myself out of this mess."

"That's fine," Nathan said. "But do us all a favor? Don't forget your friends."

Early the following morning, Ben took the Metro to Union Station and headed to Mailboxes & Things. As he approached the store, he wondered if everything would work out with Eric. It's the only way, he reassured himself. This is the best solution to the problem. Just sit tight and see what happens.

At the store, he pulled an unsealed envelope from his back pocket, removed the typed letter inside, and reread it for the fourth time. "Dear Rick: Since we're almost three weeks away from decision time, I thought it would be appropriate for us to get together. As we discussed in the limo, I have what you requested, and you have what I want. Please pick an appropriate time and place as soon as possible."

Stuffing the letter back into the envelope, Ben placed the envelope inside his empty P.O. box. He wondered if Rick would believe that he was interested in the money. After locking the box, Ben walked to the front of the store. Maybe we should stake out this place, he thought. Rick will have to come here to pick up the letter—unless he sends a messenger to get it. Deep in thought, Ben pushed open the door and accidentally bumped into an incoming customer.

"I'm sorry," the customer said. "My fault."

Ben recognized the voice with shock and looked up. It was Rick.

"Don't look so surprised," Rick said. "It makes you look like a little kid." As Rick stepped into the store, Ben turned around and walked in behind him.

"You followed me here, didn't you?" Ben asked.

Ignoring the question, Rick pulled out his own key and opened the P.O. box. He removed Ben's letter, opened it, and read its contents. "I agree," he eventually said. "Now where would you like to meet?"

"I asked you a question. Did you follow me here?"

"Why so upset?" Rick asked with a thin smirk.

"Because you piss me off. And don't think I've forgotten about Thanksgiving. I know that was you with my dad. If you ever go near my family—"

"Can you please stop with the threats?" Rick asked, waving Ben off. "You're worse than the guys in my office." Looking past Rick's shoulder, Ben couldn't help noticing the other customers filling up the store. Following Ben's glance, Rick turned around. "Makes you want to scream, doesn't it? You finally have me in broad daylight and there's not a single camera in sight. If you were really bright, you would've had one of your friends follow you here."

"Maybe I did," Ben said.

"Not even in your dreams," Rick said, amused. "Face facts—until you're able to I.D. me, you need me. Now, as far as where we're meeting, I'd like to do it in the airport. At five o'clock next Saturday, go to Washington National. Pick up the white courtesy phone, and there'll be a message waiting for you. Follow those instructions, and I'll see you soon after that."

"I don't want to meet in the airport," Ben said, hoping to stall. "It's too crowded. Let's pick someplace else."

"It's the airport, or it's not happening," Rick shot back. "And if I were in your position, I'd stop screwing around. After that lie detector test, you're going to need a new job anyway." Rick slid the letter into the inside pocket of his camel-colored coat, turned around, and headed to the door. "See you next week."

Following Rick outside, Ben frantically looked around the parking lot, hoping to at least get a look at Rick's license plates. "Damn," he whispered to himself when he saw Rick hail a passing taxi. Ben attempted to hail another cab, furiously waving his hands in the air. "TAXI!" he yelled. Watching Rick's taxi fade down the block, Ben struggled to keep it in sight. When it eventually made a left-hand turn, he knew Rick was gone.

Ben walked down his block, cursing himself for not anticipating Rick's actions. Wondering what he should do at this point, he realized that he now had only a week to come up with a plan. As Ben turned onto the front path to his house, he tried to predict where in a busy airport Rick would most likely want to meet. Maybe someplace private, like one of those executive lounges. When he opened the front door, Ben saw no one in the living room or the kitchen. He took off his coat, put it in the closet, and headed upstairs. By the time he reached the second floor, Ben heard the sound of running water coming from the upstairs bathroom. Unconcerned with who else was home, he was deep in thought about how Rick knew about the lie detector test. Ben's thoughts were interrupted when he opened the door to his room and saw Eric rummaging through his top desk drawer.

"What the hell are you doing?"

"Jesus!" Eric said. "You scared the crap out of me."

"How about answering my question? Why the hell were you going through my drawers?"

"I was looking for a stapler," Eric said. "I wanted to put up some flyers in the coffee shops up the street. I do have to find some new housing. Now, do you want to see my flyers, too?"

Ben pulled open a desk drawer, pulled out a stapler, and handed it to Eric.

Eric took the stapler and started for the door. "Thanks for all your help."

Rick glanced at his watch as he strolled through the lobby of the Washington Hilton. Stepping into the elevator, he readjusted his tie and rested his hands in the pockets of his brown tweed suit. When he reached the tenth floor, he was exactly fifteen minutes late. As he wandered through the corridors, he caught sight of his visitor, waiting outside room 1027.

"You're late."

"I'm sorry. I just wanted to make sure none of your friends were lying in wait for me," Rick explained as he opened the door to the room. "I'm a very popular guy, you know." Walking inside, he waited for his visitor to follow. When they were both in the room, Rick closed the door. "Stand right there."

"Wha'?"

"It's just a precaution," Rick said as he pulled a thin, black metal detector from his briefcase. Waving the detector across his colleague's body, he said, "I'm sure you understand." When he was satisfied that there were no recording devices present, Rick headed to the living room of the suite, where he took a seat on one of the room's two identical couches and motioned for his guest to be seated as well. Rick got right to the point. "I don't mean to be short, but do you have the decision?"

"I have it. Do you have the money?"

"Most of it," Rick said.

"What do you mean, *most of it*? How much is *most*?"

"So far, exactly one million is in the account. Naturally, you can call to verify."

"And what about the other five hundred thousand?"

"I'll deposit that after our next meeting—as long as you keep me informed about Ben."

"That wasn't part of the deal."

"Yes, it was," Rick said matter-of-factly. "When I first approached you, I said that part of the deal was for you to keep Ben at bay. The best way for you to do that is to keep me informed of his whereabouts. Simply stated, when I tell him I don't need his help, he's going to be livid. And he'll make every attempt to figure out how I got the decision without him."

"So you want me to rat on him for another month?"

"Believe me, it's no worse than what you've done so far."

"Thanks, I appreciate the moral advice."

"Do we have a deal?" Rick asked.

"Not yet. First, I want the money within the next two weeks. I'll tell you what Ben's up to, but this isn't going to be an ongoing job. Once the decision is announced, you're on your own."

Rick crossed his legs and leaned back on the sofa. "That's fair."

"Second, I want you to know that I am not simply the least expensive option. If you went with Ben, you'd not only spend more money to get the decision—you'd also have to worry about his resourcefulness during every meeting. The only reason he continued to deal with you was so he could I.D. you. And it was only a matter of time before he succeeded."

"Believe me, Ben was never close to succeeding."

"I doubt that. I saw your mouth drop when I explained about his yearbook plan."

"Believe what you want," Rick said. "But you should know that the only reason I went with you is because Ben was becoming too unstable. When it came right down to it, I didn't think he would hand over the decision."

"You may be right," Rick's visitor said, pulling the *Grinnell* decision from a paper bag. "Fortunately for you . . ."

When the thirty-page document hit the glass coffee table, Rick leaned forward and picked up the pile. He flipped through it. "Unbelievable. The Court actually found that the regulation was a taking. I didn't think Justice Veidt had it in him." Reaching the last page, he added, "It's too bad Grinnell doesn't know he's sitting on a gold mine. If he did, he wouldn't be as excited about taking on new partners."

"That's great. Now, when would you like to get together next?"

As he put the document in his own briefcase, Rick said, "I'll be in touch." Rising from the sofa, he walked to the door and opened it. When they were both in the hallway, Rick said, "If you don't mind, I'm going to take the elevator on the other side of the building."

"Whatever makes you happy."

As he headed down the hallway, Rick turned around. "By the way, congratulations. You're now a millionaire."

CHAPTER 13

"WASHINGTON NATIONAL AIRPORT EXECUTIVE CENTER. CAN I help you?" the operator asked.

"Yes, I have a silly problem that I was hoping you could help me with," Ben said in his most ingratiating tone. "I was supposed to attend a meeting this Saturday in one of the airport's executive meeting rooms, but I lost my daily planner and now I have no idea where the meeting is."

"I'm sorry, sir, but the airlines are responsible for scheduling space in the meeting rooms. Do you know which airline you were dealing with?"

"I have no idea," Ben said. "It was all in my planner."

"What about the company's name? Maybe I can find that."

"It's a start-up company," Ben explained, hoping to convince the operator that she was his only hope. "They haven't incorporated yet, so it's all under the CEO's name—which I can't remember for the life of me. And since I can't remember his name, I can't find him in the telephone directory. Believe me, I've tried everything."

"I'm sorry, but I don't think there's anything I can do to help you."

"Please don't hang up," Ben pleaded. "You have to do something. If I don't show up for this interview, I'm dead. Isn't there a master list somewhere? Anything you have may save my life."

"I'm sorry," the operator said. "I'm not supposed to give out that information."

"Please." Ben tried to sound pleasant. "I'm not some kind of lunatic. I'll give you my name and address and home phone number. I'll give you my mother's number. You can call her and ask her how nice I am. I just don't want to lose this job over something stupid."

"Well . . ."

"Please. If you help me, I'll be forever in your debt. I'll send you flowers. And chocolates. And individually wrapped kielbasa from Hickory Farms. Anything."

"Here's what I can do," the operator finally said. "I can give you a list of the companies that are meeting in the suites that are run by the airport. There are only six of those, but you may find your company in there. If not, you'll have to call all the airlines and beg each of them individually for the information."

"You're the greatest," Ben exclaimed. "How can I thank you? Name your price. Diamonds? Pearls? Kielbasa?"

"How about you just leave me alone," the operator answered.

"You got it."

"These are the companies that have reservations," she said. "Texaco has one room. And Brennan, Leit and Zareh has the other."

"Isn't that a law firm?" Ben asked as he put a star next to the firm's name.

"I'm not sure," the operator said.

"Are there any other companies?"

"That's it," she said. "The other four rooms are still open."

"Oh, well," Ben said. "I guess I'm off to beg. Thanks for all your help."

"You're welcome," the operator said, sounding relieved.

Fourteen phone calls later, Ben had a list of thirty-four reservations for executive suites. Twenty-two of the reservations were made by major companies, eight were for individuals, three were for law firms, and one was for Congressman Cohen from Philadelphia. Ben pulled up the Lexis database on his computer, logged onto the Periodicals bulletin board, and entered the name "Stewart Moore," one of the eight in-dividuals who had reservations for Saturday. As the computer scanned through more than four thousand current periodicals, Ben knew the search was futile. Rick's too smart to make a reservation in his own name, he thought, staring at the computer screen.

Eventually, the words "Twenty-six items found" appeared on the screen. Scanning the first item, Ben read a *Wall Street Journal* article about Stewart Moore, a Chicago bank president who recently restruc-tured his company's finance division. When he read that Mr. Moore was fifty-five years old, he knew he hadn't found Rick. As he typed the second name into his computer, Lisa entered the office. "What's going on?" Ben asked, looking up from his screen.

Lisa was silent.

"Hello! Earth to Lisa! What's going on? How are you doing? Why aren't you responding?"

Again, silence.

"Oh, c'mon, Lisa. Lighten up already. I said I was sorry about a dozen times."

"Then I completely forgive you," Lisa said coldly.

"Be serious."

"Okay, the truth? I'm pretty pissed off that you don't trust me any-more."

"What are you talking about?" Ben asked. "I trust you."

"Ben, look at it from my perspective: For the past three months, we've spent every waking minute talking about how we were going to catch Rick. Now I can't get a single word out of you. What the hell am I supposed to make of that?"

"You can make of it whatever you want. But the truth is that there's nothing to tell. I haven't heard from Rick in weeks, and until I do, there's nothing to talk about."

"You're a liar," Lisa said.

"What do you mean, I'm a liar?"

"I'm not a moron. I know when you're lying, and I know what you're thinking. But if you think I'm the one who's leaking information to Rick, you're crazy. I'd never do that to you."

"I don't think you'd—"

"Just do me one favor." Lisa walked over and sat on the corner of Ben's desk. "Look me straight in the eyes and tell me you trust me."

"But you're not going to believe—"

"If you tell me the truth, I'll believe you."

"Lisa, I swear I trust you," Ben said, looking directly at his co-clerk. "If I had anything to tell you, I would."

"One last question. What were you working on when I walked in?"

"What?"

"On your computer," Lisa pointed. "What were you working on?"

"I was reading *The Wall Street Journal* on-line. Is that okay?"

"Then how come you're reading a week-old paper?" Lisa asked.

Ben looked at the top of his computer screen and saw that the on-screen article listed the previous week's date.

"It sucks to be caught in a lie, doesn't it?" Lisa challenged. "I bet you wish you could take those words back."

"I don't believe it," Ben said. "You didn't care what I said to you. You sat on my desk just to see what I was reading."

"I definitely did," Lisa said, hopping off Ben's desk. "And now I finally have my answer."

"But—"

"Don't bother. It'd be a waste of both your breath and my intelligence. And when you see Rick, tell him I hope he kicks your ass."

An hour later, Ben and Lisa were silent, each of them reading a third version of Osterman's *Grinnell* opinion. Ben's phone rang, startling them both. "Hello?" Ben answered. "Justice Hollis's chambers."

"Hello, Ben. How's your day been?"

Recognizing Rick's voice, Ben tightened his fist around the receiver. "What do you want?"

"I wanted to talk about our meeting on Saturday," Rick said.

"Then I'm glad you called," Ben said. "Because I don't like the airport. I want to—"

"I really don't care what you want," Rick interrupted. "I just wanted to tell you that our meeting is canceled. I no longer need what you have to offer."

"But I thought—"

"Like most of your theories, you thought wrong," Rick said smugly. "So have fun searching through your little yearbooks, and good luck on your lie detector test. I don't believe we'll be speaking again—although I'm sure I'll hear about all the results."

"Wait, I—" Before Ben could even get the words out, Rick was gone.

"Who was that?" Lisa asked, noticing Ben's panicked look.

Ben said nothing. He pushed himself away from his desk, stormed toward the door, grabbed his jacket from the closet, and left the office. He walked down the main steps of the Court, down First Street, and approached the nearest pay phone. Picking up the receiver, he inserted a few coins and dialed Nathan's phone number.

"Andrew Lukens. Can I help you?"

"I'm sorry," Ben said, recognizing neither the voice nor the name. "I was trying to reach Nathan."

"Nathan's been promoted to another office. Can I help you instead?"

"This is his roommate, Ben. Do you know his new extension?"

"Hey, Ben," Andrew's voice warmed up. "I've heard a lot about you. How's everything at the Supreme Court? Change any laws today?"

"No, nothing today," Ben said. "We only change laws on Wednesdays. On Mondays we just try to speak to our roommates."

"Yeah, Nathan said you had a sarcastic sense of humor," Andrew said, showing no sign that he intended to transfer Ben's call. "By the way, I've been meaning to ask Nathan—how'd that prank go with your other roommate?"

"Which one?"

"You know, the one you needed the microphones and cameras for. Nathan said you guys were trying to catch your roommate doing the deed."

"Oh, yeah," Ben said, quickly remembering how Nathan had swindled the high-tech equipment out of the State Department. "It went fantastic. I'll have to remind Nathan to bring you some of the pictures. They were a bit blurry, but they're pretty funny."

"Well, if the pictures suck, tell him to bring in the audio. I'm sure the briefcase mikes picked up every moan and groan."

Ben paused. Briefcase mikes? "How do those mikes work again, Andrew?"

"The same as the cordless ones. The only difference is that they're built into a briefcase. They're used when someone is concerned that the regular microphones might get exposed. Pound for pound, I'd say they're about as close as we get to a James Bond movie. They're still only at the prototype stage, but Nathan thought you'd get a real kick out of them."

"Oh, they sure were awesome," Ben said as a cold sweat covered his brow. "We got to hear everything we wanted to hear."

"Well, let me transfer you to Nathan," Andrew said.

"I'll tell you what," Ben said. "I'm running late, so I'll just give him a call later."

"Do you want me to tell him you called?"

"No, no," Ben said. "I'm going to be busy all day. I'll see him at home."

Ben hung up the phone and leaned his head against the phone booth. Shutting his eyes, his mind searched for a reasonable explanation. When he couldn't come up with one, his breathing quickened. With his eyes still shut, he slammed his head against the metal booth. "I don't believe this!" he screamed. He picked up the receiver and searched his pockets for more loose change. As he was about to deposit the money, he paused. "Damn!" he screamed, slamming the receiver back in its cradle. Rubbing his forehead, he mentally replayed his conversations with Rick and Andrew. Struggling to make sense of both exchanges, he stood silent.

Ten minutes later, Ben stepped out of the shadow of the phone booth and returned to the Court. When Lisa heard the door of the office slam shut, she quickly turned her head. After throwing his coat into the closet, Ben stood directly in front of Lisa's desk.

"What?" she asked. "What'd I do now?"

"Listen, I'm going to tell you this, but I'm only telling you because I need your help," Ben explained. "A week ago, Rick contacted me—"

"I knew it," Lisa interrupted. "I knew he—"

"Lisa, please give me a chance to explain," Ben pleaded. "When I spoke with Rick, he asked me for the *Grinnell* decision. In exchange, he was going to give me three million dollars. Obviously, I would never give him the decision, but I was hoping that when we met for the exchange, I'd be able to finally I.D. him. Our meeting was supposed to be at the airport this Saturday, probably in one of the executive lounges."

"And now you need my help to make a plan?"

"I already had a plan," Ben said. "I had called all the airport lounges to see which ones were reserved for this Saturday. When I got that list, I started doing background checks on any names I didn't recognize—that's why I was reading a week-old newspaper. I figured if I could anticipate which room Rick and I were supposed to meet in, I'd be able to wire the room, or bug it, or do something to it in advance. Anyway, just as I start feeling confident that this'll be the time I nail Rick, I get a surprising phone call from our favorite scumbag."

"That was Rick who called before?"

"Yep. And he told me that I can go scratch myself because our meeting is canceled. He said he didn't need my help and then he hung up on me. Obviously, he got the *Grinnell* decision from someone else."

"If you think he got it from me, you're on crack."

"To be honest, I did think it was you," Ben admitted. "I figured you were the only other person who had access to the decision."

"Ben, I swear—"

"Let me finish. After I got Rick's call, I went to a pay phone to call Nathan. I ended up talking to one of his co-workers, who asked me how the briefcase microphone worked."

"What briefcase mike?"

"Exactly," Ben said.

"And now, just because Nathan withheld a piece of equipment, you think he's the one talking to Rick?"

"What else can I think? This wasn't just any piece of equipment—if I had the briefcase mike, I would've been able to get Rick on tape when we met at the restaurant. I'd have everything documented by now: Rick's offer, his explanation of the original CMI scam—everything I needed to get me off the hook. But Nathan somehow managed to not include it in his little bag of tricks. You don't think that's suspicious?''

"I don't know."

"I've tried to come up with a reasonable explanation. But I can't for the life of me explain why Nathan wouldn't say word one about it. Especially when it's such a cool thing to talk about."

"But if Nathan was working with Rick, Rick would've known about the briefcase mike, so it wouldn't have posed any real threat."

"I thought about that," Ben said as he walked toward the file cabinet. "But I keep coming back to the idea that Rick couldn't have kept the briefcase out of the limo. If he hadn't let me bring it in, I wouldn't have gotten in myself. I'd have said that I couldn't abandon the briefcase in an alley since there were vital Court documents inside. And at that point, Rick had to get me in the car."

"That's not a bad theory," Lisa agreed.

"So now I have to figure out if it's really Nathan," Ben said, leaning on the cabinet.

"Ben, let me ask you one question. Fifteen minutes ago, you thought I was selling your soul to the devil, and now you walk in here and pour your guts out to me. Why the change of heart?"

"Lisa, the God's honest truth is that I have absolutely nothing to lose by telling you. Rick's cut me loose; he presumably has the *Grinnell* decision; I don't have any more meetings with him, and therefore I have no hope of catching him. Even if you are working with Rick, there's nothing to tell him. I'm lost. I have no suspect, no clues, and a lie detector test in two days. More importantly, I have no one else I can trust."

"What about Ober?"

"Believe me, he was the first person I thought about. But I realized he really wouldn't be able to help. Ober's great, and I love him like a brother, but he couldn't find his ass with a map and a pickax. I need an extra brain to figure out what to do from here."

"So if Nathan is in on it, how'd he get the decision?"

"For all I know, he could've used some State Department supercomputer to break into our computers here. Or he could've just as easily gotten it from my briefcase—all he had to do was take it out in the middle of the night, photocopy it, and return it before I got up."

"Don't you have a lock on your briefcase? Especially after what happened with Eric?"

"Of course I have a lock. But Nathan knows the combination—he used it for his interview at the State Department."

"Well, no offense, but your choice of friends is worse than Julius Caesar's."

"Thanks for the advice," Ben said, returning to his desk. "Now, will you help me?"

"That depends," Lisa said. "Do you trust me?"

"At this point, I don't trust my own mother. Last time I was home, she started looking a little shifty."

"Are you at least sorry for your accusations?"

"More sorry than you'll ever know," Ben said, tearing the corners off Osterman's *Grinnell* opinion. "Now will you please help me?"

"Of course I'll help you." Lisa pulled the *Grinnell* opinion out of Ben's hands, put his hands flat on the desk, and covered them with her own. "Regardless of what you may think, I really do care about what happens to you. If you were booted out of here, I'd have double the amount of work."

"That's funny," Ben said dryly. "You sure do crack me up."

"You can hide behind all the sarcastic remarks you want, but I know you appreciate my help."

"Of course I appreciate it. My life is falling apart, my career is approaching meltdown, and my friends are acting like the charter members of the Benedict Arnold Fan Club. At this point, I'd appreciate election tips from George McGovern. What the hell else am I supposed to do?"

"Well, I just hope you realize that you still have some real friends that care about you."

"Thank you, Lisa Marie. I really do appreciate the help. I mean it."

"It's okay," she said. "But don't think for a second that I forgive you. You have to get raked over another twenty sets of coals before I forget about the emotional distress you've caused me."

"That's a deal. And you can pick out the coals personally."

Taking a few steps backward, Lisa sat on the office sofa. "Now, are we going to catch this motherfucker or not?"

Smiling, Ben pulled a legal pad from the corner of his desk. "I think our only option is to make a list of people Rick might approach at Grinnell and Associates.''

"I can take care of that," Lisa said. "I'm pretty sure the Clerk's Office keeps a record of every party's ownership interests. That should give us a likely list of possible sellers. If we keep an eye on those individuals, we'll know when Rick makes his move."

"We don't even have to keep an eye on them," Ben said, clearing his computer screen for a new search. "Lexis has its own public records database. All real estate transactions and deed transfers have to be reported to the county clerk's office. If we have the names of the sellers, we should be able to track them directly from here."

"Perfect," Lisa said. "I'll be back with the names."

As Lisa left the office, Ben called out, "By the way, I do trust you!"

"I know," she shouted back.

When the door closed, Ben pulled his chair toward his desk and dialed the number of the phone company. "Hi, I was wondering if you could help me out. By mistake, my wife threw out all of our phone bills. Since we need them for tax purposes, I was hoping we could get copies of them."

"That shouldn't be a problem, sir," the operator said. "I just need your name and phone number."

"The phone is under my wife's name: Lisa Schulman." Ben told the operator Lisa's phone number and added, "I was also wondering if you could send the bills directly to my accountant, since he needs them as soon as possible."

"We're not supposed to—"

"It's my phone," Ben said. "It's just under my wife's name. If it makes it easier for you, I'd be happy to talk to a supervisor."

"It should be fine. Let me just make a note of that, and then I'll need the address."

After giving the operator Ober's work address, Ben said, "Thanks for the help. I really appreciate it."

Late that afternoon, Ben stared intently at his computer screen.

"Y'know, you'll probably go blind if you keep staring like that," Lisa said.

"I should be so lucky."

"Stop worrying. You keyed in every name on the ownership papers. If someone sells, you'll see it change."

"We'll never see it," Ben said, turning away from his computer. "You saw those documents. Grinnell is owned primarily by four limited partnerships, which are owned by eight more limited partnerships, which are owned by sixteen S corporations . . ."

"We pulled out every name we could find. And if we couldn't find them, what do you think the chances are that Rick could find them?"

Ben shot Lisa his you-must-be-joking look.

"Okay," Lisa said, "so Rick could probably find anything. But that doesn't mean we're not on the right track."

"It's not that I don't think we're on the right track," Ben said. "I just feel like this is a very passive plan. We're just sitting here and waiting."

"Well, that's all we can do now. If you're so anxious, why don't you start looking through the Harvard and Michigan yearbooks?"

"What are you talking about?" Ben asked. "They haven't arrived yet."

"Yes, they have. I told you earlier that there were two boxes in reception for you."

"You never said that," Ben said, rising from his seat.

"I definitely did. When I got back from getting the ownership documents, I told you there were two boxes waiting for you. You were probably too caught up in your computer screen."

Ben walked to the closet and pulled out his coat. "Rather than bring the yearbooks home to Nathan, I think I'm going to leave them here. I'll go through them tomorrow."

"Where are you going now?" Lisa asked, noticing that it wasn't even five o'clock yet.

"I want to speak to Ober before Nathan gets home. Can you cover for me in case Hollis calls?"

"Don't worry about it. I'll take care of it."

* * *

When Ben arrived home, the hum of silence revealed that the house was empty. Taking off his coat and throwing it on the sofa, Ben checked the kitchen, peeked into the first-floor bathroom, and opened the door to the basement. "Is anybody here?" he called out. When he got upstairs, he peeked into Eric's and Ober's rooms, as well as his own. After looking in the second-floor bathroom and every hall closet, Ben opened the door to Nathan's room. Without turning on the lights, he slid open Nathan's closet and poked his head inside. Convinced that he was alone, Ben then approached Nathan's desk, focusing on the small stack of papers arranged in a neat pile. Not making a sound, Ben flipped through the pile. Grocery list, things-to-do list, birthday list, movies-to-rent list. Nothing of consequence. After returning the papers to their original position, Ben held his breath and cautiously pulled open the center desk drawer. Picking up the organizer that kept all the pens, pencils, and erasers in place, Ben slowly and methodically searched for anything that might lead to Rick's whereabouts. After closing the drawer, Ben picked up the address book on Nathan's nightstand. Reading each entry, he struggled to account for every name in the book.

"What the hell are you doing with my address book?"

Startled, Ben dropped the book and looked up, surprised to see Ober laughing in the doorway. "Don't do that!" Ben yelled, picking up the book and returning it to its place.

"You should've seen your face. You were—"

"Is anyone with you?" Ben asked, rushing out of Nathan's room.

"No. Why? What's wrong?"

"Listen, I'm going to tell you something, but you have to swear you'll never say a word."

"I swear," Ober said, pulling off his tie.

"I'm not joking," Ben warned. "Not a word to anyone. Not Nathan, not your parents . . ."

"I swear," Ober repeated as they walked down the stairs toward the living room. "Just tell me."

After explaining the entire story to his roommate, Ben said, "So tell me: What do you think?"

"I can't believe what you're saying." Ober's eyes were wide with disbelief. "You expect me to believe that Nathan is in on this whole thing?"

"What else am I supposed to believe?"

"No way," Ober slumped into a chair at the kitchen table. "Now you're crazy. I mean, if you said Eric, I'd understand. In fact, last week I saw him in your room going through your garbage."

"Did you ask him what he was doing?"

"He said someone took his classifieds section, so he wanted to see if it was you."

"Well, it wasn't," Ben said. "You should've sent him to Nathan—he's the untrustworthy one around here."

"There's no way in hell Nathan would do that," Ober insisted. "I don't believe it for a second."

"Well, I do," Ben said. "And at this point, that's all that really matters. Lisa and I are trying to find—"

"How can you suddenly trust Lisa with everything?" Ober interrupted. "I mean, you always say I'm dense, but you must be a moron to tell her stuff again."

"Listen, I don't trust her for a second," Ben said, walking over to the sink. He turned on the water and splashed some on his face. "As soon as she left the office, I started investigating her as well."

"Then why tell her anything at all?"

"It's simple. First, she can't do me any real harm. Second, and I know you'll never understand this, but she helps me think better."

"I don't understand."

"I really can't explain it, but when I brainstorm with her, I wind up with my best ideas."

"Well, I hate to be the one to break it to you, but this isn't just some Supreme Court decision you two are working on. This is your life, buddy-boy."

"It is?" Ben said sarcastically. "And here I thought it was just a big ol' game of Parcheesi. Dang."

"I think you're way off in space with this one," Ober said, shaking his head.

"Fine. I'll take your advice into consideration. Now, are you going to help me or not?"

"I'm surprised you trust me. I mean, I may be in on it, too."

"No offense, but I thought about it."

"Thanks," Ober said. "I really appreciate the vote of confidence."

"Listen, don't get offended. I'm telling you, aren't I?"

"I just don't understand why you're telling me."

"Because I need you to do me a favor," Ben said. "I had all of Lisa's phone bills sent to your address at work. It was the only address I could think of that Nathan, Rick, and Lisa don't have access to. When you get the bills, will you let me know so I can go through them?"

"Of course," Ober said. "One last question, though: If the house is bugged, why are you still telling me all this?"

"There's nothing Rick's heard that he can use against me," Ben explained. "Lisa's bills are already on their way, and if Nathan's on his side, he already knows—" Ben heard a key in the lock of the front door and fell silent. "Don't say a single word," he warned, whispering over his shoulder as Ober followed him into the living room. "You promised."

When the door opened, Nathan walked into the room. "My friend, you are going to be thrilled with me," he said to Ben as he hung his jacket in the closet. He put his briefcase on the coffee table and sat down next to Ober. "Thanks to yours truly, you are now going to pass the marshal's ever-alarming lie detector test."

"And how's that?" Ben asked.

"Well, let's just say that I made a number of phone calls today, and I was able to get everything we need to beat the test." Nathan opened his briefcase and pulled out a single sheet of paper. "I spoke to some of the technicians in the security division and they explained it all. First and foremost, you're right about the test not being admissible in court."

"I know," Ben said curtly. "They've never been admissible."

"What's wrong with you?" Nathan asked.

Ober looked at Ben. "It's nothing," Ben said. "I'm just nervous about it. What else did they say?"

"This is the way the test works," Nathan said, consulting a sheet of paper. "When you first walk in, they almost always have the machine set up in the middle of the room. They try to make it look imposing since the theory is that most people will confess because they're so terrified of the machine. They then ask you questions for at least an hour before the machine is even hooked up and turned on. On average, this is where most people crack," Nathan said, looking up from the paper to accentuate his point. "They said that the shadow of the box is enough to intimidate the average criminal."

"Hey, Ben's far more than average," Ober said. "He's at least in the ninetieth percentile of criminals."

Ignoring his roommate, Nathan continued, "The machine itself measures three things: respiratory rate, blood pressure, and galvanic skin response, which is the skin's response to electric current. Lying usually has a positive correlation with sweating, so the machine picks up your sweat levels. Not that you'd have any problem with that."

"Just tell me how to pass the test," Ben said impatiently.

"Relax," Nathan said. "After the hour of questions, they'll hook you up to the machine. And when they attach it, the machine will take baseline readings of your breathing and respiratory levels. This is the place where the undereducated always try to cheat the machine. They'll try to breathe heavy and fidget around—doing anything they can to convince the machine that their heart rate is higher than it actually is. But the guys in security said that a good machine operator will easily recognize this and will quickly account for it.

"After the initial adjustment, they pull out a deck of cards, and they ask you questions about the cards. This is just to convince you that the machine works. Then they ask you three questions, and you're supposed to answer no to each one, even if the real answer is yes. That's how they see if you're lying. They ask if you're over the age of twenty-one, if you smoke, and if you've ever done anything you're ashamed of. After that, finally, they ask you a maximum of three questions about whatever it is you're accused of."

"And that's it?" Ben asked skeptically.

"That's it."

"But what about the way it works in the movies?" Ober asked. "Where you see the suspect getting grilled with dozens of questions while the needle thrashes across the scrolling paper."

"Doesn't happen in real life," Nathan said. "In the real world, it can only test the truthfulness of three statements in a session."

"So how does that help me?"

"Ah, I'm glad you asked," Nathan said, reaching back into his brief-case. He pulled out a small brown medicine vial and threw it to Ben. "Those're the pills that I told you the military uses to beat the tests."

Ben read the label on the vial. "Prynadolol?"

"It works," Nathan said. "You're supposed to take one pill as soon as you wake up in the morning, and if your test is after three o'clock in the afternoon, you should take another pill at lunch."

"How did you get these?" Ben asked, pulling off the cap to see five pills inside.

"I told the technicians that my younger brother had to take a lie detector test for his job in the mall. When they heard that, they just offered the pills to me."

"How do they work?"

"They're supposed to moderate your heart rate and blood pressure," Nathan explained. "Doctors usually give them to people who have re-curring heart attacks, and politicians use them to beat stagefright, but the military realized that they could put them to much better use."

"Are these experimental or are they FDA approved?"

"If they were approved, everyone would have access," Nathan said.

"So they're experimental," Ben said.

"They're fine," Nathan said. "Do you really think they'd give me something that was potentially dangerous?"

"I think it'd be cool if they were dangerous," Ober said. "Then you'd grow an extra nostril in your forehead and we could sue the govern-ment for billions."

"Or maybe it'd cause me to grow a brain," Ben said. Looking back to Nathan, he continued, "Now tell me how this helps me pass the test."

"It doesn't guarantee you'll pass," Nathan said. "It significantly in-creases your chances, but it's still primarily up to you. While you're in the room, you have to be as calm as possible. Don't fidget and don't get nervous. The technicians said that if you're a good liar, you should do fine. If you're a bozo, you'll probably freak out and fail regardless."

"Oh, man, you're dead," Ober said to Ben.

Ben put the vial in his pocket and stood up from the couch. "I'm going to make some pasta," he said coldly. "Anyone else want some?"

"Hey, you're welcome," Nathan said, making a face.

"I'll say thank you if I pass the test," Ben said, heading to the kitchen.

"What the hell is that supposed to mean? What's wrong with you anyway?"

"I just want to be sure I can trust you about these," Ben said. He turned around and looked directly at Nathan. "I mean, they're not placebos, are they?"

"What are you talking about?"

"Ben, don't accuse—" Ober began.

"No, let him finish," Nathan said, standing from his seat. "Accuse me of what?"

"Well, today I got a phone call from Rick, who said that he no longer needs my help. Apparently, he already got a Court decision from someone else."

"And you think I'm the one that gave it to him?" Nathan asked, his voice rising with anger. "Have you thought about your little friend Lisa, or is all the blood that was once in your brain still being used by your dick?"

"I actually did think it was Lisa," Ben shot back as he returned to the living room. "And when I called you so that we could talk about her, I had an enlightening conversation with one of your office mates, named Andrew. He was telling me all about the briefcase microphone that we were supposed to use during our first meeting with Rick. He told me how great they work, and how wonderful they are, and how they pick up everything. So you can imagine my surprise when I realized that I hadn't heard a single word about this marvel of technology."

"And now you think I'm the one who's in on it with Rick?" Nathan asked, laughing.

"I'm not joking," Ben said. "Look at the facts."

"The facts show nothing!" Nathan yelled. "And beyond that, have you even thought about actually asking me why we didn't use the briefcase mike?"

"And I suppose there's a perfectly logical explanation."

"Of course there is. The briefcase mike is a prototype, and regardless of what Andrew said, it works like crap. The leather muffles the sound, and you can't hear a thing. The only reason we have it around is because everyone likes the idea. I just figured that we might as well go with equipment that works—I'm crazy like that."

"And I'm supposed to believe that?"

"Believe what you want," Nathan said. "But that's the truth."

"Nathan, let me tell you something," Ben said, pointing a finger at his roommate. "I know you. I probably know you better than I know myself. And if you even had the chance, just the *possibility,* of using a briefcase that concealed a microphone, you'd grab it in a second and bring it right to us, even if it hadn't ever worked."

"And how do you figure that?"

"Because I know you love to show off. And I know you love to strut like a peacock when you have something no one else has. You would've loved walking into Lisa's with that briefcase mike—you'd have looked like Q from James Bond. And even if you couldn't get it to work, you'd have brought it home just to show us you could. I mean, think about it logically. Any of us would've loved to show off with that thing. But now you want me to believe that not only did you not want to bring it home, but you didn't even think it was worth mentioning? Please, Nathan. You're way too competitive and your ego's way too big for me to believe that you'd ever keep it quiet."

"Are you done?" Nathan asked calmly, his arms crossed in front of him.

"I think so."

"Then you can go fuck yourself, you paranoid little piece of shit! I busted my ass to get you that equipment! I risked my job by lying to everyone in my office, and I drove myself crazy trying to figure out a way for you to get out of this nightmare. But when you have the gall to accuse me before you actually even speak to me—well, you can ride the *Hindenburg* alone. I know you're in a tough situation, but I have better things to do than take abuse from you."

"Listen—"

"No, you listen! This thing has made you absolutely insane. And the fact that you accused me and not Lisa shows me that you're not only way beyond reason, you're also only a few beats away from the nuthouse. When you regain your senses, I hope you'll have the integrity to apologize." Nathan turned away from his roommates and walked

out of the living room. As he approached the stairs, he turned around
and added, "And when he and Lisa shatter your existence, just know
you'll be sweeping up alone."

When Nathan was out of sight, Ben remained silent.

"You shouldn't have accused him like that," Ober said. "That was
dead wrong."

"What was I supposed to do? No matter how I started, I knew we'd
wind up in this position."

"Still, there are better ways to pick a fight. Some of that stuff you
said is unforgivable."

"I don't want to hear it," Ben said. "If Nathan were in my position,
he'd have done the exact same thing."

"Y'know, Eric said the same thing to you when he wrote his story.
And just like Nathan, you told him to fuck off," Ober said. He got up
from the sofa and moved toward the stairs. "Pretty eerie, huh?"

"So are you going to take the pills?" Lisa asked, sipping coffee at
her desk the following morning.

"Of course I am," Ben said, flipping through a Michigan Law School
yearbook. "What choice do I have?"

"You can decide not to take them."

"And I can also decide to fail the test," Ben said. "Even if they have
no effect, I might as well take them. It's not like they're mini-cyanide
pills and they'll kill me."

"How do you know what they are? They can contain anything: cya-
nide, No-Doz, truth serum—"

"That's enough," Ben interrupted. "I'll take my chances, thank
you."

"I'm serious," Lisa said. "Who knows what Nathan gave you?"

"You don't believe that. You're just mad because I told you he was
the one who suspected you."

"Of course I'm mad about that. Screw him."

"C'mon now—be nice."

"Be nice?" Lisa asked. "*You* want *me* to be nice? You're the one who
spent last night alienating your closest friends."

"Thanks for pointing that out. I had almost gone a full two minutes without thinking about it."

"I'm surprised they're still letting you live there. If I were them, I'd have thrown you out on your ass."

"It definitely wasn't happy town at breakfast this morning. Eric, Nathan, Ober, and I were all eating at the same time and no one said a word to anyone else. If someone wanted more milk or more napkins, they just pointed at them. It was like living with a family of mimes."

"If you want, you can stay at my place for a while," Lisa said.

"I appreciate the offer. But if I'm home, I can keep an eye on things."

Lisa took another sip of coffee. "Have you ever thought that you might be wrong? That your friends really aren't against you?"

"Of course I have," Ben said, looking up as he turned a page of the yearbook. "Why do you think I couldn't sleep last night?"

"So . . . ?"

"So I keep coming back to one idea: What if I'm wrong? As soon as I ask that question, I'm back where I started."

Nodding, Lisa motioned toward Ben's reading material. "Does anyone look familiar?"

"They look familiar in the sense that everyone looks like a boring lawyer. But beyond that, nobody looks like Rick." Ben closed the yearbook. "It's hopeless—he's gone, and I'm lost."

"Don't say that. Pick up the next book and keep looking."

"I don't even know why I bother," Ben said, opening another yearbook. "This plan is ridiculous."

"Listen, don't put all your faith in the yearbooks. If you find him, great. If not, we'll find him when someone at Grinnell decides to sell. Besides, finding Rick should be secondary at this point. If you fail that lie detector test, you'll have bigger problems than Rick."

"I'll pass the test."

"Suddenly you're so self-assured?"

"I'm serious. The average person fails the test because they're terrified of the machine."

"And naturally, you're much more competent than the average person," Lisa said.

"I am. I may be scared shitless, but that doesn't mean I'm going to let a silly piece of machinery intimidate me. If the machines were so great, they'd be admissible in court. Until then, they're obviously beatable. Besides, the nature of being a lawyer is arguing what you don't necessarily believe."

"But you're not a lawyer. You're a clerk."

"Did I pass the bar exam?" Ben asked. "I'm a lawyer."

"You're terrified is what you are. Whenever you get scared, you start acting like a pompous ass—as if that's a solid form of defense."

"Okay, maybe. But I still know that I haven't done anything wrong. Rick tricked me out of that first opinion. I didn't give it to him intending for him to use it to make money. I was a pawn. A fool. A knave. In my wildest dreams, I never thought Rick would use the information for personal gain. I thought I was speaking in the closest confidence. So if anyone is the victim here, it's me."

"That's a nice speech," Lisa said, applauding. "You should write it down somewhere."

"And why's that?"

"Because if you fail that test tomorrow, you're going to need it for the opening arguments of your dismissal hearing."

After work, Lisa and Ben left the Court, walked up First Street and made a right on C Street. Passing the Dirksen Senate Office Building, they saw a band of young Senate staffers empty onto the sidewalk, all of them dressed in tan overcoats and toting leather briefcases. Ben counted the months until spring, when the sun would shine again. Although it hadn't snowed for a week, the leftover slush, blackened from automobile exhaust and other pollution, covered Capitol Hill with a filthy winter veneer. Ten minutes later, the two clerks reached Sol & Evvy's Drug Store, the oldest operating pharmacy in the entire city. "Are you sure they have it here?" Ben asked, opening the door that was covered with peeling white paint.

"I'm positive," Lisa said as she walked inside.

In the small, cramped store, sun-faded maps and decade-old advertisements decorated the walls. "It smells like my grandmother's house," he said.

"This place is historic," Lisa said as she headed to the back of the store. "Have some respect."

"Trust me, I love places like this. Where else can you find expiration dates that match your birthday to the year?"

"You have to take a look at these maps," Lisa said as she pointed to the walls. "I don't think a single one lists Alaska or Hawaii as states."

"I believe it," Ben said. "The one near the front door didn't even have the Louisiana Purchase on it. Ah, those thirteen states of ours."

When Ben and Lisa reached the back of the store, the pharmacist behind the counter rose from his rusted metal folding chair. "What's your ache?"

"Just her," Ben said, motioning to Lisa.

"We're okay, thanks," Lisa said. She pointed to the freestanding blood pressure machine next to the counter. "Here it is. I told you they had one."

"Do you really think this'll work?" Ben asked, handing his overcoat and suit jacket to Lisa.

"How should I know?"

"Do I have to get undressed for this?" Ben asked, already rolling up his sleeve.

"Read the directions."

After glancing at the paragraph of directions, Ben pulled a quarter from his pocket, unrolled his sleeve, put his arm into the cuff, and inserted the coin in the machine.

"You can do it over your shirt?" Lisa asked.

"According to the directions." Suddenly, the cuff tightened around Ben's arm. Breathing deeply and remaining silent, he waited as the cuff slowly loosened. A set of red numbers appeared on the screen of the machine: 122 over 84.

"Crap," Ben said.

"What are you normally?"

"One twenty-five over eight-five. The damn pills had almost no effect. My heart rate's the same, my pressure's the same. I'm a dead man."

"Don't say that. Besides, you only took them two hours ago. Maybe they haven't kicked in yet."

Ben put on both of his coats and grabbed his briefcase. "Maybe. But for some reason, I doubt it."

"Don't let it get you upset," Lisa said as they left the store. "If you expect to pass the test, you have to focus on being calm."

CHAPTER 14

AT TEN A.M. WEDNESDAY, BEN STRETCHED OUT ON THE DEEP red office sofa. With his eyes closed, he stroked his favorite polka-dot tie. "How do you feel?" Lisa whispered.

"I'm okay," Ben said, sitting up and taking a long, deep breath. He looked at his watch. "I guess it's time."

"Just stay calm. Think of long walks in the woods, scuba diving— anything that keeps you relaxed."

"I'm focused," Ben said, standing up. "I'm a picture of calm. I'm intensely Zen."

"Good luck," Lisa said as Ben walked out the door.

Thinking it would be the least traveled route, Ben took the spiral marble staircase to the basement. Slowly, he descended into the heart of the building, counting each step to take his mind off his destination. When he reached the basement, he walked to the Marshals Office and told the receptionist that he had an appointment with Carl Lungen.

"You can go right in. He's expecting you."

When Ben entered Lungen's office, he was hit by the stench of cigars. "Nice to see you, Ben," Lungen said, leaning back in his leather chair. "Have a seat."

"I thought this was a smoke-free building," Ben said, refusing to look Lungen in the eye. "It is a historic monument, you know."

"Well, you know how it is," Lungen said, rubbing his beard. He pointed to the chair in front of his desk. "Sit."

"No offense, but can we get on with this?" Ben asked. "I have work to do. Besides, cigar smoke gets my blood pressure worked up."

Lungen got up from his seat and headed for the door. Following him out of the office, Ben was led back to the receptionist's desk. "I'll be in the interrogation room if anyone needs me," Lungen announced. He then led Ben back to the main area of the basement. Walking toward a door marked STORAGE, Lungen pulled a wad of keys from his pocket and opened the door.

The large, windowless, musty room measured about fifty feet in both length and width. The walls were lined with surplus desks, chairs, file cabinets, and other office equipment. Fluorescent bulbs illuminated the dust-filled air. "So I guess this is a storage area for most of the year, and an interrogation room when you need to scare people," Ben said.

"That's it," Lungen said. "You've got us all figured out."

In the center of the room were a wooden desk and three wooden chairs. On the desk was the lie detector machine, which reminded Ben of his office's laser printer, except with more wires. Dennis Fisk was untangling the large cluster of wires and didn't look up until they approached the equipment.

"Are we ready yet?" Lungen asked.

"Almost there," Fisk said. He glanced at Ben with a smirk. "Take a seat, buddy."

Ben sat down, crossed his legs, and said nothing.

"So tell us what's been happening with your life," Lungen said. "How's your friend Eric?"

"I have no idea," Ben said. "I haven't spoken to him in weeks."

"That's too bad," Lungen said, sitting in one of the two chairs behind the desk. Lungen leaned forward, so that his elbows rested on his knees. "But you still live together, don't you?"

"Not for long," Ben answered. "He's moving out the first of the year."

"I guess he's moving to a bigger place now that he's a hot shot at the paper. I saw that he's covering all Supreme Court stories."

"He's moving out because I'm making him move out," Ben said, struggling to remain composed.

"I know what you mean," Fisk said, still fidgeting with the wires. "If I were you, I'd definitely be mad that my roommate wrote about my involvement with the whole CMI thing."

"Listen, you better control your sidekick," Ben said to Lungen. "If he wants to make an accusation like that, he'd better have proof. Otherwise, I'd be thrilled to slap your office with workplace harassment and defamation suits."

"Fisk didn't mean anything," Lungen said defensively. "We're all just a little anxious."

"Well, I told you before and I'll tell you again, I was as surprised about the CMI fiasco as you were."

"But you do still admit that you leaked information to Eric about Blake's resignation?" Lungen asked.

"I definitely did," Ben said, his voice even-tempered and steady. "And as far as I know, there's nothing illegal about that. I was just trying to help my friend."

"So now Eric's your friend again?" Fisk interrupted.

"No, not at all. The Blake incident took place before Eric wrote the CMI story. In case you're having trouble with temporal relationships, that means it happened *before* I was mad at him." Smiling, Ben watched as Fisk's jaw shifted slightly off-center. "Now, I know you're supposed to intimidate me with an hour of questions, but can we get on with this?"

"Hook him up," Lungen told Fisk.

Fisk rolled up Ben's sleeve and wrapped a Velcro pad around his arm.

"I thought you needed an expert to administer the test," Ben said.

"I'm trained to do it," Fisk shot back.

"Oh, then I know I'm in good hands," Ben said sarcastically. "Your middle name is Impartial. Dennis Impartia—"

"Shut up."

When the rest of the instruments were attached, Fisk sat in the empty seat on the other side of the desk. "I want you to take ten deep breaths," Fisk instructed. "On the tenth, just remain as calm as possible. Then we'll take your baseline reading."

Following Fisk's instructions, Ben took ten deep breaths. When he saw Lungen pull a sheet of notes from his jacket pocket, Ben tried to remain tranquil; closing his eyes, he ignored the image and thought about hang-gliding in the South of France.

When he heard the machine whir with electronic buzzes and beeps, Ben opened his eyes and looked straight ahead. Out of the corners of his eyes, he saw Lungen writing on the sheet of paper.

Fisk opened one of the drawers in the desk and pulled out a deck of playing cards. "Look over here," he said to Ben.

So predictable, Ben thought, struggling to remain in control.

"Here's the thing," Fisk explained. "I'm going to hold up a card and you're going to tell me what the card is. If you tell the truth, you'll see the little pencil on the machine stay still. If you lie, the pencil will scribble a bit wider."

"Are you sure you're trained to tell the difference?" Ben asked.

"That's funny, smart-ass. We'll see who's laughing in an hour."

"Calm down," Rick said, cradling the telephone between his shoulder and chin.

"I'm serious—I want my money."

"I told you, you'll get the rest as soon as I'm sure Ben is out of my hair."

"How much more out of your hair do you want him? I told you everything he knows, everything he's doing, everything he's thinking—"

"And when I complete my transaction, you'll have your money."

"I can't believe how scared you are of Ben. For such a know-it-all, you can be a real coward."

"It has nothing to do with fear," Rick said, switching the telephone to his other ear. "It has to do with being realistic. Ben's too resourceful to be left unchecked."

"Listen, you can call it anything you want. But take it from me—just because you complete your transaction doesn't mean Ben is going to give up the trail. If he has to, he'll be after your ass forever. He's stubborn like that."

"You're definitely right about that," Rick agreed. "But if Ben can't find me in Washington, what makes you think he'll be able to find me when the search goes global?''

In her office, Lisa stared at the government-issue, oversized wall clock above the sofa, wondering what was taking so long. She'd already had two cups of coffee and was now on her first cup of tea. The phone rang. Lunging at the receiver, she picked it up before the first ring finished. ''This is Lisa,'' she said. Listening for a moment, she continued, ''No, of course I remember. I'll have it to you as soon as possible.'' Looking back at the clock, she continued, ''Ben should be back any second. I'll make sure he—''

The office door flew open and Ben stepped in. He looked haggard, his face even whiter than his usual winter pale. Staring at the floor, he walked right past Lisa and collapsed on the sofa.

''He just walked in. I'll speak to you soon,'' Lisa said. Hanging up the phone, she raced from her seat. ''So what happened?''

''I failed,'' he said.

''You failed? Are you kidding me?''

''I absolutely am!'' he said, jumping from the sofa. He raised his hands in the air. ''I passed with flying colors!''

''That's fantastic!'' Lisa screamed, hugging him as they both jumped up and down.

''Whoa, whoa, whoa,'' Ben said, breaking their embrace. ''I think I'm getting excited. My penis is expanding.''

Laughing, Lisa pulled away. ''So tell me what happened. What'd they say? Were they mad?''

''They were so pissed. Fisk was biting his nails so much, I thought he was going to gnaw all the way to his knuckle.''

''How'd you pass? What'd you say?''

''They made me look at all these playing cards,'' Ben explained. ''And if the card was an ace of spades, and I said it was an ace, the machine just scrolled forward. But then when I lied and said it was a king, nothing different happened. Both Lungen and Fisk were beyond irate. They couldn't believe it. So they unhooked me and started all over. They asked me about ten minutes of questions without the machine on, and then they hooked me up again. And this time, when they got to the cards part, the machine went nuts when I lied. I think it was because I was so excited about beating the machine the first time around."

"You must've been dying." Lisa sat on the sofa.

"I was," Ben said, unable to stand still. "I thought I was going to wet my pants. When Fisk was putting away the cards, I closed my eyes and just thought about G-rated movies. I don't know how it happened, but I started regaining the calm I had when I walked in there."

"Do you think it was the pills?"

"It could've been," Ben said. "To be honest, that's what I was thinking about when I closed my eyes—I just imagined that the pills were working, and I started thinking about the day of my brother's funeral. With those two thoughts in my head, my body basically shut down."

"That sounds terrible."

"It was no thrill," Ben said. "But it did completely calm me. Whenever I need to bring anything in perspective, all I have to do is think about death. Everything else pales in comparison."

"Whatever works," Lisa said, leaning on the arm of the sofa. "So what did the marshals ask you?"

"I have to admit, Nathan was right on the money. They asked me if I was over twenty-one years of age, and I had to answer no. When the machine didn't do anything out of the ordinary, I knew I was home free."

"Did the marshals say anything?"

"To be honest, I did everything in my power to avoid looking at them. I was worried that if I saw their disappointment, I'd get excited and fail the last part."

"So then what'd they ask?"

"After my age, they asked me if I smoked. When I said no, the machine didn't do anything. Then they asked if I had ever done anything I was ashamed of. That's when I thought about having sex with you. The machine was so silent, I thought they had shut it off."

"That's very funny."

"Then, finally, they asked me whether I knew about the information that was leaked to Eric or whether I knew anything about Eric's story—

to be honest, I'm not exactly sure what they asked. Whatever it was, I tried to zone out of it. Then, when I heard silence, I just answered no. After the third question, when the machine didn't go crazy, I turned toward the marshals. At that point, I could actually feel the rage seething from Fisk's little pea-brained head. I asked them if I checked out okay, and Lungen said I was all finished. He thanked me for my time and apologized for the inconvenience."

"Do you think they knew you were lying?"

"Hold on a second," Ben said opening the door to their office. "Maybe you can say that a little louder. I don't think everyone in Maryland was able to hear you."

"You know what I mean."

Ben let the door close. "Let's put it this way: I don't think for a second that they think I'm completely innocent. But until they find some proof, they really can't do anything." Walking to his desk, Ben said, "By the way, who were you talking to when I walked in?"

"Huh?" Lisa asked.

"When I came in, you were on the phone with someone. You said, 'He just walked in,' and then you hung up the phone. Who were you talking to?"

"Oh, that was Nancy calling from Hollis's office. Hollis sent his final version of *Grinnell* and he wants both of us to do one more read on it. He needs our final copy by Friday. He wants to submit it to the Clerk's Office by the end of the week so they can announce it this Monday."

"And that's all she said?"

"That was it." Lisa noticed the skeptical expression on Ben's face. "Don't give me that bullshit."

"What bullshit?"

"I know what you're thinking," Lisa said, rising from the sofa. "Sorry to disappoint you, but I wasn't speaking to Rick."

"Who said you were speaking to Rick?"

"Believe me, I know your suspicious look. I don't care how well you did with the marshals downstairs, I can always tell when you're lying."

"Well, you don't have to worry. I'm not suspicious. If you say it was Nancy, it was Nancy."

"Well, it *was* Nancy."

"Then I believe you," Ben said.

"It really was!"

"I said I believe you."

"Ben, I—"

"Listen, if I really thought you were lying, I'd pretend to go to the bathroom and then I'd go up to Nancy to ask her if she called you. I trust you, Lisa. If you say it was her, it was her."

By late Friday afternoon, Ben had been staring at his computer screen for three consecutive hours. "I can't believe he hasn't made a move yet," he said, rubbing his now bloodshot eyes. "The only way to make money is to buy the property."

For the eighth time since Wednesday, Lisa reread the final draft of *Grinnell.* "Maybe Rick never got the *Grinnell* decision. Maybe he got a different decision."

"No way," Ben said. "He definitely got *Grinnell.* I can feel it."

"Oh, you can?" Lisa asked, her eyes still glued to the page. "And assuming your supernatural powers are correct, what makes you so sure that Rick's seller will even report the sale? He may just hand over the deed and run."

"The seller may do that, but Rick won't. It's in Rick's best interest to report the sale. Otherwise, the seller might be able to reneg on the deal. By reporting the property, Rick will guarantee the transaction, and he's too smart not to do that."

Intrigued by the logic of Ben's hypothesis, Lisa put down the decision and turned toward her own computer, which was also logged onto Lexis's Public Records database. As the two clerks sat mesmerized in front of the property records, their silence was interrupted by the ringing of Ben's phone.

"Hello. Justice Hollis's chambers," Ben answered.

"Hey, is this Ben Addison? The same Ben Addison that worked at Wayne and Portnoy two summers ago?"

Rolling his eyes, Ben recognized the voice of Adrian Alcott. He forced a congenial tone. "How're you doing, Adrian? Great to hear your voice."

"Yours too," Alcott said. "We haven't spoken in a while. How's everything at the Court?"

"Busy, busy, busy," Ben said, annoyed that his attention was taken from his computer screen.

"So I hear," Alcott said. "I've heard it gets really crazy there as the year comes to a close."

"Absolutely. They try to get out as many decisions as possible so everyone can enjoy their holidays."

"Don't I know it," Alcott said. "Even here, we try to—"

"Ben, you better take a look at this!" Lisa yelled, pointing to her screen.

Ignoring Alcott's ramblings, Ben turned back to his screen, where he struggled to find the source of Lisa's outburst.

"So have you decided on your career plans for next year yet?" Alcott asked. When he didn't get an answer, he added, "Ben, are you there?"

"Yeah, yeah. I'm here," Ben said, scrolling through the list of more than a hundred identifiable owners. "I'm sorry, I didn't hear that last part."

"I just wanted to know if you had decided on your career plans for next year," Alcott repeated.

"Not yet. I've been too busy to think about next week, much less next year."

"Go to the top of the list!" Lisa called out.

"I totally understand," Alcott said. "As long as you're keeping us in mind, that's all I ask."

As he scrolled to the top of the alphabetical list, Ben searched for the most recent addition to the register of Grinnell property owners. When he finally saw the newest entry, his heart dropped. He didn't want to believe his eyes, but there it was at the top of his screen: Addison & Co. "Listen, Adrian, I have to go."

"Is everything okay?" Alcott asked. Before Alcott finished the question, Ben was gone.

"I don't believe this," Ben said, his hands pulling at his hair. "I can't believe this is happening. I'm completely screwed."

"Don't say that," Lisa said, walking over to calm her co-clerk. "It's not—"

"Lisa, when this decision comes down on Monday, a company with *my* last name attached to it is going to make millions because of a decision *I* worked on. You don't think that's something to worry about?"

"Ben, there's no way to link that company to you. You didn't create it; you have nothing to do with it. Besides, who else besides us is actually watching the Public Records database for current changes in Grinnell ownership?"

Ben's phone rang. Frozen, he looked at Lisa. Again, the ring cut through the room.

"Are you going to answer it?" Lisa asked.

Again, the phone rang.

"It's the Marshals Office," Ben said. "They know." He raced toward the closet and grabbed his coat.

"Where are you going?" Lisa asked.

"I have to get out of here," Ben explained, picking up his briefcase and heading for the door. "Switch I.D.s with me."

"What?"

"I said, switch I.D.s," Ben demanded, throwing Lisa his Court I.D. "Hurry!"

Lisa ran back to her desk, pulled her I.D. from her desk drawer, and threw it to him. As soon as he caught it, he was gone.

"Call me when you get home," Lisa yelled as the phone continued to ring.

Running full speed down the main staircase, Ben was in a deep sweat. When he reached the main floor, his pace slowed and he tried his best to maintain a casual walk. Avoiding the main exit, he stayed in the north wing of the Court and headed for the only unmanned door in the building. As he approached the exit, he thought he heard someone behind him. He turned around and saw no one, but he picked up his pace. His heart racing, Ben reached the I.D. machine that would grant him access to the locked exit. He pulled out Lisa's card, held his breath, and swiped it through the machine. Nothing. With shaking hands, he ran it through again. Finally, a click of recognition. He pressed forward and pushed open the side door of the building. Once outside, he let out his breath and dropped his briefcase on the ground, relieved to feel the bitter wind on his face. Bent over, with his hands on his knees, Ben took a minute and struggled to compose himself. Running his fingers through his hair, he closed his eyes and tried to think. He picked up a handful of snow from the ground, rubbed it across his forehead, and put the rest in his mouth. Walking a few blocks up Maryland Avenue, Ben stopped at a pay phone and dialed Lisa's office number.

"Hello, Justice Hol—"

"Lisa, it's me."

"What the hell happened to you?"

"I'm sorry. I just had to get out of there. I felt sick to my stomach."

"What the hell did you need my I.D. for?"

"I thought the marshals were going to put a lock on mine so I couldn't leave the building. That's how they got me last time."

"So now I'm stuck here?"

"No," Ben said, checking over his shoulder. "You can still use mine. If the marshals lock you in, it means they know about *Grinnell.* If not, I'll know they're clueless."

"But that doesn't answer my question. If they lock me in, how am I supposed to get out of here?"

"Just walk to the main exit and tell them you can't find your I.D. They'll look you up manually and you'll get out. Meanwhile, have you figured out who Rick bought the property from?"

"I went through the list we printed out last week and there was only one name missing. Addison and Company replaced a company called the Micron Group."

"And the Micron Group is?"

"I ran a Lexis search on them and it came up blank. All I could find was that they were a limited partnership chartered in Delaware about five years ago. The original incorporation papers were registered to a Murray Feinman, but when I looked up Feinman, the only story on him was his obituary. He died late last year at the age of eighty-four. Micron was probably created solely to make predeath investments, and I have no idea who runs it now."

"And you couldn't find anything else?"

"What the hell else do you want? I mean, all I have to work with is

Lexis, which means I'm limited to periodicals and public records. I was impressed I found as much as I did."

"I'm sorry. I'm just freaking out," Ben explained as a small crowd of guided tourists walked past him. He waited until the last of the group was gone before he said another word. "Do you think we can find Rick by looking at Addison and Company?"

"I don't know. I looked up the name, and it's not incorporated anywhere. My bet is he's either incorporated in another country or Addison and Company is a subsidiary of a company that we don't know the name of. Obviously, Rick used the Addison part just to piss you off."

"I think it was more than that. Shining a light on me means that no one will be looking for him."

"That may be true. So what are you going to do now?"

"I'm going to wait here until you get off work. That way I'll know if the marshals are after me."

"You're going to wait there for two hours?"

"Screw two hours. Just leave now. Hollis doesn't care. The *Grinnell* decision is fine—send it to Nancy. Besides that, we have nothing else to do."

"So I guess we don't have about fifty cert petitions to go through?"

"C'mon, Lisa, it's Friday. Just leave."

"Fine, fine," she said. "Tell me where you are."

"I'm at the pay phone on the corner of Maryland and D."

"You got it. I'll see you in ten minutes."

When Lisa arrived on the corner, she was concerned when she couldn't find Ben. Looking around, she saw a few dozen people fighting their way through the recently shoveled sidewalks, none of them resembling him. Spotting the pay phone on the corner, she approached it and was surprised to see a sheet of paper sandwiched between the receiver and its cradle. She picked up the phone and removed the paper, which contained a note written in Ben's handwriting: "Hail the black and beige taxi across the street."

Lisa crumpled up the paper and looked over her shoulder, wondering if she was being followed. Crossing the street, she saw the black and beige taxi. "Taxi!" she yelled. When the driver nodded back, she opened the back door and got inside. Before she could say a word, the car headed down Maryland Avenue. "Excuse me, but do you know where we're going?" Lisa asked.

"So was there a problem?" Ben asked as he popped his head up from the front passenger seat.

Lisa jumped back in her seat. "Holy crap, you scared the hell out of me!" she yelled. "Why the hell were you hiding on the floor?"

"I didn't know if someone was going to follow you or if you were going to come out alone."

"Well, you don't have to worry. Your I.D. worked with no problem. I think the marshals are lost."

"Or maybe they knew I was already gone."

"Ben, you have to calm down. No one but us knew to watch that database. The marshals don't know dick. You said it yourself: They're morons."

"Whatever." Ben's eyes were focused on the back window behind Lisa.

Lisa turned around. "Stop it already. No one is following us."

"I just can't believe this is happening," Ben said, shaking his head. "My life is ruined."

"Let's not talk about it now," Lisa said, motioning with her chin toward the taxi driver. "We can discuss it when we get home."

Fifteen minutes later, they arrived at Ben's house. "See, you're home free," Lisa said as Ben put his key in the door. "If the marshals really wanted you, they would've jumped us as soon as we got out of the taxi."

When Ben opened the door, he was surprised to see Ober watching TV in the living room. "Hey, why are you home so early?" Ober asked. "Oh, now I see," he added when he saw Lisa follow Ben inside. "What's new with you, missy?"

"Nothing really," Lisa said, taking off her coat. "You?"

"Not much," Ober said.

"What are you doing here, anyway?" Ben asked his roommate. "Aren't you supposed to be working?"

"I am," Ober said, shutting off the TV. "I'm just taking a long lunch."

"It's almost three-thirty," Ben said.

"It is?" Ober said, turning the television back on. "Then I have at least another half hour before I have to show my face."

"Do you realize that our tax dollars are paying for you to sit around?" Lisa asked as she took a seat on the couch. "Go back to work."

"Hey, my tax dollars are paying your salary, too," Ober said. "Aren't they?"

"It doesn't matter," Ben said, collapsing next to Ober on the couch.

"What happened?" Ober asked, still staring at the TV.

After explaining the entire story, Ben said, "And once the decision comes down on Monday, Grinnell and Associates is going to make millions and every finger is going to point to me."

"And they should," Ober said. "You are the president of Addison and Company."

"This is not the time for jokes," Ben said.

"Then can I ask you a favor?" Ober said. "If Monday is going to be your last day at the Court, can I come along to watch the decision being announced?"

"Do you really want to come?" Ben asked.

"Absolutely," Ober said. "If you're not going to be there anymore, I figure this's the last time I'll be able to get backstage."

"There's no stage," Lisa said. "The justices sit behind a bench."

"Then backbench," Ober corrected himself. "So will you take me?"

"Sure," Ben said, shrugging his shoulders. "Why not?" He turned toward Lisa and added, "By the way, I guess the Addison and Company purchase answers your question about whether Rick was going to take part in *Grinnell*."

"I just don't understand it," Lisa said. "How could Nathan do that to you?"

"You have no proof it was him," Ober interrupted, suddenly angry.

"Oh, yeah?" Lisa asked. "Then how come we never saw that briefcase mike?"

"Don't ask me," Ober said. "But if you want to talk about Nathan, do it elsewhere. I don't want to hear that crap anymore."

"That must make you Hear No Evil," Lisa said. "Now if we only could've gotten Nathan and Eric to play Speak No Evil and Print No Evil."

"Listen you bony little bitch, you can—"

"Both of you, stop it!" Ben interrupted. "I don't have time to play mediator now. Save it for later."

"How can you let her get away with that?" Ober asked. "These people are still your friends."

"Me?" Lisa asked, pointing to herself. "What about you?"

"Listen, I don't care if it's Nathan," Ben said. "I don't care if it's either of you. In fact, I don't even care if it's my own damn mother at this point. The bottom line is that come Monday, it's all over."

Ober pulled his jacket from the couch. "Ben, I'll talk to you about it later, when she's gone. I really have to get back to work."

"Good riddance," Lisa shouted as Ober slammed the door. "Listen, I really should get going, too. We'll talk about this later?"

"Sure," Ben said. "Just abandon me now. It's okay."

"C'mon, Ben, don't give me guilt. You know that we have to get those cert petitions done. At least this way, one of us will be working on them."

"No, you're right," Ben said. "It'll be good for me to have some time alone. That way I don't have to share my burden with anyone else."

"Don't say that," Lisa said. "You know I care about—"

"I'm just joking," Ben interrupted. "Go ahead. We'll talk about it later."

Avoiding the main lobby of the Washington Hilton, Rick slid his coded key into the computerized lock and walked into the side entrance that adjoined the parking lot. As he headed straight for the elevators, his pace was brisk and confident. Getting off on the tenth floor, he made a sharp right turn toward room 1014. Sliding his key into the lock, he turned the knob and stepped inside.

"Where the hell have you been? You're a half hour late."

"Where I've been is none of your business," Rick said, a faint smile lighting his features.

"So you made a lot of money. Big deal."

"It was definitely a big deal," Rick said. He sat back on one of the canary-yellow couches and kicked his feet up onto the coffee table. It was a plush suite: three rooms, oil paintings on the walls, deep cream carpet, and a full bar. "Did you know that President Reagan was shot at this hotel?"

"I didn't know that. But I'm sure the information will someday come in handy."

"It's true," Rick said. "Locals still call it the Hinkley Hilton."

"That's great. I'm thrilled."

"What're you so pissed about?" Rick asked.

"Listen, I don't have time for this. I have to get back to work. Is the money transferred or not?"

"The last five hundred thousand will be there at the end of business today," Rick said. He reached into his jacket pocket, pulled out a small sheet of paper, and slapped it on the coffee table. "Here's the account number. I hope you enjoy your winnings."

"I definitely will."

"And to think," Rick said, "all of this happened because you don't like your roommate."

"You have it all wrong. Just because I took a decision from Ben's briefcase doesn't mean I don't *like* him. I just saw a golden opportunity that I couldn't walk away from."

"Sure, sure. And you're a great friend otherwise. That's the real reason you told me about the lie detector and the yearbooks and the—"

"I meant to ask you: How come Ben couldn't find you in the yearbooks? I thought that was a foolproof plan on his part."

"Then you're as big a fool as he is," Rick said. "The flaw with the yearbook plan is that it assumes I went to a top law school. Being the intellectual snobs you are, you can't fathom the possibility that smart people exist at non–Ivy League schools as well."

"You're definitely right. You fooled me." Slapping himself on the knee, he rose from the couch. "Oh, well, you win some and you lose some."

"Well, I guess you won this time."

"That's for sure."

"It's been a pleasure doing business with you," Rick said, extending his hand.

"You, too," Eric said as he walked into the hallway. "Maybe I'll see you on the beach."

CHAPTER 15

AT NINE-THIRTY MONDAY MORNING, LISA AND BEN PREPARED to go down to the courtroom to watch the justices announce the decisions to the public. "I still think you should turn yourself in," Lisa said, putting on her beige-and-black-striped suit jacket.

"No way." Ben tightened his gold and navy tie. "Not at this point."

"Why not? I'm sure they'd go easy on you."

"It doesn't matter. That's not a viable option as far as I'm concerned. Even if I don't go to jail, they'll have to fire me from the Court. And if they're going to take me out of this place, you better believe I'm going out kicking and screaming. I refuse to serve myself up on a platter."

"It's your life. I just think you're making a mistake."

A light knock on the door interrupted the debate.

"Come on in," Ben said.

The door opened and Nancy entered. "Ben, your visitor's here."

Ober moved around Nancy and walked into the room with his arms outstretched. "Bubby! So this is where the big boys play, huh?" Ober asked, his hands brushing over everything he passed: the books on Lisa's desk, her computer monitor, Ben's pencil sharpener, his telephone.

Ben pointed to the sofa and offered Ober a seat. "I guess you had some trouble getting in."

"Not at all," Ober said, taking off his coat and throwing it on the sofa. "It was easy. The security guard downstairs said that the courtroom was full today. And then I told him that I was here to see Ben Addison. Well, let me tell you, the man checked his clipboard and, bingo, I was inside and at the front of the line. After I got through the metal detector, another guard led me up here." Ober looked around the room. "This is a pretty good setup here. It feels like the White House—everything is old and serious."

"It *is* the Supreme Court," Lisa said. "Perhaps you've heard of it?"

"Did someone say something?" Ober asked, looking at Ben. "I thought I heard a whiny bitch, but it must've been my imagination."

"Ober, you promiscd," Ben scolded.

"Fine, fine, I'll be good," Ober said, sitting on the sofa. "How are you today, Lisa?"

"I wish a pox on you."

"Why, thanks for saying so. I just had it cut last week," Ober said, touching his hair. "This is a great sofa," he noted, bouncing up and down on its springy cushions. "And you guys have a lot of privacy. So have you ever, you know . . . late at night after the cleaning lady leaves . . . ?"

"Can you please show some decorum?" Ben begged.

"Can I ask you a question?" Lisa said to Ober. "How can you be so damn festive when you know your friend is scared to death?"

"Don't judge me," Ober warned. "You help Ben your way and I'll help him mine."

"Both of you, stop it," Ben said, heading for the door. "Let's go downstairs."

In the Great Hall, the slowly diminishing crowd filed through two metal detectors, while Ben, Lisa, and Ober walked straight into the main courtroom. "He's with us," Ben explained to a security guard who was staring at Ober.

"This is amazing," Ober said when he finally entered the room packed full of spectators, reporters, and Court staff.

"If you want pomp, we've got pomp," Ben said as they walked to a roped-off section of seats on the right side of the room.

"Is everyone in front of us a clerk?" Ober asked, noticing that they all seemed to be his age.

Ben nodded. "Only clerks and roommates of clerks can sit here."

As the remaining spectators were ushered into the room, Ober said, "Well, Ben, I have to admit, the Court looks the same as when I worked here."

The clerk in front of Ober turned around. "Who'd you clerk for?"

"Osterman," Ober said.

"Me too!" the clerk said, clearly excited. Extending a hand, he said, "I'm Joel."

"Nice to meet you, Joel," Ober said, his voice growing deeper.

"What's he saying now?" Lisa asked Ben.

"Nothing," Ben said, amused. "Let him go."

"Hey, if he puts you in a good mood, I'm in a good mood," Lisa said.

"So what'd you think of the big man?" Joel asked Ober.

"He was always the nicest in my book."

"Really?" Ben asked. "Because Osterman's usually known as being the biggest asshole on the Court."

"Well, that's what I meant," Ober said. "He was nice in that 'mean asshole' sort of way."

"Your friend wasn't a clerk, was he?" Joel asked Ben. When Ben smiled, Joel said, "Fuck you, Addison. You think you're so funny, don't you?"

"No, Joel," Ben replied. "I *know* I'm funny."

"He is very funny," Ober said. When Joel turned around and ignored him, Ober continued, "Nice to meet you, too."

A buzzer sounded, ending every conversation in the room. "Is this where I'm supposed to be quiet?" Ober whispered.

"Shhhhh," Ben said.

The marshal banged his gavel, and every person in the room stood at attention. "The Honorable, the Chief Justice and the Associate Justices of the Supreme Court of the United States!" the marshal announced. Within seconds, the nine justices strode through openings in the burgundy velvet curtain and moved to their respective seats on the bench.

"Very cool," Ober whispered.

When the justices took their seats, the marshal announced, "Oyez!

Oyez! Oyez! All persons having business before the Honorable, the Supreme Court of the United States, are admonished to draw near and give their attention, for the Court is now sitting. God save the United States and this Honorable Court!'' Once again the gavel fell, and everyone took their seats.

From the center seat, Chief Justice Osterman said, "Today we have a longer docket than usual. We will be handing down the decisions of *Doniger* v. *Lubetsky; Anderson* v. *United States; Maryland* v. *Schopf; Galani* v. *Zimmerman;* and *Grinnell and Associates* v. *New York.* Justice Blake will be reading our first three decisions, and Justice Veidt will be reading the remainder.''

"Get comfortable,'' Ben whispered. "Blake's going to take his own sweet time.''

"Thank you, Mr. Chief Justice,'' Blake announced in his signature Southern drawl. Reading from his prepared statement sheet, he announced with painful slowness each of the decisions of the Court.

"How do they pick who speaks?'' Ober asked.

"It depends,'' Ben whispered. "Blake wrote the first three decisions, while Veidt was chosen because he was instrumental in the last two.''

When Blake finished, Osterman said, "Thank you, Justice Blake. Justice Veidt.''

Justice Veidt pulled his microphone close to his mouth and announced the first of his two decisions. A small man with stark dyed-black hair and gaunt features, Veidt was known for his writings on American legal realism, which made him popular with legal scholars and uninteresting to the popular media. Although he had heard that Veidt was one of the nicest justices sitting on the Court, Ben, at this moment, couldn't muster anything but hate for him.

"How are you doing?'' Lisa asked, noticing the lack of color in Ben's face.

"I'm fine,'' Ben whispered back.

With his hand still on the microphone, Veidt cleared his throat and announced the decision. "In the case of *Grinnell and Associates* v. *New York,* we agree that the burden borne by the plaintiffs is a great one indeed. However, the importance of historical preservation of this country's landmarks cannot be overstated. The historical value of the property, combined with the limited expectations of the plaintiffs when the property was purchased, leads us to conclude that New York City's Landmark Law does not constitute a taking of the plaintiff's property. We therefore find for the defendant and reverse the Appellate Court's decision.''

The marshal banged his gavel to close the session, the tourists left the room, and Ben leaned back in his chair, a wide smile of relief flushing his face.

''Congratulations!'' Lisa said, hugging her co-clerk.

''I don't understand,'' Ober said, confused. ''I thought you said that *Grinnell* was—''

''Not here,'' Ben interrupted, holding up his hand and indicating the other clerks who were still filing out of their seats. Ben rose from his chair. ''Let's get out of here.''

''Wait a minute,'' Ober said. ''What the hell is going on?''

''Just shut up and walk,'' Lisa said, pushing Ober from behind.

The three friends fought their way through the crowds that lingered in the Great Hall and made their way to the stairs on the north side of the building. As they walked upstairs to Ben and Lisa's office, Ober struggled to make sense of the last five minutes. ''Hold on a second,'' he demanded, stopping on the stairs.

''Just wait,'' Ben said, refusing to stop for his roommate. ''I'll explain in a second.''

When they entered the office, Ober waited for the door to close behind him. ''Now tell me what the hell just happened down there.''

Ben's phone rang. ''I knew it,'' Ben said to Lisa. ''I told you it wouldn't take ten minutes.''

''You were right,'' Lisa said as Ober looked on, still bewildered. ''I thought for sure he would try to sell the property first.''

''Hello,'' Ben said. ''Justice Hollis's chambers.''

''You're a dead man, Ben.''

''Ah, Rick, how're you doing? Everything's just swell here.''

''Make all the jokes you want,'' Rick said, ''but you're now—''

''Let me tell you something, you piece of shit,'' Ben interrupted. ''*You're* the one who picked this fight. *You're* the one who approached *me. You're* the one who lied to gain my trust, and *you're* the one who screwed me at the first opportunity you got. If you thought for a second that I wouldn't try to screw you back, then you never understood me. You thought you were so damn smart that you'd make fools of the Ivy League imbeciles. Well, I've got news for you, my friend, you were outsmarted! I'm not some spoiled, gullible rich kid! I wasn't born with a silver spoon! I was born with an iron foot, and right now, I'm sticking it straight up your non–Ivy League ass! In the future, pick your opponents more wisely. Now, I have to go celebrate with my real friends, so enjoy your shitty property and know that we beat you." Ben slammed down the receiver, caught his breath, and then looked at his colleagues.

"Wow," Lisa said. "Why don't you say what's on your mind? The catharsis will do you good."

"Rick was, how shall I say, concerned, but otherwise thoughtful," Ben said, struggling to catch his breath. "And he sends his love to everyone."

"Just tell me what the hell is happening," Ober demanded, shaking Ben by the shoulders. "I thought you said Grinnell was supposed to win."

Ben sat down in his seat. "He *was.*"

"Are you saying that you knew the decision was going to come out the other way?"

"Of course I knew," Ben said. "Lisa and I wrote the opinion."

"But I thought you wrote the dissent," Ober said, scratching his head. "I'm completely confused."

"Here's the deal," Ben explained. "When the justices first voted on the decision, it came down four to four. Justice Veidt was undecided. Then Osterman convinced Veidt that if he voted for Grinnell, the decision, when it was written, would barely limit future government regulation. At that point, Veidt sided with Osterman, who now had enough votes to form a majority. Since Hollis was in the minority, Lisa and I started writing the dissent."

"And at that point, Grinnell was supposed to win." Ober leaned on the corner of Ben's desk.

"Exactly," Ben said. "Now, when the majority opinions are finally written, they're passed around to all the justices, so they can all see what it is they're actually voting for."

"And that's when Veidt switched sides," Ober said.

"Exactly," Ben said.

"Omigod, I think he's actually learning," Lisa said, patting Ober on the back.

Ben couldn't contain his smile. "When Veidt saw Osterman's opinion, he realized that the decision was taking a bigger step than he had signed on for. Osterman had basically written a ranting condemnation against government regulation. So Veidt told him that if he didn't rewrite it, he was going to jump ship. Eventually, Veidt realized that there would be no way to take a small step, so he came over to our side. With that extra vote, our dissent became the majority opinion."

"It happens all the time," Lisa interrupted. "Justices say one thing in Conference, but when it comes down to putting it on paper, they don't agree, so they switch sides."

"So wait a minute. What does this do to Rick?"

Ben put his feet up on his desk. "Let's put it this way—he just paid a great deal of money for a crappy piece of property."

"Is the property worthless?"

"It's not worthless, but the only thing that pushed the price up so high was the possibility that the owners could turn it into a giant, revenue-creating mall. And as you could see from my conversation with Mr. Scumbag, *that* possibility is totally shot."

"There's still one thing I don't understand," Ober said. "How did Rick get the wrong decision?"

"Eric took it from my briefcase," Ben said.

"Eric?"

"The one and only," Lisa said.

"I don't believe it," Ober said. "So since you knew the decision was going to be stolen, you planted the wrong decision in your briefcase."

"Exactly," Ben said, as someone knocked on the door. "I just left it in the old dissent form."

"Come in!" Lisa yelled.

Nancy walked in. "I have someone here who says he has an appointment with you." Stepping aside, she let Eric enter the room.

Ben rose from his seat. "Yes, I know him," Ben said to Nancy. "Thanks for bringing him up."

When Nancy left the room, Eric stared at Ben. "I just heard that Grinnell lost their case."

"Can you believe it?" Ben asked as he rushed toward his roommate.

"Congratulations!" Eric embraced Ben.

"You, too," Ben said. "We couldn't have done it without you."

Eric hugged Lisa. "Thanks for all the help."

"Did you have any trouble getting in downstairs?" Ben asked.

"Not at all," Eric said. "I told them I was Nathan, just like you said."

"Wait a minute," Ober said, his eyes darting to everyone in the room. "What the hell is going on here? Yesterday, everyone hated each other, and today you're having a love-in?"

"Take a seat, Sherlock." Ben pointed to the sofa. "This is where it gets good."

Looking at Eric, Ober asked, "So you've been—"

"Just listen," Ben interrupted, sitting on the edge of Lisa's desk. "If you remember, Rick and I were supposed to meet—so I could give him the *Grinnell* decision. Apparently, Rick was worried that I'd try to trap him, which I would've, so he started looking for other sources that could get him a decision."

"And since he knew Ben and I were on the outs, he approached me," Eric said, sitting down next to Ober. "I guess he figured that if I wrote the CMI story so I could get a promotion, I'd definitely steal some documents for one and a half million."

"He offered you over a million bucks?" Ober asked. "He should've come to me."

"Funny," Eric said. "So a few days before Thanksgiving, I'm sitting at my desk, and I get a call from Rick. He tells me that he wants to speak to me about our mutual friend Ben, and he asks me to meet him at this hotel. When I get there, he offers me over a million and a half to keep an eye on Ben and to somehow snag the decision."

"Are you kidding me?" Ober asked. "What'd you say?"

"I can't believe you didn't tell him to screw off right there," Lisa said.

"No way," Ben said. "Eric's way too opportunistic to do that." Turning to Ober, Ben continued, "That night, Eric slipped a note under my door telling me the whole story. He said he was sorry about what happened between us, and he wanted to make it up to me. We were so afraid that the house and all of our phones were bugged, we started communicating through notes, until we eventually worked out this plan.''

"That's what I was looking for when you caught me rummaging through Ben's garbage,'' Eric said to Ober.

"So you knew all along that you were giving Rick the wrong decision?'' Ober asked.

"Yes,'' Eric said.

"And Rick believed you since he thought you hated Ben.''

"Exactly.''

"And all of you were in on it?''

"Yep.''

"And now you've basically screwed Rick to the wall since he bet on the wrong decision?''

"You got it.''

"THIS IS THE GREATEST PLAN OF ALL TIME!'' Ober screamed, throwing his hands in the air. "You guys are geniuses!''

"We try,'' Lisa said.

Ober jumped from the sofa. "We have to celebrate! This is the best ever!''

"So you're not mad we didn't tell you?'' Eric asked, knowing the answer.

"Yeah,'' Ober said, calming down. "Why didn't you tell me?''

"We just wanted to keep you safe,'' Ben said.

"That's not it,'' Ober said.

"He didn't tell you because you're a bonehead who can't act, and you probably would've screwed up the whole plan,'' Lisa said.

"Oh, give me a break,'' Ober said. "I'm a great actor.''

"I'm sure you are,'' Ben said. "But there was too much at stake to fool around. For the past month, Eric and I had to act like we were still at each other's throats. We couldn't risk involving everyone.''

"Did Nathan know?'' Ober asked.

"No,'' Ben said, looking at Lisa.

"You can say it,'' Lisa said. She turned to Ober and explained, "That part was my idea. I'm the one who said not to trust Nathan. There, it's out. Are you happy now?''

Ben looked back at Ober. "Believe me, I was dying to tell him. But in the end, I felt the fewer people who knew, the better. And when we found out about that briefcase mike—well, that sealed it. We were convinced that Rick had contacted Nathan as well.''

"So you really did suspect him," Ober said.

"Absolutely," Ben said. "Especially when Eric told me that he never told Rick about the yearbook plan, but Rick somehow knew about it on his own. I was terrified. I thought Rick was using Eric to get the decision and that he was using Nathan to keep a closer eye on me.''

"But why couldn't Rick get that information from Eric?" Ober asked, sitting in Ben's desk chair. "Why pay two friends?''

"Because at that point, I wasn't speaking to Eric anymore," Ben explained. "And Nathan was the person I was spending the most time with.''

"We still don't know Nathan's innocent," Lisa pointed out.

"Oh, man," Ober said to Ben. "He is going to be pissed at you for not telling him. And when you combine that with what you said to him last week—you'll be lucky if he ever forgives you.''

Ben stuffed his hands in his pockets. "Thanks for the reminder.''

"Don't worry about it," Eric said, waving his hand. "You can deal with Nathan later. We should be celebrating right now. This was a tremendous victory.''

"I'm telling you," Ober said, pulling open Ben's desk drawers, "I've got to get a job here. This is the most exciting day of my life. Where can I pick up an application?''

"The brass polishers have their own union," Lisa said. "My guess is you'll have to go through them.''

Ignoring the comment, Ober asked Eric, "So what was it like being the inside man? Risking your life, seeing danger around every corner, but forging ahead because you knew that . . . wait a minute." He stopped. "What happened to all the money you got?''

"It's in some bank in Switzerland. It was supposed to be released to me after the decision came down. I called a minute after the decision was announced, and I still couldn't get access. My guess is we'll never see that money.''

"Do you know what we could've done with a million bucks?" Ober groaned. "We could've bought a small nation. We could've owned Guam. We could've built the world's biggest hoagie as a monument to the sandwich gods.''

"Darn," Eric said sarcastically. "I never thought about the hoagie monument. Maybe I can get it back." Turning toward Ben, he added, "Meanwhile, I'm surprised you haven't heard from Rick yet. I thought for sure—"

"He already called," Ben said.

"He did? When?"

"About a minute after we got back here. He was completely dumbfounded."

"You should've heard it," Ober said. "Ben tore him apart! I just wish we had a videophone so we could've seen his expression."

"I don't know if you should've told him off like that," Lisa said, taking a seat in her own chair.

"To be honest," Ben said, "I really don't give a shit right now. I'm just happy to have my life back."

"Whatever you say," Lisa said. "But I suggest that you watch your back. He's not going to just go away."

Eric looked at his watch. "I want to hear exactly what you said to him, but I really have to get back to work. We'll talk about it later?"

"Definitely," Ben said with a smile. "But don't think that just because you saved my ass, I'm not still pissed at you for writing that story."

"Yeah, yeah, you'll never forgive me," Eric said as he walked to the door. "I've heard it all before."

"Hold on," Ober said to Eric. "Did you drive here?"

"Yeah, why?"

"Because you have to drop me off at work," Ober said, grabbing his jacket and following Eric to the door. "By the way, Ben, thanks for bringing me in today. It wasn't as exciting as you said, but it was okay."

"I'll see you guys later," Ben said.

When the door closed behind Eric and Ober, Lisa looked at Ben. "So how do you feel? Top o' the world, Ma?"

"I feel unbelievable," Ben said, banging his desk. "You should've heard Rick on the phone. He was so pissed."

"I still think you shouldn't have—"

"Lisa, I don't want to hear it. I don't want to lose this mood. I feel mighty. I feel authoritative. I feel like I can command a small army of rebel soldiers on a quest for the perfect tetherball court."

"I have to admit, the ego boost suits you. I haven't seen you this happy since I let you drag me into bed."

"That's funny," Ben said. "Because the way I remember it, you were the one doing the dragging. Or was it begging?"

"That's right, I forgot your major in college was revisionist history. I should've known better."

"Trust me, the facts have not changed," Ben said as he strolled to the sofa. "You were the one who was begging for it. In fact, as I remember it, the quote was, 'I've been waiting to jump your bones since the moment I met you.' Does that ring any bells?"

"Oh, please," Lisa said. "I just made that up to make you feel better. It was a lie and you know it."

"Let me ask you one question," Ben said. "If you were so reluctant to get into bed with me, how come you were the one who wasn't wearing any underwear that night?"

Lisa flushed red. "I told you, I forgot to pack extra. I ran out on the first day. That was the only reason."

"Sure it was," Ben said, amused. "And if I were a complete moron, I might even believe that."

"Good thing you're only a partial moron, then."

"Ha. And what else did you say that night?" Ben asked. "That whenever I wanted to go again, you'd be ready?" Stretching out on the sofa, he announced, "I'm ready."

Lisa approached the sofa. "You're serious, aren't you?"

"I am."

"Are you wearing your lucky underwear?"

"I most certainly am. Today was a big day for me." As Lisa sat down on the sofa, Ben said, "You know you want to—it's all over your face."

"It is?" she asked as her face approached his.

"It definitely is. Besides, you heard what I said before: I'm ready."

"You're dreaming, is what you are," Lisa laughed as she pulled away. "Do you really think that just because you had your macho victory, you can get your hormones worked up and talk me into bed?"

"Pretty much," Ben said.

"Then you're on some serious hallucinogens," Lisa said, heading back to her desk. "You may've pulled off one miracle earlier today, but that doesn't mean you can do two."

Sitting up, Ben readjusted his tie. "Does this mean we're not having sex on the sofa?"

"That was unbelievable," Ober said as he and Eric stepped out of the elevator and into the Great Hall. "I can't believe you guys pulled it off."

"It was all Ben," Eric said. "The moment I told him about Rick, he had the whole plan designed within a few hours."

"The boy's no dummy," Ober said.

"All I can say is, thank God he's no longer mad at me. He can be a devious bastard when it comes to revenge."

"Do you think Nathan will forgive him?"

"Not a chance in hell," Eric said as the two friends walked past the security guard station and out the front entrance of the Court.

"Are you sure that was him?" Lungen asked as Eric and Ober left the building.

"Are you kidding?" Fisk said. "Of course that's him. I had my friend point him out last time I was at the *Herald*."

"And he didn't sign in under the name Eric Stroman?" Lungen asked the security guard who manned the main entrance.

"Nope," the guard said, flipping through the pages of his clipboard. When he found what he was looking for, he pointed to the sign-in sheet. "See, he said his name was Nathan."

"That's the other roommate," Fisk said. "Ben's been blowing smoke since the beginning. I told you he's a liar."

"I want you to call our friend at the *Herald*," Lungen said. "If Eric and Ben are on speaking terms, I want to know why."

Returning home from work, Ben dreaded his inevitable confrontation with Nathan. Maybe he won't be home until later, Ben thought, slowly walking up the never-shoveled, ice-covered front path. As he opened the door, he wondered how he would break the news to Nathan.

"So you set up the whole thing and trusted everyone but me and Ober?" Nathan asked before Ben could pull his key out of the lock.

"I guess you heard the good news," Ben said.

"I have one question for you," Nathan said, standing face-to-face with Ben in the middle of the living room. "Why did you trust Lisa over me?"

Ben stepped around Nathan and toward the kitchen, hoping to somehow defuse the situation. "I didn't trust Lisa over you. In fact, I didn't tell her about the plan until three days ago, when Rick finally invested his money in Grinnell. When I found out Rick bet on the wrong decision, I knew Lisa was innocent. If she was working with Rick, she would've told him that he had the wrong decision."

"But that didn't mean you had to tell her everything."

"Yes, it did," Ben said. "Otherwise, she wouldn't have stopped talking about how Rick bet on the wrong decision, which was something I didn't want anyone saying out loud."

"Fine. Thank you," Nathan said, heading for the stairs. "That's all I wanted to know."

"Wait," Ben said, turning back toward the living room. "Where are you going?"

Nathan didn't answer.

When Nathan was out of sight, Ben looked at Ober. "What did he want me to say?"

"Oh, c'mon," Ober said. "You're a grown-up. You know what you did. Did you really expect to hug and make up?"

"Yeah, but please, the silent treatment?"

"It'll only last a while," Ober said. "Don't worry. I'm sure he'll come around eventually. I mean, he's still your friend."

"But that's such an immature way to—"

"Look at it this way," Ober said. "At least he's not asking you to move out and find a new roommate."

"Ho-ho. That's very funny," Ben said sarcastically. "I just hope he comes around in time for New Year's."

"Why? Are you actually going to have some time off to enjoy it?"

"Well, we still have piles of cert petitions to go through, but the justices are gone for the next few weeks. We're basically closed down until the second week of January."

"Do you still have to go to work every day?"

"Are you kidding? Justice never sleeps. It doesn't even nap. And if it does doze off, you can bet it never hits the snooze bar."

"I get the idea," Ober said, getting up from his seat. "Just tell me when you're going to be off, so I can figure out where to make plans."

"I'll probably take off on Christmas Day and New Year's Day, but that's it."

"Then I guess we'll make plans around here," Ober said as he walked to the kitchen to make dinner.

"I don't care where we celebrate," Ben said, following Ober to the kitchen. "All I want is for next year to be less stressful than this one."

Striking a match, Ober turned on the gas and lit the stove. "Don't count on it."

CHAPTER 16

TWO WEEKS LATER, AT SEVEN-THIRTY IN THE MORNING, BEN read through the newspaper at his desk. Wearing jeans and an old wool crewneck, he was thrilled that the absence of the justices also meant casual dress for all Court staff. Reaching the op-ed page, he leaned forward and pored over the opinions of Washington's top columnists. He looked up when Lisa entered the office.

"Happy New Year," she said. Lisa had spent the previous week in California, celebrating Christmas and New Year's with her family. Although she was wearing a stark black sweater and faded jeans, the first thing Ben noticed about his co-clerk was her deep brown tan.

"You look great," Ben said, kissing her on the cheek.

"Thank you. You look pale." She opened her briefcase and dumped a six-inch pile of paper on her desk.

"You got through all of those?" Ben asked, amazed.

"What can I say? I'm that good." As she started to organize the pile of papers, Lisa noticed a memorandum on the corner of her desk. "What's this about?"

"Clerk lunches," Ben explained. "Since we're halfway done with our term, they're starting to organize private lunches with the justices so we can get to know them better."

"That's really nice," Lisa said.

"It should definitely be interesting," Ben said. "Besides Hollis, I don't think I've said two words to any of them."

"So we get to rub elbows and the Court picks up the tab? What a deal." Leaning on the back of her chair, Lisa stared at Ben. "Speaking of deals, I can't stop thinking about this whole *Grinnell* thing."

"What can I say? It was a great plan."

"No, it wasn't," Lisa said coldly. "It was completely stupid. The more I think about it, the more I realize it was the dumbest thing you could've done."

Ben sat up straight in his chair. "What's wrong with you?"

"Nothing's wrong with me," Lisa said, shuffling papers. "I just think the plan was stupid."

"How was it stupid?" Ben asked, annoyed.

"It was stupid because all you did was piss off Rick. When everything was said and done, the plan accomplished nothing else."

"It did more than that."

"Really?" Lisa challenged. "Tell me what else it did."

"It got Rick off my back."

Lisa stopped shuffling the papers on her desk. "Let me ask you a question," she said. "When you designed the whole *Grinnell* thing, what was your actual goal?"

"What was my goal?"

"Your goal," Lisa repeated. "What did you hope to accomplish?"

"There wasn't a true goal," Ben explained. "Rick approached Eric, then Eric approached me. From there, I kinda planned it out so Rick wouldn't win."

"But what was your number-one concern? What was going through your head?"

"Tons of things were going through my mind," Ben said. "Excitement, fear, anxiety, anger, revenge—"

"Exactly," Lisa interrupted, pointing a finger. "Revenge."

"What's wrong with revenge? After everything Rick put me through, I was pissed."

"And you have every right to be pissed," Lisa said. "But since this thing started, you've been so obsessed with revenge, you've stopped thinking about how you'll actually get yourself out of this mess."

"Don't give me that," Ben said. "Getting out of it was my first priority."

"Then why didn't you try to get Rick arrested? If you knew where Eric was meeting with him, why didn't you stake the place out with the authorities?"

"We didn't know where they were meeting," Ben explained. "Rick always called Eric moments before they met. Eric would be in the lobby of one hotel, and then he'd get a phone call to go to the lobby of another. It was impossible to track Rick down. Besides, even if I wanted to, I couldn't go to the authorities—they'd arrest me in a heartbeat."

"See, there's the main flaw in your thinking. You *can* go to the authorities; you just don't want to."

"You're damn right I don't want to. No offense, but I like my job."

"Forget about your job. Your life is more important."

"Lisa, I don't know why you're so crazy. The past three weeks have been perfectly calm. I have no worries. Nothing's hanging over me. Rick is gone—"

"Rick is not gone!" Lisa said, raising her voice. "When are you going to get that through your head? Rick may be pissed off, and he may be broke, and he may be angry, but he is certainly not gone! And if you just screwed *me* over for a few million dollars, you can bet your ass that I'd be plotting some serious revenge of my own from the moment it happened."

"What are you getting so nuts about?"

"I just want you to see what's going on. You're not safe."

"So what do you want me to do? Run to Hollis and ask for help?"

"I don't know if Hollis is the right person, but I think that's the right idea. Otherwise, you're never getting out of this mess. I mean, this guy has already slashed your father's tires—do you really want to wait to see his next move?"

Saying nothing, Ben grabbed a calculator from his desk. Nervously, he started tapping its keys.

"You know I'm right," Lisa added. "Throughout this whole disaster, you really haven't been thinking about getting out of this mess—you've just been obsessed with the fact that Rick outsmarted you."

"That's not true," Ben said as he continued to tap at the calculator keys.

"It is true," Lisa insisted, picking up Ben's calculator and throwing it in the garbage can next to his desk. "You hate the fact he beat you. And you're obsessing over revenge. But let me tell you, getting revenge is easy. Screwing Rick was cake. The hard part is catching him. To do that, you have to make some sacrifices. So for once in your life, you'll have to admit you can't do it alone."

"Maybe *I* can't, but *we*—"

"No, *we* can't," Lisa said. "We can't do anything. No offense, but you, me, and all your friends, even with all their little spy toys, do not have the resources to anticipate where Rick's going to turn up next. No matter how smart we are, we're not that good. And until you're willing to admit that, you're never going to get out of this."

Ben stared silently at his desk. "You think I should turn myself in?"

"Yes," Lisa said. "For the past week, I've been thinking about every possible outcome of this scenario. No matter what happens, the authorities are going to find out somehow. That's the one truth you have to accept."

"Unless we get something on Rick."

"It doesn't matter if we get something on Rick. Rick doesn't care if we tell the police he's the mastermind. They can't find him. But they can always find you. And as long as Rick's out there, you'll always have that hanging over your head."

"But what if we catch Rick ourselves?"

"It wouldn't matter," Lisa said, impatiently. "Even if we caught Rick on our own, we'd have to turn him over to the police at some point. It's not like we can lock him in our basement forever. And the moment we turn Rick over, you can be sure he's going to blame everything on you."

"Then I'm screwed no matter what."

"That's my point," Lisa said. "So you might as well go to the police and preempt whatever Rick can do to you."

"Maybe they'll go easier on me because I'm the one approaching them."

"Possibly," Lisa said. "And if we give them a solid enough plan, they might let you walk away so they can catch Rick in the act."

Pausing as he processed the information, Ben eventually said, "If I go in, I can kiss my job good-bye."

"Not necessarily," Lisa said. "For all we know, you may get a medal for your bravery."

"You know what? Let's just stop, okay?" Ben said, turning his chair away from her.

"What's wrong? What'd I say?"

"Nothing," Ben said, refusing to turn around.

"Are you mad at me?"

"I'm not mad at you. I'm mad at myself. I should've ended this weeks ago."

"That's easy to say now. Things were different weeks ago."

"Sure they were," Ben said sarcastically.

Lisa walked back to her desk. "So what are you going to do?"

"I don't know yet," Ben said. "Let me think."

At a quarter to eight that evening, Ben left the Court and made his way to Union Station. He took the escalator down into the dimly lit, underheated, advertisement-decorated hall and was surrounded by fellow overachieving, business-clad Washingtonians. Ben started counting blue pin-striped suits, brown leather briefcases, and black wing tips in his immediate vicinity. The majority of those with all three were losing their hair, and only one had actually loosened his tie since leaving work. Ben suddenly felt claustrophobic and walked to the far end of the platform. *What the hell am I doing to myself?* he wondered, staring at his peers. When the silver train hissed into the platform, Ben got on board and found an empty seat. Two minutes into the ride, the train came to an abrupt halt.

"We regret the inconvenience, but we have another train in the station ahead of us," a grainy voice announced through the public address system. "We'll be moving again in a few minutes."

The crowd let out a simultaneous groan, and Ben settled back in his seat.

"*Every* day," sighed the passenger sitting next to Ben. "I mean, can't they ever time it right? It's not like there's never been a rush hour before."

"Yeah," Ben muttered, glancing an acknowledgment at the young man. He couldn't have been more than sixteen, even though he was wearing a suit and tie.

"Why is it the same story every night?" the boy asked. "Why can't they fix it?"

"I have no idea," Ben said. "And I'm too tired to think about it."

"Don't talk to me about tired," the boy said in a slight Massachusetts accent. "Run from the Senate buildings to the House buildings twenty times a day and then talk to me."

"So you're an intern?"

The boy proudly pulled open his coat and showed off the laminated Senate I.D. card that hung around his neck. "I prefer to be called a page. And just so you're aware, if you need to know the coffee preferences of any senator, I know them all by heart."

"The pee-ons of the People, huh?"

"That's what they say. But I won't be for long."

"And why's that?" Ben smiled.

"Because I'm good at what I do. I solve problems." The boy motioned to the front end of the train. "That's what's wrong with the people who set the train schedules. None of them are problem solvers. They're boring, staid, *reactive*. That's why we're sitting here right now. No one goes after the problem proactively."

"So what's your solution?"

"It's not so much a solution as it is an approach. In my mind, if you really want to deal with a problem, you have to go straight to the heart of it. But no one in this city ever does that. They just dance around everything defensively."

"And that's your grand plan?"

"I never said it would change rail travel as we know it," the boy snapped. "I'm just telling you my approach."

"You planning to go to law school?" Ben asked.

"How'd you know?"

"I can smell lawyers a mile away. They have a distinctive scent."

"Don't mock what you don't understand. Being a lawyer is the only way to be taken seriously these days. Without a law degree, no one will listen to a single thing I say, but if I'm a lawyer, they'll give me real responsibility."

"You think so?"

"I know so," the boy insisted as the train started moving. "Good ideas can only get you so far. You need credibility to get real work. If you're suffocating at your job, you should think about it. Law school's for everyone. It'll open up your future."

"I appreciate the advice," Ben said, as the train arrived at its next stop. "I'll give it some thought."

"I hope you do," the boy said. "It may change your life." The boy got up and walked to the door. "Well, here's where I get off. Enjoy the rest of your night."

"You, too," Ben said as the boy stepped out. Seconds later, the subway doors slid shut and the train pulled away.

When Ben arrived at home, Eric and Ober were washing dishes in the kitchen. "Finally," Ober said the moment he saw Ben.

"Don't tell him," Eric said, running a dish towel across the outside of their large ceramic pasta bowl. "He'll hate it."

"No, he won't," Ober said, his hands foamy with soap. "He'll love it." As Ben put away his coat, Ober called across the room, "We thought of a whole new way to organize the judicial system."

"That's great," Ben said dryly, as he approached the kitchen.

"What happened to you?" Eric asked when he caught sight of Ben. "You look terrible."

"Thanks," Ben said.

"Everything okay at work?" Eric asked.

"It's the best," Ben said, pulling some leftover Chinese shredded beef out of the refrigerator. "Every day's a pleasure."

"You didn't hear from Rick, did you?"

"Not yet." Ben grabbed a fork from the utensil drawer.

"Screw Rick. He's gone," Ober said, rinsing a plastic mug. "Now listen to this idea. Here's what we propose: To make the judicial system more efficient, wouldn't it be great if everything—every case, every motion, every hearing—was decided by arm wrestling?"

"Just think about it for a second," Eric said. "Don't dismiss it too quickly."

"Consider the possibilities," Ober said. "Law firms would be populated with huge wrestlers; they'd recruit at all the best gyms."

"It'd be a return to Darwinism," Eric interrupted. "Survival of the fittest! Instant justice!"

"Your Honor, I object. One, two, three—case dismissed," Ober said, pretending to be beaten by an imagined arm-wrestling opponent.

"So?" Eric asked as Ben sat down at the kitchen table. "What do you think? Pretty good idea, eh?"

Ben stared down into the carton of shredded beef. "Do you think I should turn myself in?" he asked.

"What?" Eric asked.

"You heard me. Do you think I should turn myself in?"

"Why would you do that?" Eric asked.

"So I could get out of this mess."

"You wouldn't get out of this mess," Eric countered. "All you'd do is get in deeper. The moment you told anyone, you'd be fired."

"So what? Is my job worth all this headache?"

Eric threw his dishrag on the counter and approached Ben. "Are you feeling okay?" he asked. "You have the best legal job on the planet. Why would you want to jeopardize it?"

"What do you think?" Ben asked Ober.

"If you're actually serious, I agree with Eric. Why risk it all now? Rick's beaten. He's gone. What's to worry about?"

"What if he comes back?" Ben asked. "What do I do then?"

"I have no idea," Ober said. "But if you're going to wreck your life, I'd at least wait until Rick showed his face again. Otherwise you're throwing it all away for no good reason."

"Maybe," Ben said as he stabbed at his shredded beef. "Although I'm not sure that's true."

Lying in bed that evening, Ben tried to fall asleep. His feet were clammy from sweat, and he searched endlessly for a comfortable sleeping position. Lying on his back, he thought about open green meadows. Shifting to his side, he pictured the tumbling of sapphire ocean waves. Turning on his stomach, he fantasized about sex with a long-legged redhead. But in the end, the meadow always became the Supreme

Court, the waves always crashed too loudly, and the redhead always became Rick. His eyes long since adjusted to the darkness of his room, Ben eventually got out of bed and sat down at his desk. On one of his bookshelves, he spotted the cheesy metal scales of justice his mother had bought for him when he first got his clerkship. He grabbed the scales from the shelf and smiled.

Alternating his fingers, he tipped each side of the scale, hoping the repetitive movement might lull him to sleep. Five minutes later, he was still wide awake. He opened his top drawer looking for a new distraction and pulled out erasers, paper clips, highlighters, and other desk accessories. He placed a staple remover on the left balance of the scale and watched justice tip toward the left. Adding a paper clip to the same side, he said, "This is all that is good in the world." Adding a highlighter, he said, "This is all that is bright." Smiling as he added a small bottle of white-out, he whispered, "This is my honesty." Slowly, he added pencils, extra staples, rubber bands, and an eraser to the balance: his intelligence, his integrity, his happiness, and his future. He grabbed his wallet from the corner of the desk and held it over the still-empty right side of the scale. "And this is the Supreme Court," he announced as he dropped the wallet into place. When it hit the scale, the desk accessories flew through the air.

"Are you sure?" Lisa asked, surprised.

"Not entirely," Ben said early the following morning. "But I'm ninety percent there. Just tell me what you think the next step is."

"It depends who you trust," Lisa said, sipping her coffee. "You can probably go to Hollis."

"I was thinking about that," Ben explained, hoping that his cup of tea would calm his nerves. "But I don't think he's the right person to turn to. He may be able to smooth things over if he takes me to the authorities, but he certainly won't be able to help me catch Rick."

"I agree. Hollis may be a great justice, but there's no way he'll let you use your position on the Court to trap Rick."

Ben wrapped the string of the teabag around a pencil to squeeze the teabag dry. "So who does that leave?"

"I wouldn't go to Lungen and Fisk. They'll never help you."

"No question about it. They'd arrest me the moment I opened my mouth."

"What about going over their heads? Go talk to the head of the marshals."

"That's what I was thinking last night. I need someone with authority who isn't looking for a promotion. That way, they'll be more concerned with catching Rick than with simply turning me in."

"Then you've got to go to the head of the marshals."

"Then that's that."

Lisa leaned back in her chair. "I can't believe you're going to turn yourself in!"

"What are you talking about? You're the one who suggested this whole thing."

"I know. I just can't believe you're doing it. What put you over the top?"

"The next head of the D.C. Transit Authority."

"What?" Lisa asked.

"Nothing. Forget about it," Ben said. "When it came right down to it, I thought your argument yesterday really made sense. For the past few months, I haven't been in control."

"So when are you going to do it?"

"I think during lunch. I just have to find out the name of the chief marshal."

"Have you thought about how you're going to get in to see him?"

"I'll tell his secretary that I have to personally deliver a vital message from Justice Hollis. The moment I get in his office, I can explain the real story and ask him if he'll help us catch Rick." When Lisa nodded her approval, Ben continued, "So that means we only have one more thing we need to do."

"Which is what?"

"We have to figure out how to catch Rick."

At noon, Ben grabbed his coat and headed for the door.

"So this is it?" Lisa asked, handing Ben his briefcase.

"It could be," Ben said. "If he buys the plan, we'll have some more time, but if they arrest me—"

"I'm sure they'll buy the plan," Lisa interrupted. "It's their best option."

"Maybe I should call my parents first," Ben said. "That way they won't be surprised if they see their son on the news tonight."

"You're not going to be on the news," Lisa said. "The marshals will love the plan." Lisa noticed the panicked crease in Ben's forehead. "But are you okay with all this?"

"I guess I am. I mean, this is what we planned. I shouldn't be so worried. . . . "

"But you are."

"Of course I am," Ben said. "It's my life. In the next hour, I'm going to take it and flush it down the toilet. For some silly reason, that doesn't sit well with me."

"Do you want me to come down there with you?"

Ben paused. "No."

"I'm coming," Lisa said, opening the closet.

"No. I'm fine," Ben insisted, his voice shaking. "There's no reason to get you involved."

"Are you sure you're okay?" Lisa asked, coat in hand.

"I'm perfect," Ben said firmly. "You don't have to come."

"Be careful."

"I will," Ben said, noticing that his briefcase handle was damp with sweat. "Just be sure to look for me on the news tonight. I'll be the one in leg irons."

"Don't say that," Lisa said. "You'll be fine."

"Thanks for lying," Ben said. "And thanks for all the help."

"Anytime," Lisa said as Ben walked out the door.

As Ben rode the Metro to Pentagon City in Virginia, his stomach churned with both anxiety and anticipation. For months, he had done everything in his power to avoid this moment, and now he was actively riding toward it. As the subway crossed into Arlington, Ben wondered if he was crazy and if this current plan was really the best way to solve the problem. Steeling himself against indecision, he reassured himself that he was right. There was, after all, no other way.

Ben got out of the train and stood facing the Pentagon City

Mall. Following the instructions he had been given by the receptionist, Ben walked toward the offices of the United States Marshals
Service. Housed in a twelve-story contemporary office building, the
U.S. Marshals Service was headquarters to ninety-five presidentially
appointed marshals, including the director of the Marshals Service.
Responsible for protecting the federal judiciary, they ensured the
safety of federal judges as well as federal witnesses. Although Carl
Lungen and Dennis Fisk protected the Supreme Court justices
while they were in the District of Columbia, the main office assigned individual marshals to protect those justices who ventured
outside the District.

Ben took a deep breath and pulled on the glass doors of the office
building. Walking inside, he was stopped by a security guard. "Can I
help you?" the guard asked.

"I have an appointment. Ben Addison."

"With who?" the guard asked suspiciously.

"Director Alex DeRosa."

Checking his clipboard, the guard turned to his desk and picked up
the phone. "I have a Ben Addison here to see DeRosa," the guard said.
"Okay, I'm sending him up." Looking at Ben, the guard said, "It's the
twelfth floor. You can't miss it."

Minutes later, Ben exited the elevator on the twelfth floor.

A receptionist was seated in front of the glass entryway that led back
to a series of offices. "Can I help you?" she asked.

"I have an appointment with Director DeRosa. I'm Ben Addison."

"Yes, he said to leave Justice Hollis's message with me."

"I'm sorry, I can't. I have strict instructions to deliver the message
personally."

"You can deliver it to me, sir. Director DeRosa is very busy today."

"Let me explain something to you," Ben said, his agitation turning
to annoyance. "Justice Mason Hollis is also very busy. He has three
personal assistants and two legal clerks. Not to mention the three hundred Supreme Court employees who are also under his direct authority.
Any of those people could have typed up the message and sent it over
here. But Justice Hollis decided I should deliver it verbally. Now, if a
Supreme Court justice has a message that is so important he's not even

going to put it on paper, do you really think it's okay for me to simply leave it with you?"

Ben stared at the receptionist until she picked up her phone. "I have a Mr. Ben Addison to see you, sir. Justice Hollis asked that the message be delivered in person." The receptionist paused. "Yes, he is quite serious about it." Listening for another minute, the receptionist hung up the receiver and pushed a small button that unlocked the glass doors to the offices. "You may go in, Mr. Addison. He's in the far right corner."

Following the hallway, Ben tried to act as calm as possible. As he reached for the handle to DeRosa's door, the door flew open. "This better be damned good," DeRosa said, blocking the entrance to his office. Short and squat, Alex DeRosa was known for both his ruthless intellect and his lack of patience. With his sleeves rolled up to reveal thick, hairy forearms, DeRosa pointed to the single chair that was in front of his desk. "Sit."

Military awards decorated DeRosa's office: framed medals, ribbons, commendations, and diplomas from the Naval Academy and Columbia Law School. On the right wall of the office were photographs of DeRosa with two past presidents.

"So tell me this top-secret message," DeRosa barked, sitting down behind his desk.

"This is a matter of great importance, but it's not from Justice Hollis—" Ben began.

"Then what the—?" DeRosa asked, rising from his seat. "Get your ass out of here! I'm going to call Hollis personally and make sure that you—"

Ben stood as DeRosa rounded his desk. "No one knows this, but a clerk's been leaking information from inside the Court!" he blurted. "Charles Maxwell knew about the CMI merger before it came down!"

DeRosa stopped in his tracks and narrowed his eyes. "Sit." Ben sat. "Now start from the beginning. Who's the clerk?"

Ben paused. "I am."

"I'm still listening," DeRosa said.

"A few weeks into the fall term, a guy named Rick Fagen, who said he was one of Hollis's former clerks, called the office to help ease us into the position. Lots of old clerks do the same thing. It's hard getting started there and—"

"I know how it works," DeRosa interrupted.

"Anyway, thinking Rick was an old clerk, I was talking to him one day, and he asked me the outcome of the *CMI* case. I told him I couldn't tell him, but he promised he'd keep it secret. He knew all about the ethics code we signed, and he had helped us for over a month with all our Court stuff." Sensing DeRosa's impatience, Ben continued, "So I casually told him the outcome of the *CMI* case. A few days later, Maxwell bet on a legal victory. When I tried to find Rick, he'd disappeared. His number was disconnected; his apartment was abandoned. When I tried to track him down, I found out that Rick Fagen was never a Supreme Court clerk. And for the past four months, he's been trying to get another decision out of me."

Still standing, DeRosa scratched his chin. "Have you given him anything else?"

"Last month, I purposely gave him the wrong outcome to the *Grinnell* case. But that was just to piss him off."

DeRosa snickered.

"It got him off my back for a while. But I'm sure he's going to approach me again."

Silent as he thought about Ben's predicament, DeRosa finally said, "So you violated the foremost rule of our highest Court, and now you want me to save your ass? Give me one good reason why I shouldn't have you taken into custody and charged with judicial interference?"

Ben looked straight at DeRosa. "I can help you get Rick."

DeRosa walked to his chair and sat down. "Keep talking."

Two hours later, Ben returned to the Court. "What happened? Did you do it? How'd it go?" Lisa asked before Ben was even through the door.

"I did it. I told them."

As Ben sat in his chair, Lisa sat on the corner of his desk. "What'd they say? Tell me already!"

"Calm down, I will," Ben said, his voice sedate.

"Don't tell me to calm down. Tell me what happened."

"I think it went okay. He wanted—"

"Who's 'he'? DeRosa?"

"Yes," Ben said. "He's the big man there. He wanted to hear every detail. And I mean everything. How I beat the lie detector, how Eric was contacted by Rick, how Rick reacted to *Grinnell*. It took me over an hour to tell it all. And after that, I told him our plan."

"Did he like it? Was he impressed?"

"I don't think he's ever impressed. He's one of those stone-cold, ex-military types. No matter what I told him, I couldn't get a reaction."

"He obviously wants you to help him catch Rick, though. If he didn't, he wouldn't have let you walk out of there."

"That's what I'm hoping. But all he said was he wanted to think about it."

"He's definitely going to go for it," Lisa said. "If he didn't believe you, you would've left his office in handcuffs."

"Y'know what I was wondering?" Ben asked. "What if Rick was watching me today? What if he saw me go into the marshals' building?"

"I doubt it," Lisa said. "That was the whole purpose in being proactive. Rick's too busy setting things up to waste time watching you."

"I hope you're right."

"So did DeRosa say when he'd be in touch?"

"He said he'd get back to me, and he told me not to go to anyone else with the story. He knew the media would freak if they got wind of it."

"So that's it. For the time being, you're set."

"For the time being," Ben said.

"Don't worry about it. You did the smartest thing you could do— you finally put your head in front of your heart. This is the first step in the best direction."

Later in the week, Ben squeezed into a crowded subway car heading downtown. Ben always arrived at the Metro station at exactly six-forty-five in the morning and had started to recognize many of his equally early-rising co-commuters. Though they shared fifteen minutes of every day together, few, if any, of them actually spoke to each other. On most mornings, like this one, they spent their time lost in thoughts of the business day ahead. Ben, however, was thinking about the marshals. Why the hell haven't they called? he wondered.

After the train unloaded a handful of commuters at Farragut North, Ben found an empty seat and sat down. He stared at his briefcase in his lap. Maybe they're not going for it, he worried. When the train reached Metro Center, dozens of commuters crisscrossed through the car. The woman standing directly in front of Ben reached into her pocket and handed him a letter-sized envelope. "Did you drop this?" she asked.

"I don't think so," Ben said, studying the blank white envelope.

The woman stared insistently at him. "I saw you drop it." Switching to a warm, congenial tone, she repeated, "Are you sure it's not yours?"

"Actually, it is," Ben said, taking the envelope and putting it in his briefcase. "It must've slipped out of my coat. Thanks." As the train once again started moving, Ben looked up. The woman was gone.

As the Metro pulled into Union Station, Ben calmly stepped out of the train and headed for the escalator. Although he was dying to open the envelope, he knew that whatever was inside was something he shouldn't read in public. He slowly weaved through the hundreds of commuters flooding Union Station until he spotted a sign for the men's bathroom. He looked over his shoulder before going in. No one was behind him. He checked under each of the five stalls. No one there. Walking into the corner stall, he locked the door and ripped open the envelope. Trying not to skip to the end, he read:

Finding Rick is our foremost concern. However, our agreement is wholly contingent on your promise to aid us in our search. Your protection is guaranteed only so long as you help us find *everyone* involved with Rick.

We have included a list of potential suspects. You must not tell anyone on the list about our agreement. We believe this is necessary to ensure the arrest of all parties involved. *If you ignore this restriction, our deal is off.*

When Rick asks you for a new decision, you must stall him until the Sunday before the decision comes down. Only then should you actually hand over the decision.

If you decide to accept our agreement, you will be under our surveillance. As long as Rick acts as predicted, we see no reason for further concern.

From this point on, communication will be limited to when we contact you. If something goes wrong, call the 800 number at the end of this letter. It will notify our field agents that you need their immediate assistance. *This should be used only in the event of an emergency.*

Your complete assistance will ensure your future. I hope the next time we talk, it is under better circumstances.

Ben turned the page to see the list of potential suspects. Suddenly, the door to the bathroom flew open. Through the space between the door hinge and the stall, Ben saw a figure rushing toward him. The man banged on Ben's stall, screaming, "Get the hell out of there! I know who you are!"

Panicking, Ben crumpled up the letter and stuffed it down the front of his pants.

"Get the hell out!" the man shouted. "I know you're trying to find me out!"

Ben noticed a slight slur in the man's voice. "Who are you?" Ben asked.

"You know damn well who I am!"

Ben stepped out of the stall with his briefcase. Before him was a shabbily dressed street person with a long, dirty beard.

The man banged on the next stall. "I know you're in there!"

Ben approached the man. "Are you—"

"Give me a dollar!" The man pushed his palm under Ben's nose.

Convinced that the man was neither a marshal nor a threat, Ben opened his briefcase and pulled out his regular turkey sandwich. "It's not a dollar, but—"

"Thank you," the man said, grabbing the sandwich. "You're a good man."

After rushing through Court security, Ben avoided the elevator and ran up the stairs to the second floor. When he arrived in his office, he threw his briefcase on the sofa, reached into his underwear, and pulled out the letter. He smoothed it flat and passed it to Lisa.

"I hope you don't expect me to touch that," Lisa said from her desk.

"Someone passed me this on the subway," Ben explained, his voice racing with excitement. "The marshals went for it!"

Quickly reading through DeRosa's missive, Lisa flipped the page and scanned the list of potential suspects. Included were Lungen and Fisk, Nancy, fellow legal clerks, and a variety of other Supreme Court employees. The first three names on the list were Nathan, Ober, and Eric. "Do you think this is real?" Lisa asked, looking up at her co-clerk.

"What do you mean, is it real? Of course it's real."

"The only reason I'm asking is because it's so cryptic. I mean, it's not addressed to you, it's not signed by anyone. It makes no reference to the fact that you already met. For all we know, it could be from Rick."

"It can't be from Rick," Ben insisted, snatching the letter back. "It's from the marshals."

"Hey, if you're satisfied, I'm satisfied," Lisa said.

"Well, I'm satisfied," Ben said. "Completely satisfied."

"What do you think of their list?"

"I don't know what to think," Ben said, rereading the list of suspects. "But I don't think my roommates are the ones we should be worried about."

"I don't know about that," Lisa said. "I mean, who else could've told Rick about our plan with the yearbooks?"

"Who knows? It might've been the people in the mailroom. They received the packages. Anyone could've gone through them before we picked them up."

"Maybe," Lisa said. "But you're not telling your roommates about this, are you?"

"No way," Ben said. "You read the letter. Without my full cooperation, we don't have a deal. In the end, my roommates will be pissed for being left out, but what they don't know won't hurt them."

"Exactly," Lisa said. "That's—"

Ben's phone rang. "Hold on a second," Ben said, picking up the receiver. "Justice Hollis's chambers. Can I help you?"

"Hi, I'm looking for an Alvy Singer."

"This is Alvy," Ben said hesitantly, remembering the fake name from his P.O. box.

"Hey, Alvy. This is Scott over at Mailboxes and Things. I wanted to let you know that your payment is once again overdue on your second P.O. box, and we need a payment as soon as possible or we'll have to turn it over to a collection agency."

Ben realized that Scott was talking about the box that Rick had opened. "I'm real sorry about that," Ben said. "It just slipped my mind. When do I have to make the payment?"

"All it says here is that they want it by the end of the month," Scott explained. "And if I can give you a piece of advice, I'd make it as soon as possible. If the owner doesn't get her payments, she'll confiscate the mail that comes in for you. It's not my policy, but that's the way it works."

"You know that's against the law," Ben said matter-of-factly.

"It doesn't matter what it is—that's her policy. In fact, she wanted me to tell you that you're not getting your package until you pay your bill."

"What package?"

"Oh, I'm sorry—I thought you knew. We have a package here for you. That's probably why she had me call."

"Can you see what the postmark says?" Ben asked nervously. "I want to know if it's anything important."

"Sure. Hold on a second."

Ben turned to Lisa. "You won't believe this one."

"Alvy, are you there?" Scott asked.

"I'm here," Ben said.

"It's postmarked a few days ago, but it probably came in yesterday."

"Thanks for the help," Ben said. "I'll be in to pay the balance by the afternoon."

"You got it. We'll have your package waiting behind the counter."

Ben hung up the phone and headed straight for the door.

"What's wrong?" Lisa asked. "Where are you going?"

"There's a package waiting in my P.O. box."

"So what? That doesn't mean anything."

"Of course it does," Ben said. "Rick's the only one who communicates that way."

"Big deal. The marshals have it covered."

"I don't know about that," Ben said, his hand on the doorknob. "The package has a postmark from a few days ago. The marshals may not've put everything in motion until today."

"I'm sure they—"

"I wouldn't be sure of anything," Ben shot back as he opened the door. "If Rick started before we did, we're in serious trouble."

Twenty minutes later, Ben returned to the office holding a small manila envelope. Before he could say a word, he noticed the disturbed look on Lisa's face. "What's wrong?" he asked.

"Dennis Fisk from the Marshals Office was just up here. He said he wanted to speak to you as soon as you got back."

"Did he say anything else?" Ben asked, throwing the envelope on his desk.

"He asked me why Eric was in our office the day *Grinnell* was announced."

"I don't believe this," Ben said as he picked up his phone. "Could more things go wrong today?" Furiously dialing their number, he waited for the receptionist to answer. "Hi, this is Ben Addison. I want to speak to Carl Lungen."

Moments later, Lungen picked up. "Hi, Ben. Long time no speak. How was your New Year?"

"Let me tell you something," Ben said, enraged. "If you suspect me of something, I expect you to have the decency to tell it to my face.

Don't send Fisk up here to scare me. I passed your damn lie detector test and answered every one of your questions.''

"First, why don't you take a deep breath and calm down," Lungen said.

"I don't want to calm down. I want to know what this is all about."

"Fisk wasn't trying to scare you. He was just passing along a message."

"I have voice mail. I assume you've grasped the function of a phone."

"Listen, Ben, I think we've been more than fair with you since this whole thing started."

"What *thing*?" Ben interrupted. "You're always talking about some *thing*, but you can never exactly say what this mysterious *thing* is."

"Let me put it to you this way," Lungen said. "Three weeks ago, you swore to us that you and Eric weren't speaking. A couple days after that, Eric was in the Court and in your office. Not only that, but he also used Nathan's name to get in here. Now, do you want me to tell you what I think, or do you want to finally tell me the truth?''

"You got me," Ben said. "You figured it all out. Eric and I are friends again. Alert the local militia."

"This isn't a joke."

"You're damn right it's not a joke," Ben interrupted. "It's my life you're playing with. For the past two weeks you've obviously been racking your brains trying to come up with my crime. But let me tell you, it's not against the law to make up with your roommate. So until you can actually prove something, I'd appreciate it if you just stayed the hell away from me."

"Tell me why Eric was in the Court that day."

"He's the reporter who's assigned to the Court! What do you think he was doing here?"

"Why did he use Nathan's name?"

"To be honest, because I told him that if you guys found out we'd made up, you'd be all over our asses. What a surprise—I was right."

"That still doesn't—"

"Listen, I'm done with this conversation. No matter what I say, you're still going to suspect me. I've done nothing wrong, and I have nothing to hide. If you don't believe that, I'm sorry. But if you're committed to interfering with my life, you'd better get proof or go away. Because I swear, if this doesn't stop, I'll slap your office with a workplace harassment suit faster than you can say, 'Forced retirement and bye-bye pension.' Now if you don't mind, I have to go do some work. I hope I won't hear from you soon." Before Lungen could respond, Ben slammed down the phone. When he noticed Lisa staring at him, Ben asked, "What?"

"Nothing," she said. "I'm just admiring your ambassadorial abilities—always calm and level-headed; never once losing your temper."

"What the hell was I supposed to do?"

"Take it easy," Lisa said. "Forget about the marshals. They don't have anything on you."

"Of course they don't. If they did, I'd be out of here by now." Ben grabbed the manila envelope from his desk and threw it to Lisa. "Now, back to the original crisis."

Dumping the envelope's contents on her desk, Lisa saw a miniature cassette tape and a small stack of photocopies. She picked up the copies and looked at the first page, which resembled the first page of a bankbook. There was a single entry for $150,000, and the words "City of Bern" were in fine print at the bottom of the page.

"As far as I can tell, it's a Swiss bankbook," Ben said.

"Is this Rick's account?"

"In truth, it is," Ben explained. "But take a look at the last page."

Lisa reached the final page in the stack, titled "Registration of Account," and saw that the account holder's name was Ben Addison.

"I know," Ben said, noticing Lisa's distressed reaction. "He took out all the vital information like the bank's name and the account number, but he made damn sure we saw my name in there."

"November seventeenth?" Lisa looked at the date of the first and only deposit. "What happened then?"

"I wanted to check that," Ben said, grabbing his desktop calendar. He flipped back toward November. "It's what I thought. That's the day the *CMI* decision came down."

"Any idea what's on the cassette?" Lisa asked, putting down the papers.

"None," Ben said. He reached into his desk drawer and pulled out his Dictaphone. "But I bet it's not *James Taylor's Greatest Hits*." Ben put the tape in the small recorder.

"What's happening with the CMI merger? Doesn't that come down next week?"

"Actually, it probably won't come down for another few weeks. Blake and Osterman asked for more time to write their opinions. You know how it is— merger cases always wind up confusing everyone. It takes forever to sort through all the regulatory nonsense."

"So who wins?"

"It was actually pretty amazing. When the justices were voting in Conference, it was five to four against CMI. At the last minute—"

"Shit," Ben said, stopping the tape. "He taped the whole conversation."

"Was that when you first told him the decision?"

"No, it was when we were exchanging recipes. Of course it was the time."

"Don't—"

"Damn!" Ben said, slamming his desk with his fist. "How could I be so stupid?"

"Listen, there's no way you could've known," Lisa said. "You thought Rick was a friend."

"But if I never said anything—"

"You probably wouldn't be in this mess. You're right—you wouldn't. We've been through this before. The point is, for the first time you're finally in a position to get out of it."

"I don't even know if that's true anymore. What if the marshals didn't set everything up in time?"

"I'm sure they did," Lisa said. "I'm sure they started working on it the moment you left DeRosa's office."

"I hope so," Ben said, staring at the small tape player on his desk. He looked up at Lisa. "You have to admire the way Rick set it up, though. Before today, the only thing at risk was my job. All he could prove was that I broke the Court's Ethics Code. But by combining the tape with the bankbook, Rick's created a whole new reality: Now it looks like I was paid for the information. He's *created proof* that I was paid.

That's more than an ethics violation. Accepting a bribe as a public official is a federal offense.''

"I wouldn't worry about it," Lisa said, walking over to Ben's desk. She opened his Dictaphone and pulled out the tape. "We'll send this to DeRosa just to be safe.''

"Do you think DeRosa would ever believe it happened that way?'' Ben asked. "That he'd see this and think I really took a bribe?''

"Not anymore," Lisa said, dropping the tape in an envelope. "By going in and being honest about it, you've preempted that conclusion. Mailing him this just seals the deal.'' As Ben wrote a quick note to DeRosa, Lisa asked, "Do you think DeRosa is listening to us talk right now?''

"No way," Ben said. "He'd only bug us if he thought I was lying. And if he thought I was lying, there's no way I'd still be working at the Court. They can't risk another breach like that. This is the one place we can actually feel safe.''

Lisa went to her desk, picked up the copies of the bankbook pages, and handed them to Ben. He inserted the copies in the envelope. "So what do we do now?'' Lisa asked.

"We sit here and hope Rick calls.''

"Oh, he'll definitely call," Lisa said. "Mark my words. He's going to make sure you got his package of incriminating evidence, and then he's going to blackmail you. My guess is he'll threaten to distribute the tape and the bankbook unless you give him a new decision.''

"I never thought I'd say this, but I hope he does.''

At six-thirty that evening, Ben returned to the office. "Anyone call for me?''

"Not yet," Lisa said. "How are you holding up?''

"I'm okay," Ben said. "Antsy, but okay. By the way, in case you were wondering, I flipped through the U.S. Code and confirmed that accepting a bribe usually carries a sentence of five to fifteen years.''

"Great," Lisa said wryly. "Any other vital bits of—''

Ben's phone rang. When he didn't grab it, she said, "What are you waiting for? Pick it up.''

"Should I—''

"Pick it up!''

Hesitantly, Ben lifted the receiver. "Hello, this is Ben."

"Hey, Ben. It's Adrian Alcott calling." Before Alcott even identified himself, Ben had recognized the voice of Wayne & Portnoy's most persistent recruiter.

"It's not Rick, is it?" Lisa asked.

"I should be so lucky," Ben whispered, covering up the mouthpiece of the phone.

"So how is everything in the ol' Court?" Alcott asked.

"It's fine. We're super-busy."

"I'm sure you are," Alcott said. "I just wanted to make sure you were okay there. Last time we spoke, we got cut off abruptly."

"Yeah, sorry about that," Ben said. "We had to get something directly to Hollis, so I had to run."

"No apology necessary," Alcott said. "I mean, who's more important, me or a Supreme Court justice?" When Ben didn't respond, Alcott added, "By the way, the reason I'm calling is that I wanted to tell you that we're going to be there in three weeks. We're arguing for the respondent in *Mirsky.*"

"That's great," Ben said, struggling to act surprised even though Alcott had told him the news on three previous occasions.

"It looks like it's going to be a hard one, too," Alcott said. "After Osterman's majority in *Cooper,* no one's had any luck with Sixth Amendment cases up there."

"No comment," Ben said coldly. "You know I can't talk to you about pending cases."

"Oh, that's right," Alcott said. "I apologize. I didn't mean to—"

"No apology necessary," Ben said. "It's just one of the perks of working here."

"Well, I hope you'll let us show you the perks of working here," Alcott said, sounding proud of his transition. "It's not the Supreme Court, but we do okay for ourselves. Speaking of which, the other reason I called was to set up another lunch meeting. We haven't seen you in a while."

"I'd love to. But can I get back to you in a week or two? I've got so much on my plate right now, I'm afraid I'd be a terrible guest."

"Definitely," Alcott said. "You take care of whatever you need to. I'll give you a call in the next few weeks."

"That'd be much better," Ben said, doodling a picture of a gun pointed at the head of a man in a suit. "Hopefully, things'll be calmer by then."

When Ben hung up the phone, Lisa asked, "Wayne and Portnoy?"

"You got it."

"Let me guess—they're hoping to stick their head farther up your butt, and they want to give you another ten grand to do it?"

"They just want to take me to lunch," Ben said as he added another gun to his doodle.

"Hey, cheer up," Lisa said. "You should be happy that prestigious firms are still interested in you. There are worse things in life."

"You mean like having a psychopath dangling your biggest fuckup in front of the whole world?"

"Exactly. Having a personal psychopath is so much better," Lisa said. "Meanwhile, are you going to tell your roommates about the cassette Rick sent?"

"Probably not," Ben explained. "If I do that, I have to act upset all night."

"And you're not upset?"

"I'm trying not to be," Ben said as he added a third gun to the doodle of himself. "Hopefully, everything's going according to plan."

Ben walked up the block toward his house and took in the silence that winter brought to the city. It was cold but clear; no snow and all stars. Taking deep breaths of crisp air, he paused on the front steps. It's almost over, he thought. He eased his key into the lock and turned the knob.

"Where the hell were you?" Nathan asked. "Lisa said you left the Court almost an hour ago."

"We're in deep shit," Ober added from the couch.

"This is the final straw for me," Nathan yelled, waving a piece of paper in front of Ben's face. "I'm done."

"What's going on?" Ben asked, dropping his briefcase on the floor.

"Read this," Nathan said. He handed Ben the piece of paper.

"Dear Mr. Bachman," Ben read to himself. "Since October of last year, Nathan Hollister has illegally used the following equipment for his own personal use:" Scanning down the list that included the telescopic camera lens, the wireless microphones, and even the Prynadolol for the lie detector test, Ben's eyes darted to the letter's closing paragraph. "Although I am unwilling to reveal my identity, you can rest assured that this information can be verified by checking the equipment records in the Office of Security. There is no reason for a member of the Policy Planning Staff to have access to such equipment. I hope you will investigate this matter. A copy of this letter has been sent to your supervisors, as well as the Secretary of State."

"Crap," Ben said, looking up at his roommate. "Mr. Bachman is your boss?"

"He's the general counsel," Nathan said. "Which means that if Rick sent this letter, it was entered into Bachman's correspondence log the moment it was opened. And that means Rick can get proof the letter was received."

"So Bachman will *have* to start an investigation," Ben said.

"Exactly," Nathan said. "If Bachman doesn't investigate, he's at risk since there's clear proof that his office opened the letter. It'll look like he ignored the whole thing. And after that disaster with his confirmation hearings, he's terrified of looking like he sat on a scandal. Rick did his homework here."

"When'd you get that letter?" Ben asked.

"It came in the mail today," Nathan explained accusingly. "One for me, another for Ober, and a third for Eric."

"Damn," Ben said, pushing the letter back in Nathan's hands.

"As soon as I got the letter I tried calling you," Ober explained, holding his own letter. "When I heard you left, I called Nathan and Eric and told them to rush home."

"Did Rick send anything else with it?" Ben asked, terrified by the fact that his friends were not only deeply involved, but were in serious trouble.

"Nothing," Nathan said. "No instructions. No explanation. Just the letter. It's not clear whether he sent it to Bachman or not."

"What'd yours say?" Ben asked Ober.

"I'm dead," Ober said. He passed Ben the sheet of paper. "Mine's addressed to my staff director. It tells her that the death threat written to Senator Stevens was written by me. And it says I did it to get myself a big promotion.''

''Which you got,'' Nathan said indignantly. Looking at Ben, he continued, ''You better do something, because this just got out of hand.''

''What do you want me to do?'' Ben asked as the room started to spin. ''I got my own letter today—in the form of a cassette tape and a bankbook.'' Ben sat on the sofa and wiped his brow with his shirtsleeve. ''But there's no reason to believe that anyone else has gotten copies of any of it. What'd Eric's letter say?''

''Eric's was addressed to *The New York Times*,'' Nathan explained, ''but I'm sure Rick plans to send it out to everyone in the national press.''

''What'd it say?'' Ben asked, putting his hands to his head.

''Eric's letter explains the whole story start to finish. It talks about how you leaked the information about CMI, and it names you as Eric's source for his first story. As far as I can tell, it doesn't really have any devastating effect on Eric—''

''Except it shows that he was lying to his bosses about not knowing anything,'' Ben interrupted. ''Does Eric even know yet?''

''He was out on assignment when I called,'' Ober said. ''He'll wander in soon.''

Letting Ben have a minute of silence to process the information, Nathan said, ''So I guess this means you're finally going to the authorities.''

''What?'' Ben asked, looking up at his roommate.

''You are going to turn yourself in now, aren't you?'' Nathan asked.

''No,'' Ben said coldly. ''I'm not.''

''Ben, don't get mad at me,'' Nathan said. ''What choice do you have?''

''We can wait for Rick to make his next move. I'm sure he hasn't sent the letters out yet. If he wanted to get us all fired, he could've done that months ago.''

''Who do you think you are?'' Nathan demanded. ''This isn't just your life you're playing with anymore—this is mine, and Ober's and Eric's.''

''But if I go to the authorities, Rick can still mail the letters,'' Ben pointed out. ''Which means you're implicated no matter what I do.''

"Not if you tell the police you're the one at fault. If you cooperate with them, we have a better chance of getting off."

Before Ben could respond, the front door opened and Eric walked in. Looking around the room, he asked, "What's wrong? Who died?"

"We got some mail today," Nathan said, as he and Ober handed Eric the letters.

When he was finished reading all three, Eric asked, "What are we going to do?"

"*We* don't have to do anything," Nathan said. "It's up to Ben."

"He thinks I should turn myself in and take my punishment," Ben explained.

"No way," Eric said. "You'll be fired in a heartbeat."

"Forget about being fired," Ben interrupted. "If the bankbook gets out, I'm going to jail."

"If that's the case, then you should take your chances trying to catch Rick," Eric said, finally taking off his overcoat.

"Don't give us that macho bullshit," Nathan interrupted. "You have the least to lose."

"How do you figure that?" Eric asked.

"If your letter gets out, you'll probably get credit for breaking the story," Nathan pointed out. "Which means it's in your best interest to egg Ben on."

"You are unreal," Eric said, shaking his head. "Do you really think I'm that much of a scumbag?"

"It wouldn't be the first time your self-interest interfered with your judgment."

"You can go fuck yourself," Eric shot back.

Looking at Ober, Ben said, "You've been way too quiet. What're you thinking?"

"I guess I lean toward Nathan," Ober said. "I'm sorry."

"That's crazy—" Eric began.

"It's ridiculous to argue," Ben interrupted, hoping to end the conversation. "I can't do anything until I hear from Rick."

"But—"

"I'm sorry, but that's my decision for now," Ben said. "All I can say is trust me. I would never do anything to put you guys at risk."

"Do you have a plan in the works?" Nathan asked suspiciously. "Because if this is like *Grinnell*—"

"There's no plan," Ben interrupted. "I don't have a plan. But I want you to know that I wouldn't do anything to hurt you guys. I swear. I wouldn't."

"Fine," Nathan said. He grabbed his coat from the closet and headed for the door.

"Where are you going?" Ben asked.

"Out," Nathan said. "I'm hungry and I need to get some dinner."

When the door closed, Ober turned to Ben. "Ben, you're forgetting what's right. You better talk to him when he gets back."

"But if you talk to him, be careful what you say," Eric pointed out.

"What's that supposed to mean?" Ober asked.

"It means that if I were Ben, I wouldn't trust anybody."

"So you still suspect Nathan?"

"Not at all," Eric said. "I just think a better friend would've offered a bit more support."

"You can be a real jerk," Ober said as he got up from the couch. "You of all people should never talk about what a *better friend* would do." Before Eric could respond, Ober was halfway up the stairs.

"Let him go," Ben said, grabbing his coat from the closet.

"Where are *you* going?" Eric asked.

"I need to get some air," Ben said, closing the door behind him.

As he inched up the block, Ben kept looking over his shoulder. Scrutinizing every person he saw, he wondered where DeRosa's agents were, and if they were even in place. When he reached the commercial section of his neighborhood, Ben ducked into Jumbo's, the area's best late-night eating spot. He sat down at the counter and ordered one of the daily specials. He then got up and walked to the pay phone at the back of the restaurant. Ben inserted the required change and dialed Lisa's number. "C'mon, be home. Be home, be home, be home."

As the phone rang, Ben thought about everything he wanted to tell Lisa: how scared he was about Rick's new letters; how apprehensive he was about lying to his friends; how nervous he was for their safety; how anxious he was to talk to someone he could trust. But when the answering machine picked up, Ben knew Lisa wasn't home. He was alone.

His eyes rapidly scanning the customers in the restaurant, Ben hung up the phone. He reached into his back pocket and pulled out the phone number from DeRosa's note. Maybe I should call, he thought, and picked up the receiver. No, nothing terrible has happened yet. The plan should still work. He hung up the phone. For all I know, Rick will do everything else as expected. Agitated, but ever-cautious, Ben stepped away from the phone and walked back to the counter. But if anything else goes wrong, I'm pounding that panic button.

CHAPTER 17

"I CAN'T TAKE IT ANYMORE," BEN SAID. STARING INTO THE mirror in the office closet, he picked at a deep shaving cut on his chin. "Why hasn't he called?"

"It's only been a week," Lisa said.

"The longest week of my life," Ben said as the cut started bleeding. "You'd think by now he'd tell us what he wants."

"Maybe he's trying to wear you down."

"He's obviously trying to wear me down. The longer he waits, the crazier I get. Typical Rick mindgame."

"I'm not surprised Rick hasn't called—I'm more surprised you haven't heard from DeRosa."

"Don't even start me on that. The guy promises to keep me informed, and then he doesn't send a single message. For all I know, the marshals aren't even out there."

"Do you feel like you're being watched?"

"Not at all. Which means they're either extremely good, or they lied to me."

"You better get moving," Lisa said, looking at her watch. "You're going to miss your first free lunch."

"They're lucky it's free."

"Don't give me that," Lisa said. "You're about to go to lunch with the Chief Justice of the United States. Don't pretend you're not excited.''

"No, you're right,'' Ben said. "I'm very excited. I mean, who wouldn't want to spend an hour having their intellect crushed?''

"Don't pay attention to what his clerks say. Their backbones are so weak, they barely stand erect.''

"Well, I'll have you know, I stand very erect,'' Ben said proudly, sticking out his chest. "Super-erect.''

"You're a one-man erection,'' Lisa said as Ben walked to the door. He paused when his phone rang and looked at Lisa. "Let it ring,'' she said. "Go enjoy lunch.'' When she saw him turn around and head for the phone, she added, "Relax. It's not him.''

"Hello. Justice Hollis's chambers,'' Ben said as he picked up the receiver.

"Hi, Ben,'' Rick said. "How's everything in the big house?''

Closing his eyes, Ben said, "Tell me what you want.''

"What I want?'' Rick asked. "Who says I want anything? I called to say hello.''

"C'mon, Rick, I really don't have the time for this. What's the story this time?''

"What's the matter there?'' Rick asked. "You don't sound as confident as the last time I spoke to you.''

"I'm fine,'' Ben said through clenched teeth.

"I assume you and your roommates got my package?''

"Yes, we got the damn package. Now what do you want?''

"Down to business,'' Rick said. He cleared his throat. "I want the *American Steel* case, and I want it tonight.''

"But that case comes down Monday,'' Ben said, panicking.

"I know when it comes down,'' Rick said. "And I want it personally delivered by you, to me.''

"I need to think about this,'' Ben said.

"You have a half hour.''

"I won't be here in a half hour. I'll be at lunch with Osterman.''

"I'll call you back at exactly two o'clock,'' Rick said. "At that time, I want an answer. Obviously, from my recent mailing, I'm sure you understand the consequences.''

"Wait a minute," Ben said. "What about—"

"There's nothing else to talk about," Rick said. "Good-bye."

"What'd he say?" Lisa asked as Ben hung up.

"I have to go," Ben said, looking at his watch. "I'm late for Osterman."

"Tell me what happened," Lisa said.

Ignoring her, Ben left the office and ran down the stairs to Osterman's office on the first floor.

"You're two minutes late," the secretary said. "Expect him to mention it."

"Great." Ben walked into Osterman's office, the largest in the Court. Across the sea of burgundy carpeting, Osterman was seated at his desk, which was a perfect replica of the one used by John Jay, the first Chief Justice. In an ornate gold frame on the desk was Oliver Wendell Holmes's 1913 description of the Court: "We are very quiet there, but it is the quiet of a storm centre. . . ." In no mood to acknowledge the accuracy of the quotation, Ben stood in front of the desk and waited for the Chief Justice to look up from his stack of papers.

After waiting almost a minute, Ben cleared his throat.

Osterman abruptly looked up at his guest. "You're late. Now give me a moment." Small and lanky, Samuel Osterman had thick glasses and a thin comb-over of black hair. At fifty-nine, he was one of the youngest Chief Justices in history, but his poor selections in eyewear and hairstyle made him look old beyond his years. Looking back up at Ben, he said, "Rather than facing the weather outside, I've asked that our food be delivered to us." He pointed to the antique table on the right side of the room. "I figured we'd eat up here."

"That's fine with me," Ben said.

"Sit, please."

"Thank you," Ben said, easing himself into the leather chair opposite Osterman's desk.

"Columbia, Yale Law, and some time with Judge Stanley," Osterman said, recalling the facts from memory. "So how has your term been so far?"

"Very enjoyable," Ben said.

"Nervous about something?" Osterman asked, pointing to Ben's foot, which was tapping against the carpet.

"No," Ben said as he stopped tapping. "Just a bad habit. How was your vacation?"

"It was fine. And yours?"

"Wonderful," Ben said dryly.

"Tell me," Osterman said, "any new cert petitions come through that sound worthwhile?"

"Actually, there's one that challenges the president's new farm subsidy program. It seems intriguing."

"Farmers are Jeffersonian reactionaries who haven't had a progressive thought in their lives," Osterman said.

"That's one way to look at it," Ben said, surprised by Osterman's reaction. "But don't you feel that—"

"Ben, don't *feel.* Law is not about *feeling.* If you learn one thing during your time with the Court, you should learn that life is a tragedy for those who *feel* and a comedy for those who *think.*"

"And it's a musical for those who sing," Ben offered. When he saw Osterman's eyebrows lower behind the rim of his eyeglasses, Ben quickly added, "I know what you mean, though."

Before Osterman could say another word, the office door opened, and his secretary walked in. "Lunchtime."

An hour later, Ben returned to his office. "Finally," Lisa said. "Tell me—what'd Rick say? What'd he want? How was lunch?"

"Taking the easiest question first, I'd say lunch was a complete disaster," he said, collapsing on the sofa. "And y'know how everyone says Osterman has Coke-bottle glasses? He doesn't. He has bank-teller windows attached to his face."

"Forget about him," Lisa said. She had picked up a huge salad from the deli and was eating it at her desk. "What happened with Rick?"

"Oh, yes, asshole number two. He wants *American Steel.*"

"But that comes down Monday," Lisa said. "It's already Friday."

"I assume that's the point," Ben said, slumping on the sofa. "I'm sure the last thing Rick wants is to have us try to scheme around him."

"Do you think everything will be ready?" Lisa asked through a mouthful of greens.

Ben paused. "I honestly have no idea."

"What do you mean, you have no idea?"

"I have no idea," Ben said, raising his voice. "I have no idea where the marshals are; I have no idea if they're doing anything right; I don't even know if they're on my side anymore. For all we know, they could be the ones working with Rick."

"That's bullshit."

"How is that bullshit?" Ben asked defensively. "They promised to contact me, but I haven't heard from them in a week. Rick is demanding a brand-new case, and he wants it two days earlier than we can give it to him. He has information that'll get my friends fired and put us all in jail. I'll be disbarred, and every single thing we've worked for will be gone. If the plan doesn't work out perfectly, I face those consequences. Now where's the bullshit part?"

"It can still work out perfectly."

"It's already screwed up. Involving my roommates makes the whole thing a mess."

"I don't want to have this argument. It can still work out. Now what else did Rick say?"

Ben looked at his watch. "He should be calling back any minute. That's when I have to tell him whether I'll hand over the decision."

"Was he adamant about getting it tonight?"

"He seemed to be."

"Try and stall until Sunday. That way we can contact—" There was a knock at the office door.

"Come in," Ben yelled. Nancy stepped into the room.

"And how are you two doing today?" Nancy asked, carrying a small pile of books and papers. "Don't you look tired," she said to Ben as she handed Lisa a thin manila folder.

"Are these the corrections for the commercial speech dissent?" Lisa wiped the salad dressing off her hands with a napkin before she picked up the folder.

"You got it," Nancy said. Walking past Ben's and Lisa's desks, she approached the back wall of the office and straightened the framed picture of the justices. She then turned toward Ben, who was still stretched out on the sofa. "Have you been getting enough sleep?"

"Oh, yeah. I got a full hour last night."

"You really should take a day off," Nancy said. "Every year I watch the clerks here kill themselves. It's just not worth it."

"I know . . ." Ben began. His phone started ringing. He jumped from the sofa and put his hand on the receiver.

"Thanks for the delivery. I'll give you the rewrite before the end of the day," Lisa said to Nancy.

"Take your time. He doesn't expect it until Monday," Nancy said, leaning on Lisa's desk. "So do you have any interesting plans for the weekend, or are you working?"

Convinced that Nancy was not leaving the office anytime soon, Ben reluctantly picked up the phone. "Justice Hollis's chambers," he said. "This is Ben."

"Are you ready to deliver?" Rick asked.

"Hey, how are you doing?" Ben said, as he struggled to sound as cheerful as possible.

"I'm not joking anymore."

"I'm fine," Ben forced a laugh. "I'm just visiting with some colleagues."

"What's your answer?" Rick asked.

Ben turned his chair away from Lisa and Nancy. "I need more time."

"This isn't *Grinnell.* You don't need more time."

"I do," Ben said. "It's not done yet."

"Don't bullshit me," Rick warned. "I know that decision is finished."

"I swear—" Ben began.

Rick hung up.

"Hello? Are you there?" Replacing the receiver, Ben turned around and faced Lisa and Nancy, who were staring at him.

"Is everything okay?" Nancy asked.

"Yeah. Fine," Ben said nonchalantly. "I got disconnected."

"Don't worry," Nancy said. "They'll call back." Walking to the door, she added, "Lisa, I'm serious about the corrections. I can tell Hollis won't look at it until Monday."

"Thanks," Lisa said as Nancy left the room. As soon as the door closed, Lisa looked back at Ben. "What'd he say?"

"The son-of-a-bitch hung up on me!" Ben said. "He asked for the decision, I tried to stall, and he hung up. I don't believe it.'' Ben and Lisa waited for the phone to ring again. After a full minute, Ben said, ''He's not calling back. What the hell is going on?''

''He's just trying to make you crazy,'' Lisa said.

''It's working,'' Ben said. ''What should I do?''

''Relax. I'm sure he'll call back.''

"He's not calling back. What the hell is going on?"
"He's just trying to make you crazy."
"It's working. What should I do?"
"Relax. I'm sure he'll call back."

Smiling as he paced across Lungen's office, Fisk was thrilled that the microphone was finally working. ''I don't know what they're up to, but there's no way this kid is innocent.''

Lungen's eyes were focused on the small charcoal-gray speaker on his desk. ''I don't know,'' he said. ''Whoever this Rick is, he's got Ben terrified. It sounds like he's being blackmailed.''

''Blackmailed or not, he broke the law.''

''We don't know that,'' Lungen said. ''I still think we're missing half the story.''

''You must be kidding,'' Fisk said as he stopped pacing. ''Within the first five minutes we put this thing on, we hear them talking about leaking a decision to an outside party.''

''We shouldn't jump to conclusions.''

''Who needs to jump? The answer is staring us in the face. Regardless of how they got involved, these two are up to no good.''

''The microphone was just installed last night. It took us until lunch to finally get it working, and we've heard a total of five minutes of conversation. All I'm saying is that we should give it a bit more time. I want all the facts before we run in with guns blazing.''

''Trust me, we'll get the facts,'' Fisk said as he turned up the volume on the speaker. ''The way these two are talking, by next week, Justice Hollis will be interviewing new clerks.''

*   *   *

"That's it," Rick said, slapping shut his cellular phone. "I've had enough of his shit." He opened the passenger-side door and got out of the car.

Getting out of the driver's side, Richard Claremont, American Steel's executive vice president of marketing, asked, "What'd he say?"

Slamming the car door shut, Rick looked up the block, where he had a perfect view of the Court. "He was trying to stall." Unfazed by the frigid wind that whipped down First Street, Rick didn't even button his overcoat. "He sounded nervous, but he was definitely trying to stall."

"He should be nervous. From everything you've said, it sounds like his life is ruined."

"I don't want him to be scared, though," Rick explained, approaching the Court. "If he's scared, he'll go to the authorities. But if he still thinks he has a chance of catching me, we have a better chance of getting the decision."

"So you think he may still go to the police?" Claremont asked.

"Actually, no," Rick said, watching a busload of bundled-up tourists snap pictures of the nation's highest tribunal. "Ben's too concerned about his résumé to do that. That's the reason I picked him in the first place. He's got a great deal to lose."

"Then why didn't you pick Lisa? From your file on her, she's got a similar background."

"Ben's a much better mark. Between the two, Lisa's smarter. She never would've given up the original decision. Ben's more anxious to please. I knew he'd bite."

"If you say so," Claremont said. "Though it sounds like he hasn't been as predictable as you'd hoped."

"He's had his moments," Rick said. "But this week has really worn him down. He's exhausted." Rick reached into his pocket and pulled out his phone. "Besides, he's about to realize that this is no game."

Even two-dimensional, you look good, Ober thought as he admired the most recent photocopy of his face. Sitting at his government-issue desk, he pulled open the bottom-left drawer, removed a thick file folder and added that day's photocopy to the three hundred and twenty-six

316 • BRAD MELTZER •

other photocopies already in the folder. Every day, Ober placed his face on the photocopier and posed for the world's quickest portrait in an attempt to create a photo album unlike any other. After writing the date on his newest copy, he placed it in the folder with the others. As he returned the file to its drawer, he saw Marcia Sturgis, the staff director for Senator Stevens, standing in the doorway of his office.

"Ober, can I see you in my office?" Marcia asked abruptly. A Capitol Hill veteran, Marcia had started as a receptionist for Senator Edward Kennedy soon after she had graduated from college, then spent almost twenty years working her way through the bureaucratic ranks. In her view, the years of toiling in obscurity were well worth it—she was currently the most important member of Senator Stevens's staff. With a workday that began at six in the morning and ended at eleven at night, Marcia controlled most of what the senator saw and heard. She attended committee meetings, organized floor appearances, and edited the senator's speeches and press releases. She was also responsible for the most important decisions affecting the senator's staff.

Following Marcia to her office, Ober tried to guess what he had done wrong this time. Since his promotion to administrative assistant, visits to Marcia's office had become commonplace. There was one when his reply letter to an irate constituent simply said, "Relax." There was another when he misspelled Mrs. Stevens's name on a letter to another senator. And there was another when Marcia caught him making prank calls to Republican staffers, telling them to "Give up."

As he stepped into Marcia's office, Ober noticed the stiff-shouldered stranger sitting in one of the chairs facing Marcia's desk. When he saw the solemn look on the man's face, Ober knew this visit wasn't about the coffee he had spilled on Marcia's computer.

"Take a seat," Marcia said, pointing to the empty seat next to the stranger. "This is Victor Langdon, from the FBI."

"Nice to meet you," Ober said, extending his hand.

"Can we get to the point?" Victor asked.

Marcia's eyes were focused on Ober. "I wanted to tell you about an anonymous fax I got a few hours ago," she explained. "It said that the death threat you investigated a few months ago was actually written by you. The fax also accused you of writing the threat to Senator Stevens

in an attempt to advance your own career. Considering that your promotion *was* based on your handling of that situation, we were wondering what you had to say for yourself."

"I don't know what you're talking about," Ober said. Crossing his
legs, he tried his best not to panic.

"I don't want to play that game," Victor said, pointing a finger at
Ober.

"Ober, don't lie about this one," Marcia pleaded, her hands in tight
fists on her desk. "This is serious."

"It's not the way it looks. . . ." Ober stuttered.

"Do you deny it?" Victor asked.

"If you didn't write it, and you know who did, tell us," Marcia said.

Ober leaned away from Victor. "It wasn't a real death threat. The
senator was never in danger."

"I already told the FBI that," Marcia said. "Just tell them who
wrote it."

Trying to figure out a way to avoid implicating Ben, Ober was silent.

"If you don't tell us who wrote it, I'll be forced to ask for your resignation," Marcia said.

"Attempted assassination means you'll get life in prison," Victor
added, grabbing Ober's armrest.

Ober pushed Victor's hand away. "It was never an assassination."

"Then tell us what happened," Victor said. "Who wrote the letter?"

Again, Ober fell silent.

"Ober, please make this easier on yourself," Marcia said, leaning on
her desk.

"That's it," Victor said, standing up. "It's clear we can't do this here.
I'm taking him in for questioning."

Marcia shot from her chair. "No, you're not. You promised me full
jurisdiction with this. It's clear the senator was never in danger."

"Why are you protecting this kid?" Victor asked.

"I'm not protecting him. I just—"

"I wrote it," Ober interrupted, whispering into his chest.

"What?" Marcia asked.

"I wrote it," he repeated, his eyes focused on the floor. "I wrote the
letter."

"You did?" Marcia asked.

"I knew it," Victor said, returning to his seat.

"Why would you do that?" Marcia asked.

"I can't explain it," Ober said, refusing to look up. "I wrote it. That's it. That's all I want to say."

Victor grabbed his notepad from Marcia's desk and started taking notes. "Was it a real threat to the senator?" he asked.

"No," Ober said. "Not at all. The senator's been nothing but terrific to me."

"So it was for the promotion?" Marcia asked. "The fax was right?"

"It's not a hundred percent right, but it might as well be true," Ober said. "I wrote the letter, and the letter got me the promotion." As silence filled the room, both Marcia and Victor stared at Ober. Looking up at his two interrogators, Ober's eyes welled with tears. "What?" he asked. "What else do you want me to say? I wrote it."

Victor turned to Marcia. "If you like, I can take him down to—"

"Leave him alone," Marcia said. "We'll handle this in-house. And I expect you to keep your promise—I don't want to see one word about this in the press."

"Playing it safe before the election?" Victor asked.

"What do you think?" Marcia asked, returning to her seat. She scribbled some quick notes to herself and then looked up at Ober. "If you tender your resignation, we won't file charges."

"What if I want to keep my job?" Ober asked, his face now pasty white.

"That's not an option," she said. "At this point, you're fired. If you'd like to tender your resignation first, I can save both of us a great deal of headache. Otherwise, we'll have to formally release you, which means documenting the entire story for your personnel file."

"But—"

"That's the deal," Marcia said as she resumed her writing.

Ober realized he had no choice. "I'll resign."

"Fine," Marcia said, putting down her pen. "You have ten minutes to clean out your office. Leave your Senate I.D. with me."

*   *   *

As he walked back to his office, Ober's mind was flooded with the repercussions of the past half hour. After two years in Washington, he had nothing to show for it—his first professional success was now gone. His short-lived promotion had given him the slightest taste of victory, but once again, he felt himself sliding back toward failure. He could never show his face in the office again. When he saw his colleagues on the street, he'd have to lie about why he quit. His parents and relatives would also have to hear the fabricated excuse for why he no longer worked in the Senate. And it better be a good excuse, he thought as he reached his desk, because my mother is going to kill me.

As he collected his personal belongings, Ober's hands were shaking. Removing his diploma from the wall, he was afraid he'd drop it. Although he had been instructed not to take any files from his office, Ober opened his desk drawer and pulled out the only folder that was definitely his. Flipping through the three hundred and twenty-seven photocopies of himself, he thought about the day he started working for Senator Stevens and how he'd sneaked into the copy room to make the first picture in the pile. He remembered the excitement of starting the photo album and how he wanted to keep it a secret from his roommates until it was finished. I guess it's finished, he thought, staring at the pile of paper in his hands. It's all finished. Now I can finally show Eric and Nathan and Ben. Ben. Ben. Ben. Simmering in the silence, Ober took the folder and hurled it against the wall, causing three hundred and twenty-seven pages to fly through the air. What's wrong with me? he wondered, collapsing in his old chair. Then, amid the remains of the paper hurricane that covered his former office, Ober cried.

This can't be happening, Ben thought as he sprinted from the Metro station to his house. Maybe Eric heard the story wrong. Rounding the corner of his block, Ben stepped on a sheet of ice, which sent his body skidding and his right hip smashing into the frozen pavement. Ignoring the pain as he stumbled to his feet, he resumed his mad dash toward the house. He threw open the front door, ran inside, and saw Ober sitting on the sofa. Still dressed in his navy suit, with his tie loosened,

Ober glared directly at the television, refusing to acknowledge Ben's entrance.

"I came as soon as I heard," Ben said, dropping his coat on the floor. "How're you doing? Are you okay?" Pausing, but getting no response, Ben tried again. "C'mon, Ober, talk to me. I'm here to help."

"There's nothing to talk about," Ober said, his voice quiet and spiritless. "I helped you. My boss found out. I got fired."

Crossing over to the couch, Ben took a seat next to his friend. "Ober, you know I never meant—"

"I know you didn't mean for this to happen," Ober said as his shoulders sagged in defeat.

"I swear, I thought Rick was bluffing. I never thought he'd actually do it, and I thought—"

"It doesn't matter what you thought," Ober interrupted, his voice still barely above a whisper. "I lost my job. That's all that really matters."

Ben stared up at Eric's painting, unable to face his roommate. Searching for the perfect reason, the perfect explanation, and the perfect apology, he was silent. In an argument, Ben was never at a loss for words. But when it came to apologies, he was awful. Finally, he came up with "I'm sorry."

Ober's eyes welled with tears. He covered his face with his hands.

"I'm so sorry," Ben said, putting a hand on Ober's shoulder. "I can't apologize enough for this."

"My life is ruined. . . ."

"It's not ruined," Ben insisted, struggling to get Ober's attention. "You'll get a new job. A better job."

"No, I won't," Ober sobbed. "It took me five months to find that job. How am I going to get a new one?"

"We'll help you find a new one," Ben said. "It really isn't as bad as you think. Between the five of us, we can—"

"That's not even true," Ober interrupted, wiping his eyes. "You know I'm not like you guys. I wasn't a straight-A student. I'm not a genius. I'm a moron."

"Don't start with that. You're as bright as any one of us."

"No, I'm not," Ober said, his voice still hushed. "You said it and it was true: I'm really not."

"You are."

"No, I'm not," Ober said. "This's the sixth job I've been fired from. It'll take me months to find another job. And it'll be worse than the last one. My life is just like our board-game company—one big bust."

"Ober, don't be so rough on yourself," Ben said, his hand still on Ober's shoulder. "Life doesn't revolve around SAT scores and grade-point averages. Once you start looking, a sharp personality will carry you just as far. And if you have anything, you have that."

"I don't even have that," Ober said, pulling away from Ben. "I'm not bright; I'm not resourceful; I don't work well under pressure. Why do you think I can't hold down a job? I've been failing at this one for months—they would've fired me soon anyway. This whole thing with Rick just sped up the process."

"That's not true," Ben said.

"How do you know what's true?" Ober asked, his eyes once again filling with tears. "You weren't there. You've never seen me at work. Half the time, *I* don't even know what I'm doing there."

"You were an administrative assistant," Ben interrupted. "That was a good job."

"It was a below-average job," Ober said, wiping the tears from his face with the back of his hand. "And the only reason I had it was because I investigated a death threat that *I* wrote. If it wasn't for that, I'd still be answering phones." Catching his breath, he looked into Ben's eyes. "Why did this have to happen?"

Surprised by Ober's emotional collapse, Ben almost didn't recognize the friend he'd known since grade school. But as Ober became more hysterical, Ben instinctively stepped forward. "This was all my fault," Ben said, embracing him.

"I just want it to be like it was when we first got here," Ober said, his face buried in Ben's shoulder. "Just the four of us. No fighting. No arguing."

"It will be," Ben said. "I promise."

"It won't," Ober said. "It never will again. It's over. We're finished."

"No, we're not," Ben said. "We're all still friends. We'll get through it."

"No, we won't!" Ober sobbed. "Nathan and you barely speak. Eric and Nathan never speak. I'm having the worst day of my life, and both of them are too damn busy with work to even come home to see me. That's not a friendship. It's a joke.''

"We're not finished," Ben insisted. "Rick won't—"

"It doesn't matter what Rick does anymore," Ober wailed. "The damage is done. Nathan will never forgive you for getting me fired. And as long as Nathan is mad at you, Eric will be mad at him. You can't change that."

Silent as he stared at Ober, Ben knew his friend was right. "What about you?" he finally asked. "Will you forgive me?"

Ober wiped his eyes. "I don't know."

"But—"

"Please don't say anything," Ober interrupted. "I don't want to hear it right now."

Before Ben could respond, the phone rang. Ben glanced at it, then looked back at Ober.

"Pick it up," Ober said. "You know you want to get it."

"It's not that," Ben said. "It's just—"

"Pick it up," Ober insisted.

Ben grabbed the receiver. "Hello."

"So, you still interested in Wayne and Portnoy?" Alcott asked enthusiastically.

"Adrian?" Ben asked, annoyed.

"Of course," Alcott answered. "You had said to give you a call so we could set up a lunch, so I figured—"

"Adrian, why are you calling me at home?" Ben asked, rising from the couch. His movement sent the base of the phone crashing to the floor.

"I apologize," Alcott said. "The secretary at the Court said you were gone for the weekend, and I wanted to set up something for Monday."

"Let me tell you something," Ben said, gripping the receiver. "Don't call me at home. If I'm not at work, I don't want to be bothered by you. In fact, even when I'm at work, I don't want to be bothered. I know all about the firm, and an extra lunch isn't going to get me to go there."

"I'm—" Alcott stuttered.

"I don't want to hear it," Ben interrupted. "If I want to go to lunch, you'll hear from me. Otherwise, leave me alone. I'm busy." Without waiting for Alcott's response, Ben slammed down the phone.

"Who was that?" Ober asked.

"No one," Ben explained. "It was a—" The phone rang again. Ben picked it up. "Adrian, I'm sure you're sorry, but I don't want to hear it right now."

"This isn't Adrian, and I'm certainly not sorry."

"Rick?" Ben asked, knowing the answer to his question.

"Sounds like you're having quite a night," Rick said. "Ober gets fired; he's on the verge of a breakdown; you scream at the one person still recruiting you. I have to be honest; if I were in your shoes, I wouldn't yell at someone who was offering me a job."

Ben turned to Ober. "Rick's been listening all night. The whole place is bugged." He turned back to the phone. "What do you want, Rick?"

"You know what I want," Rick said. "The only question is whether you're going to deliver."

Ben sat down on the couch. "What do you think?"

"I think Ober's breaking your heart. So my guess is you're thinking of turning yourself in," Rick said. "I just want you to know that if you give me the decision, you can still walk away from all this."

"Thanks for the tip," Ben said. "I'll take it under advisement."

"If the decision works out, you'll never hear from me again. Case closed. You get to keep your job. Nathan gets to keep his. I get what I want. All parties are happy." Without giving Ben a chance to respond, Rick continued, "If you're interested, go to the Museum of American History at noon on Sunday. There's a courtesy phone next to the information desk. Wait there, and I'll leave a message where you can meet me. If you're not there, your bankbook and Nathan's letter will be hand-delivered to your respective superiors."

"I'll see you there," Ben said coldly. Without another word, he hung up.

"What'd he say?" Ober asked.

"I hate that bastard," Ben said. "He's so damn smug."

"Just tell me what he said."

"Not here," Ben said, looking around the room. "Not another word in this place." Ben got up from the couch. "Let's get out of here."

"No way," Ober said. "I'm done with this nonsense. You're on your own."

"I'm only going to Lisa's. It's a safer place to talk."

"I don't care where you're going. I've had enough."

"Are you okay with everything?" Ben asked, picking up his coat from the living room floor.

"Would you be?" Ober asked. "I just need to get some sleep."

Knowing there was nothing he could say, Ben buttoned his coat, picked up his briefcase, and walked to the door. As he was about to leave, the door flew open and Nathan stormed inside. "Where the hell are you going?" Nathan asked Ben.

"Out," Ben shot back, aggravated by Nathan's accusatory tone.

"Hold on a second," Nathan said. He turned to Ober and asked, "Did you really get fired?" When Ober nodded, Nathan turned back to Ben. "You're not going anywhere."

"Really?" Ben asked. "Watch this." Within seconds, Ben was out the door.

Running up the block, Ben headed directly for the nearest pay phone. Finding one a few blocks away, he pulled a scrap of paper from his jacket pocket, grabbed the receiver, and punched in DeRosa's 800 number. "Answer the damn phone," Ben said before the call had even registered.

Impatiently waiting for someone to pick up, Ben was alarmed to hear a recorded voice say, "The number you have reached is no longer in service. Please check the number and dial again." Within seconds, he hung up and redialed the number, carefully checking to make sure he dialed correctly. Once again, he heard "The number you have reached is no longer in service. Please check the number and dial again."

"I don't believe this," Ben said. With his eyes closed and his hands locked around the frame of the pay phone, he tried to think of a rational explanation for why the number had been disconnected. There was none. "Son of a bitch!" he yelled, slamming the phone with his fist. His heart pounding, he turned around and screamed, "ARE YOU GUYS OUT THERE? WHAT THE HELL IS GOING ON?"

Hoping for a response, but expecting none, Ben silently waited. Nothing. His eyes scanned the area, inspecting every tree, shrub, and hiding spot within his sight. Still nothing. He was on his own. Spotting the "on duty" roof lights of an approaching emerald-green taxi, Ben jumped in front of the car, which screeched to a halt to avoid hitting him.

"What's wrong with you? You crazy or something?" the cabbie shouted as Ben opened the door.

"Do you know any cheap motels?" Ben asked, climbing inside.

"I know a few," the driver responded, unnerved.

"Take me to one," Ben demanded.

Following Ben's instructions, the driver headed toward Connecticut Avenue. "You okay?" the driver asked.

Ben was staring out the back window, checking to see if anyone was following him. "I'm fine," he said. "Perfectly fine."

Ten minutes later, the cab pulled up to the Monument Inn, a plain-looking, one-story building with a neon VACANCY sign. Ben paid the cab driver, walked into the motel, and approached the front desk. "I need a room."

Packing her briefcase with three soon-to-be-released decisions, Lisa prepared for a long work weekend. Well accustomed to the fact that as long as she worked in the Court, every weekend was a work weekend, Lisa also added three floppy disks, Hollis's written comments, and photocopies of a dozen already-released decisions that she thought were relevant. She locked her briefcase and scrambled the small combination lock near the handle. As she went to grab her coat, the phone rang.

Fearing that it might be Hollis with a new assignment or another rewrite, Lisa didn't immediately answer the phone. As always, however, she couldn't help herself. She had to pick it up. "Hello. This is Lisa."

"Lisa, I need you to meet me as soon as possible," Ben demanded.

"What?" Lisa asked. "Where are you?"

"I'm at the Monument Inn. It's on Upton, near the Van Ness Metro. I'm in room sixteen."

"What happened with Ober? Is he okay?"

"I'll tell you about it later," Ben said. "Now please come over here. I don't know what to do."

Forty minutes later, Ben heard a knock on the door. "Who is it?" he asked suspiciously.

"Open the door," Lisa said.

He looked through the eyehole and let her in.

"What happened?" she asked, walking inside.

Ben peered out of the room to make sure Lisa was alone, then slammed the door and locked it.

Lisa scrunched up her face in disgust. "Nice place," she said, noticing the peeling wallpaper. "Why didn't we just meet in a sewer? It's cleaner *and* safer."

"Rick has my house bugged," Ben said, his face glued to the eyehole on the door. "And I wouldn't be surprised if yours was, too. I figured we needed a neutral place to talk."

"Then tell me what happened," Lisa said, sitting on one of the room's twin beds.

Turning around, Ben leaned on the door. "They're not out there," he said. "They're gone. I think they switched sides. That's the only way—"

"Slow down—one thing at a time," Lisa said. "Who's not out there?"

Ben walked over to the other bed and sat down across from Lisa. "The marshals. DeRosa. They're not out there," he explained. "After talking to Ober, I pushed the panic button and—"

"You dialed the number in your house?" Lisa asked. "Are you crazy? Rick probably heard—"

"I went to a pay phone," Ben interrupted. "The number's out of service. It's been disconnected."

"Are you kidding me? But DeRosa said—"

"I know what he said. But it's clear he lied. I think he's been working with Rick from the beginning. Think about it: DeRosa wouldn't let Lungen and Fisk know what's going on, even though they're the marshals assigned to the Court. He didn't want me to tell anyone else what I had done. He never took an affidavit from me. He even told me to turn a decision over to Rick. I think Rick approached DeRosa before we did."

"I don't know," Lisa said, grabbing one of the pillows on the bed. "Do you really think Rick has the resources to meet with the head of the Marshals Service?"

"Are you kidding?" Ben asked. "*I* walked right in to see him. You don't think Rick can do the same thing?"

Lisa nodded. "But that doesn't mean they're necessarily working together."

"So where does that leave me?"

"There aren't many options. If I were you, I'd spend tomorrow trying to contact DeRosa. For all we know, the plan is still in effect, and his secretary simply mistyped the phone number."

"And what if I still can't contact him?"

"Then I'd think about ending it. Go to the press, go to Hollis, go to anyone that'll listen, but get the story out there."

"That's what I've been thinking for the past hour. If both DeRosa and Rick are against me, I'm dead."

"Then there's your answer," Lisa said as she threw the pillow aside. "If you find DeRosa, great. But if he's switched teams, you'll go to the press and take them all down with you. Either way, you'll be done with this by Sunday."

"Great," Ben said sarcastically. "Now all I have to do is figure out what I'm going to say to my friends."

"Eric, it's me," Ben said, still sitting on the bed in his motel room.

"Where are you?" Eric asked. "Nathan said—"

"I'm at Lisa's," Ben lied. "I didn't feel comfortable talking in the house."

"Are you coming home tonight?"

"No. I'm sleeping here."

"That's probably a good idea," Eric said. "Tell me what's happening. I heard Rick called again."

"Forget about Rick. I want to get together with you guys so we can talk about what's going on."

"Tell me the place. I'll be there."

"I want everyone there," Ben said. "You, Nathan, and Ober."

"Fine. Where and when?"

"Tomorrow night at eight o'clock. And I want to meet at the place where we celebrated our first night in D.C."

"At the—"

"Don't say it," Ben interrupted. "The phone's not safe."

"Oh, yeah. Ober told me."

"Exactly," Ben said. "Meanwhile, how is he holding up?"

"He's a mess. I've never seen him like this before. Nathan and I spoke to him for almost two hours, and he's still crying like crazy."

"Has he told his parents yet?"

"He's terrified to call them. You know how his mom is. She'll be on his back the moment she hears what happened."

"I know. I was thinking about that. To be honest, I think that's what he's most scared of."

"I don't think he's scared of anything," Eric said. "I'm not even sure he's upset about his job. I think he's more devastated by the fact that all of us aren't getting along."

"He was saying that when I was there."

"It's because he's such a social animal," Eric explained. "He's like a puppy—if everyone's happy, he's happy. But if everyone's sad, he's miserable."

"Keep talking to him. I'm sure he'll be fine."

"I agree. It's just that—"

"Ben, is that you?" Nathan asked angrily as he picked up the phone in the living room. "Where the hell have you been for the past three hours? Get your ass—"

"Don't tell me what to do," Ben shot back. "If you want to kick and scream, come meet me tomorrow. I told Eric where." Ben hung up the phone.

Early Saturday morning, Ben sat up in bed, unable to sleep. In the second bed was Lisa, who was having no such trouble. He looked at his watch and saw that it was seven in the morning. After taking the longest shower of his life, he turned on the television with the sound off, hoping to be distracted by cartoons. Unimpressed, he shut off the TV and returned to his bed. For a full hour, Ben stared at the white stucco ceiling.

At nine o'clock, Ben took the phone into the bathroom. Sitting on the closed toilet, he called information and asked for the number of the Marshals Service. He dialed the number and asked for Director DeRosa.

After a moment, a woman answered the phone. "Director DeRosa's office. Can I help you?"

"Is the director in today?" Ben asked in his most genial tone.

"I'm sorry, he's not. Is it anything I can help you with?"

"You probably can," Ben said, recognizing the voice of DeRosa's receptionist. "My name's Ben Addison. I'm the guy who hand-delivered that message from Justice Hollis a couple of weeks ago. I have another message I'm supposed to relay, and I was wondering if you knew how to contact Director DeRosa." For effect, Ben paused for a second. "It's an emergency."

"Hold on a moment," the receptionist said. "I can try to transfer you to his home number."

Ben prayed that DeRosa would explain everything: that it was a clerical error, that everything was fine, and everyone was still in place.

"Mr. Addison?"

"I'm here," Ben said.

"I'm sorry, but the director won't take your call. I just spoke to him, and he said he doesn't know what you're talking about. He has no idea who you are."

"He knows who I am," Ben said. "*You* know who I am. I met you two weeks—"

"I'm sorry, Mr. Addison. I spoke to him personally, and that's what he said."

"What are you talking about? What's your name?" Ben asked.

"Have a good day, Mr. Addison," the receptionist said as she hung up.

As Ben put down the phone, reality set in. That's it, he thought. I'm done. Staring down at the stark linoleum floor, Ben wondered exactly what his next move should be. His thoughts were interrupted when the bathroom door swung open. He looked up and saw Lisa, who had obviously been listening.

"What'd they say?" she asked.

"DeRosa's gone," Ben said, his voice shaking. "He's denying he ever met me."

"Then that's it—it's over," Lisa said, leaning on the door frame. "Are you going to go to the press?"

"I don't know about the press, but I have to tell someone."

"You should tell Hollis."

"Maybe," Ben said as his mind worked through all the consequences. "I was thinking that I should also put my story in writing. That way, no matter what happens, it'll all be documented."

"I wouldn't be so worried about the writing part," Lisa said. "Before you face the world, you have to face your roommates."

At seven-thirty that evening, Ben braved the late January chill and sat on one of the few concrete visitor benches surrounding the Jefferson Memorial. Unable to sit still, he repeatedly shifted his weight, searching for a comfortable position. As he stared blankly at the waterfront walkway leading to the Memorial, his eyes danced across the landscape—focusing on nothing in particular while looking at everything. Fifteen minutes later, he was checking his watch at thirty-second intervals, impatiently waiting for the arrival of his roommates. Slowly becoming convinced that they wouldn't show, he looked up at Jefferson's ebony silhouette and wondered why he'd let Lisa talk him into this.

"Why the hell did we have to come out here?" he suddenly heard from the western side of the monument. "It's freezing." As Eric and Nathan approached Ben, Eric stared at the giant bronze rendering of the country's third president. "Let me say, meeting like this—late at night at one of the world's most famous monuments—I feel like I'm in an overblown spy movie."

"I'm so glad you're amused," Nathan said indignantly.

"Listen, I know you're upset," Ben said. "We're all upset. It's been a bad week. So let's start over and—"

"No offense, but I'm not in the mood for touchy-feely right now," Nathan said.

"Give him a chance, tight-ass," Eric interrupted. "He called you down here to talk—the least you can do is listen."

"I came here to find out one thing," Nathan said, crossing his arms. "Are you going to turn yourself in?"

Ben ignored the question. "Where's Ober?"

"He said he'd be late," Eric explained. "He was on the phone with his mother when we were leaving."

"I don't know what you want me to do," Ober said, struggling to fight back his tears.

"What kind of question is that?" Barbara Oberman asked. "I want you to get that job back."

"Mom, I can't get it back. They fired me. They didn't like my work, and they fired me."

"Don't give me that. Go back and tell them you'll change your ways. Tell them you'll work for less money, and that you'll double your hours. It doesn't matter how you do it, but get that job back."

"What's so important about my old job?"

"What's so important? Get this through your head, William: You need that job. It was the only place that ever promoted you. The only place that ever respected you. The only place that didn't fire you within the first six months. You've spent over four years failing at everything else you've tried, and now you've turned this into a disaster as well."

"I'll find a new job," Ober said. "Ben and Nathan said they'd help me look for one."

"Forget Ben and Nathan. You're always obsessed with Ben and Nathan. I don't want to hear about them. For Ben and Nathan, finding a job is simple. Employers love them, their college professors loved them, the high school principal loved them, their kindergarten teachers loved them. For them, finding a job is simple. But *you*—you're going to have a harder time."

"But they said—"

"I don't care what they said," she interrupted. "They're not you. What makes you think they'll be so eager for a job search?"

"They're my friends."

"Big deal, they're your friends. They don't know what a job search entails. They've never lived in the real world. Looking for a job requires hours and hours of legwork. You remember how hard it was to find the position with Senator Stevens.''

''Yeah, but—''

''But nothing. You said it yourself a few months ago: The three of them are always at work—they don't have the time to find you a job.''

''Yeah, but Ben helped me find this job. Maybe he can—''

''He can't do anything for you,'' she said. ''You have to learn to do things for yourself. They may be your friends, but they're certainly not your equals. When it comes to finding a job, like everything else in this world, you have to suck it up and do it yourself. Now hang up this phone and think about what I've said. I don't want to hear from you again until you have that job back.''

''I asked you a question,'' Nathan said, his breath lingering in the cold air. ''Are you going to turn yourself in or not?''

''I'll get to that,'' Ben said. He pointed to the empty spaces on his bench. ''How about taking a seat first?''

''I'm fine standing,'' Nathan said as Eric sat down.

''Fine. Stand,'' Ben said as he glanced over his shoulder.

''What're you so nervous about?'' Nathan asked.

''What do you think?''

''Can you both shut up?'' Eric asked. ''Stop fighting and relax for a second.'' Pointing at Ben, he added, ''Talk.''

''Thank you,'' Ben said, lowering his voice. ''I didn't want to say this on the phone, but tomorrow morning, I'm turning myself in. Since the decision affects all of us, I wanted to discuss it with you first.''

''I don't need to discuss it,'' Nathan said. ''I made my decision the moment I heard about Ober.''

''Good for you,'' Ben said. ''Eric, any thoughts?''

''It's your call. I just hope you can handle the consequences.''

''I don't see what choice I have,'' Ben said. ''What happened to Ober ripped my heart out. I got him fired; I put the rest of you in jeopardy. I have to end it.''

''That's real noble of you,'' Nathan said. ''But I'm warning you, you better end it tomorrow.''

"Or what?" Ben asked defensively. "You'll do it for me?"

"You're damn right I will," Nathan shot back. "And I won't feel a single bit of guilt doing it. In fact, you're lucky my boss doesn't work weekends, or I'd have turned you in today."

"Why don't you relax a second?" Eric said.

"Why don't you shut up?" Nathan said. "No matter how hard you stick up for Ben, he still isn't going to forgive you completely."

"What's wrong with you?" Ben asked.

"What's wrong with me?" Nathan replied, forcing a laugh. "Let's see: My friend got fired yesterday; it was all your fault; my job's on the line; and I don't trust you or Eric. Other than that, I'm peachy."

"Listen, you can—"

"No, you listen for once!" Nathan yelled as the wind whistled through the monument. "You have to get over this golden-boy complex. For once in your perfect life, you screwed up. You blew it. You choked. You made a big mistake, and now you have to take responsibility for it. If you were the only one at risk, I'd say do whatever you want. But if you think I'm going to stand around, with *my* career on the line while you continue your futile hunt for Rick, you're out of your head. Face facts, Ben—you're outsmarted. You lost. Give up."

"Shut the hell up!" Ben flew from the bench and grabbed Nathan by the front of his jacket.

Immediately, Eric pulled the two roommates apart. "Ben, relax a second. Calm down."

As Eric attempted to keep Ben at bay, Ben yelled at Nathan, "If you'd shut your damn mouth for a second, you'd realize that I didn't come here to plot against Rick. I came here to talk to my friends."

Ober walked into the living room and placed a pile of books on the coffee table: four high school yearbooks and one overstuffed scrapbook. Picking up the ninth-grade yearbook first, Ober flipped to his roommates' class portraits and smiled at the furry block that was Nathan's hair. When he reached Ben's picture, he laughed out loud. It had been at least four years since he'd last opened his yearbook and looked at the messy-haired, brace-faced, gawky nerd named Ben Addison. Turning to Eric's picture, Ober remembered his desire to sleep over at Eric's house, inspired primarily by the fact that Eric's brother had the largest collection of pornographic playing cards in the neighborhood.

When he opened the tenth-grade yearbook, Ober again skipped to the class portraits. He remembered the year they got their driver's licenses. Eric was not only the first to drive, he was also the first to crash—directly into Nathan's mother's car as she pulled out of her driveway. Thumbing through the eleventh-grade book, Ober remembered their first college party at Boston University. He laughed as he thought about Ben, who spent the whole night trying to convince the ladies he was "Ben Addison, Professor of Love."

Opening his personal scrapbook, Ober was proud he had so thoroughly documented his friends' achievements. He had the articles that appeared in *The Boston Globe* when Nathan was photographed with the secretary of state and when Ben received his Supreme Court clerkship. He had the first news story Eric wrote for the high school newspaper, as well as his first stories for *Washington Life* and the *Washington Herald*. He had the *Herald*'s first word jumble, as well as Eric's article about a leak at the Supreme Court. He even had Ben and Lisa's engagement announcement. Everyone's famous, he thought, closing the book. They're all superstars.

"Don't act like you're the victim here," Nathan said, straightening the front of his jacket. "That's the last thing you should—"

"I never said I was the victim," Ben retorted, as Eric kept him away from Nathan. "I know I screwed up. I admit it—it's my fault Ober lost his job. What else can I say?"

"There's your problem," Nathan said in a soft and slow voice. "You think you're only responsible for Ober losing his job. But you have to realize that you're responsible for much more than that. It's your fault this whole thing started, Ben. And more important, it's your fault it's still going on."

"You think I don't know that?" Ben's voice cracked. "It kills me that I—"

"Oh, so now you feel guilty?"

"I've felt guilty since the first day I met with Rick. What else do you want me to say? This thing's been eating away at me for months."

"It should be," Nathan said. "And I hope—"

"We get the picture," Eric interrupted. "Now can you let up a little?"

"No, I can't," Nathan said. "I want to make sure he knows how I feel about this."

"I know how you feel—" Ben began.

"No, you don't," Nathan insisted, his voice growing louder. "If you did, we wouldn't be fighting right now. Since the day we got those letters from Rick, you knew this might happen. At that moment, you should've had the decency to turn yourself in—if not for your own sake, then certainly for ours. The fact that you let it come to this tells me one thing . . ."

"That I'm an evil person with no redeeming qualities?" Ben asked.

"No," Nathan said, regaining his composure. "That I want nothing more to do with you. Ever." As Ben and Eric fell silent, Nathan continued, "This isn't high school anymore. We can't always be on your side. And don't think this is about me being selfish. You let Ober take the beating for your mistake. That's something I can never forgive you for. He's your friend, and you owe him more than that."

"I know," Ben said despairingly. "And I'll deal with him."

"You better," Nathan said. "This is bigger than some dumb slipup with *CMI,* or *Grinnell,* or—"

"Can you keep your voice down?" Ben interrupted.

"What's wrong?" Nathan asked. "You're still worried Rick is listening in on us? That he's making tapes of our conversations?"

"Shut up," Ben said.

Nathan ran to the edge of the monument. "HEY, RICK! ARE YOU LISTENING? I HOPE YOU CAN HEAR THIS. . . ."

"Shut the fuck up!" Ben screamed.

". . . BECAUSE THIS IS YOUR LAST WARNING! STAY THE HELL OUT OF MY LIFE! IF YOU KNEW BEN WAS SCARED OF GOING TO THE AUTHORITIES, YOU SHOULD ALSO KNOW THAT I'M NOT!"

"Nathan, stop it!" Eric yelled. "We get the point."

Nathan turned back toward Ben and pointed a finger at him. "I'm not joking about what I said before. I don't care what you do. I'm going to my boss Monday morning."

"You do that," Ben said, staring intently at the statue of President Jefferson.

"Don't be mad at me," Nathan said. "This one's not my fault." He wiped his forehead with the sleeve of his jacket. "Eric, you ready to go?"

"I'm going back with Ben."

"He doesn't have a car," Nathan pointed out.

"We'll take a cab."

"Suit yourself." Nathan walked down the stairs and headed toward the parking lot.

As Nathan's car pulled into the driveway, Ben and Eric's taxi pulled up to the house. "That made a lot of sense," Nathan said as the three roommates headed for the door.

Ignoring the comment, Ben opened the front door and stepped inside.

"You should tell Ober what's going on," Eric suggested.

"I know," Ben said. "But I don't want to say anything in the house." He noticed the yearbooks on the coffee table. "What was he doing tonight?"

"Probably reminiscing about better times," Nathan said.

"I wasn't asking you," Ben said. Atop a pile of yearbooks, Ben saw a single sheet of white paper and picked it up.

"Dear Ben, Nathan, and Eric," he read to himself. "I'm so sorry. I can't possibly explain my actions to you, but I didn't know what else to do. You'll probably think this is another stupid Ober idea, but please understand that there's no other way I'd be happy. For as long as I can remember, you have carried me forward, and I have held you back. Tell my mother she can go to hell, and tell Rick that I hope he drops dead. Also, tell my boss that I wasn't trying to advance my career—I really want her to know that. If I can ask you one last favor, please take it easy on each other. I will miss you more than you'll ever know. You're my best friends and I love you. Ober."

"Oh, my God," Ben said, running toward the stairs. "OBER!!" he screamed.

Instinctively, Nathan and Eric followed.

"OBER, ARE YOU IN THERE?" Ben screamed, pounding on the locked door to Ober's room. Ben turned to Eric and Nathan. "I think I found a suicide note!"

"OBER! OPEN UP!" Nathan screamed, pounding on the door.

"Break it down," Ben said frantically.

"Move out of the way." Nathan took a couple of steps back, then threw all his weight against the door.

"Again!" Ben said.

Once again, Nathan rammed his body into the door.

"KICK IT!" Eric shouted. "HURRY!"

Nathan rammed his foot into the door, and the door frame buckled. He rammed it again, and the door flew open. They all ran inside.

Ober was dangling against the closet door, a belt taut around his neck. "Omigod!" Eric said. "Omigod! Omigod!"

"Help me get him down," Ben said as he and Nathan grabbed Ober's legs and struggled to support his body. "Eric, open the door."

Eric was hysterically crying. With his hands shaking and the tears rolling down his face, he didn't even hear Nathan's request. All he could see was Ober. "He's dead!"

"OPEN THE DAMN DOOR!" Nathan screamed.

Eric pulled open the closet door, and Ober's body slumped forward and fell to the floor. Instantly, Nathan rolled Ober on his back and started CPR.

"Hurry!" Ben said as Nathan pinched Ober's nose. Taking a deep breath, Nathan tried to breathe life back into his friend.

"Look at his eyes!" Eric said, unnerved by the blank stare on Ober's face. "He's dead."

Nathan shut Ober's eyes and looked at Ben. "Get Eric the hell out of here."

"Eric, go downstairs," Ben said. "Call an ambulance."

As Eric ran out of the room, Nathan pumped Ober's chest and then listened for a heartbeat.

"There's no pulse!" Ben said, holding Ober's wrist.

"He's all white," Nathan said, looking at Ober's pallid complexion.

"Keep trying," Ben demanded. "Do it again!"

Futilely filling Ober's lungs with air, Nathan continued to administer CPR.

"DON'T STOP!" Ben screamed, reading the disheartened look on Nathan's face. "DO IT AGAIN!"

Once again, Nathan tried to bring back his friend. He pumped against Ober's chest with his full strength, and did everything he could to elicit any sign of life. He listened closely for a heartbeat, but eventually pulled away. "Forget it. It's over."

"Let me try," Ben said, pushing Nathan aside.

"Ben, it's over."

"Help me take him downstairs!" Ben demanded, lifting Ober's feet. "Maybe the ambulance can revive him. They have that shock machine—"

"It won't do any good," Nathan said, sitting on the floor and leaning against Ober's bed. "He's gone."

As the paramedics rolled the stretcher out of the house, Ben gave the suicide note and the leather belt to the policemen assigned to the scene. After interviewing the three roommates, one of the officers gave Ben his card. "I'd like to talk to you more about this."

"We'll come down tomorrow," Ben said. He felt emotionally drained. Shutting his eyes, hoping to somehow shut out reality, Ben attempted to quell the throbbing pain at the back of his neck.

"I'm really sorry about your friend," the other officer said.

"Thanks," Ben said, walking the two officers to the door. When the police car and the ambulance pulled away from the house, Ben shut the door. Collapsing on the floor, he rolled on his back and tried his best to think clearly. A minute later, he turned toward Nathan, who was sitting at the glass table in the dining room. "Where's Eric?" Ben asked.

Nathan peered through the glass, staring at his feet. "He's in his room talking to his mom."

"Is he okay?"

"Under the circumstances," Nathan said. "When he gets off the phone, you should call Ober's parents."

"*I* have to call?" Ben asked. "I can't do that."

"Oh, yes, you can." Nathan got out of his seat and headed for the stairs.

"Why me?" Ben asked, following his roommate.

"You're the one responsible," Nathan said curtly.

"Don't you dare say that," Ben warned.

Nathan turned from the stairs and looked at Ben in disbelief. "You're not responsible?" he asked, approaching Ben. "Whose fault is it, then?" Nathan stood face-to-face with Ben in the living room. "Is it Ober's fault? No, it can't be Ober's fault. Maybe it's Rick's fault. Maybe it's my fault. Maybe it's Senator Stevens's fault."

"It's nobody's *fault*," Ben interrupted.

"So no one's to blame?" Nathan asked. "This is something that just happened out of the blue?"

"Obviously, it didn't just *happen*. And if it weren't for me, Ober would probably still be alive. But that doesn't mean I killed him."

"No, you just put the belt around his neck."

An angry silence filled the room. "You can really be a bastard, y'know that?"

"I just want to make sure that you—"

"That I what?" Ben interrupted, his eyes filled with tears. "That I blame myself? That I think it's my fault? Don't worry—I do. I hold myself one hundred percent responsible. I'm the one that put this whole thing in motion, and it'll haunt me for the rest of my life. Until the day I die, there won't be a single day that I don't feel guilty about this."

"You should feel guilty."

"Don't tell me how I should feel," Ben said, his voice shaking. "Ober was my best friend! I would've done anything to save him."

"You *could've* saved him," Nathan said. "All you had to do was open your mouth."

"What the hell is wrong with you?" Ben lashed out. "How can you be so callous? I was going to the authorities! That's what tonight was all about! I didn't *know* Ober'd kill himself! I didn't *know* he was suicidal!"

"And I don't know what you expect me to say. Do you think that just because you admit it's your fault, I'll absolve you of your sins? It doesn't work like that. You killed him. Now you have to deal with it."

Enraged, Ben punched Nathan in the stomach. "I DIDN'T KILL HIM!"

Bent over in pain, Nathan struggled to catch his breath.

"I DIDN'T KILL HIM," Ben repeated. "HE KILLED HIMSELF!"

Still heaving, Nathan ran toward Ben, tackling him and sending them both crashing into the coffee table. The homemade table splintered in two, the yearbooks and the scrapbook sliding onto Nathan and Ben.

Sitting on top of Ben, Nathan grabbed him by the shirt. "Why did you let this happen?" he screamed.

Ben pushed Nathan back and staggered to his feet. "I never wanted this to happen!"

"Then why didn't you—"

"I wish I could've done a million things!" Ben yelled.

"You didn't have to do a million things," Nathan said. "All you had to do was one."

"I swear, I was going to turn myself in tomorrow!"

"Who cares what you were *going* to do?" Nathan screamed, tears streaming down his cheeks. "Ober died *tonight*! He's gone, Ben! We'll never see him again! Because of you, he's dead! Ober is dead!"

"Nathan, I—"

"I don't want to hear it," Nathan said, storming toward the stairs. "Enough of your damn excuses. No matter what you say, I know you killed him. And I hope that thought haunts you forever."

"I told you already," Richard Claremont told Rick. "I never touched him. I spent the whole night watching the other three at the Jefferson Memorial."

"If you're lying, the police will find you," Rick warned. "They dusted the entire place for fingerprints."

"I'm not lying! I didn't know he killed himself until I got back here." Taking off his coat, Claremont asked, "And since when are you so concerned about what happens to these guys?"

"I'm not concerned when one of them loses his job, but I am concerned when one of them winds up dead."

"I don't know why you're so shaken by this," Claremont said, sitting on the plush hotel sofa. "You put them in an impossible scenario—you should've expected one of them to snap."

"I never meant for this to happen!" Rick shouted.

"But you should've known—"

"Don't tell me what I should've known," Rick interrupted. "You can't anticipate something like this."

"But—"

"I don't want to hear it," Rick said. "Drop it."

"Consider it dropped," Claremont said. "Now, what are we going to do about the decision?"

"I've been thinking about that." Rick pulled a miniature bottle of white wine from the hotel refrigerator. "I'm afraid Ben's no longer running in the maze."

"You don't think he's going to meet us tomorrow?"

"Not a chance," Rick said, opening the wine. "He'll be talking to the authorities by noon."

"But if he—"

"Don't worry about it," Rick reassured his colleague. "He'll never get there."

Wrapped in a haze of anguish and remorse, Ben walked into the bathroom and turned on the shower. He undressed and stepped into the hot stream of water, anxious to wash away the past few hours. With his arms outstretched in front of him, he leaned against the front wall of the shower, letting the water glide over his body. For a full three minutes, he stood there, motionless. Slowly and without warning, a quiet fit of weeping overcame him. "I'm sorry, Ober," he sobbed, as his crying became hysterical. "I'm so sorry." As the water rushed over him, he imagined carrying Ober's coffin, and remembered carrying his brother's. He imagined Ober's mother's face when she heard her son was dead, and remembered his own mother's wails. He imagined the future without Ober, and knew how much he'd miss his brother.

CHAPTER 18

AT A QUARTER AFTER NINE ON SUNDAY MORNING, BEN PUT on his coat and picked up his briefcase. Still reeling from Ober's death, he tried not to think about the unnerving silence that now filled the house. Instead, he turned around and walked out the front door. A new layer of snow blanketed the neighborhood. He stepped outside, carefully maneuvering into the footprints left behind by Eric and Nathan. As he headed toward the Metro station, he periodically looked over his shoulder. After the events of the past few nights, Ben's watchfulness had become instinctive. When he rounded the corner he saw a man in a navy winter coat and a brown fedora coming toward him. He was bothered that the brim of the hat blocked the man's face. In the street, a gray car pulled up and stopped. Ben immediately recognized it as Eric's.

"How're you doing?" Eric asked, rolling down his window.

"Okay, I guess," Ben said unconvincingly. He stepped into the street and leaned in the window. "I slept about five minutes last night."

"Me too," Eric said. "I can't get him out of my head. Just the thought of him dangling there . . ."

"Please, let's not talk about it," Ben said, his gloved hands gripping the metal door frame.

"Did you tell Lisa?"

"I called her late last night. Before I finished my first sentence, she was crying. I never heard her like that. She offered to help with the eulogy."

"That was nice of her." Noticing the briefcase in Ben's hand, Eric asked, "Where are you headed now?"

"The U.S. Attorney's Office."

"So this is it?"

"I hope so," Ben said. "By this time tomorrow, I should be done with this nonsense."

"I know I didn't say this last night, but I think you're doing the right thing."

"Thanks," Ben said as the stranger in the navy coat passed behind him. Ben turned around to watch him walk down the block. "Does that guy look suspicious to you?"

"Not really. Why?"

"He looked a little weird to me."

"I wouldn't worry," Eric said. "I'm sure he's no one."

"Yeah," Ben said, pulling out of the window.

"Do you want a ride to the Metro?" Eric asked.

"I'd prefer a ride downtown."

"No time. I have to do some quick edits at the house, then I need to get back to work. The Metro is as good as it gets."

"Don't worry about it," Ben said, heading back to the sidewalk. "I think I can handle the two blocks."

"Your choice," Eric said, rolling up his window. "See you tonight."

"I hope," Ben said. "If you don't hear from me by dinner, it means I'm still in the middle of my plea bargain."

As the car pulled away, Ben continued his walk up the block. When he reached the commercial section of the neighborhood, his eyes darted everywhere. At the old man pulling his grocery cart along the snow-covered sidewalk. At the undeterred athlete jogging with her black labrador. At the supermarket employee shoveling the sidewalk. At the overweight woman struggling to keep her footing. Still jumpy, Ben reached his favorite bakery. I really have to calm down, he told himself as he stepped inside. There's no one following me. After a quick bagel and a fresh banana, Ben wiped his mouth, zipped his coat, and stepped back into the cold. Immediately he saw that the only thing between him and the Metro station was the man in the navy coat and the brown fedora.

Cautiously, Ben inched up the block, trying to identify the approaching stranger. The man appeared to be Rick's height, but heavier. But then, it was a heavy coat, Ben thought. As his heartbeat accelerated, Ben tried to convince himself that it was just his imagination. Relax, he told himself. There's no reason to get crazy. When they were ten feet apart, Ben pulled off his right-hand glove and made a tight fist, determined to swing if the man made a suspicious move. When he was five feet away, Ben was sweating furiously. As they were about to pass each other, Ben was frantic, his mind preparing for every possible scenario.

Holding his breath as the man walked by him, Ben fought the urge to turn around. It wasn't until he was well past the stranger that he finally breathed a sigh of relief. All that perspiration for nothing, Ben told himself, forcing a laugh. As he was about to turn to get one last look at the man, Ben's neck snapped back as he was grabbed from behind. He felt an arm wrap firmly around his neck, while a hand in a navy coat sleeve shoved a pungent handkerchief into his face. Instinctively, Ben threw his head back, slamming it into his attacker's nose.

"Son of a bitch!" the man yelled, releasing Ben and grabbing his bleeding nose.

Coughing as he ran up the block, Ben struggled to catch his breath. As he passed the supermarket, he looked back and saw that his attacker was in pursuit. Ben dropped his briefcase and grabbed the snow shovel from the hands of the supermarket employee. As the man approached him, Ben swung the shovel wildly. "Stay the hell away from me!"

"Calm down," the man said. "I'm not here to hurt you." As the man tried to keep Ben's attention, Rick turned the corner and was slowly sneaking up behind Ben.

"Who are you?" Ben asked. "Who sent you?"

"I'm on your side," the man said. "I swear. I'm from the Justice Department." His eyes were locked over Ben's shoulder.

Following the man's gaze, Ben spun around, swinging the shovel blindly as he turned. To his surprise, the flat side of the shovel connected with Rick, who would've otherwise grabbed him. "I don't believe it," Ben said. When Rick fell to the ground, Ben took the shovel and hit Rick once more in the head. "Who the hell do you think you are?" Ben screamed. "This is my life!"

Ben yelled at the supermarket employee. "Call the police!"

"We are the police," Rick's accomplice said to the employee. "Don't call anyone."

"Grab him already, Claremont!" Rick yelled, holding his ear, which was covered in blood.

Throwing the shovel at Claremont, Ben turned around and ran down the block.

"Follow him!" Rick yelled, even though Claremont was already in motion.

Faster and more athletic than either of his attackers, Ben ran back toward the residential part of his neighborhood. Hopping fences and racing through backyards, Ben crisscrossed between houses so his pursuers never had him in sight for longer than a few seconds. He turned down one driveway, made a left when he reached the backyard, hopped over a fence into the next-door neighbor's garden, ran to the back of the garden, hopped over a fence that put him in a connecting backyard, and ran back out another driveway. Weaving through the neighborhood, Ben knew that the only house he had to avoid was his own. If his two attackers had split up, one of them would definitely be waiting there. As the cold air packed his lungs, he worked his way back toward the supermarket, staying off the main streets and navigating through the garbage-filled alleys. Hoping he had lost his pursuers, he ran toward Boosin's Bar, the only place he knew that had a pay phone and, more important, a back door. He took one last look around and then entered the bar.

Ben headed directly for the back of the bar. He shoved open the door to the men's rest room, entered a stall, and locked it. He bent over and tried to catch his breath. As the warmth of the bathroom replaced the cold of the outdoors, Ben felt like he was burning up. He pulled off his jacket, then lifted the toilet seat and vomited the banana and bagel he had just eaten. When his stomach was empty, he convulsed with dry heaves, as his body reacted to the panic that flooded his mind. He flushed the toilet and sat down, shaking. *I can't believe this,* he thought, his elbows resting on his knees. *What the hell is happening?* As he dabbed his forehead with toilet paper, Ben's body temperature eventually returned to normal, and the color slowly returned to his face.

Twenty minutes later, convinced that Rick and his colleague were long gone, Ben left the rest room. He searched his pockets for change and pulled out a few coins, which he inserted into the pay phone. As he dialed Lisa's number, his eyes darted through the bar, which was filled with a few basketball fans who were eating breakfast before the first game of the day.

"Hello," Lisa answered.

"You will not believe what just happened to me," Ben said, his voice racing. "I just got attacked by Rick and some other guy. They jumped me and tried to kidnap me. I slammed them in the head with a shovel and ran for—"

"Whoa, whoa, whoa," Lisa said. "One thing at a time. Start over." After hearing his explanation of the past half hour, she said, "I don't believe it."

"Believe it," Ben said.

"Did you get a good look at Rick's partner?"

"Not really. My mind was running at full speed. All I remember is that he was trying to tell me that he was from the Justice Department."

"Do you think he was?"

"Of course not," Ben said. "The Justice Department doesn't attack people with chloroform. He just didn't want them to call the cops."

"Who was he, then?"

Ben's eyes were focused on the front door of the bar. "Either Rick's lackey or the guy Rick's using to make money on *American Steel.*"

"Why would Rick need a new person? American Steel's a public company. Rick can buy all the stock he wants."

"But you need money to buy stock. And presumably, Rick was wiped out from *Grinnell.* He needs someone who already has a lot of American Steel stock or who's willing to put up the funds. Otherwise, he's—" Ben looked at his coat on the floor. "Damn," he said. "I just realized I left my briefcase by the supermarket. I'm sure they grabbed it."

"You didn't leave the decision in there, did you?"

"Of course not. But the letter I was working on is in there. Which means they know that I'm turning myself in."

"They knew that the moment you didn't show up at the museum yesterday," Lisa said. "Meanwhile, have you called Nathan and Eric?"

"Not yet. Why?"

"Call them," Lisa demanded. "If Rick's running around your neighborhood, the first place he's going to check is your house. Are they still home?"

"Nathan's at work, but Eric might be." Ben hung up and searched his pockets for more change. He was a nickel short. Undeterred, he anxiously entered his calling card number into the pay phone. As his fingers danced across the buttons, he realized he'd misdialed the number. "Damn," he said, hanging up. He picked up the receiver and frantically reentered his calling card number. "C'mon, c'mon," he said as he waited for the tone. He heard it and entered his home number, praying Eric had finished his editing and left the house.

"Hello," Eric said.

"Eric, it's me. Get out of the house. Rick and that guy in the navy coat—"

"Have you spoken to Lisa?" Eric interrupted.

"Don't worry about Lisa," Ben said. "You have to—"

"Shut up a second," Eric insisted. "Rick called here looking for you. He said it was an emergency. And he wanted me to tell you that he was going over to Lisa's."

Ben's heart sank. "How long ago did he call?"

"About a half hour ago. Do you need any—"

Ben hung up the phone, reentered his calling card, and dialed Lisa's number. "Shit, shit, shit," he said as the phone rang five times without an answer.

Finally, Lisa picked up. "Hello."

"Get out of your apartment," Ben said. "Rick's on his way over."

"Or maybe I'm already here," Rick said. "How are you doing, Ben? Long time, no see."

"Oh, my God."

"Why so sad?" Rick asked. "It's just me."

"If you hurt her, I swear I'll—"

"Spare me the threats," Rick demanded, his voice growing suddenly serious. "I now have both Lisa and Nathan—"

"Nathan?"

"Shut up and listen for once," Rick said. "I have both of them, and I'm sick and tired of playing games. Now tell me where you are."

Ben was silent.

"This is no time to be stupid," Rick said. "You already lost one friend this weekend. Do you want to go for two?" Getting no response, he added, "How about three?"

"I'm at Boosin's Bar," Ben finally said. "It's on New Hampshire."

"I know where it is," Rick said. "I expect you to be standing outside in ten minutes. And if you happen to feel the urge to call the authorities, your parents, Eric, or anyone else, I will be extremely upset with you. Do you understand?"

"Yes," Ben said, fighting his rage.

"Good. Now, one last question," Rick said. "What's the outcome of *American Steel*?"

Again, Ben was silent.

"I asked a question," Rick said.

Still, silence.

"This is just about money," Rick warned. "Don't turn it into anything that requires violence."

"American Steel wins," Ben snapped. "Are you happy? Now you can go make your millions."

"I'm extremely happy—that's exactly the same answer Lisa gave us," Rick said. "We'll see you outside in ten minutes."

Hearing Rick hang up, Ben exploded. He grabbed the receiver and slammed it against the pay phone. The few patrons who were in the bar looked up when they heard the crashing noise. Again, Ben banged the receiver against the metal base of the phone. And again. And again.

Suddenly, someone grabbed him from behind. "What the hell is wrong with you?" the bartender asked, pulling the receiver from Ben's hand.

"Get off me!" Ben screamed, struggling against the bartender.

The bartender dragged him to the front door and pushed him outside. "If you're going to be a psycho, go someplace else."

*   *   *

Waiting outside of Boosin's, Ben teemed with anger. With his hands shoved deep into his jacket pockets, he despondently kicked at a small pile of snow next to the building. Within ten minutes, a red Jeep pulled up to the curb. The only person in it was Claremont. "Wait right there," Claremont said as he got out of the Jeep and approached Ben. Now that Claremont was no longer wearing his brown fedora, Ben studied his attacker's features. With a round face that was highlighted by a worn, floury complexion, Claremont looked much older than Ben had expected.

"Take off your jacket," Claremont said, pointing with thick, stubby fingers.

When Ben obliged, Claremont patted him down. "Still worried about microphones?" Ben asked.

"I'm told you have a habit of wearing them." After establishing that Ben was clean, Claremont opened the door for Ben. "All aboard," he said.

Thirty-five minutes later, the Jeep pulled into the back parking lot of the Palm Hotel, in Bethesda. "Follow me," Claremont said as he walked toward the back entrance of the building. "And if you say one word to anyone . . ."

"I get the picture," Ben said.

They took the elevator to the twenty-fourth floor and walked down the hallway to room 2427. Claremont slid his coded card into the electronic lock, pushed open the door, and entered the lavishly decorated suite. The main room was empty.

"Where is everyone?" Ben asked.

"Shut up and follow," Claremont said. He led the way through the bedroom and opened the door that connected the suite to the one next door. They walked through the second suite and reached a door that connected that suite to a third. Finally, they entered the largest of the three suites, where Rick, Lisa, and Nathan were waiting.

When Ben and Claremont entered the room, Rick got up from his seat on the sofa. "Well, well, the gang's all here," he said. "Lisa, Nathan, I believe you know Ben. Ben, this is Lisa and Nathan."

Ben was surprised to see Nathan and Lisa sitting calmly at the large glass dining-room table. Looking through the glass tabletop, he noticed that they were both handcuffed to their chairs. A swollen black eye colored the left side of Nathan's face.

"Are you okay?" Ben asked.

"Fuck off," Nathan said, turning away.

"Children," Rick scolded. "No fighting."

"You didn't have to hit him," Ben said.

"Yes, we did," Rick said glibly. "Otherwise he wouldn't have come with us."

Looking at Lisa, Ben asked, "They didn't hit you, did they?"

"Are you kidding?" Rick interjected, showing off the scratch marks on the side of his neck. "She did more damage than you." When he approached the small mahogany desk in the corner of the room, Rick reached into his briefcase, pulled out two sets of handcuffs, and threw them to Claremont.

Claremont pushed Ben toward the large wooden chair next to Nathan. "Take a seat."

"Let them go first," Ben demanded.

"And let them run to the police?" Rick laughed. "Take a seat, Ben. You're in no position to argue."

When Ben sat down, Claremont used both sets of handcuffs to fasten Ben's arms to the chair.

"And if you're thinking about screaming," Rick said, "you can save your lungs the wear and tear. We have most of this floor, and the manager promised us complete privacy. You can buy just about anything these days."

"I don't know why you're so smug," Ben said. "Eric's still out there. When we don't come home tonight, he'll head straight to the police."

"No, he won't," Rick said coldly.

Lisa looked at Ben. "Nathan called Eric and told him that he was working late tonight. And then I called him and told him that we were both okay—that the phone call from Rick was just a fake threat." Seeing the bewildered look on Ben's face, she added, "Rick said he would kill you if we didn't make the calls."

Surprised by the gravity of Rick's threat, Ben looked up at his captor.

"Satisfied?" Rick asked.

*   *   *

"Are you going to stop the decision?" Fisk asked, sitting impatiently in Lungen's office.

"I don't see how," Lungen said. "We have no more proof than we did on Friday. Ben and Lisa haven't been in all weekend."

"I knew we should've staked out his house," Fisk said, pointing at Lungen. "Now we have no idea where he is."

"For all we know, he's out shopping."

"I still say we pull the plug on the decision. Tell the justices we don't want it announced until we find Ben."

"Will you listen to what you're saying," Lungen demanded. "You want me to hold up the Supreme Court of the United States because one of their clerks didn't work this weekend? Do you know how fast we'll be standing on the unemployment line?"

"What if he doesn't show up tomorrow?"

"It doesn't matter," Lungen said. "Until we have all the facts—and I mean every last detail—we cannot bring this Court to a screeching halt. Believe me, when we have the information, Ben Addison's ass is mine. But until that point, we just sit and wait."

"And listen," Fisk said, turning up the speaker on Lungen's desk.

Ben's arms were growing stiff from being restrained. "You made a mistake taking only three of us."

"Oh, we did?" Rick sat on the plush sofa and flipped through the paperwork laid out on the coffee table.

"I mean it," Ben said. "Eric won't believe those stories. I bet he's talking to the police right now."

"That's a pretty crappy theory," Rick said, his eyes still focused on his paperwork.

"And why's that?"

"You expect Eric to run to the police?" Rick asked, looking up at his captives. "Is this the same Eric who told you to avoid the authorities at all cost? The same Eric who said you could catch me all by yourself? This is the person who's going to blow this wide open?

Even Ober was more resourceful." Ben's jaw tightened. "Hit a raw nerve, huh?"

"If it wasn't for you, he'd still be alive," Ben said. "I'll kill you for that."

"Sure you will. And if you believe that, I can see why you think Eric's coming to your rescue." Making himself comfortable on the sofa, Rick added, "I hate to break it to you, but you're on your own this time."

Sitting at his desk in the political bureau, Eric was annoyed. For the past three hours, he had tried to locate his roommates. Nathan wasn't at work, Ben wasn't at the Court, and Lisa wasn't at home. Those phone calls had to be a setup, Eric thought as the crumbs of his late lunch fell into his computer keyboard. Wiping his hands on his jeans, he flipped through his Rolodex. No more playing around, Eric thought as he dialed the number of the Marshals Office at the Supreme Court. I need real help.

"U.S. Marshals Office," a man answered. "This is Carl Lungen."

"Mr. Lungen, this is Eric Stroman—Ben Addison's roommate."

"How'd you get my private line?" Lungen asked, sounding annoyed.

"I stole it from Ben's Rolodex—you never know when you're going to need a marshal," Eric explained. "I'm only calling because it's an emergency. I think Ben's in trouble."

"I'm listening."

"Well, without getting into the whole story, Ben was being black-mailed by this guy named Rick. A few hours ago, I got a call from Ben telling me to get out of my house because Rick was after us. A half hour after that, Lisa called and told me everything was okay. Maybe I'm just being neurotic, but I think something happened to them."

"Eric, I'm very glad you called," Lungen said. "Now start from the beginning and tell me the whole story."

At ten o'clock that evening, Rick and Claremont sat in the center suite, picking at the remains of their room-service dinner. "Only twelve more hours," Rick said, nibbling on a french fry. "We're almost there."

"You promise we'll cash in the options by noon?" Claremont asked.

"How many times do you need to hear it?" Rick asked. "It'll all be done by noon."

"Don't look at me like that," Claremont said. "If you were in my position, you'd be just as concerned. It'll only take a few hours before the SEC realizes that an American Steel executive cashed in all of his stock and risked it all on a long-shot bet. This deal is going to raise one hell of a lot of eyebrows over there."

"We'll be long gone by the time they put it together," Rick said. "Don't get crazy over it."

"I'll just be happy when it's over," Claremont said.

"You'll be more than happy," Rick said. "You'll be rich. Those options will be worth millions."

"What if Ben's lying and Steel actually loses?"

"Don't worry," Rick said. "After what happened with *Grinnell*, I'm not putting a dollar down unless I know he's telling the truth."

"Nathan, will you stop it already?" Ben begged. "Talk to me."

"Leave him alone," Lisa said. "He'll talk when he's ready."

"Silence doesn't help anyone at this point," Ben said. "Get over it."

"Get over it?" Nathan asked, looking up and facing Ben. "Ober is dead. That's not something I'll just *get over*. Not today. Not tomorrow. Never."

"Enough with the fighting," Lisa interrupted, pulling on her restraints. Leaning to her left, she peered over the armrest and saw that her handcuffs were attached to the wooden supports that connected the front and back legs of the antique chair. "I say we focus on getting out of here."

"Let me guess." Nathan said. "You have a bobby pin in your hair and you're a master lockpick?"

"I wish," Lisa said, tipping her chair forward until she could stand. Hunched over, she shuffled toward Ben. She then lowered her chair, sitting in front of him. "See those supports?" she asked. "I bet if you kick them hard enough, they'll break in half."

Ben looked at the width of the supports. "There's no way," he said. "It'll never—"

"Don't give me that," Lisa demanded. "Try. Kick the shit out of it. Just don't kick my hand."

Ben jerked his chair into position and prepared to kick the support. "Hold on a second," Lisa said, waving her handcuffed hand. "Give me your other foot."

"Why?"

"Because if you don't, the moment you kick this chair, you'll go flying backward."

Nodding, Ben let Lisa get a good handhold on his left ankle. With his right leg primed for impact, he counted, "One, two, three," and slammed his foot against the support.

"Again," Lisa said as Ben hit the support. "Keep going." Wildly kicking over a dozen times, Ben felt the wooden support start to splinter. "You're almost there," Lisa said. After one more blow, the support snapped, allowing Lisa to slide the handcuff off the chair. With one arm still tied down, she turned her chair around. "Do the other one."

"Quietly," Nathan warned, carefully watching the door that connected to the other suite.

When Ben had kicked through the other support, Lisa was free. With the handcuffs still dangling from her wrists, she walked to Ben's chair and prepared to start kicking.

"Screw the chair," Ben said. "Run and get help."

"No way," Lisa said.

"Don't argue, just go," Ben said as the handcuffs pulled against his wrists. "There's no way we'll all get free without them hearing."

"They didn't hear you, did they?" Lisa asked. "Besides, if I leave and they find out I'm gone, who knows what they'll do to you?"

"We'll be fine," Ben said. "Go get help."

"I'm not going," Lisa said. She started kicking at Ben's supports. "I don't need your death on my head."

"They won't kill us," Ben said.

Lisa stopped to look Ben in the eye. "Are you kidding me? You think they'd beat us, kidnap us, and chain us up, but not kill us?"

"Go get help," Ben said.

"Nathan?" Lisa asked.

"Kick the chair," Nathan said. "I watched them dance on my face. Rick enjoyed it."

Standing on one leg, Lisa slammed her foot against the support. It refused to buckle. "Damn."

"Get out of here," Ben said.

"Shut . . . up," Lisa said, pounding the support. Slowly, it began to fracture. After six more kicks, it broke in two. Lisa ran to the other side of the chair.

"Hurry," Ben said.

"What do you think I'm doing?" she asked as she started working on the other side. Within a minute, the second support broke. Quickly running to Nathan's chair, the two clerks each took a side and kicked the old wood.

Nathan's adrenaline was pumping. "It'll give," he said. "It'll definitely give."

Her legs tired from the attack, Lisa stopped to catch her breath.

"Keep kicking," Nathan said. "You're almost there."

As Ben shattered the wood on his side, Nathan pulled his arm free. Running around to help Lisa, Ben heard a quiet click.

They all looked up.

"Shit," Nathan said.

"Why do you even bother?" Rick asked. Standing in the corner of the room, he pointed a gun at the three friends. "I want them separated," Rick demanded as he and Claremont walked toward the large glass table. He pointed the gun at Lisa. "Put her in the bathroom. Lock the cuffs to the pipes under the sink."

As Claremont grasped her left handcuff, Lisa swung her right one through the air, smashing him in the side of the head. Gripping both her hands in one of his, Claremont smacked Lisa in the face and sent her flying to the floor.

"I'll kill you!" Ben screamed, racing toward Claremont.

Rick pointed his gun at Ben. "DON'T MOVE!"

Suddenly frozen in fear, Ben stared down the barrel of Rick's gun.

Just then the door that connected to the second suite crashed open.

"EVERYBODY FREEZE! U.S. MARSHAL!" Carl Lungen screamed as

he ran into the room, erratically pointing his gun in every direction. Ben's mouth dropped open. "You're all under arrest!" Lungen yelled.

"Where the hell have you been?" Rick asked, unfazed by the entrance. "You were supposed to be here hours ago."

Lowering his gun, Lungen looked over at Ben and started laughing. "Oh, man, you should see your face," he said. "You really thought I was coming to your rescue, didn't you?"

"Help us tie them up," Claremont said. "They almost got out."

"How's it feel to be the fool, Addison?" Lungen asked, pointing his gun at Ben. "Now get your hands up."

"What the hell is going on?" Ben asked, raising his hands in the air. "You're working for him?"

With his gun in Ben's back, Lungen led Ben to a chair that wasn't broken. "Don't take it personally," Lungen said. "Money's money."

"Was Fisk in on it as well?" Ben asked as Lungen handcuffed him to the chair.

"I should be so lucky," Lungen said. He turned toward Rick and added, "That's where I was all day. Sorry I couldn't help you bring these three in."

"Fisk giving you a hard time?" Rick asked.

"Are you kidding? It's taken every excuse I can think of to keep him from rushing in and arresting everyone. He's more anxious than a virgin on prom night."

Rick smirked as he watched the shock on Ben's face. "Will he stay quiet?" Rick asked.

"He seems okay now, but I'm worried he'll go nuts when Ben doesn't show up for work tomorrow."

"He won't do anything," Rick said. "From what you've told me, Fisk won't take a crap without your permission."

"I don't believe this," Ben said as Lungen turned his attention to Nathan.

Lungen reattached Nathan's loose handcuff to the armrest on Nathan's chair. "C'mon, Ben," Lungen said, "did you really think you were that good? Without me, Fisk would've bugged your office weeks ago instead of days ago. And that lie detector test—you would've never passed without my help. The way I see it, you should thank me."

"I don't get it," Ben said. "Fisk administered that test."

"But who do you think rigged the machine?" Lungen asked, sitting on the couch next to Rick. "You couldn't fail that test if you tried."

"And you thought your roommate gave you placebos and you passed anyway," Rick said.

Ben turned toward Nathan. "I never thought . . ."

"It's okay," Nathan whispered, his voice trembling. "It doesn't matter anymore."

"Oh, man," Lungen laughed, slapping Rick's knee. "Did you see their faces when I ran in here? They thought it was all over."

"It will be," Rick said. "In less than eleven hours."

By four in the morning, all but one of the lights in the suite had been turned off, and an eerie silence pervaded the darkened room. A small tabletop lamp next to the sofa provided just enough reading light for Lungen to see his newspaper. In the bathroom, Lisa was asleep on the tile floor, her fear overwhelmed by sheer exhaustion. In the living room, Nathan struggled to keep his eyes open, even as his head bobbed down with sleep. Ben was wide awake in the corner of the room, his eyes blazing as he stared at Lungen.

Sitting on the sofa and flipping through his newspaper, Lungen stood guard over the three friends. When he looked over his shoulder, he caught sight of Ben. "If you're going to stare like that, you might as well say something," Lungen said. Getting no response, he added, "Why don't you just go to sleep?"

"I'm not tired."

"Fine, stay awake," Lungen said, turning back to his paper. "Like I care."

"I hope the money's good."

"The money's great."

"How much does integrity go for these days?" Ben asked. "A million? Two million?"

Lungen folded up his paper and turned back toward Ben. "I don't need morality lessons from you."

"That's fine," Ben said. "But I hope you realize you'll be a fugitive for the rest of your life."

"What are you talking about?" Lungen asked. "This isn't some rinky-dink operation. When this is over, I'm going right back to my job. And when I walk in with Ben and Lisa, the two most wanted clerks in America, I'll probably get a promotion.''

"Sure you will," Ben said.

"Believe what you want," Lungen said. "But by tomorrow night, Ben Addison is going to be a wanted man. When the SEC traces our stock sales, guess whose name will be attached to the transfer? And that bank account Rick opened for you during *CMI*—don't think that baby's not getting another big deposit. When you put that together with the tape of you giving out the decision, there's not a person in the world who will believe your story.''

"You don't have a prayer."

"I won't need one," Lungen said. "Who do you think America is going to believe—the clerk with the million-dollar bank account, or the marshal who brought him in? And if you try to finger Rick, what proof do you have? At this point, you can't even prove he exists."

Ben was silent. As his shoulders tensed, the handcuffs pulled against his wrists. "No matter what you say, Rick is out for himself. And that means he doesn't give a damn about you. In fact, I wouldn't be surprised if some of his information points a finger at the Marshals Office. If I were in your position, I'd get out now."

"C'mon, Ben, do you really think you can trick me into switching sides? I'm not some simpleminded, misunderstood lackey. I'm fully aware of every possible consequence. Rick and I planned this a long time ago, and I plan to see it through to the end.''

"So you've been in on this since *CMI*?"

"How do you think Rick knew so much about the Court?" Lungen asked. "Without an inside man, it'd be impossible to pull this off."

As the door in the corner of the room opened, the bright light of the connecting suite cut through the darkened room. Rick followed. "Are you two bonding?" Rick asked as he walked toward the center of the room.

"Absolutely." Lungen got up from the sofa and moved toward the second suite. "Ben convinced me to switch sides. I've realized what a fool I've been, and now I'm going to turn us all in."

"That's great," Rick said, patting Lungen on the back as he passed him. "Just make sure to get some sleep first. We have a busy day to-morrow."

Stopping as he reached the door to the connecting suite, Lungen turned around. "Have a good night, Ben."

"I hope you choke in your sleep," Ben said as the door slammed shut.

"It looks like it's just the two of us," Rick said, noting that Nathan was fast asleep.

"So what?" Ben snapped, trying to look over his shoulder. Standing behind Ben, Rick slowly tipped back Ben's chair. "What are you do-ing?" Ben asked.

Rick didn't answer. Dragging the chair to the center of the room, Rick made sure that Ben faced the sofa. With a better view of his most resourceful captive, Rick took a seat. "Don't pout," Rick said. "Every game has to have a winner and loser. You just happen to be the loser in this one."

"And you're the winner?"

"I am," Rick said. "You could've been a winner too. The offer was there from the beginning. You simply refused to accept it."

"There was no offer," Ben said. "You didn't ask me. You just ma-nipulated my trust."

"So sue me. Would you have given me the information otherwise?" Ben said nothing.

"Exactly."

"Well then, I guess that's it—you must know everything about me."

"Ben, do you have any idea what the main difference is between us?"

"Besides the fact you're a psycho?"

"I'm serious," Rick said. "It's a subtle difference, but an all-important one."

"Oh, I get it," Ben said. "This is where you tell me some cheesy story—like how we're opposite sides of the same coin or something."

"Not at all. We may have similar qualities, but as far as I'm con-cerned, we're not even part of the same currency. And it all stems from our one major difference: You think society's right, while I think soci-ety's a joke."

"Aren't you the maverick."

"Think about what I'm saying and you'll understand I'm right," Rick said. "You scheme and lie and manipulate just as much as I do. But you love the way society's set up. You stick to the rules. Work hard, get the perfect job, find the perfect wife, buy the perfect house, lease the perfect car. You'll be chasing that carrot for the rest of your life. As long as you follow that path, no matter how smart you are, you'll always be the predictable pragmatist, and I'll always have the advantage. And that's the real reason I picked you."

"You don't know me at all," Ben said coldly.

"Really?" Rick asked. "Then let me ask you the question I've always held back on: How about being my partner?"

"What?"

"I'm not joking," Rick said, his tone deadly serious. "We become partners. I let you go. You go back to the Court. You finish out your term, and you feed me all the lucrative decisions. By summer, we'll be swimming in money. You'll never have to worry again."

"Are you serious?"

Rick smiled. "No. Not at all. Do I look that stupid?"

Ben swung his right leg forward and kicked Rick in the shin. "You're an asshole."

"I sure am," Rick responded. With a swift shove, Rick kicked Ben's chair. As the chair fell backward, Ben struggled against his handcuffs. Unable to stop the momentum, he braced for impact. With a loud crash, the chair fell back, slamming Ben's head against the floor. Lying on his back, Ben kept his eyes closed, refusing to show any sign of pain. "Get a good night's sleep," Rick said, leaning back on the sofa. "Tomorrow's a big day."

"Wake up! Wake up! Wake up!" Rick shouted out at a quarter to nine the following morning. Jarred awake when she heard Rick bang on the bathroom door, Lisa jumped and slammed her head against the pipes directly above her head. Groggy as she sat on the floor and leaned against the bathtub, she rotated her wrists to encourage circulation to her pale white hands.

In the living room, Nathan slowly rotated his neck. Still lying on his back, Ben had slept the best of the three friends. He licked the morning film from his teeth. "I have to go to the bathroom."

"Hold it in," Rick said, lifting Ben's chair and setting it upright.

"You two look terrible," Claremont said to Ben and Nathan, who had matching bags under their eyes.

"Where's Lungen?" Ben asked, glancing around the room.

"At work," Rick said as he walked toward Nathan. "Placating Fisk."

"When are you going to call the broker?" Claremont asked impatiently. "It's almost nine."

"I'll call him in a minute." Rick tipped back Nathan's chair and dragged him to the center of the room.

"What's going on?" Nathan asked. "What are you doing?"

"Testing a theory," Rick said, letting the chair down. Turning to Ben, who was now facing Nathan's side, Rick asked, "Do you have a clear view of your friend?"

"Don't touch him," Ben warned. "I told you the decision."

"You also told me the *Grinnell* decision," Rick said as he rolled up the sleeves of his white, button-down shirt. "And look where that got me." Rick pulled his arm back and cracked Nathan in the side of the face.

"Stop!" Ben screamed.

"Does American Steel really win?" Rick asked as Claremont looked on.

"It wins. I swear."

Rick smashed Nathan in the jaw. "Are you sure that's the right outcome?"

"Stop it!" Ben yelled. "It's right."

As blood dripped from Nathan's mouth, Claremont said, "He's telling the truth."

"We'll see," Rick said, walking toward the bathroom. He dragged Lisa out by the handcuffs.

"Don't you dare!" Ben yelled, seething.

"Shut up," Rick said. Claremont pulled Nathan's chair away and brought an empty one to the center of the room. Lisa kicked and fought furiously against Rick.

"Get the hell off me!" she screamed. "I'll kill you!"

"Quiet," Rick said as the two men forced her into place. When they had handcuffed her to the armrests of the chair, Rick stepped back to watch Ben's expression.

Ben exploded as he felt his face turn a bright crimson. "Stay the hell away from her! I told you the damn decision!"

"My," Rick said. "I didn't realize you were so attached."

"Hurry up," Claremont said, looking at his watch. "We don't have time for this."

"Believe me," Rick said, "if we don't have the right decision, all the time in the world won't mean a thing." Turning back toward Ben, he continued, "Now, Ben, does American Steel really win?"

"Don't tell him," Lisa said.

Rick punched Lisa in the face. "No one asked you." A red patch blossomed around her left eye. "Now you and Nathan match each other."

"Get away from her!" Ben screamed, his arms struggling against his handcuffs and his body convulsing in a rabid rage. "I'll kill you!"

"I asked a . . . question," Rick said as he hit her again.

As blood and saliva flew from Lisa's mouth, Ben fought uncontrollably to break free. "I'll fucking kill you!"

"That's not the answer," Rick said. He slapped Lisa across the face. Her head flew sideways.

Enraged and screaming, Ben couldn't contain himself. In a mad frenzy, he fought against his restraints. "IT'S THE TRUTH!" he shouted as tears rolled down his face. "WHAT ELSE DO YOU WANT TO KNOW?"

"What's the vote?" Rick asked.

"Five to four," Ben said. "Dreiberg's the swing vote."

Rick pulled out his gun and pointed it at Lisa. "Are you sure?"

"C'mon, Rick, that's enough," Claremont interrupted.

"Shut up," Rick said. Holding Lisa by the hair, Rick shoved the barrel of the gun in her mouth and repeated his question. "Are you sure?"

"I swear," Ben pleaded. "On my life."

As he pulled back the hammer, Rick put his finger on the trigger. "I'm not joking. I'll do it."

"I swear it's true," Ben said, his body tensed. "Steel wins."

Rick paused, searching Ben's face for a glimmer of deceit. "Fine," he said, removing the gun from Lisa's mouth. "I believe you." Rick walked to the desk in the corner of the room and picked up his cellular phone. Quickly dialing a number, he said, "Hello, Noah? It's me. Here's the story. The moment the market opens, I want you to liquidate all those preferred stock certificates I gave you. Then take the proceeds and buy every American Steel option you can find." Listening for a moment, he continued, "Exactly. I'm positive. Then at noon, I want all the proceeds cashed in and sent to my usual account. Exactly. You got it." Rick hung up the phone and turned to Claremont. "Now all we have to do is wait."

Spitting blood all over the carpet, Lisa struggled to stop the room from spinning.

"Lisa!" Ben called. "Over here!"

"She's coming around," Nathan said. "Give her a second."

"What the hell happened?" Lisa asked. "My face feels like a balloon."

"Are you okay?" Ben asked. "Talk to me."

"I'm fine," she said, shutting her eyes tightly to stop the vertigo. "Let me catch my breath." She remained quiet for a minute, then asked, "Does my eye look as bad as it feels?"

"It's just a black eye," Ben said.

"I know what it is," Lisa snapped. "Tell me how it looks."

"It looks pretty bad."

"Did Rick do all the damage or did Claremont take some shots also?"

"It was Rick," Ben said.

"He's a dead man when I get out of these handcuffs." Lisa looked over her shoulder and saw Nathan. "How are you doing?"

"I'm fine," Nathan said, his voice barely above a whisper.

"Does my eye look as bad as his?" Lisa asked Ben, pointing her chin at Nathan.

"It will in a few hours," Ben said.

"Great," Lisa said.

"Hey, Rick," Ben yelled across the room. "Can we at least get some ice over here?"

"No," Rick said, pulling his laptop computer from his briefcase.

*   *   *

A few minutes before ten, Rick hooked up his cellular phone to his laptop and logged on to the Westlaw Supreme Court database. Looking over Rick's shoulder, Claremont asked, "We can watch the decision from here?"

"No," Rick said sarcastically, "we're going to take a field trip to the Court so we can all see it in person." His fingers pounded the keyboard. "The moment it's announced, the Information Office releases the decision, and Westlaw puts it on-line."

Across the room, Ben asked Lisa, "Are you sure you're okay?"

"For the tenth time, I'm fine," Lisa said as the area surrounding her eye continued to swell and darken. "I get punched in the face all the time."

"Nathan?" Ben asked. "How's your eye?"

"It's fine," Nathan said. "Stop asking about it."

"All of you, shut up," Rick said, turning toward his three captives.

At exactly ten o'clock, the Court marshal banged his gavel, and every person in the room stood at attention.

"The Honorable, the Chief Justice and the Associate Justices of the Supreme Court of the United States!" the marshal announced. Immediately, the nine justices stepped out from behind the burgundy velvet curtain and moved to their respective chairs.

"Oyez! Oyez! Oyez!" the marshal announced. "All persons having business before the Honorable, the Supreme Court of the United States, are admonished to draw near and give their attention, for the Court is now sitting. God save the United States and this Honorable Court!" Again, the gavel fell, and everyone took their seats.

"Today we will be ruling on three decisions," Osterman said to the packed courtroom. "*Alvarez* v. *City of Gibsonia, Katz and Company* v. *Nevada,* and *Richard Rubin* v. *American Steel.* Justice Veidt will be reading our first two decisions, while Justice Dreiberg will read the third."

*   *   *

"What's taking so long?" Claremont asked, staring at Rick's blank computer screen. "It's almost a quarter after."

"Relax," Rick said. "They have three decisions to get through. It'll be here."

"Does it come out the moment it's announced, or do they wait until they're done with all three?" Claremont asked.

"I said it'll be here," Rick said. "Now shut up."

". . . is constitutional under the First Amendment. Therefore, in the case of *Katz and Company* v. *Nevada,* we find for the defendant and uphold the Supreme Court of Nevada."

"Thank you, Justice Veidt," Osterman said. "Justice Dreiberg will announce our final decision."

"Why don't you let us go?" Ben asked from across the room. "You have your decision."

Rick stared intently at his laptop. "I'll believe it when I see it."

"What if he was lying?" Claremont asked. "We could've bet on the wrong outcome."

"Pull it together," Rick demanded. "He was telling the truth."

"How do you know?"

"Because if he didn't, he knows I'll kill him."

"Thank you, Mr. Chief Justice," Dreiberg announced, leaning forward on both elbows as she spoke into the microphone. In a slow, monotone voice, she read: "In the case of *Richard Rubin* v. *American Steel,* we find that American Steel's board of directors was not required to seek the approval of its minority shareholders before its merger proceeded. The shareholders' claim is, therefore, insufficient to establish a private cause of action under the Securities Exchange Act. We find for the respondent and affirm the Court of Appeals for the Ninth Circuit."

*   *   *

"Did we win?" Claremont asked.

Rick's eyes skimmed through the decision as it scrolled up his computer screen. "Hold on. It's coming." He paused. "Looks like American Steel just won itself a huge lawsuit. Congratulations, Addison. You finally did something right." After he shut his laptop and unhooked his phone, Rick walked over to the couch and placed both items in his briefcase.

"What do we do now?" Claremont asked, elated. "Where are we meeting Lungen? When do we leave?"

"One thing at a time," Rick said. He pulled a key from his pocket and moved toward Ben. "Help me uncuff these three. Then we can get out of here."

"Where are we going?" Ben asked as Rick unlocked his handcuffs.

Rick didn't answer. Instead, he pulled Ben out of the chair and pushed him toward Claremont. "Lock them up again," Rick said to Claremont.

"Stick your hands out straight," Claremont said. When Ben obliged, he handcuffed him.

Lisa was unlocked and recuffed in turn. Holding their shoulders, Claremont continued to watch over the two clerks as Rick approached Nathan. "Don't move until I say," Claremont warned.

Glaring at Ben until she got his attention, Lisa motioned toward Claremont with her eyes while subtly pointing to her crotch. Ben leaned backward. "I'm not feeling so good," he moaned. "I think I'm going to faint." Claremont let go of Lisa to catch Ben as he fell. Lisa spun toward Claremont and slammed her knee into his groin. As Claremont and Ben fell to the floor, Lisa rushed to the door. Realizing what was happening, Rick turned away from Nathan, pulled his gun, and started shooting. Two bullets had ripped through the door by the time Lisa grabbed the doorknob.

"DON'T MOVE!" Rick screamed.

The door slightly ajar, Lisa stood there motionless, her hands still cuffed.

"I'll do it—I'm not kidding. I'll kill them all," Rick threatened.

Lisa knew this was her last chance to escape. She darted into the hallway. Three more bullets plowed through the door.

Lisa headed straight for the emergency exit, but when she opened the stairwell door, she was surprised to see two other doors—one leading upstairs and one leading down. Opening the heavy metal door with her still-handcuffed hands, Lisa opted to run downstairs.

"Get her!" Rick screamed to Claremont, who was already staggering to the bullet-ridden door. Rick pointed his gun at Ben. "If you leave this room, I swear you'll have two dead roommates to deal with."

Ben looked over at Nathan, who was still handcuffed to his chair. "I'm not going anywhere," Ben said. "I swear." Seconds later, Rick was out the door.

Thrown off-balance by her handcuffs, Lisa had trouble navigating the first flight of stairs. Searching for a less awkward running position, she realized it was easier to move when she held her elbows close to her body. When she reached the twenty-third floor, she found another door blocking the stairway that led to the twenty-second floor. "Damn," she said. Pulling open that door, she heard Rick and Claremont following behind her.

Racing down the stairs, her hands clenched and her elbows tight against her, Lisa fought with a door on every floor. As she grew fatigued, each door was heavier to open, and each staircase took longer to descend. At every landing, she was tempted to run back into the hallway, but fear and skepticism kept her to the stairs. As she opened the door to the sixth floor, she wondered how quickly Rick and Claremont were gaining on her.

When Lisa reached the fifth floor, she was exhausted. The lack of sleep combined with her circular descent caused a return of her morning vertigo. Refusing to surrender, though, she gritted her teeth against lightheadedness and plowed forward. Only four more, she told herself. Once I'm in the lobby, I'll scream like a banshee. By the time she reached the door that led to the fourth floor staircase, the dizziness had returned and her body was covered in a fearful, fatigued sweat. Off-balance, she lurched for the doorknob. It was locked. Looking up, she saw a stenciled sign painted on the door: TO REACH LOBBY LEVEL, PLEASE USE SOUTH STAIRWELL. No! Not now! she thought, wildly kicking the door. Grabbing the doorknob again and putting her foot against the wall, she desperately pulled on the door.

She heard the pounding of Rick's and Claremont's footsteps closing in on her.

Turning toward the door that led to the hallway, Lisa yanked it open and left the stairwell. In the sudden calm of the carpeted hallway, she looked through the plate-glass window on her right and caught a glimpse of a crystal-blue indoor swimming pool below. She ran down the corridor, banging on every door with her cuffed hands. "Fire! Everybody out! Fire!" she screamed. Not a single door opened. When she reached the elevators, she repeatedly pounded the down button with her fists. The digital display above the elevator doors showed one at the nineteenth floor and the other at the twenty-sixth. Too long to wait, she thought as she continued running. Heading toward the far end of the hallway, she saw a small sign marked: SOUTH STAIRWELL—LOBBY LEVEL. Praying for an escape, she grabbed the doorknob. Once again, it was locked. "SON OF A BITCH!" she screamed.

From the north stairwell door, Lisa heard Claremont shouting back to Rick. Their voices were loud. Lisa knew they couldn't be more than a few floors away.

As she raced back to the elevators, Lisa could barely catch her breath. Furiously, she punched both call buttons. "C'mon, you piece of crap! Get here!" One elevator was now on the seventeenth floor and the other was still at the twenty-sixth; they had barely moved. Convinced that Claremont and Rick would be there in seconds, she looked down the hall and remembered the swimming pool outside the window. She took a deep breath. It's only four stories, she calculated. I can probably make it if I go through fast enough. Before she could talk herself out of it, Lisa tucked her elbows in tight and ran full speed, barreling down the hallway toward the huge window next to the stairwell. Shoulder first, shoulder first, shoulder first, she repeated to herself as she raced toward her target.

Lisa hurled her body against the glass just as Claremont emerged from the stairwell. He grabbed the chain of Lisa's handcuffs, even as the glass started to shatter. Propelled forward by her momentum, Lisa cleared the threshold of the window, as thousands of tiny glass shards rained down on her. The weight of her fall had brought Claremont down flat on his stomach and dragged him to the edge of the window. But something had stopped his slide: Rick.

"Are you okay?" Rick asked, holding Claremont by the belt.

Looking over the edge, Claremont struggled to hold on to Lisa, who was dangling outside the window. "Y-yeah," Claremont said.

"No! Don't!" Lisa screamed as her hands grabbed Claremont's wrist. Her face and arms were covered in hundreds of tiny, bleeding cuts. "Please don't drop me!"

Without the momentum to reach the pool, Lisa would fall directly onto the tiled atrium, where a crowd had already started to gather. "Drop her," Rick said.

"What?" Claremont asked.

"Please don't!" Lisa screamed. "Don't drop me!"

"Drop her, and let's get out of here," Rick said. "I've had enough of this nonsense."

Still, Claremont held on to Lisa's handcuffs, his arm tensing from the weight.

"I said drop her," Rick demanded. "What's wrong with you? We were going to kill them anyway."

With all his strength, Claremont held tight.

Rick pulled his gun from his waist and pointed it at Claremont's head. "You're not Richard Claremont. Who the hell are you?" Lifting his arm, Claremont started to pull Lisa to safety. Rick pulled back the hammer on his gun and pressed the gun against Claremont's head. "You have three seconds to tell me who you are. At the end of three, you're both going out this window. One . . . two . . ."

"Ben!" Lisa screamed. Rick spun around to a blast of white foam. As Rick rubbed his burning eyes, Ben ran into the corridor wielding a fire extinguisher. With his wrists still handcuffed, Ben swung the fire extinguisher like a baseball bat and slammed Rick in the side of the head. Rick stumbled backward and fell to the floor. He fired his gun, and a jagged pain ripped through Ben's left shoulder. He'd been shot. Staggering forward, Ben swung the fire extinguisher again, this time knocking the gun out of Rick's hands.

Ben struggled to swing the fire extinguisher one more time, but the pain in his shoulder was impossible to ignore. Seeing the blood that rushed down his arm, he felt faint and dropped the extinguisher.

"Hurts like a bitch, doesn't it?" Rick asked, stumbling to his feet. "The next one's going in your head."

Holding his shoulder, Ben looked down the hallway and saw Rick's gun lying on the floor by the elevators. He looked back at Rick, who was almost standing.

"GET THE GUN!" Claremont screamed, pulling Lisa to safety.

Ignoring the gun, Ben raced toward Rick. Grasping his hands together, Ben swung wildly at Rick's head. When his handcuffs struck Rick's face, Rick staggered backward. As Ben moved in to hit him again, Rick slammed his fist into Ben's gunshot wound. Ben screamed, clutching his shoulder. Rick looked down the hallway at the gun.

Fighting the urge to collapse, Ben saw Rick move toward the gun. Once again, he ran at Rick, plowing into him from behind and knocking him to the floor. Rick turned on his back and tried to fight his way free, but Ben stayed on top of him. Ben grabbed Rick by the throat and pinned him against the floor. "You greedy bastard!" Ben screamed as Rick thrashed wildly. "You killed Ober!"

"He killed himself," Rick coughed.

"NO!" Ben screamed, banging Rick's head against the floor. "YOU KILLED HIM!" Ben tightened his grip around Rick's throat. "YOU WANT TO SEE HOW OBER FELT? YOU WANT TO FEEL HOW HE DIED?" Rick swung at Ben's head, attempting to remove his attacker. Ben wouldn't budge. Rick punched at Ben's bloody shoulder. Ben didn't move. The more Rick fought, the tighter Ben's grip. Eventually, the coughing stopped and the struggling ceased—Rick was finally unconscious. But Ben didn't let go of Rick's throat. "You killed my friend!" Ben sobbed as rage slowly erupted into tears. "I'll kill you for that!"

As tears rolled off Ben's cheeks, Rick's face turned beet red. Ben clenched even harder. With Rick's life in his hands, Ben remembered his last conversation with him. "You want to see me break the rules?" Ben growled as blood continued to flush Rick's face. "Here's what I think of your damn rules." Holding fast to Rick's throat, Ben remembered Rick's boasting. And Nathan's beating. And Lisa's bleeding. And Ober's hanging.

Ben sobbed and, staring down at Rick's swollen face, he let go: "Ober! I'm so sorry!"

A small cough emerged from Rick's lips. Mentally and physically exhausted, Ben collapsed on the floor, his ragged breathing punctuated by sobs. It was finally over.

As Ben lay on the floor, holding his shoulder, the elevator arrived. When the doors opened, Alex DeRosa got out with half a dozen armed U.S. marshals.

"Everybody out," DeRosa yelled as his men fanned into the hallway. Two of them handcuffed Rick, while two others ran to check on Lisa and Claremont.

"Are you okay?" DeRosa asked Ben, helping him to his feet.

"What the hell is this?" Ben asked, confused. "You were here all along?"

"Sorry about that," DeRosa said as he unlocked Ben's handcuffs. "Rick was watching you full-time this whole week. We didn't want to risk anything."

"Risk anything?" Ben yelled, rubbing his wrists. "We were almost killed! You lied to my face."

"I didn't lie," DeRosa said. "I needed you to act normally." DeRosa put his hand on Ben's shoulder. "It was the only way—"

"Don't touch me!" Ben yelled, pulling away from DeRosa's hand. "You lied and put all of our lives at risk! Who the hell do you think you are?"

"Ben, I couldn't get through to you. Rick was always watching."

"That's bullshit," Ben snapped. "You could've passed me a note on the subway. You could've passed me something at the Jefferson Memorial. At the very least, you should've passed me something when Ober died."

"I'm sorry about that—"

"I don't want to hear it," Ben yelled, walking past DeRosa. Holding his shoulder, he headed up the hallway.

Ben approached Lisa and Claremont. "Thanks for the save," Claremont said.

"Fuck you," Ben said, pushing Claremont aside to get to Lisa, who was collapsed against the wall. He grabbed her bloodied hand and looked at her battered face. "How're you doing?" he asked.

"I've had better days," she said.

"Did you get pushed through the window?"

"No way," Lisa said with a pained smile. "This was by choice. Great idea, huh?"

"One of your best," Ben said.

"Let's get them both to a hospital," one of the marshals said. "They're pretty banged up."

"Did you really get shot?" Lisa asked, looking at Ben's shoulder.

"No way," Ben smiled back. "This was by choice."

CHAPTER 19

HOLDING A BAG OF ICE TO HIS EYE, NATHAN WAITED INSIDE a small room that connected to DeRosa's office. For two hours, Nathan hadn't moved, sitting in the same hard chair and leaning on the same small conference table. Throughout the ride to DeRosa's office, the marshals wouldn't say a word to him. When Nathan asked questions, they wouldn't respond. When he threatened them, they weren't fazed. All they would tell him was that Ben and Lisa were safe.

Finally the door to DeRosa's office opened. Taking his bag of ice with him, Nathan walked inside. Ben sat in one of two chairs that faced DeRosa. A sling held Ben's left arm in place. Nathan pulled the bag of ice from his eye and scowled at his roommate. "This's why I've been locked up for two hours?" Nathan asked. "So you could interrogate Prince Charming over here?"

"Take a seat," DeRosa said, pointing to the chair next to Ben.

"I'd rather stand," Nathan replied shortly.

"Whatever you want," DeRosa said.

"How are you doing?" Ben asked.

"How am I doing?" Nathan asked sarcastically. "Let's see, my eye is a melon, my head is ringing, and no one's told me a damn thing. Other than that, I'm superb."

"What was the last thing you saw at the hotel?" DeRosa asked.

"The last thing I saw was a dozen marshals busting into the room. They confiscated all of Rick's equipment, shouted about tracing Rick's cellular phone, and then they unlocked me—obviously their lowest priority. Then you come over, introduce yourself, and disappear. A medic checks me out and gives me some ice and some aspirin, and the next thing I know, two of your Secret Service wannabes drive me here and lock me in that little room."

"I'm sorry I had to leave," DeRosa explained, scribbling notes as he spoke. "Now what happened before that?"

Before Nathan could respond, the door to DeRosa's office opened and Claremont walked into the room. Carrying a cup of coffee, he sat in an empty chair near the window. Staring at his former captor, Nathan was enraged. "Who's he, and what the hell is he doing here?" Nathan asked.

"That's Michael Burke," DeRosa said, pointing to Claremont. "He's a U.S. marshal."

"You're a cop?" Nathan asked.

"I'm a marshal," Burke said.

"You're a marshal, but you let Rick beat the shit out of us?"

"Sorry about that," Burke said. "We wanted to wait until Rick bought the stock before we did anything."

"Then where were you after he bought the stock?" Nathan asked, his voice growing louder.

"Don't blame me for that," Burke said. "That was your fault. We were ready to storm in, but Lisa bolted out the door."

"Oh, and that's *my* fault?" Nathan laughed. He walked to the empty chair next to Ben and sat down. "How the hell were we supposed to know you guys were out there?"

"Ben and Lisa knew," Burke said.

"You knew?" Nathan turned to Ben.

"I swear I didn't know," Ben insisted. "I thought they gave up on me."

"Hold on a second," Nathan said. "I thought I was about to die a few hours ago! Now what the hell is going on?"

"Here's what—" Ben began.

"I want the full story," Nathan demanded. "From the beginning."

"Drop that tone and shut up," DeRosa ordered. Nathan put his ice back on his eye. Ben then took a deep breath and explained how he'd initially approached DeRosa and how he'd thought he'd been abandoned by the Marshals Office.

"Are you telling me they could've grabbed Rick weeks ago?" Nathan asked in disbelief. He looked back at DeRosa. "Why did you wait until now?"

"We wanted to get everyone Rick was involved with," DeRosa explained. "From his broker to everyone else on his payroll."

"And we wanted to catch Carl Lungen," Burke added.

Nathan stared coldly at Burke. He then turned back to Ben. "Did you know he was a marshal?"

"Not at all," Ben explained. "That's why I smashed him in the face. I didn't know he was on our side until he saved Lisa."

"What about Ober getting fired?" Nathan asked. "Did anyone know—"

"We didn't know Rick was going to get Ober fired," DeRosa said.

"And if it makes you feel any better," Burke added, "I didn't know Rick was going to kidnap you. He decided that at the last minute when he thought Ben was turning himself in. Remember, we were counting on Ben handing over the decision early yesterday morning."

"The kidnapping thing really messed us up," DeRosa said. "We didn't think—"

"No, you didn't think," Nathan interrupted. "The moment Rick grabbed us, you should've blown the whistle. Instead I got my face kicked in for no reason."

"There was nothing I could do," Burke said.

"That's bullshit," Nathan said. "You could've revealed who you were. That would've forced everyone to rush in the room and save us all."

"I couldn't do that," Burke said. "It would've jeopardized all of our lives. I didn't know where the backup was hiding. I just knew they would be there if things got out of control."

"You don't call this out of control?" Nathan yelled, pointing to his black eye. "And what about when Rick put a gun in Lisa's mouth? That wasn't out of control enough for you?"

Ben put his hand on Nathan's shoulder. "Nathan, calm down," he said. "If everyone came charging in at that moment Rick *would've* blown Lisa's head off. As it is, we should consider ourselves lucky nothing else happened."

Nathan pulled away from Ben and stood up. "What else could possibly happen? This was the worst weekend of my life!" Ben reached over to calm him, but Nathan continued to pull away. Eventually, Nathan was standing in the middle of DeRosa's office. "When Ober lost his job, they already had Rick in their hands! And *you* didn't say a word! You could've blown the whistle on all of this! You could've—"

"I did what I thought was best for everyone," Ben said. "If I had blown the whistle early, Rick would've disappeared. The only way to deal with Rick permanently was to catch him."

As his fists tightened, Nathan could no longer contain his rage. "YOU SELF-CENTERED SON OF A BITCH! THE ONLY THING YOU DEALT WITH PERMANENTLY WAS OBER! BY KEEPING YOUR MOUTH SHUT, YOU KILLED HIM!" Blindly, Nathan threw his ice pack across the room, sending it flying toward DeRosa's neatly organized desk. As it landed on the desk, the ice bag sent a stack of papers crashing to the floor.

"I understand you're upset," Burke said, "but you have to look at the big picture—"

"Screw the big picture," Nathan yelled. "My life isn't there for you guys to play with! You used us! And Ober paid the price for it!"

"That's enough," DeRosa interrupted, his voice booming through the office. "Ober acted on his own. And if suicide was his best solution, he had more problems than the ones Ben gave him. As for you, you should be thrilled you're alive. If you're not, you can drop a note in the suggestion box on your way out."

Silent as DeRosa picked up his papers, Nathan remained motionless in the center of the room.

"Nathan, I'm so sorry," Ben said. "I tried my best to—"

"I don't want to hear it," Nathan interrupted. Walking over to DeRosa, he added, "I guess you knew about the blackmail letters Rick sent us."

"All about them," DeRosa said. "Don't worry. We'll let your office know that your participation in this case was invaluable. There's no way they'll fire you after I'm done with them."

"Great. Fine," Nathan said, walking to the door of DeRosa's office.

Burke followed Nathan to the door. "You're not going anywhere," Burke growled. "We still have questions for you to—"

Nathan opened the door and stormed out.

"Let him go," DeRosa said. "It's been a long day." When the door closed, DeRosa turned to Ben, who looked exhausted. "Well, that's one battle lost—you ready for Hollis?"

Sitting outside of Hollis's private office, Ben anxiously waited for the door to open. What's taking so long? he wondered. Restlessly, he fidgeted with the sling on his left arm. Not since his first day on the job had he been this nervous about an encounter with Hollis. Twenty minutes later, the thick mahogany door opened, and Lisa walked out.

"How'd it go?" Ben asked. "What'd he say?"

"He's ready to see you," Lisa said.

"But how'd—"

"Go in and talk to him," Lisa said. "He's the boss. Not me."

Uneasy as he stepped inside, Ben forced a smile and took his usual seat in front of Hollis's desk. "Nice to see you," Ben said.

With eyes that had watched the evolution of the law for more than thirty years, Justice Mason Hollis was the most accessible of the nine. The oldest of seven children and the father of five, he radiated a paternal presence. As a college baseball player at Yale, he was rumored to strike out on purpose when he felt the other team was losing by too wide a margin, and as a judge on the D.C. Circuit, he'd once granted an extension so that counsel could "get some sleep." According to the employees of the Court, Hollis was the one justice no one feared. At this moment, however, Ben Addison was terrified.

"How are you doing?" Hollis asked. As his hand slid over his sparse white hair, his fingers brushed against the numerous liver spots that dotted his head.

"I'm fine," Ben said, unable to look his boss in the face.

"Sounds like you're lucky to be alive, yes?"

"I suppose."

Hollis picked up a pencil and started nibbling on the eraser. "Don't be so downcast," he said. "You should be proud of yourself—quick thinking and all that." Getting no reaction, he added, "A lesser person would've been beaten by this."

"I'm just glad it's finally over."

Hollis smiled at Ben. "I have to tell you—when I hired you and Lisa, I knew you'd be a lively team. I didn't expect you to be this lively, but that's neither here nor there."

Tapping his foot against the thick burgundy carpet, Ben wished Hollis would get to the point. He wanted to know Hollis's decision. "Can I ask you a question?" he blurted. "Do I get to keep my job?"

"Ben—"

"Since I helped catch Rick, I'm not going to be criminally charged," Ben said, his voice shaking. "The marshals said my record would stay completely clean, and they want to give me a commendation for helping them catch Lungen. They arrested him early this morning."

"Ben, I'm sorry . . ."

"They said I could—"

"Ben, listen to me," Hollis demanded. "Theoretically, you may be innocent, but you still violated the Code of Ethics of this Court. I have no choice but to let you go."

At eight-thirty that evening, Ben returned home. Eric was in the dining room, hunched over a small canvas. Flicking drops of red, blue, yellow, and green paint from his fingers, Eric was trying to re-create the splatter painting that he had done directly on the wall. It was Eric's fourth attempt to duplicate his earlier work; only a close match would be suitable to go in Ober's coffin. Seeing Ben walk through the door, Eric rubbed his fingers with a turpentine-covered rag and headed toward the living room, rattling off questions: "What happened? Are you okay? How's your shoulder? What'd they say? What took so long?"

Ben took off his coat and put it in the closet. He then turned toward Eric and gave a single answer. "I was fired."

"What?" Eric asked as Ben moved into the kitchen. "I don't believe it. Tell me what happened."

Ben poured himself a tall glass of water. "There's nothing to tell. They fired me. I told my story to Hollis. He listened. He tried to soften the blow. He fired me. Then he took me to see Osterman. After a long lecture, they let me leave. That's it. I no longer work at the Supreme Court.''

Ben drank the entire glass of water.

"What else did they say?''

Ben ignored Eric's question. "Where's Nathan?''

"He drove back to Boston. Ober's funeral is tomorrow.''

Slowly rotating his shoulder, Ben felt a heavy ache setting in. "Did he say anything?''

"He told me the story about Rick, packed up his stuff, and left.''

"Was he still mad?''

"I wouldn't call him until we get to Boston. He's pretty pissed off.''

"I understand,'' Ben said. Pulling a small vial from his pants pocket, he read the directions for his pain medication. Ben poured some more water and took one of the tiny pink pills.

"So tell me what happened,'' Eric demanded. "I just saw the story on the news.''

"Great,'' Ben said sarcastically. "Did they mention my name?''

"No. It was just a short clip. They said someone named—''

"Mark Wexler,'' Ben said as Eric struggled to remember the name.

"That's it. Mark Wexler,'' Eric repeated. "They said he was arrested for insider trading using confidential Supreme Court decisions. They didn't have much information, so I wasn't sure—''

"Mark Wexler is Rick's real name,'' Ben explained, turning back to the living room. "Apparently, he used to work in a high-powered Seattle law firm that did high-tech legal work for CMI and Charles Maxwell. About a year ago, he was fired for ethics violations—they thought he was buying stock in one of the cases he was working on.''

"So he has a criminal record,'' Eric said as he sat on the small couch.

"No, he's clean,'' Ben explained. "The law firm could never prove anything. Whatever Rick was doing, he was good about keeping it secret. Even though they couldn't find proof, the firm asked him to leave. It looks like he moved to New York after that, and he's been living there ever since. When he needed to do business in D.C., he was only a shuttle away.''

"Amazing,'' Eric said.

"I really don't want to talk about him anymore," Ben said. "He's been the topic of conversation all afternoon."

"Well, at least tell me what happened with Hollis."

"There's nothing to tell. Since the story was going to be announced to the public, they couldn't just turn their backs on the whole thing. And if they let me stay, I'd be a stigma on the Court. I violated the Code of Ethics. If I wasn't asked to step down, no one would take it seriously."

"But you weren't fired," Eric clarified. "They asked you to step down."

"There's no difference," Ben said.

"Was Hollis at least nice about it?"

"He couldn't have been nicer. He told me how much he appreciated my work for him, and how he hoped we'd stay in touch. He said he'd write me a recommendation for my next job. He even said he was impressed with how we caught Rick. But it didn't change his decision."

"What's going to happen to Lisa?"

"Nothing," Ben said. "I made sure she was left out of it. As far as anyone's concerned, she's the co-clerk who designed the plan and helped me through the hard times. Otherwise, she had nothing to do with the original leak." Ben rested his arm on one of the couch's pillows and wondered how long it would be before the pain medication kicked in.

"What did Osterman say?" Eric asked.

"He was a typical jackass. He gave me a big lecture about the aims and ideals of the Court and how they could never be compromised. I really wanted to reach over and mess up his pathetic comb-over. I don't know why they brought me to see him. Hollis had already fired me."

"You should've grabbed the comb-over," Eric said. "What's the worst thing he could've done? Fired you again?"

"I guess," Ben said, distracted.

"One last question?" Eric said, unable to shake his reporter's instincts. "How did Burke convince Rick that he was Claremont?"

"After *Grinnell*, Lisa and I knew that Rick was going to try to get his money back. So we isolated all the cases on the Court's docket that he could potentially make money on."

"How many cases were there?" Eric asked, intrigued.

"There were only four involving major dollars."

"So how'd Burke find Rick?"

"He didn't," Ben said. "Rick picks his own partners, so we had to figure out a way to make Rick find Burke. We staked out—"

"*You* staked out?" Eric asked.

"Actually, the marshals did all of the legwork, but Lisa came up with the idea," Ben explained. "The Marshals Office watched the top executives at all four corporations—"

"But there are hundreds of executives at each one," Eric pointed out.

"Not when you're only looking at the ones with criminal records," Ben said. "We figured that if Rick was going to look at a hundred executives and pick one, he'd probably go for the one who was most likely to break the law."

"So they watched every executive until Rick made his move?" Eric asked.

"Better," Ben said. "The marshals *replaced* every executive until Rick made his move. Burke stood in for Richard Claremont, American Steel's executive vice president of marketing, who was previously convicted of tax evasion."

"How many executives did they replace?"

"They couldn't afford to do everyone," Ben explained. "Especially if they wanted to keep it quiet. So we picked the twenty most likely candidates and we waited."

"Wasn't the real Claremont's life disrupted?"

"All they did was take over his phone line. The real Claremont didn't even change offices. The only difference was that his calls were routed to Burke. If it was a real client, he passed the call back to Claremont. If it was Rick, he kept it."

"And you weren't sure any of this was going on?" Eric asked.

"We didn't know a thing," Ben said, distracted by the throbbing pain that ran down his arm. "Lisa and I gave DeRosa the plan and the list of corporate suspects, but we never knew if it was implemented. I didn't know how it played out until the car ride over here."

"Unreal," Eric said, leaning back on the couch. Noticing the vacant look on Ben's face, he asked, "Are you okay?"

"I'm just feeling a little out of it. Between the pain and the medication . . ."

"You look like hell. Maybe you should get some sleep."

"I feel like hell," Ben said, rising from the couch.

"Cheer up. You had a huge victory today."

Ben slowly made his way to the stairs. "Doesn't feel like it."

Eric pulled his notepad from his back pocket. "Ben, can I ask you one last favor? I don't mean to be inconsiderate or obnoxious, but would you care if I wrote the story on this?" He looked at his watch and added, "I can probably make page one if I hurry."

"Eric, go fuck yourself," Ben said, climbing the stairs. "And you can quote me on that."

EPILOGUE

TWO WEEKS LATER, ON SATURDAY NIGHT, BEN WALKED INTO Lisa's building. "Nice to see you," the doorman said enthusiastically.

"You, too," Ben said, trying not to make eye contact.

"Nice job with that whole thing," the doorman added. "You've become quite the celebrity."

"Thanks," Ben said, stepping inside a waiting elevator. Getting out at the fourth floor, Ben went down the hallway to Lisa's apartment and rang her doorbell.

"Who is it?" Lisa asked, peeking through the eyehole.

"It's me," Ben said.

"Wait a minute. Aren't you that guy I saw on the news? That genius legal clerk who redeemed himself by catching the criminal mastermind?"

"Just open the door," Ben pleaded.

When Lisa opened the door, Ben saw that most of the cuts on Lisa's face and hands had fully healed. All that remained were a few thin, pink scars in the places where the glass cut deepest.

"Nice to see you," she said. As Lisa leaned in to give Ben a kiss, she was surprised when he turned his cheek. "That's what I get? A peck on the cheek?"

Ben walked inside and sat on Lisa's couch. "Please don't start," he begged.

"What's wrong?" Lisa asked.

"Nathan's definitely moving out. He found an apartment, and he's leaving this week."

Lisa pulled out her desk chair and sat down. "I don't know why you're surprised. He said he was moving out when he got back from Boston."

"I know," Ben said, "but I thought he'd get past it. I figured—"

"You figured what?" Lisa interrupted. "That he'd forget about the fact that Ober's dead? That he'd forgive you for almost getting him killed? That he'd eventually look back and laugh about the whole thing? This was a big deal, Ben. It's been all over the news for the past two weeks. It's not something that just goes away."

"But I can still be upset when he leaves. He's one of my closest friends, and he won't talk to me."

"You should be upset," Lisa said. "But you should also give him some space. If you're that close, he may eventually come around."

"I don't know," Ben said. "I really think I've lost him."

"That's the problem with competitive friendships—they shatter at the slightest impact."

"I don't think this impact was slight. This was more like a freight train running over us."

"Either way, it's going to take a long time to put back together," Lisa said. "How is Eric reacting? Is he taking sides?"

"He could care less," Ben said. "You've seen what's happened to him. He's in his glory. As far as his boss is concerned, he broke this story wide open."

"Are you still mad he used your quotes?"

"I'm not thrilled he quoted our private conversation, but what am I going to do? Besides, if it wasn't for the slant Eric put on the original story, I don't know if everything would've worked out as well. He's the one who first called me the King of the Court."

"King of the Court," Lisa repeated, shuddering. "Is that the stupidest thing you ever heard?"

"It makes me sound noble and honorable," Ben said, sticking his chest out.

"It makes you sound like an overhyped basketball star."

"Make fun if you want, but that corny title has served me well. The media loves it."

"Whatever you say, Your Lordship."

Smiling, Ben asked, "How's everything at the Court?"

"It's fine," Lisa said. "Same as yesterday. The new clerk sucks. He's about as exciting as sawdust."

"He can't be that bad."

"Trust me, he's that bad. I brought him a sesame-seed bagel from the cafeteria last week, and he said he couldn't eat it because he has a gap in his back teeth. He said the seeds would get caught."

"I don't believe it," Ben said. "And you didn't kick his ass right there?"

"I'm serious," Lisa said. "You try and spend the day with someone who's allergic to cheese. The guy's a loser."

"Is he smart?"

"Academically, yeah. He's brilliant. But he can't operate in the real world. He wouldn't recognize a daring thought if it got lodged in his back teeth."

"If he's so drab, why'd Hollis pick him?"

"I think it's because he was so drab. After you, they couldn't afford another dynamic personality. They needed someone safe. And allergic to cheese."

"Well, at least he has the job," Ben said.

"Don't give me that. Who cares about the job?"

"I care."

"You of all people should not care. The only reason you worked there was to be in the position you currently occupy. Every clerk wishes they were in your shoes. You're the talk of the entire town—the center of every legal circle. Wayne and Portnoy offered you another extra ten thousand even though you told their recruiting chair to drop dead. Every damn lawyer in America wishes they had the savvy of Ben Addison. What could you possibly miss about the Court?"

"I miss working with you," Ben said matter-of-factly.

Surprised by Ben's comment, Lisa asked, "You really miss me?"

"Of course I miss you," Ben replied. "I miss you. I miss Ober. I miss his lottery stories. I miss . . ."

Lisa raised an eyebrow. "Ben, Ober's gone, and there's nothing you can do to change that."

"And Nathan's gone. And Eric's not worth keeping."

"I know it's hard," Lisa said. "But you have to focus on the future. You're starting a job at the U.S. Attorney's Office—filling a position that usually requires at least two years' experience. You jumped ahead of every damn applicant and got one of the best jobs in D.C. You're going to be a prosecutor! You'll be going after guys like Rick full-time. Isn't that what you told me when you accepted the job? That you were thrilled because you loved to be in the chase? Now you'll be in the chase every day."

"And I'm still thrilled about that," Ben agreed. "Considering everything I went through, I could be in a lot worse shape. But I can't help it. I miss them."

"You still have me," Lisa said.

"I know," Ben said warmly. "And that's the luckiest thing that's happened to me."

"I'll tell you why you're lucky," Lisa said. "You're lucky I never told anyone who really designed the 'secret Addison plan.' "

Ben laughed. "Don't bring that up now."

"I'm serious," Lisa said. "You know I was the one who thought up that entire—"

"I know," Ben interrupted. "You came up with the plan. You were the one who said to go to the marshals. You were the one who said it was my only hope. You were the one who said we should replace the executives. You were the one who said to isolate the criminal records. . . ."

"I was the one who said you should be proactive."

"Absolutely," Ben agreed. "You were the aggressive one. You had the idea. I was cocky about *Grinnell,* and you're the one who wound up saving my ass."

"Yet we had to share the credit," Lisa said.

"Are you going to bring this up every time we get together?" Ben asked.

"Pretty much."

"I never said I designed the plan," Ben pleaded. "All I said was that I wrote it up for DeRosa."

"Based on my idea."

"Based on your idea," Ben repeated. "I told them that. What else do you want me to say?"

"I want you to say: Lisa deserves all the credit—I'm just her meek and lowly servant."

"Y'know, there are worse things than sharing the spotlight. I mean, it's not like you've been completely ignored."

"I have too been ignored."

"How many job offers did you receive this week? A dozen?"

"Fourteen, actually. And *The New York Times* is doing a profile that runs next Sunday. But that doesn't mean I don't feel slighted. The way I see it, you shouldn't have opened your mouth in the first place."

Ben grabbed a nearby pillow and whipped it at Lisa's head. "Don't give me that! Eric was the one who screwed up—he was the one who gave both of us credit for designing it. And when the rest of the press picked up on it—"

"You couldn't deny it."

"I tried to deny it," Ben laughed. "But at that point it was too late. The King of the Court was born."

"Don't say those words in front of me," Lisa warned.

"If it makes you feel better, you can call me Sovereign."

"I should call you Court Jester."

"Fine, call me Jester. Whatever makes you happy," Ben said. "But if you have to know the truth, I really am sorry. *And* grateful."

"I know you are. I just want you to learn your lesson." Pleased to see Ben smiling, Lisa said, "Y'know, I like you much better when you're happy."

"Me, too," Ben said. "The way I see it, though, there are two types of people in this world . . ."

"Don't start," Lisa begged.

"I'm serious. There are two types of people in this world: winners and losers."

"Let me guess which one you are."

"In this situation, I'm both," Ben explained. "That's the only way to look at it."

Lisa paused for a moment. "That's fair. I'll agree with that."

"Thank you," Ben said.

Lisa jumped from her seat and walked toward the couch. "Now that we've heard your wonderful analysis, can we get out of here? You said we'd have fun tonight."

"I don't want to have fun," Ben said with a smile. "I'd rather stay in."

"So you want to have a different kind of fun?" she asked, sitting down next to him.

"No," Ben said, pulling away. "I just want to sit here and mope. Trust me, it'll be tons of fun."

"Moping is not an option. Get it out of your mind."

"Is sulking an option? Because I can just as easily sulk if I can't mope."

"You're not doing either." Slowly, Lisa moved closer to Ben on the couch.

"Then what are we going to do? Pout? Brood? Fret?"

"Let me put it to you this way," Lisa said. "In my mind, there are two types of people in this world: those who will sleep with me, and those who won't."

"Relax. I'm not in the mood."

"Don't give me that. You said when everything calmed down—"

"It hasn't calmed down yet," Ben said. "Besides, who says I'd even want to sleep with you?"

"Oh, that's funny," Lisa said. "But that game doesn't work anymore. I saw you crying when Rick was slapping me around. You were worried about me."

"Those tears had nothing to do with you. They were tears of anger. They were angry, hateful tears."

"Sure they were," Lisa said, inching closer to Ben.

"I'm serious," Ben said. "Anyway, I can't do it now. I have a lot on my mind. You saw me before—I'm depressed."

"You're not depressed."

"I am depressed. And it's going to take me a long time to get over it."

"How long?" Lisa asked.

"A very long time. A long, long time."

"So when are we going to fool around?"

"I'm not sure. Maybe never."

"Ben—" Lisa warned.

"Fine. You talked me into it. But I want you to know I'm not going to like it."

"You'll like it."

"Fine. I'll like it. But the moment we're done, this relationship is over. I've had enough of this nonsense."

"Whatever you say," Lisa agreed. She kissed Ben's neck. "You're in control."

ABOUT THE AUTHOR

BRAD MELTZER HAS WRITTEN SPEECHES FOR BILL CLINTON'S national service program; developed marketing strategies for *Games* magazine; earned credit from Columbia Law School for writing his first novel; and married his high school sweetheart, also a lawyer. They live in Washington, D.C., where Brad is at work on his next novel.